Red Dream

Red Dream

An Exotic Novel

VICTORIA BROOKS

Greatest Escapes
PUBLISHING

06 05 04 03 02 1 2 3 4 5 6

First published in 2002 by
Greatest Escapes Publishing
P.O. Box 48503
595 Burrard Street
Vancouver, B.C.
Canada V7X 1A2
E-mail: *marketing@greatestescapes.com*
www.greatestescapes.com and *www.literarytrips.com* and *www.RedDream.info*

With the exception of a few deceased actual historical personages the characters and story of this novel are entirely the product of this author's imagination and have no relation to any person in real life. In a few cases the historical events have been rearranged and names changed.

National Library of Canada Cataloguing in Publication Data

Brooks, Victoria.
Red dream

ISBN 0-9686137-2-1

1. Title.
PS8553.R667R42 2002 C813'.6 C2002-910159-7
PR9199.3.B6972R42 2002

Typeset by Jen Hamilton
Design by Adam Swica
Maps by Alex Ignatius

Printed and bound in Canada

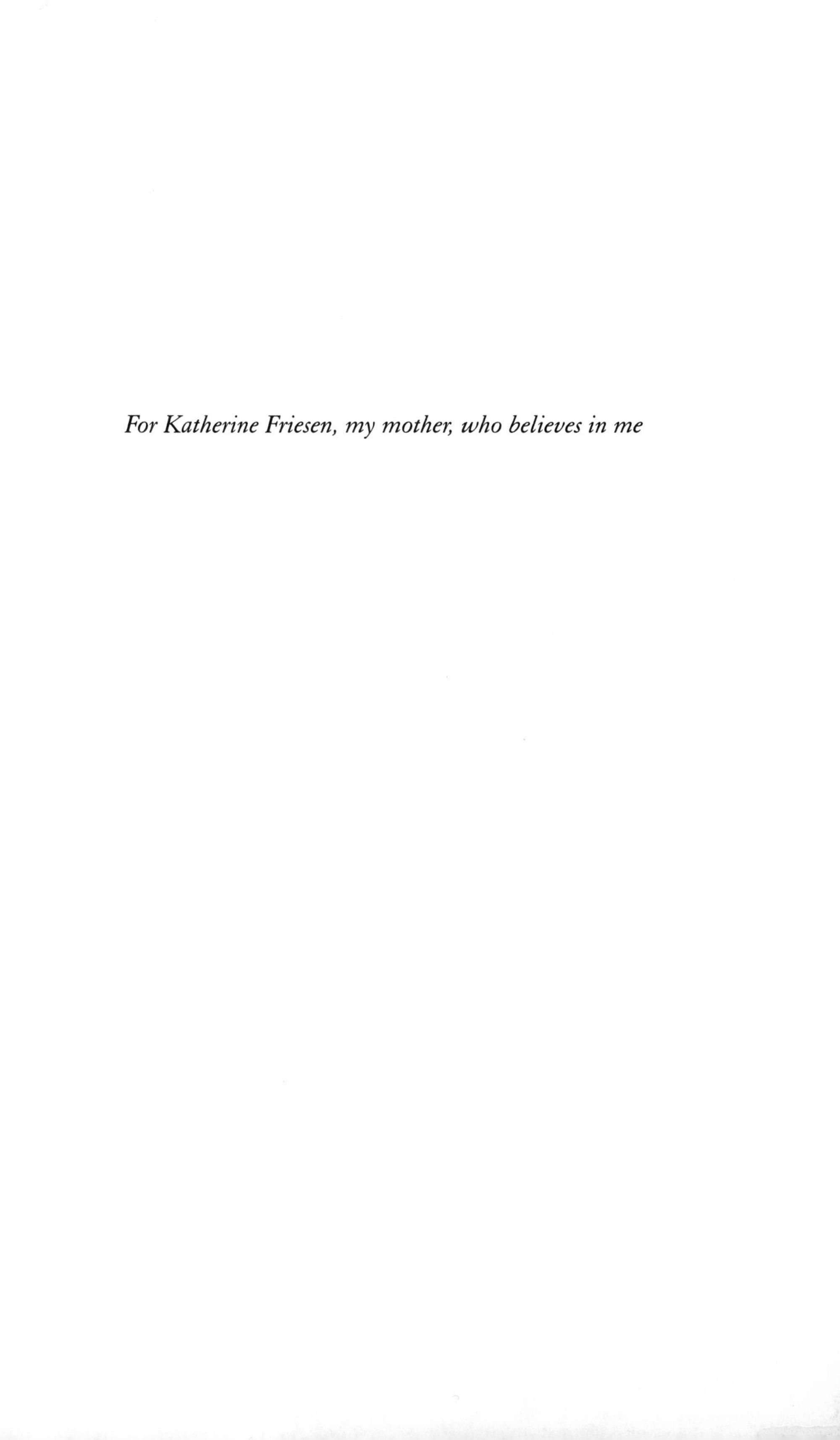

For Katherine Friesen, my mother, who believes in me

ACKNOWLEDGMENTS

I would like to thank Thanh Nguyen who was kind enough to give me the seed of the story as "a gift" with typical Vietnamese generosity and aplomb and who set me on the path to Vietnam. I would also like to acknowledge the following: Stanley Karnow for his *Vietnam: A History*, the historical work that became my Bible; Mike Ruffle for his generous help with details of South Vietnamese army uniforms; the Majestic Hotel whose staff and setting sparked my imagination; and my friend Nancy Beckham for providing a retreat at Tensing Pen where I can slip away from my own world and write.

Thanks and more thanks to the talented Bob Shacochis for "making me fret" and then helping me out as best as he could. Eternal thanks to Guy and Tyson for their enthusiasm, support, and generous help with research. Thanks to my parents, David and Katherine Friesen, for the part they play in all aspects of my life, and thanks also to my sister Ruth Hastings and her family. More thanks go out to Michael Carroll for his friendship and his editorial advice; to Kathryn Means, as always; to Adam Swica for his cover and design work; and to Jen Hamilton for her creative layout. And, finally, I must thank the city and people of Saigon, or Ho Chi Minh City, for throwing all who visit them back in time and forward with hope.

CHRONOLOGY

1945: Japanese occupy French Indochina and Emperor Bao Dai proclaims an independent Vietnam under Japanese auspices. Japanese transfer power to the Vietminh with Ho Chi Minh as leader of provisional government in Hanoi. Emperor Bao Dai abdicates to Ho Chi Minh. British forces land in Saigon and return authority to the French.

1946: War between Ho Chi Minh's Vietminh and France begins in earnest.

1947: Bao Dai living in Hong Kong, commences negotiations with France to achieve Vietnam's independence.

1949: Bao Dai and the French president sign an agreement making Vietnam an "associated state" within the French Union. France retains control of Vietnam's defenses and finances.

1950: Emperor Bao Dai returned to the throne by France. United States funds French efforts in Vietnam. Bao Dai's French-backed government is recognized by the United States and Britain. Ho Chi Minh declares that the Democratic Republic of Vietnam is the only legal government and is recognized by China and the Soviet Union.

1954: Ho Chi Minh's war against the French culminates in the Vietminh victory at Dien Bien Phu. The French surrender. Vietnam becomes a divided country under the Geneva Agreements, partitioning Vietnam along the Seventeenth Parallel. Ho Chi Minh formally assumes control over North Vietnam. Ngo Dinh Diem becomes leader of the South.

1955: Diem, who had been appointed by Bao Dai to represent him in the South, beats Bao Dai in a referendum and proclaims the Republic of Vietnam, with himself as president. Diem calls off the 1956 all-Vietnam elections called for by the Geneva Agreements.

1959: North Vietnamese government steps up infiltration of guerrillas and weapons into South Vietnam via the Ho Chi Minh Trail. Major Dale Buis and Sergeant Chester Ovnand, the first American military personnel to die in Vietnam, are killed by Communist guerrillas at Bien Hoa.

1960: Military coup against President Diem fails. Hanoi cadres form National Liberation Front for South Vietnam, which Saigon regime dubs the Vietcong.

1961: Newly elected U.S. President John F. Kennedy decides to send more American advisers into combat in Vietnam.

1962: American Military Assistance Command formed in South Vietnam. By mid-1962, American advisers have increased from seven hundred to twelve thousand. Two South Vietnamese military pilots bomb Independence Palace, but Diem and his family survive.

1963: On May 8, South Vietnamese troops and police shoot at Buddhist demonstrators in Hué. Crisis mounts in June when Buddhist monk commits self-immolation. In August, Ngo Dinh Nhu's forces attack Buddhist temples. American support for mutinous generals against Diem and Nhu becomes evident. On November 1, bloody coup by South Vietnamese army generals against their leader, President Diem, takes place. On November 2, Diem and his brother,

Nhu, are murdered after their surrender. General Duong Van Minh, leading the Revolutionary Military Committee, takes control of South Vietnam. John F. Kennedy assassinated in Dallas, Texas; Lyndon B. Johnson becomes president of the United States.

1964: American aircraft begin bombing of North Vietnam. Johnson is reelected president of the United States.

1965: First American combat troops in Vietnam. Two U.S. Marine battalions land to defend Da Nang airfield. By the end of the year, U.S. troops in Vietnam number almost two hundred thousand.

1967: General Nguyen Van Thieu becomes president of South Vietnam.

1968: Tet Offensive begins. U.S. President Lyndon Johnson halts bombings in North Vietnam. Johnson announces he won't run for reelection. Richard Nixon is elected president of the United States.

1969: United States secretly bombs Vietcong bases in Cambodia.

1970: American and South Vietnamese troops attack Communist sanctuaries in Cambodia. President Nixon declares that United States will withdraw from Vietnam by 1973.

1973: Last U.S. combat troops leave Vietnam.

1974: Richard Nixon resigns as U.S. president. Vice President Gerald Ford becomes president.

1975: Saigon falls to the North Vietnamese on April 30. Saigon renamed Ho Chi Minh City. North and South reunited into single country with Communist leadership.

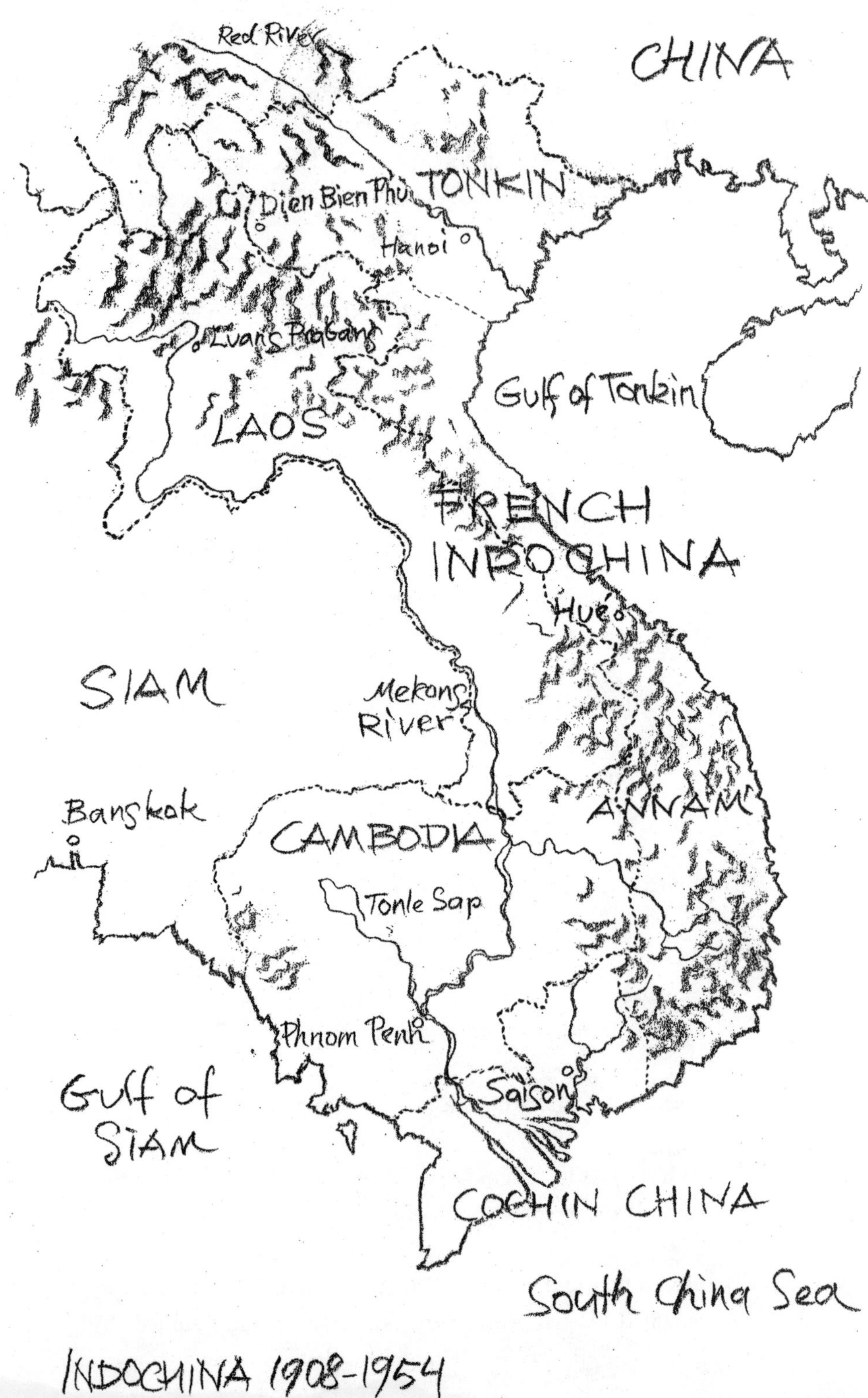
Red River
CHINA
TONKIN
Dien Bien Phu
Hanoi
Luang Prabang
Gulf of Tonkin
LAOS
FRENCH INDOCHINA
Hue
SIAM
Mekong River
Bangkok
CAMBODIA
ANNAM
Tonle Sap
Phnom Penh
Gulf of SIAM
Saigon
COCHIN CHINA
South China Sea
INDOCHINA 1908-1954

Red River
CHINA
Can Bang
Dongkhe
Dien Bien Phu
Langson
Hanoi
NORTH VIETNAM
LAOS
Gulf of Tonkin
Vientiane
Demilitarized Zone July 22, 1954
Hué
THAILAND
Mekong River
Bangkok
CAMBODIA
SOUTH VIETNAM
Tonle Sap
Phnom Penh
Gulf of Thailand
Saigon
South China Sea

VIETNAM 1954–75

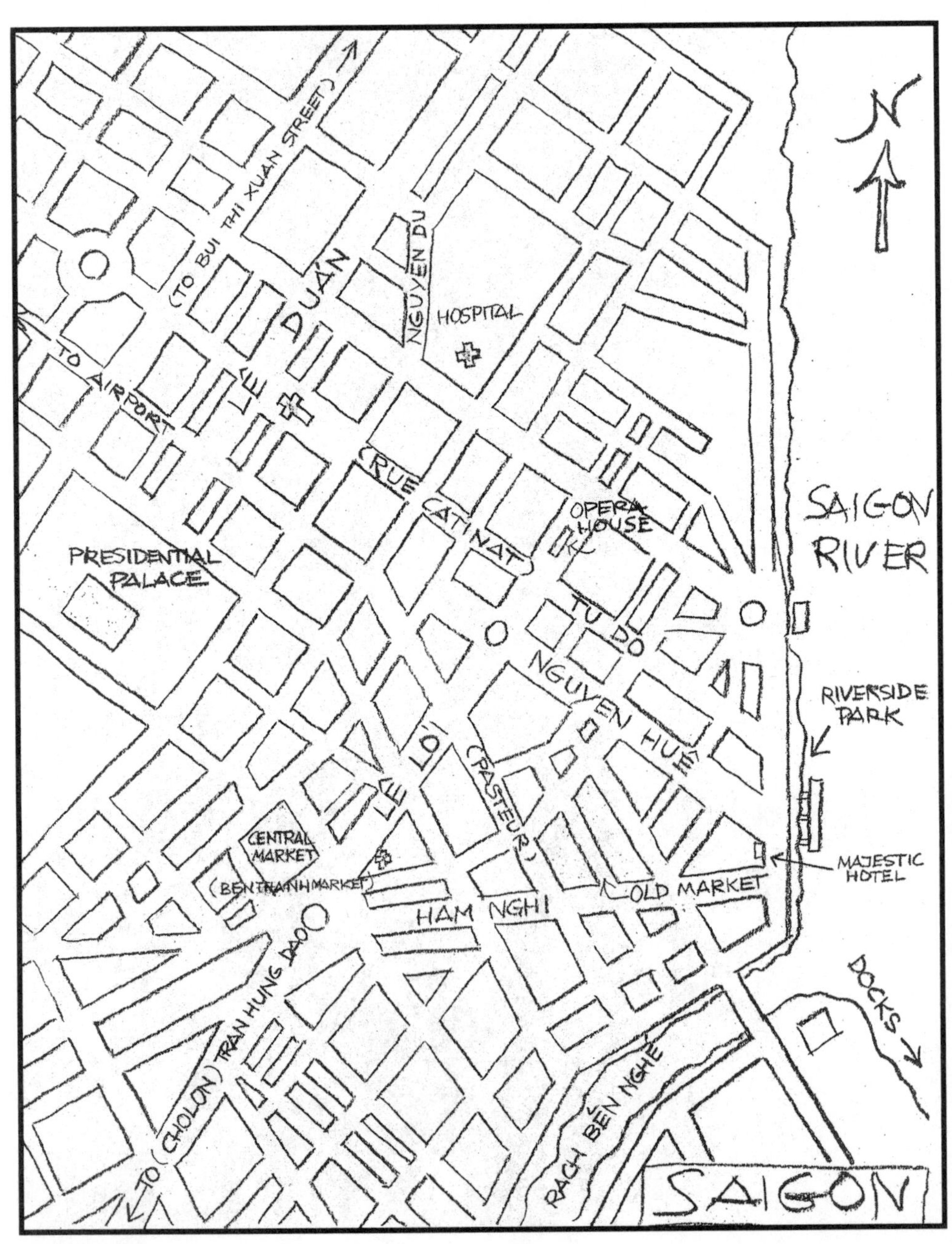
N
(TO BUI THI XUAN STREET)
NGUYEN DU
HOSPITAL
LE DUAN
TO AIRPORT
(RUE CATINAT)
OPERA HOUSE
SAIGON RIVER
PRESIDENTIAL PALACE
TU DO
NGUYEN HUE
RIVERSIDE PARK
LE LOI
(PASTEUR)
CENTRAL MARKET
(BEN THANH MARKET)
OLD MARKET
MAJESTIC HOTEL
HAM NGHI
TRAN HUNG DAO
TO (CHOLON)
RACH BEN NGHE
DOCKS
SAIGON

BOOK I
JADE

We are slaves to our past, our circumstances, and our surroundings.

—Somerset Maugham
Wit and Wisdom of Somerset Maugham

PROLOGUE

Who has twisted us around like this, so that
no matter what we do, we are in the posture
of someone going away?
—Rainer Maria Rilke, *Duino Elegies*

Paris: April 1955

Jade Tu Minh lazed, her body a single floating lily on the night pond of her bed. Looking petulant, she didn't bother removing her shoes or the duvet from the bed she would sleep in alone. One calf and tiny pointed foot kicked at the air and off came her Dior shoes, first the left, then the right. They flew inelegantly across the room. She gave no thought to the walls of her expensive Paris apartment overlooking the dreaming Seine River. Her red stiletto shoes landed on the oriental carpet without a sound. Nestling her head against the pillow, Jade sighed and rested a recently lacquered nail against her prettily bowed upper lip. A chance ray of light from the chandelier above struck the center of the green stone she wore on that finger. As she flung her hand from her face in a fit of pique, a loose claw in the ring caught at the flesh of her cheek. A single droplet of blood stood at attention.

she turned
she stared
her life was bare
there was no one
to touch her hair
the woman lay alone

1

THE MYSTERY

It was France that educated me, France that taught me value, beauty, distinction, wit, and good sense.

—Somerset Maugham

Wit and Wisdom of Somerset Maugham

Paris: April 1955

La Doctoress Jade Minh was attending the ritual Monday-afternoon staff meeting in her role as translator for the South Vietnamese embassy. The room was a costly and eclectic mix of French provincial and Ming Dynasty Chinese antiques.

Jade was only vaguely aware of the talk around her. She was thinking of her husband, Van, back in Saigon, when the bell of the telephone jangled in the outer room. Uncrossing her silk-stocking-clad legs, she pushed her chair away from the boardroom table. Without a word of excuse she moved toward the door, her hair a coiled black knot against the nape of her slim neck. Her small, high breasts jutted from the smooth front of her Chanel suit as if they were proud to point the way but knew it would be vulgar to make any real commotion.

On Jade's face there was no trace of annoyance at the interrupting telephone. Her features were as expressionless as they were perfect. She took no notice of her colleagues, although the all-male staff caressed her retreating back with greedy eyes. Her black patent high heels flashed them a low smile as they tapped rhythmically across the room. Shutting the doors to the boardroom behind her, Jade threw herself into the swivel chair at the reception desk, sighed for effect, crossed her legs, and lifted the receiver from its cradle.

"Hello," she cooed, and immediately recognized the voice of Chou Yang-shu, who was the legal adviser to the embassy and had known herself, her father, and Van ever since she could remember.

"I'll keep you only a moment, Honorary Doctoress," Chou enthused. "We must arrange a private interview. It's a matter that may concern you personally. Come to my office at six o'clock."

"Chou, I'm a very busy woman. It's already close to five." She knew Chou well and disliked him with an instinctive unreason. He, on the other hand, went out of his way to become part of her family.

"Dear Doctoress, I insist on that arrangement and for your benefit alone."

"Is this matter of such urgency that you disturb the afternoon meeting?" Jade retorted, a winter chill in her voice.

"Not for me, my dear Doctoress, but for you. It's in *your* interest to meet with me." Chou then changed tack and continued in a whisper. "Trust me, my dear, I'm your friend. It's better we say nothing over the telephone."

Jade heard a soft click and the line went dead. She returned to the staff meeting, confused and a little frightened. Jade had never understood Chou and wondered how much he knew about her past. A corner of her mind suspected him of a voyeurism that resulted in his own personal collection of the private details of his friends' and acquaintances' lives. Chou enjoyed deluding those he was, or pretended to be, fond of by silently giving the impression he knew more about "things" than he would say. And worse, he had an annoying way of tapping his nose with his index finger and saying, "Chou knows..." When Jade would ask, "Knows what?" Chou would nod, tap, and say it again. Jade always wondered if he gave a sly wink when he turned away.

Taking her chair at the long rosewood table and sitting once again among the embassy staff, Jade tried to concentrate on matters at hand and look animated, but a voice smothered her thoughts and pushed at her, repeating the words, *Chou called. What does it mean? Chou phoned. What does he know?* In her mind's eye she could see Chou's face hovering close to hers, his fingers tapping, one narrowed eye winking.

Jade was awakened from her paranoid reverie by the ambassador, a man of manners, of the old school, who asked her if she was ready for her honorable duty.

"Yes, I shall translate the minutes and tally the vote," she replied as she always did. And with those words she finally put pen to paper.

Jade's red Renault, a 1954 two-door automatic sports model purchased direct and duty-free off the show-room floor with a purse full of francs, sped along the scenic riverside road that hugged the slow-drifting Seine. The traffic, like the late spring rain, was thin, and a record twelve minutes later the four-story La Tour building was in sight. Jade slowed, expertly threw her car into first gear, and maneuvered it over the curb in a seamless motion. Her Renault slid to a stop. Luckily the cobblestones were empty of passersby. Above the closed canvas of her cabriolet, the overhanging leaves from a stand of poplars were magnified to silver-green by their new skin of rain and the polish of the neighboring gas lamps. She twisted the rearview mirror to a suitable angle, applied face powder liberally, especially to the areas where she noticed telltale lines, put on fresh lipstick, and checked her tiny white teeth for smears. Leaving the mirror askew, La Doctoress, as she preferred to be called, locked the automobile and prepared to face Chou.

As was their habit, Chou greeted Jade in French. His voice, a drawl of lazy elegance, called to her, hollowly masculine through the entrance of his private office. His only staff, a revolving door of female receptionists whose curriculum vitae were based on their physiques, had left for the day. Jade studied Chou for a moment for any clue to his cryptic and potentially dangerous summons, but he appeared nonchalant to her behind his opulent desk. He'd been marking a passage in *Paris After Dark,* Art Buchwald's popular guide to the city's raunchy nightlife.

Chou's thick hair, blue-black and heavy with pomade, was slicked back from a wide forehead. His eyes were small ebony beads, and his handsome slat of a mouth turned up at one corner, giving the impression of a perpetual and charmingly derisive smile. His perfectly manicured goatee waggled as he spoke, drawing further attention to his smile.

"Hello, *Madame la Doctoress*," Chou said as he raised his lean body from his chair. Jade insisted on being addressed La Doctoress, having received a doctorate in the Romance languages and German. Plucking Jade's gloved hand from her side with practiced grace, Chou undressed it, finger by finger, then raised it meaningfully to his lips. And there he lingered. His voice and hair were flavored with charm, scent, and oil. His eyes shone.

Jade, unprepared for his aura of sensuousness, recoiled at his warm breath on her skin. Then he straightened but at first didn't let go of her hand. She felt displeasure even at the harmless sight of Chou's fingers cupping hers. Jade noticed his digits: the index and middle fingers were permanently yellowed from nicotine. One fingernail, as long as a fancy woman's, scraped her soft inner wrist. This single, elongated nail was the sign of a wealthy mandarin in Asia. As they each waited for the other to make the next move, the only sounds were Chou's breathing and the background hiss of the room's steam radiator, which stood on tiny iron feet by the paneled wall.

Finally stepping back to give Jade the distance she obviously required, Chou displayed no rancor at her aversion, only unadulterated admiration. Narrowing his eyes, and with one hand tucked in the silk pocket of his well-cut slacks, he considered her face as if she were a portrait by Rubens or Goya. His lips trembled with a connoisseur's delight as he contemplated how her skin was made delicate by the depth of her eyes that, like a child's kaleidoscope, changed dramatically with each nuance of her moods. At that moment they were cool, but then it was as if night had fallen and they shot stars of anger. Chou stood still as he took in her curvaceous form. Then, as if to conclude, he ran his eyes from her neck to the points of her shoes and back as quickly as a newly lit flame.

Jade knew what behavior Chou—any man—expected. He wanted gratitude or a womanly plea for his help with whatever problem he too obviously meant to burden her with, not the cold silence she presented him. Realizing the preliminary match was over but never admitting defeat, Chou moved his hand casually to the breast pocket of his suit. He held his stained thumb and forefinger like the closed mouth of a serpent, retrieved a folded square of paper, and handed it to Jade. It was a telegram that had been opened and read. Jade could see that it was addressed to her as Madame Jade Tu Minh.

"I hope you'll forgive me, Jade," Chou said, his devilish face sly. "I was at the embassy today on important business." One sleek eyebrow quivered as he mimicked Jade's incredulity. "You were out at lunch, I think." His eyes pinged about his office as if to check each nook and cranny. And when they returned to Jade's face, it was as if they'd hit the jackpot. "When this telegram came, I took the liberty of receiving it on your behalf." He smiled at his own audacity. "You know, my dear, I made a promise, which I take very seriously, to your honorable father that I'd look out for you here in Paris."

The too-quick use of Jade's first name and the casual endearment didn't escape her. She was accustomed to French etiquette and preferred lengthier formalities with Chou before he addressed her with *tu* rather than *vous*, or by her Christian name.

"Monsieur Chou, I appreciate the importance of pleasing my father. His position in the government makes him easy to please." Diplomacy and superiority were her weapons.

"Dear girl, I wanted to spare you pain. Telegrams often contain nasty news. You have no husband here to protect you." Chou's mouth curled, making a black show of lips. He continued coyly. "By the way, how is your husband, Van?"

Jade turned her attention to the telegram: TO: MADAME JADE TU MINH, EMBASSY OF THE REPUBLIC OF VIETNAM, PARIS, FRANCE. CONTACT CIGARETTE STAND 10, AVENUE ST-MAUR, MONTPELLIER, FOR INFORMATION ABOUT MONSIEUR JACQUES.

She spoke rapidly to cover her surprise. "Monsieur Jacques was an old professor of mine when I studied languages at the University of Montpellier. He's probably died of old age." Calming herself, she tsked, then said, "His wife and family were most kind to me in my loneliness. I missed Van a lot in those days. The family probably wants me to speak at his funeral." Jade's eyes misted at the thought she'd conjured.

Chou locked his eyes on Jade. "Why a cigarette stand?"

"A family business, a going concern in its time." Jade then ended the game, folding the telegram into a neat square. "I have to leave now, Chou. I appreciate your kindness. I'll mention you to Papa."

Depositing the telegram in her purse, she snapped the latch shut. Jade offered Chou her elegant hand. It trembled slightly as the lawyer lifted it and held it for a brief moment to his lips.

Jade knew it was her Jacques. It could be no other. Years ago she had exorcised his memory and expunged him from her existence. All he was to Jade now was an unreal and distant recollection that had no relation to her present life. During her time with Jacques, and even long after, she had thought of him as a page in a child's exercise book that had "Jacques, Jacques, Jacques" written in it in loving script with indelible ink. Jade had thought the youthful page had been erased and the fear of being found out and tarnished forgotten.

She was aware she had shown her husband in Vietnam much disloyalty by having an affair with a European man. She was aware, too, that it was a sin. Jade's Catholic schooling had prepared her for what was expected of a woman, or any moral human being. She understood the rules of good behavior within Christianity, and like most Vietnamese she had studied the rules of Buddhism, including the precept of reincarnation. But she couldn't make herself abide by those moral teachings, even the few times she decided to try. And to be truthful, her pretense both to herself and in public knew no bounds.

But what news would Jade learn of Jacques after all these years? Did he want to see her? Did he still love her? Did he want her back? Was he in financial straits and in need of money? Or was he dead?

Although Jade was certain she would never allow her heart to be Jacques's again, she reasoned she must face reality and be made aware of whatever had kicked up the dust of his buried memory. All these thoughts rushed at her as she prepared to face her past and decided to take the next day's train to Montpellier.

2

MEMORIES

To take an Annamite to bed with you is like taking a bird: they twitter and sing on your pillow.

—Graham Greene, *The Quiet American*

Paris: April 1955

Jade Minh heard the slow *chuk-a-chuk* of a horse and carriage through the window of her Paris apartment. She shoved the glass down, closing out the cold and the noise before crawling into the opulent comfort of her large bed. She would sleep; Chou's cryptic telephone call at the embassy and then the telegram had been too exhausting. She would pack for her trip to Montpellier in the morning. While she slept she dreamed.

She was a shaman. There was a tangerine sunset on the Baie d'Along, and its karst shapes rose out of the bottle-green depths and threw their strange shadows like hallucinations at the sea. The islands' shapes were spread close, like a deck of playing cards, edge upon edge. Figures shuffled. There were dragons and eagles and animist gods. There were human shapes, too: man, woman, and one was her soul. She was a shaman and she bent by the sandy shore gathering sticks that were bathed in a transcendent glow. She bundled the twigs that represented her past, and when she burned them, smoke rose, affording her a vision in a silver mirror.

Jade saw her life through her own eyes, and through her husband's softer revelations. She glimpsed Van as a young man. She was his bride and she was a vision herself in a bridal gown of embers. Jade dreamed of the way she and Van had been. Walking with him on the first day of their marriage, she felt a thrill at the novelty of being a bride. Sunlight streamed through the bamboo cages that hung from the facades of the Chinese-owned shops. The tiny captives twittered and sang as if they were free. A desire to touch her new husband, coupled with panic at the thought of their approaching night alone, made her forget the Vietnamese sense of propriety. Jade took Van's hand.

"Please, Jade, we are in public and someone will see," Van said, not returning the clasp and leaving his hand limp in hers.

Jade blushed and dropped his hand. To hide her shame, she reverted to a habit she'd cultivated in school. When she was bored, lonely, or emotional, she would stand in front of the polished mirror in her bedroom or—even better—in front of Dô, her *yaya* or nursemaid, and recite poetry. She could memorize entire stanzas at a time. Sometimes during class and on the school grounds, when she was allowed, she would stand and recite, hands curled, eyes shining, in a bid to impress her peers. Jade recited for Van now in a soft, clear voice.

> "The bloom of my complexion made all women jealous;
> a glance from my eyes, iridescent as autumn pools,
> stirred up waves of passion that would overthrow fortresses.
> The moon strained to catch sight of me through my window blinds,
> not even the trees and plants could stay indifferent to my beauty."

Van frowned. "Jade, what are you doing?"

"Don't you know that poem? It's from *The Complaint of the Royal Concubine* by Nguyen Gia Thieu, and it's as famous as it is beautiful. The poet writes about a deserted lover thinking about her past beauty."

"But, Jade, is that a proper subject for a young woman? I don't mean to appear old-fashioned, but I beg you to try to cultivate a more scientific approach to your thinking." Van fell silent.

Jade's dream continued, flashing forward to her honeymoon in Dalat with Van. She and her new husband had just arrived at the pink-plaster-and-wood-framed one-story colonial villa where they would be staying.

"Very pretty," the Vietnamese assistant manager rasped to himself behind the front desk of the Palace Villa Hotel.

Eyes lined with kohl, pelvis thrust forward, hands on slim hips, Jade swayed as she walked with Van. "This is how they do the tango." She demonstrated the steps, her ankle-length red silk dress slit to the knee and clinging as it traced her figure.

"Please stop that, dear," Van whispered. "The desk clerk is watching. They'll think I've hired a dancing girl."

Jade stepped back in place beside her husband. "Oh, but, Van, the best people dance the tango in Paris and in the finest salons."

"We are *not* in Paris, although anyone would think so to see your clothes."

She looked directly into his eyes. "Don't you like it? I had my dress copied from *La Gazette du Bon Ton,* especially to please you."

"Yes, it's beautiful. But people stare. Sometimes I think you're not of this world. We should be honeymooning in Paris. You would have had a better time."

"Don't worry. I know the Pasteur Institute wouldn't give you enough time off."

"Do you know, Jade, that Dalat was first described by a Westerner, a disciple of Pasteur's? A Dr. Yersin, who visited in 1893. Isn't that interesting?"

They made their way past the green shutters and up the stairs to their honeymoon suite. As Jade sashayed up the stairs, she said, "Van, this is *la petite Paris* and as close to the City of Light as one can get in Vietnam."

The bridal suite's carved teak bed dominated the room, and

the delicate Peranakan porcelain lamps threw shadows at the paneled walls. The bed sheets had been woven exclusively for the hotel at the silkworm farm in nearby Bao Lac. Van sat on the edge of the bed. Jade knew he was oblivious to the room but not to her as she sat at the dressing table in her tulle gown. Her back to Van, she preened like an exotic bird, one bare arm crooked as she brushed out her endless rope of hair.

"I'll just go downstairs and get a glass of arrack before bed," Van finally said.

Jade could see him in the mirror. His coarse black hair was parted in the middle of his skull, and his glasses magnified his eyes, making them enormous. Jade's recollection of her father when he reeked of arrack prompted her to say, "Why don't you bring a bottle of champagne instead?"

Van stared at her for a moment, then said, "I'll be back."

Jade was alone, and the nervousness that had begun when Van wouldn't take her hand returned. Her mind raced through the love scenes gleaned from French novels she'd read with the exquisite excitement of an uninitiated voyeur. She reached back to unzip her gown and recalled her plan to ask Van to undo her. It was too late now; he expected her to be waiting when he came back. She undressed, hanging the expertly copied dress in the closet and folding a scented pouch between the folds of her lingerie. Then she retrieved her bridal-night clothes from the armoire and pulled the sheer peignoir over her head.

Jumping into bed, Jade was a girl child in gossamer. *I must put on my perfume*, she thought as she threw back the covers she'd so recently smoothed over her body and padded across the polished floorboards to the dressing table. Taking up the stopper, scented with Ma Griffe, she dabbed the back of her wrists, her throat, the nape of her neck, and then, as an afterthought, the insides of her thighs. When she was finished, she bounced back into bed and waited.

Half an hour passed with excruciating slowness as the clock marked the seconds. After an hour, Jade extinguished the light and thought about tomorrow. She and Van were planning on touring the magnificent local waterfalls at Camly, Pongour, Gougah, and Prenn. Long ago, as a child, she'd visited them with her mother and Dô when they lived near Dalat overlooking a coffee plantation. With her eyes tightly shut, it was as if she were there now underneath the wet veil of Camly, skipping over the gleaming stones, feeling the rush of water, the droplets clinging like diaphanous jewels on her skin.

Van still wasn't back, and she tried to will herself to sleep but to no avail. Then, finally, she heard the door creak open as Van stole in on stocking feet, his shoes dangling in one hand. She watched through almost closed eyes as he pulled off his clothes and whispered near her ear, "My darling, are you asleep?" Turning her head into the pillow, Jade continued her silent vigil.

Carefully Van folded his shirt and trousers, then placed them on the chair. A filmy material fluttered to the floor from the bed. He lifted the covers to crawl in beside Jade and saw that his bride was naked.

"Why did you make me wait?" Jade complained. Moving her mouth to his, she touched Van's lips with her own. It was as delicate a move as the tentative first brush of an artist on a canvas. The smell of liquor on his breath was strong, but Jade didn't move away. She enjoyed the velvet texture of his mouth.

"My rough chin must feel like sandpaper," he said. With those words and without meaning to, Van averted his face. He was still wearing his eyeglasses.

Jade was a shaman again. She rose with spirals of smoke from the sticks she burned at the strange Baie d'Along and saw herself as a young bride desiring a new pleasure and Van as a nervous young husband. Jade could tell Van was confused about what he should do next, but his instincts made him roll on top of her.

Looking away, he whispered, "Don't be afraid. You'll be the mother of my children."

The smoke from the phosphorus sticks Jade had burned as a shaman faded and she dreamed she was back in the present, alone and bathing in the magical waters of Baie d'Along. The sea was her bauble and it ruffled azure and lapis lazuli in her hands. Then she was engulfed in a karst's shadow where a black dragon loomed, startling her into consciousness. Jade found herself once again in her ornate Parisian bed, her odd dream of Vietnam and Van rapidly fading. Strangely enough, she had never seen Baie d'Along in person, only in the pretty postcards sold by Saigon's street children. Now, though, she thought of her past with Jacques and her decision to follow the mysterious telegram to its source—cigarette stand 10 in the old university town of Montpellier.

3

SCENT OF THE PAST

I'm not the type that I seem to be, Happy-go-lucky and gay.
—Bing Crosby and Jimmy Dorsey, "I Can't Escape from You"

Montpellier, France: April 1955

Cigarette stand 10 was squeezed between a patisserie and the busiest corner on avenue St-Maur in Montpellier. A flower girl, her skirt torn at the hem from dragging against the cobblestoned street, sold a newspaper-wrapped bouquet of cut flowers to a serious young man. A tumult of pink and mauve mimosa spilled from her wooden cart.

The scene was still familiar to Jade. In the early evening she'd often accompanied Jacques on a stroll along the cobblestones to purchase his daily package of Gauloises at this very stand. Nothing seemed to have changed over the years except the proprietor. The striped canvas awning that protected the cellophane-wrapped packages of cigarettes from Montpellier's desultory winter rains might have been replaced, but Jade recalled the thin blue and white lines that differentiated the stand from another a few yards down the sidewalk.

Clicking open her purse, Jade pulled out the telegram and spoke softly. "I received a telegram from your cigarette stand. Did you send it?"

"Yes, madame." The man behind the cigarette stand had been napping upright, but he had opened his eyes and answered without hesitation.

His words were simple, but Jade sensed an overriding insolence in the man's voice and demeanor. He was unshaven and his skin had an unhealthy pallor for someone in his early twenties. Sharp cheekbones jutted over the stubble like cliffs overlooking a burnt-out wasteland. Circles from hard living formed purple pools beneath his wary yet aggressive bloodshot eyes.

Jade clutched her purse and the folded telegram like a shield, then demanded, "What does the telegram mean?"

The man feigned disinterest. "It's not mine, madame."

"It says you have information about Jacques."

The man smiled, as if that would cover his denial. "*I said*, the telegram isn't mine."

"Does your message mean Jacques has died?"

"Sorry. I can't answer any questions."

Jade waved the folded piece of paper angrily in the air. "Who asked you to send me this telegram?"

The man shifted his feet. "I was paid by a citizen whose name is unknown to me. So, as you see, I can't give you information about who you might call my paying client."

"I'll be a paying customer, too, and exchange a twenty-franc note for your client's name." Extracting a twenty from her glove, she held it up.

"Let me see the note." Bending toward her, he took it in his fingers, his eyes alight with greed. "A woman sent you the telegram. Quite a beauty in her time, but that's all the information I have for you. If I can be of service to you further, please don't hesitate to ask."

"Why have you called me here?"

But the man would reveal nothing more. Turning his back on Jade, he began the nightly task of reorganizing his shelf of neatly ordered packs of cigarettes. What could Jade do but leave?

As she walked the streets of Montpellier, Jade cast her mind back to that long-ago cool night in this city. In the glow of the streetlights she could almost feel Jacques's arm encircling her waist, her cheek brushing the worn cotton of his shirt. She imagined them alone among the unseen smiles of lovers whose mouths caressed, whose breath mixed with the air like the phosphorus in the Mediterranean Sea. Jacques and she had been like that—like the lovers, like the waves, like the cocktails made of frothy cream and spirits that they drank in the bars fifteen years ago.

She missed the pungent smell of Gauloises that clung to Jacques and remembered placing her hand in his hip pocket and digging deep for the box of wooden matches he kept by his thigh. With one sure strike, hovering close to his face, she would light his cigarette for him. And after, while seated on a lonely park bench, he would pull her onto his knee, purse his lips, and blow ring after ring of smoke as if he were a magician. One ring followed the other until the air around her was a blue haze. Jade would struggle and laugh, not used to the romantic liberties the French took for granted. The strong scent of Jacques's Gauloises was still as familiar to Jade as that of the Juan Bastos Vietnamese cigarettes Van claimed were as addictive for him as the filtered black coffee he drank. Jade now realized that her decision to check in to the Pension des Voyageurs rather than take the return train to Paris suited her nostalgic mood. She'd left no contact number with her embassy, but if someone wanted to find her, she'd be easy to trace.

When Jade entered room 202 in the pension, she glanced unhappily around it. She'd been shown two others but was too tired to keep looking. "This will do," she told the nervous bellboy.

After he was gone, Jade sighed and threw off her hat and coat. She lay on the bed to rest but quickly fell into a fitful sleep.

Jade dreamed of fresh blood—pools of it. She swam in it, and as she breaststroked through the body-temperature stickiness that had no end and no beginning, she brushed against an object that was soft, alive. The horror she felt rapidly disappeared. Instinctively she knew she'd discovered something important, something special. She was determined to find it again and, like a blind person, explore the warm liquid. With a shiver of excitement she touched it once more. It was immature and as light as a feather. Hallucinogenic trails scattered as she drew her treasure toward her. Placing her palms underneath, she lifted it high as if it were a trophy. She felt ecstasy at finding this prize and moved her mouth down to kiss it. Blood washed over her like a waterfall.

Brngg, brngg, the pension's bedside phone called through her dream. She fumbled for the receiver. "Hello…?"

"Jade Minh, I have information about a friend of yours. Are you interested in seeing me?" Her caller gave no name, but the voice was female.

"Yes, can you come to my pension?"

"That would be best. I'm sure you wouldn't want to be seen."

Hurrying, Jade straightened the bedcovers. She counted her francs, calculating that she had more than enough to pay for any information about Jacques. Taking precautions, she hid a bundle of francs in the pillowcase.

Jade then dialed the front desk. "I'm expecting a visitor. Send the lady up in twenty minutes and please ring again, just in case. You understand, she's a stranger and I'm a woman alone with valuables in my room."

She replaced the receiver and changed into fresh clothes, readying herself for her visitor. Maybe, she thought, the woman would take her to Jacques. But that wouldn't mean anything after all these years, would it? The smile that lit Jade's lips, though, belied any denial.

She was confused by the odd pleasure Jacques could still stir, and remembered a passage she'd memorized from a banned copy of D. H. Lawrence's *Lady Chatterley's Lover*: "Love is the flower…" How impressionable and how impressed she'd been by Lawrence's words. She wondered if they had affected her behavior when she left Saigon and her young husband to study so long ago in Montpellier.

4

JADE'S MISTAKE

> Love is the flower of life, and blossoms unexpectedly and without law, and must be plucked where it is found, and enjoyed for the brief hour of its duration.
>
> —D. H. Lawrence, *Lady Chatterley's Lover*

Montpellier: April 1955

Prepared for the mysterious visit and even to be taken to Jacques if need be, Jade had francs at the ready and a coat with a high collar to hide her face. She listened for footfalls but heard nothing beyond her room door. Jade paced the dusty flooring impatiently, then sat on the single bed's faded floral cover. While she waited for her past to resurface, she thought of how she had first met Jacques in this town fifteen years earlier.

Against Van's better judgment, Jade had decided to leave Vietnam in January 1940 to study for her *licencié en lettres* undergraduate degree at the university in sun-blessed Montpellier. How Jade had smiled bravely through her slowly falling tears. How Van, her husband of less than a year, had uncharacteristically grasped her hand as they moved together through Saigon's Tan Son Nhat Airport. She could still conjure up the barnlike hangar in her mind's eye: the dirt-dark corners muddied with sleeping bodies, the stink of sweaty people packed too close in the oppressive heat and humidity. Jade found herself back there again, standing behind the stained fish-oil crates that served as the Air France counter, thinking that her education was Vietnam's future and that such a future was filled with loneliness.

World War II had begun the previous summer after the Germans and Soviets invaded Poland. There were fears that the Nazis were preparing to invade France, but Jade refused to believe that her adopted land wouldn't prevail. Life went on, people toiled at their jobs, students attended classes.

Jade and Jacques met in the first week of classes halfway through the school year. A woman attending university was unusual in those days, especially a Vietnamese. There were no female quarters on campus, so Van had arranged through the Montpellier branch of a rental agency to lease a suitable apartment while she earned her degree. The spacious French Renaissance one-story flat was near the university on rue de Montaigne. Her new situation returned to Jade the freedom to do as she pleased, a freedom she had sorely missed after her arranged marriage to Van. Although it wasn't needed, Jade's father had set up a scholarship for her through his "senatorial" connections with the Vietnamese government. And later, of course, he had pulled strings again and secured Jade her translator's post at the embassy. Scholarships and foreign postings were easy to come by and handed out as rewards for the families of wealthy *colons* or government officials. Her father was adept at making and using connections.

Jade's father was a personal friend of Vietnam's playboy Emperor Bao Dai. In fact, in their younger days her father and Bao Dai had lain side by side on the wood-slatted beds in their local opium den. With the haze of opium as their guide they had dreamed their personal dreams. And, on more than one occasion, her father had arranged for the deft, pleasurable, and eminently patient twin courtesans known around town as *les Mademoiselles Deux* to minister to the men's baser instincts before they entered their opium-induced holidays.

Jade's *carte de séjour* and *certificat d'assiduité* required by the French authorities were also organized by her father, and in reality were only a simple matter of wax seals passed from desk to desk until they found relevant contact. As for Van, she knew he would miss his headstrong bride but would fill up his free time with scientific endeavors at Saigon's prestigious Pasteur Institute.

It had been Jade's decision to go to France to study Romance languages and German. She was fluent in French, as were all upper-class Vietnamese at the time, but Jade was blessed with a talent to translate immaculately from Vietnamese to French and vice versa, and had a good ear for other tongues. When Van finally agreed his wife should follow her chosen path, he insisted on giving her a generous allowance. So, ensconced in the university town of Montpellier, Jade felt as if she were a millionaire, thanks to the largesse of her father and husband.

During the first few days of classes—and before she met Jacques—Jade found it difficult to negotiate the maze of halls whose stone walls were cool and damp in contrast to the brilliant sunlight outside. Now, sitting alone at a table in the corner of the student café, the air thick with cigarette smoke and aimless chatter, she picked at a *religieuse*, an éclair shaped like a nun's hat, and sipped a double espresso in a tiny cup. A German grammar book lay open on the table.

"I see you're studying German. Are you preparing to converse with the Germans when they get here?" A pimply youth in all-black attire stood over her. His friends, who lounged at a nearby table like slothful, pop-eyed lizards, stared rudely in expectation of her response.

Jade's hands fluttered with confusion. "Are the Germans invading?"

A ripple of laughter began at one end of the nearby table and finished like the syncopated notes of a jazz piece. The young man glanced back at his friends with narrowed eyes. Then he returned his attention to Jade and blushed. "I'm just teasing you. Of course, the Germans aren't invading. But who's to say it won't happen again?" He laughed. "Come join us. Meet my friends. They're not so bad. We'll discuss life, love, and the aftermath of war."

Closing her book and holding her purse tightly to her chest, Jade stood. "Excuse me," she said, head high, cheeks burning. "I have a class to attend." Her German grammar book lay forgotten on the cafeteria table as she made her exit.

After her embarrassment at the student café, Jade made it a habit to spend as little time on campus as possible. She attended classes, then made a dash for her apartment where she felt confined and lonely but at least safe from the eyes of laughing strangers.

The sign on the student bulletin board that had attracted Jade's attention read: FREE YOURSELF FROM THE DRUDGERY OF TYPING. JACQUES DURAS TYPING SERVICE. BEST RATES ON CAMPUS. HAVE TYPEWRITER WILL TRAVEL. CALL 21-379.

Jade had three assignments due and had never learned to type. All work at Sacré Coeur Convent School, where she had received her earlier education, was done with a quill pen and in sepia ink. The dye for the ink was shipped from the Vietnamese port of Haiphong and was ejected from cuttlefish.

She agreed with the notice's sentiment about the "drudgery of typing." Typing was secretaries' work and beneath her station. Studying was a loftier pastime. But what on earth could the "have typewriter will travel" part mean? She wrote down the number. At the telephone booth conveniently located across the street from her apartment she dug for a five-franc coin at the bottom of her purse, then dialed 21-379.

"It means I'll pick up and deliver your typing to your door," the voice on the phone informed her when she asked about the curious expression in the man's notice.

"And I am speaking with Monsieur Duras?"

"But of course. Call me Jacques."

"I'll give you my address," Jade interjected quickly. "Can you come right away? My assignment's due tomorrow."

"I'm almost at your door," Jacques replied.

As Jade waited for the typist, she fiddled with the skirt her seamstress in Saigon had made for her. Her favorite color was green, and the skirt was a swirl of minute pleats.

Jade parted the curtains and glanced out the window. Standing on the steps of 5 rue de Montaigne was a tall, dark stranger, a man somewhat above middle height with a handsome face marked by deep lines on each side of his mouth. When she heard his knock, she tripped lightly toward the door. As the door swung wide and she looked into Jacques's eyes, a shadow fell across the foyer floor. She cast her eyes down. The dim light playing through the etched panes of translucent glass gave her the fleeting illusion that she was an extension of Jacques's shadow, maybe an extension of Jacques himself. When she looked up and into his eyes again, she knew her instinctive emotion was reciprocated.

"I'm studying Romance languages and German," Jade said rapidly to cover her nervousness. She felt as light as the breeze that had cooled her in the hillside honeymoon town of Dalat, where she had napped coverless and naked on the first mornings of her marriage to Van.

"I'm going to be a doctor," Jacques said in turn, smiling and pushing up the sleeves of the surgeon's jacket he wore.

Jade stomped one tiny foot and pouted. "They're making me take Biology 101 as part of my studies, and I hate it because I can't understand it. It's so technical."

"The sciences are my forte. I can help if you like."

Jade looked at the painstakingly written notes in her hand. They appeared even more like hieroglyphics than they had before.

"I'd be forever in your debt if you would." She hesitated for a second, then asked, "When can you begin?"

Jacques lifted his gaze from Jade's notes and looked deeply into her eyes. She was taken aback by the tangible excitement, no, magnetic attraction she experienced.

"There's no time like the present," he said, and together they began the short journey up her stairs that would become a familiar repetition.

From the first moment the two students felt a mutual attraction that could easily be termed love at first sight. They talked into the early hours of the morning as Jacques painted his past life and future aspirations for her. Jade could see that Jacques was as lonesome as she was. That was their bond: he had been orphaned at ten, and she was far away from her country and from Van. Jade didn't tell Jacques she was a married woman. It wasn't until much later that she told him the truth.

Jade had never been in close contact with a handsome young European man before, and Jacques had never been intimate with an Asian woman. Jacques did admit he'd witnessed a live show in Paris's place Pigalle some years back. The poster outside the cabaret had depicted a tangle of black-and-yellow flesh and proclaimed: CHINA GIRL FUCKS BRUTUS. The performance featured a sensuous young woman of Asian origin simulating sex with an incredibly well-endowed black man. She writhed across his muscled body like a fish. Jacques hadn't known such exotic creatures truly existed—until he saw Jade.

Although Jade had come to appreciate the quickening feelings and merciful release sex with Van afforded her, she hadn't realized women could actually experience sexual urges before they were at least in the middle of the sex act. Just looking at Jacques's tall frame as it drifted near her made her tingle erotically. Van might have introduced her to sex, but it was Jacques who really awakened her to the possibilities of her body.

Exquisite intimacy between the two came quickly, possibly because they were both loners. Neither ran with a gang or clique. The campus, a swarm of many young men and a few young women who dressed like wraiths in dark pants and jet-black turtlenecks in imitation of their cleverer cousins at Paris's Sorbonne, was alive with talk of Carl Jung, André Breton, surrealism, communism, and the iniquities of Adolf Hitler. Talk that Jade had no knowledge of and Jacques no time for.

When Jacques strolled beside Jade among the university's stone buildings, her books balanced on his arm, he made Jade appear tinier and more delicate than she was. His slave-trading grandfather, a man with blond hair and intense gray eyes, had dallied with an Algerian handmaiden and consequently introduced exotic blood into the family. Like his dark-skinned grandmother, Jacques was lean and moved with lazy grace. That he was handsome was unquestionable. He barbered his dark hair himself, cropping it close to his skull in the popular, easy-wear style known as a buzz or razor cut. His casually shorn hair stood straight up, like a surprise, or like the quills of a young porcupine.

Jacques's skin was so tight it was almost transparent, and Jade delighted in tracing the veins of his arms and chest with her fingertips. His gaze was that of a zealous man, but it could charm at will. His blue-gray eyes devoured all they saw: knowledge, food, even Jade.

cheek to cheek
arm in arm
they move
seeing nothing
but each other

For Jacques, medical school was a grind made slower by the fact that he had spent the previous four years working at odd jobs to put himself through school. This, his last year, would be easy in comparison. Prior to meeting Jade, he had received the Delois Scholarship, which paid two-thirds of his tuition and gave him time to enjoy life to the hilt. To be financially safe, he had kept two of his more engaging part-time jobs: working as a kitchen hand at a café in the evenings and doing typing jobs for various students. Before his scholarship, in what he already referred to as his "lean years," he had earned only enough money to cover his schooling, lodging in a third-rate rooming house, and books. Nothing was left over for spending money, and his only sure meal was in the evening at the Café Puss Puss, where he worked as busboy and dishwasher.

As the weeks passed and Jade's feelings for Jacques deepened, she decided to catch a glimpse of him working, thinking it would help her to know him better. After all, he had to fend for himself and lived hand-to-mouth while she enjoyed the spoilt existence of an ingenue.

Walking to his district, she passed over the huge *dalles*, the great elevated boardwalk where students drank, mixed, or attended the opera at the end of the place de la Comédie. Behind was the old cobblestoned town. Jacques had told Jade that its architecture dated from the thirteenth to the nineteenth centuries. Up the wide steps and behind the ancient buildings was a slum, a raw tenderloin that students frequented when drunk or on a dare. Sailors, married Frenchmen whose wives shunned them, and tourists out to relive the potent lust of youth or other long-gone sexual excitement roamed these tawdry alleys like dogs in heat.

Jade was appalled at the meanness of the area. Moving hurriedly through the quarter, she was approached by men who mistook her for an Asian *belle de nuit.* She was disgusted by the shabbiness of everything, infected by the men's fever for women, dirtied by their hot words, some of which she didn't understand. Jade would never forget the faraway looks in the eyes of the whores.

CAFÉ PUSS PUSS, the neon sign glared. Jade hesitated, then braved the alley behind in search of the kitchen and a view of Jacques. She had no intention of letting him see her. Picking her way through mounds of fish heads and food scraps that had missed the garbage tins lining the alley, Jade held a lilac-scented handkerchief to her nose. She could see the café's kitchen door. Through the steam issuing from the open door she recognized Jacques, his razor-cropped hair flat with heat. He faced a dingy wall and was stooped over a metal sink. Straining to see, she found herself mesmerized as his red hands moved in and out of greasy, steaming water, removing a dish, rinsing a glass. She imagined by the slant of his head that he was far away, dreaming about being a physician, maybe dreaming of her.

Jade lingered only for a few minutes, then secretly made her way home. She dreamed about that place for many nights after her visit. In her sleep she rescued Jacques from a groping sea of filthy hands, keeping him safe with her.

5

DECEPTIONS

There is no greater torture in the world than at the same time to love and to condemn.

—Somerset Maugham, *Wit and Wisdom of Somerset Maugham*

Montpellier: March 1940

It was difficult to focus on studies with the encroaching threat of the Nazis on their threshold. Talk in the student cafés had turned from a brazen condemnation of Hitler to palpable fear. But a sense of unreality about the situation prevailed, especially for Jade, who isolated herself from all but Jacques.

Toward the end of the semester the study load escalated and Jade knew Jacques was falling behind. It was his final semester. As well as wrestling with papers and exams, he attended an intern practicum at the limited-facility teaching hospital affiliated with the medical school. Jade insisted on seeing him as often as she could and badgered him to move into her apartment. With some difficulty she persuaded him to leave his job at the café.

Their cocoon was 5 rue de Montaigne. For the first time she could remember, Jade didn't feel alone. She loved Jacques, her Jacques, and under the guise of protecting him she hid the letters and pictures sent to her from Vietnam by her husband and her father.

Jade should have known she might become pregnant. After all, she was a married woman. But she and Jacques took no precautions and never spoke of the probability or ramifications of having a child. It never crossed her mind that it could happen. Or maybe she secretly wanted it to occur. The day she sat for her mid-term exams was the moment she knew. How, she berated herself, could she have forgotten the symptoms she'd read about in the illicit novels of love, romance, and pain she'd consumed so avidly in Saigon?

Taking a seat in the sterile environment of the exam hall, confident in her knowledge of German grammar, she was struck by nausea. She battled the feeling, but it came at her in waves. Leaving her exam paper uncovered, she bolted to the ladies' room. There, locked behind the cubicle door, she was sick. She had tried to wait for the student applying lipstick to leave, but she couldn't. Jade wretched into the dirty toilet bowl. It was humiliating, and she recognized this symptom immediately for what it was, especially since she had missed her last period. She was pregnant with Jacques's baby.

When Jade returned to the exam room, she couldn't think and felt too confused to continue. She asked the professor in charge if she could rewrite the exam when she felt better. As she did so, she fancied that the professor's face was Van's. The look of shock she imagined she glimpsed made her heart pound even harder, leaving her more nerve-racked. *Pregnant with an illegitimate child.* These words were her silent litany. Head bent in embarrassment, tears streaming, she found her way back to her apartment.

With great difficulty she fumbled with the old-fashioned key in the lock, heard it click, and pushed the heavy door open. Once in her hall, she kicked off her shoes and let her silk-stocking feet carry her noiselessly up the stairs toward her bed. It took only a split second for her to notice Marceline, the day girl, reclining while leafing through the letters and pictures Van and her father had sent her over the last while. Jade's gasp made Marceline look up.

"Your husband, madame, he isn't handsome. I always wondered if you were hiding something, especially with the airs you put on. How do you think your husband feels to be cuckolded?"

Jade was so angry that it took her a moment to find her tongue. "Give those letters to me and get out!"

"You take such pains to hide the letters each week, madame. Or should I call you mademoiselle? You seem to go by that." The day girl had never felt such power. "Are you hiding the letters from your boyfriend, or from me, or do you pretend to yourself?"

Jade turned toward the door, the light through the windowpane illuminating her anger. "I'll call the police. Your insolence is unspeakable."

"Madame, I was only cleaning the way you want me to. Each week I dust your hidden letters. I was told wealthy ladies like you give rewards for work well done."

"Are you blackmailing me?"

Marceline stroked Jade's cache of letters with possessive fingers. "Madame, if you see fit to give me something valuable, who am I to argue? I won't tell your lover you have a husband far away."

"Yes, I have a lover, but he knows everything about my past relationships. You can't tell him anything he doesn't already know."

Marceline was silent for a moment. "You have so much, madame, and my life's a struggle. If I told your husband—"

"My husband died of malaria in Vietnam only last month. The letters are old and you're too slow. I'll pay you a month's salary since, as you say, you've been thorough."

After the girl left, Jade checked her letters to see if any were missing. She couldn't be sure, but possibly the pile was thinner than it had been. Feeling ill and shocked, she ripped off the bedclothes that had been invisibly soiled by Marceline, then threw herself onto the bed.

Jacques would be home soon. Dinnertime was approaching. She pictured the deserted library, knowing he would be the last one there, no doubt studying *L'Anatomie du Corps Humain* in the enlightened atmosphere and civilized heat of the room. Jade had laid down ground rules that Jacques had said he fully understood.

He wasn't allowed to return to her apartment before five o'clock. "I need complete privacy to study," she'd explained the day he had moved in. Jacques had said that was all right with him, since it was her place and she paid all the bills. Besides, he'd told her, she was too much of a distraction. Each time she was near he burned with a desire that made him forget everything, especially his studies. That was why he was content to cram at the university library. Now Jade heard Jacques at the door, and she trembled when she thought about what she had to tell him.

"I'm home, baby," he called out as he rushed up the stairs. When Jade didn't answer, he said, "Are you here?"

She heard him pass through the kitchen and the salon. Then, finally, he entered the bedroom and grinned when he saw her. His joy quickly turned to alarm, though, when he realized she was crying.

Sitting beside her on the bed, he stroked her forehead, then her hair, as if she were ill. She listened mutely as he murmured sweet endearments, calling her his angel, his darling, his poor baby. When he called her his baby again, she cried even harder. How could she tell her husband in Vietnam she was pregnant with another man's child? There was no excuse she could give Van, no plausible lies she could tell. How could she tell Jacques, who soothed her now, that she had a husband in Saigon? Perversely Jade didn't want to lose Jacques or Van.

She tilted her eyes to see Jacques clearly, sobbed, then cleared her throat. "I'm...I'm pregnant."

Jacques looked at her intently. "I'll marry you."

"No! I don't expect you to do that."

Afterward, despite Jacques's protestations, she refused to discuss the matter further, saying she would have to sort things out in her mind first. That said, they both fell into a fitful sleep. When Jade awoke the next morning, she felt shame as soon as she realized her condition wasn't a bad dream. She was still clothed and the bed sheets were twisted around her, not unlike her own lies. Jacques had offered to stay with her, even miss his student rounds at the university hospital, but she'd declined his kindness with bad grace.

After Jacques left, Jade wrote and posted three letters. The first one was to her father. "Dearest Papa," it began, "please talk to Van. Persuade him to let me stay in Montpellier through the summer break. I have a marvelous opportunity to study international politics with a renowned American professor who will only be available through the summer term." She wrote the same to Van but added a postscript: "Although I'll miss you terribly, I'll be too busy with my studies to have any visitors."

The third letter, to her old *yaya*, Dô, was written in the peasant dialect Kinh and couched in the simplest terms. She knew Dô had family connections in a Vietnamese village famous for its medicinal herbs. Jade was sure there was a special potion that could do away with unwanted babies. That way she wouldn't have to deal secretly with a doctor, or worse, a backstreet abortionist.

The next week Jade rewrote her German grammar exam and did well. Jacques was adoring and patient, taking her at her word. Before she knew it she entered her fifth month, yet barely showed. Fashion was her accomplice. She wore the gathered French painter's shirt that was all the rage with Parisian ingenues who strolled the leafy paths on the Seine and shopped the Champs-Elysées. The shirt hid her problem well. Priding herself that only Jacques and the physician knew, Jade was genuinely surprised when she felt movement in her abdomen. Dr. Mercador, an acquaintance of Jacques, received her in a run-down office located off rue du Bras-de-Fer. He greeted her as Madame Duras, and she didn't set him straight. At first Jade had refused to go, saying Jacques's medical knowledge was enough. But on that count his sweet bullying knew no bounds and she was persuaded. The unborn baby and she were given a clean bill of health by a jubilant doctor. Jade, for her part, returned to her apartment devoid of joy.

Jacques nagged her endlessly about getting married. Her continued silence, even melancholy, stretched his usual patience to the breaking point. Storming from the apartment in response to her coldness, he turned up days later, seemingly convinced she didn't love him. When Jade questioned him, he answered, "I'm trying to be like you—the silent Asian."

Not long after, the pocket-size package of herbs from Dô for "Jade's poor friend" finally arrived. Jade knew she was probably too far along, but she tore the brown paper wrapper off the parcel, anyway, and boiled the dried roots to make a tea. With great anticipation she downed the bitter substance and waited for the miscarriage. But nothing happened, although she felt ill. She then ate the hard roots, pulling them from the bottom of the burning water with bare fingers, chewing them to a pulp, and choking when she swallowed. Still nothing. Desperate, she threw herself off the building landing and down the last set of stairs in the hall, but only twisted her ankle and bruised her knees. It was useless.

Resigning herself to the inevitable, Jade told Jacques the truth about Van and her frantic bid to free herself of the baby. Jacques was stunned.

"Don't you see?" Jade implored. "I can't have this baby. What would people think?"

Jacques scowled. "Are you trying to tell me you attempted to kill our baby to protect your reputation? What kind of woman are you?"

Before Jade could say another word, Jacques stormed out of the apartment, slamming the door behind him. Not knowing what else to do, Jade sat motionless in a wicker chair, contemplating her sorry state. Well into the night, Jacques returned with a sulky, drunken flourish. When he didn't say anything, Jade, who was still sitting in the chair, pleaded, "Please don't leave me again. I can't bear it."

"I'll stay with you until the baby is born." He shook his head. "After that, I don't know."

To sweep away his bitterness, Jade threw herself at his feet and sobbed, "I love you, Jacques. Only you. I didn't mean to hurt you. I—"

Jacques glowered but said nothing. Instead he fell to his knees and fumbled with the black velvet ribbon that held her loose blouse together. Head bent, he undid the buttons of her smock with a dexterity that belied his drunkenness. She was glad she couldn't see his face very well in the gloom. After he unfastened each button with exaggerated care, he let his lips and tongue linger beneath the fabric, his unshaven cheeks and chin grazing her bare skin.

"Stand up!" he finally ordered, and she obeyed.

Jacques tugged on her elasticized skirt, and the silk slid to the ground in a pool of wavy aquamarine. He told her to remove her underthings, and she complied, her hand moving to her back, her stomach distending farther as she unclipped her brassiere and nervously untangled the straps from her arms. Her breasts were engorged, her usually flat nipples pointed. He motioned at her panties and she pulled them to her knees. When they slipped to her feet, she kicked them off, almost losing her balance.

Kneeling, Jacques caressed her enlarged stomach with hot hands. Without looking at her he breathed, "One last time." Still on his knees, he hauled her to the cold hardwood floor.

Jade now saw Jacques's face more clearly. She hardly recognized him. His features were a mask of writhing emotion.

He whispered, "Cunt," and touched her there. She gasped involuntarily, more at his words than from his action. In reply he hissed, "Shh, I won't hurt my baby."

For a moment Jade thought he was referring to her.

Jacques took something from his pocket. She saw it flash, but only knew it was a tin of Vaseline. His other hand tore at the buttons of his fly. Shutting her eyes and trying not to cry out, Jade allowed him to maneuver her onto her side. Her body protectively took the shape of an *S*. She smelled liquor and hate on his breath as his greased finger opened her and moved back and forth. Then, with his own hand guiding his penis, Jacques entered her and closed like scissors, both against and into her, one sharp, hard time and another and another, each thrust more violent than its predecessor. Jade now knew what her father had stunk of when she was a child—stale sex that clung to him when he returned home from what he referred to as "partaking his pleasure."

Exams were on again, this time finals. Although Jacques did passably well in his internship, he failed his last semester's written exams. His hard work to become a medical doctor was all for naught. Jade knew he blamed his failure on the shock of finding out that she was married. Becoming silent and morose, he didn't speak of marriage again.

Jade was partially jealous and grateful for this. She wrote two more letters. One was to her father, asking for money. The other was to Van, saying she missed him but that her studies were onerous and took precedence. She had to stay on in Montpellier. Jade next renewed her lease and the same day dialed the number of a charitable institution, a Catholic orphanage. But she replaced the receiver in its cradle even before a female voice answered.

Jacques spent all his time with Jade. "You'd be better off without me," he once rasped, barely checking his anger. "Or are you afraid your husband will beat you, leave you, burn you, or whatever cuckolded Vietnamese do to unfaithful wives?" He would sit by the bedroom window while Jade dressed, looking down at the street, his large hands holding the impossibly delicate curtains that used to shield their love from the life below but now kept them prisoners.

Despite his behavior, Jade was afraid of losing him, and of what would happen when the baby came. "I'll leave my husband for you, Jacques. I can't live without you. Please don't leave me!" she told him time and time again. Whenever she talked like that he would fall silent, take her coolly into his arms, and once more renew their ritual of love and hate.

In June the unthinkable happened and Paris fell to the Nazis. Relatively safe in the newly formed, so-called unoccupied Vichy France, Jade and Jacques became increasingly absorbed in their own situation and found it difficult to follow the larger-than-life events unfolding in the rest of Europe.

At what would have been the beginning of their autumn semester, if they had attended classes, Jacques returned to his normal loving self. He borrowed a country cottage near Cevennes from a friend. Here, he told Jade, they would have an idyllic retreat and a secluded place for the birth.

Jacques informed Jade of the arrangements he had made: a discreet country doctor, a crony from medical school who lived in a nearby village would deliver the baby when it came. "Trust me," he told her. "No one will know anything unless you want them to. I might never be a physician, but I still have medical contacts and a favor from a friend to be repaid."

The rural days passed, they picnicked, walked, searched the forest floor for mushrooms, spent long nights before the cottage stove fire. Love seemed to return to their relationship.

Jacques treated Jade like a swollen, delicate dove. His fingers fed her, his hands soothed her. Then, a week before their idyll was to end, Jade went into labor. Jacques called his physician friend from the nearby village and they delivered the baby. Jade's labor was long and intense. When her painful ordeal was over, Jacques surreptitiously removed the bloody thing from her view. Then he sedated her, saying she needed to sleep and that everything would be taken care of to her satisfaction. Their country cottage became heavy with quiet after the commotion of the birth. When she awoke the next day, and before she could say a word, Jacques told her bluntly that her baby was dead.

6

THE SECRET UNFOLDS

I woke in the plane from Saigon, and some sexual dream compelled by the beat of the plane engine made me wonder why the cry of a woman's orgasm is always sad: the sound that seems to be torn from her unwillingly, in pain, rather than pleasure?

—Graham Greene, "Saigon Journal"

Montpellier: April 1955

The door of her pension room swung open with a creak, and the woman Jade was waiting for stood large in its frame. "Come in!" Jade said. "Are you a friend of Jacques?"

"Yes, a very old friend. Even an older friend than you are. You don't remember me, do you?"

Jade gestured toward a chair.

"I'm Monique. Now do you remember?"

Jade looked blank.

"I met you a number of times with Jacques, but I'm not surprised you don't recognize me. You looked right through me as if I didn't exist. Jacques and I worked at Café Puss Puss. We were to be married—that is, before you came along."

Jade took stock of her visitor: Monique was taller than she and had a voluptuous figure obviously trimmed to an hourglass by a boned and elasticized girdle. She wore heavy pancake makeup. A beauty mark, round and black, was penciled on her lower cheek beneath a garish sweep of rouge. Her patterned dress was purchased off the rack, a sure sign of poverty in a Frenchwoman. Jade had to admit, though, that the woman must have been attractive when she was younger.

"Jacques never mentioned a fiancée," Jade finally said.

Moisture welled in Monique's eyes. "I hated you so much. I loved Jacques more than you ever did and cried myself to sleep for months after he left. I begged him to stay with me. But he loved you more." Tears carved furrows in her powder and paint.

Jade smiled with false sympathy and edged her chair closer. "What can I say? Jacques never mentioned you. But where is he now?"

"Jacques came back to me after he left you. He brought your child with him. I looked after that baby as if it were my own."

"What baby? Are you insane? My baby died in labor. Who put you up to this? Is it money you're after?"

Monique shook her head. "Money? We're not all on your level. Jacques took the baby from you when you were sedated. He arranged everything with the help of an acquaintance in medical school who stole pharmaceuticals. Jacques had this man masquerade as the village doctor. The man lived in the village close to where you stayed. An addict, he was desperate for money." She wiped her tears. "Jacques hated you for trying to abort his unborn child, but he still wanted to keep a part of you."

"I don't believe you! You're a liar!"

Monique made a subtle motion with her damp handkerchief, sending the scent of lilacs around the room. "Believe it or not—that's your choice. If you like, I'll leave now."

"No, don't go. Tell me, Monique. Please!"

"I lived with Jacques after you left him. He adored the baby and treated her like a jewel. Jacques named her Phuong—Phoenix. He said the name Phoenix signified the happiness the baby brought him out of the ashes and ruin of his love for you."

Jade's face clouded. "I believe you now, Monique."

"At first I was happy to have Jacques back, but he was so moody. He'd say he was ruined, then spend days not speaking to me. He said he despised women, that we were all the same. He'd rant and rave that his medical career was lost, his life useless. And he drank, but only at night when the baby slept. You ruined him, Jade Minh, and no amount of love from me could change that. In the end all he did was drink, and the only contentment he had was when he played with the baby."

Jade tsked.

"One day I came home from serving at the restaurant I worked at and Jacques and his baby were gone. I was heartbroken. I had hoped time would make him forget you and let him love me again. Jacques had made some money selling drugs on the black market. He said he needed to do it to make a life for his baby. He and the child lived like Gypsies camping in the countryside.

"I didn't see Jacques again until a little less than a year ago. He was begging on a street corner in Paris. I almost didn't recognize him and I'm not sure he knew who I was. He was demented and ill. His clothes were tattered and his face was ravaged by alcohol, sickness, and loneliness. He said he was dying and the sooner the better."

Jade gasped and put her hand to her mouth.

"I asked Jacques where the baby was, though obviously she wasn't an infant anymore. When I mentioned Phuong, he clutched his heart and nearly collapsed. He said he'd been forced to leave her in the Catholic orphanage in Mont Ste-Odile. Jacques cried when he told me. I tried to console him and asked him if I should tell you about the baby. He didn't answer. Instead he said, 'I loved only her and never you.' I didn't know if he was talking about loving you or the baby. After that I couldn't bear to look at him anymore and slipped away."

Monique gazed past Jade and continued. "I'd almost forgotten how Jacques ruined me. After he walked out, I ran out of money. I was despondent and they let me go at the restaurant. I wandered the streets after dark. If a man looked at all like Jacques,

I'd tell him he resembled my old lover. These strangers would take me in cheap rented rooms. Once, against a brick wall. I could smell old wine and urine, but I didn't care. After that they would pay me."

"In the old town!" Jade said, horrified and at the same time recalling the alley behind the Café Puss Puss.

"No, in Marseille. Jacques had insisted we move to a place where no one knew him. He was afraid you would try to find him. But of course you never did."

Jade studied Monique. "Do you need some money?" She moved toward the pillow where she'd hidden her bundle of francs.

"It's always money with you. No wonder Jacques hated you."

"I'm so sorry," Jade placated. "I didn't mean it that way. I just want to help you in return for your kindness to Jacques so many years ago."

"Jacques is dead for me and for himself. I wanted you to know that you killed him."

"No, it's not true!" Only then did Jade begin to cry. "I couldn't help what happened. I was afraid for my reputation. But I loved Jacques. I loved Jacques," she said, making the words poignant.

Monique's mouth puckered with disdain, and her beauty mark hid under a fold of skin. "Your reputation—that's a good one! Everyone at the university knew you and Jacques were having an affair. Everyone knew you were married except Jacques. People respected him and didn't want to be the bearers of bad news. The two of you were the scandal of the university." She got up and moved toward the door. "I just wanted you to know the truth."

"Wait! Where is he now?"

"He's dead, or at least he might as well be."

Just then the hotel phone rang. "Hello," Jade said when she answered. "No, I'm fine." Replacing the receiver, she turned back toward the door, but Monique was gone.

Jade was stunned by her visitor's news and overcome with humiliation for her once-beautiful lover. She thought hard. How could she be blamed for his weakness? Would Monique interfere again? No, Jade was certain the woman only wanted to shame her, desired merely some measure of personal revenge. She recalled Monique's words: *He's dead, or at least he might as well be.* Jade understood. It was better to bury people in your mind, believe them dead, rather than allow them to continue hurting you.

Then another consideration took hold. What if the child came to find her? After all, she had no idea how much Jacques had told his daughter about her. But that was impossible, Jade reasoned. Her husband, and the world, knew nothing of her ancient indiscretion. Jade weighted the consequences of disclosure and they were dire. Her reputation would be ruined and Van might desert her. He was a moral man. Yes, he was kind and he loved her, but she realized the one thing he wouldn't forgive was cruelty to another human being. If Van knew she had purposely tried to get rid of a child, his love for her would die. She saw little of Van, but that wasn't the point. Even his faraway existence made her who she was. She still had a husband who supported her. And when she was old, she knew she'd need him even more. But Phuong or Phoenix wasn't her fault or her business, she figured. Jacques had told her the baby was dead.

Jade began pacing, then halted and poured water into a ceramic basin. After she splashed her face, she took inventory of herself in the cheap square of mirror affixed to the wall. A smooth, elegant countenance looked back at her. Even so, she imagined a furrow in her brow and lines marring the corners of her mouth. Demoralized, Jade turned away and began hunting frantically in her overnight case for a small vial of wrinkle cream, finally unearthing the tube in a side pocket she'd almost forgotten existed.

She placed the cream on the bed and continued her reverie.

If she were in Saigon, away from France where the child obviously lived, her secret would be safe. But then she was suddenly ashamed of herself, of Monique and the woman's dirty search for love, of her own response to the news that a child of hers existed.

Phoenix would now be fourteen. Jade couldn't stop thinking about how revolted Van would be if he found out that her child had been abandoned. And behind those thoughts, she knew in her heart she wished the girl didn't exist. Then, unbidden recollections of losing her own dear mother flooded her mind. Flinging herself on the bed, she rocked in a childlike ritual. Back and forth, she went, back and forth, her arms a self-made straitjacket around her body, repeating the motion until the act itself brought the oblivion of memories, sleep, and dreams...

7

ORIGINS

Children begin by loving their parents; after a time they judge them; rarely, if ever, do they forgive them.

—Oscar Wilde, *A Woman of No Importance*

Dalat, Indochina: July 1926

Little Jade had been spared the reality of her mother's end, although she knew Maman was ill from the solemn whispers and endless processions of somberly clad physicians who passed first through the door of their house high on Dalat's most prestigious hill, then into Maman's private rooms, making her even less accessible to the five-year-old Jade than usual. Jade's black-trousered *yaya*, Dô, who had attended to Maman in her childhood home in the colder north of Vietnam, kept the child away from the sick room with cries of "Maman too busy for you," repeated each bedtime in Vietnamese French.

Fever, malaria, and "treatment" had turned Maman's smooth complexion into the ravaged parchment of an abused book. "Curers" called hysterically to her bedside by Jade's helpless father, had mechanically rubbed the skin of her wan forehead with a spoon, hoping to remove the "bad wind" in her head and thus relieve the fever. Dô tried to help and practiced her village magic, mumbling over a hen's egg. When she cracked the egg, the viscous liquid ran black, representing the evil spirit that possessed Maman. Although Jade witnessed the egg's transformation, it was to no avail. Maman's fever and the bruises lingered, turning yellow, then deep red, marring her extraordinary beauty even in its final release. Many years earlier a fortuneteller had told Maman that red was an unlucky color that signified death and that she would be wise to avoid it at all cost. But here, on her deathbed with the leeches and the physicians, that was impossible.

Dô finally pulled the small girl into the lap of her loose trousers and said, "Maman, she gone forever."

Narrowing her eyes, Jade accepted this statement without question. Later she would think of Maman and what she had lost. Conjuring emotionally induced images of herself with her mother, she would cry inconsolably until Dô took her into bony arms and rocked her into a hiccupping sleep. In those charged memories of Maman, Jade saw herself sitting contentedly at her mother's feet, her beloved parent's waist-length hair elaborately coiffed and rolled so high that the style added six inches of height as befitted a mandarin's daughter.

Always Jade recalled the precious fabrics. Bolts of silk, some shot with gold thread, were collected from the near and far corners of the planet to be flung carelessly onto the hand-polished teak floor of Maman's room. The cloth came from the neighboring French colonies of Lao and Cambodge, from the weaving villages located in Malaya on the South China Sea, from the Kingdom of Siam with its gold-leafed temples, from China itself, and from Lyon and Paris. A lisping French, Indian, or Chinese dressmaker minced in attendance, vacuously complimenting Maman on her slender figure and her fashion wisdom. Offhandedly Maman would choose four, five, sometimes ten lengths of the costly stuff, usually remarking, "After all, little Jade, what good is having so many piastres if it isn't to buy beautiful things, and what *good* is a woman if she isn't beautiful?"

If she behaved, Jade was allowed to select two lengths of the precious material for herself, as long as she promised not to tell Papa. One piece of silk was for her dowry; the other shimmering length was transformed into clothes for mother and daughter.

Jade usually picked green, the color of the stone she was named after, while Maman always varied her selection but avoided red, the hue she so often warned Jade was unlucky.

When Jade remembered the house of her childhood and Maman, she visualized, too, the rainbow of bougainvillea and hibiscus. Dô plucked blooms with her in the courtyard. Sitting under a scarlet, tree-size poinsettia, Jade practiced counting on the petals of a stray flower. Dô squatted nearby, chewing a leaf-wrapped package of lime paste, betel, and areca palm nut and making a small pouch under her left cheek. Every so often a spray of purple saliva streamed from Dô's stained mouth. Bees buzzed and the breeze cooled the south-facing ironwood house, with its tiled four-slope roof that curved up like the corners of Jade's mouth when she was allowed to see Maman.

The days after Maman's death were quite different. Papa had no religion. Although their provincial neighbors followed Buddhism and some were staunch Roman Catholics, he had no time for spiritual trappings. Dô, like most rural Vietnamese, practiced animism, the belief that a governing spirit dwelled in living and nonliving things. Such faith meant that the beings in trees, rocks, wind, and rain must be appeased by gifts of food, incense, and prayer.

Lately Dô had discovered the all-seeing orb of the Cao Dai religion and had traveled by *cyclo-pousse*, the single-seat rickshaw, and then on sore feet to the multihued temple at Tay Ninh, a town north of Saigon. She described her experience with glowing words and excited eyes for little Jade when she returned.

Dô had marveled at a mural in the temple's entrance. It depicted the cult's "Third Alliance Between God and Man": Vietnamese poet Nguyen Binh Khiem, French novelist Victor Hugo, and the Chinese nationalist Sun Yat-sen. The peasant nursemaid and pilgrim knew nothing of these historic figures whom the congregation worshiped along with Jesus and

Buddha, two individuals Dô did know. Like the followers of the mystic who founded Cao Daism in 1919 when he communed with a spirit who called himself Cao Dai, Dô donned long white robes and wound a black turban around her shorn hair. Inside the temple she found the spectacle phantasmagoric. The outrageously costumed temple priests wore soutanes and tall hats, not unlike those sported by chefs. The hats were emblazoned with miniature replicas of the popular temple's monstrous centerpiece—an all-seeing eye.

Ritual ancestor worship, as practiced by Dô, consisted of sporadic burning of offerings and served to keep Maman's memory intact. When a full moon lit the Saigon sky, Dô and little Jade would set fire to tiny paper clothes and houses, or sometimes "Bank of Hell" money at the ancestral altar that stood at the threshold of the long stairs. This was to ensure that Maman would have the comforts of home in her afterlife. But, of course, there was no one to arrange and light the miniature paper objects and chunks of incense but the nursemaid, who took charge of the entire household.

Immediately after Maman died, Jade's father sold their home near Dalat and moved the family to Saigon where he spent a great deal of time at the opium *fumerie* on rue d'Ormay or, when he felt like slumming, in one of the boxlike establishments in gangster Bay Vien's Chinese Cholon district. He would lie on a hard leather divan and let a pipe maker knead the ball of gum over the flame. Then he would pull hard on the pipe, pursing his lips so that the crevices in the flesh of his mouth became black stripes. When he drew in, the opium in the bowl bubbled and the smoke engulfed him, sweeping him off to some faraway place. But before he sucked himself into that sated state and couldn't maintain an erection, he'd take a *cyclo* to the largest and most pleasurable brothel east of the Suez Canal—Cholon's House of Five Hundred Women, another of Bay Vien's lucrative establishments.

When Papa returned from a few days of "partaking his pleasure," he stank of cheap perfume, something ammonia-like, and the sweetish odor of opium. Jade was never sure if she enjoyed or hated the cloying smell, but Dô would mutter under her own garlic breath about Papa washing before he left his street women.

Born into a dirt-poor *paysanne* family whose one-room house of thatch stood near the backwaters of the lower Mekong River on southern Vietnam's Ca Mau Peninsula, Papa was indentured to a rice farmer at age six. Soon he was intimate with the tiny stalks he planted and cultivated, but knew nothing of the history of the nearby canal that predated the colonial period. Formerly named Kramoun-Sa under the previous rule of the Kingdom of Cambodge, the flat, forest-covered swamp was placed under the protection of the Nguyen lords of Hué in 1715. The area, one hundred miles southwest of Saigon, was renowned as a producer of honey, beeswax, and the feathers of exotic birds. But when the swamps were drained, Rach Gia became a center for rice processing.

The child who became Jade's father grew weary of his monotonous labor in the greenish water of the paddies. He took a boy's pleasure in dodging the twisting emerald pit vipers with their poisonous fangs as they slithered across the rich muck, delighting in breaking their backs with the butt of his machete. Sometimes he teased the small-eyed pipe snakes that, when molested, hid their harmless heads under thick bodies. When a pipe snake raised its tail to simulate a more dangerous and larger head, the boy chopped its body in half with a series of energetic whacks. Always, though, when he spotted a sunbeam snake, he let it live, watching in awe as it slid by, its metallic luster a zigzag of gold.

By the age of ten, the boy had had enough of the rice fields and left his village and job forever, giving no more thought to his parents or siblings. Once he glimpsed the splendor of Saigon, the humid Pearl of the Orient, he was mesmerized. The city's ochre buildings and rococo balconies of wrought iron draped with silk-clad ladies now informed his young life.

He arrived in Saigon on a cloudless morning. A white moon was still cocked in the sky, which he took as a lucky sign. With the day came traffic, mostly the whir and whirl of wheels. He was amazed by the *cyclos* and the torrent of bicycles, some with wire baskets attached to the handlebars. Girls in *aio dais* enchanted him, slit skirts streaming behind like the tail feathers of the exotic birds that were sold at the market in Rach Gia.

The boy was filthy and starved, but he easily found employment, of sorts, with the street urchins who sold postcards or sticks of gum to passersby. He purchased a small box of wholesale cellophane-wrapped gum squares from the foreign-owned chewing gum factory in the claptrap outskirts of Saigon. Shanty shacks that had sprouted like toadstools encircled the French-run factory. Inside the cavelike place a line of half-naked males of various ages sweated, turning vats of chicle into gum. The heat was unbearable and the smoke made his breath catch in his lungs. He had hoped to find work there but knew instinctively it was an even harder life than what he had run from.

When the boy from the Rach Gia canal left home, he wasn't empty-handed. While his parents and siblings had snored and swung in their greasy-stringed hammocks from their day's labor, he had stolen the few meager piastres secreted by his mother in the rice bucket by the charcoal brazier. It was this foresight that had kept him from prostitution or starvation during his first weeks in Saigon.

At night, when rain sluiced Saigon's litter into ditches that in monsoon season ran wild with storm water and reeked of human feces, the street urchins huddled under the wall of Saigon's Notre Dame, the vulgar 1880s neo-Romanesque, twin-spired church of red brick. There the half-starved children scrapped, played, and slept. Some simply rested back to back, or leaned their grimy heads on one another's bony shoulders. Others, like Papa, planned their tomorrows. Tuning his senses to opportunity, he applied for a courier job at Saigon's infamous opium factory, run by Bay Vien. The position was a simple matter of delivering the tiny pots of the oozing substance to wealthy Vietnamese and French patrons who smoked opium as Englishmen drank brandy and puffed cigars.

His timing was perfect: one of the urchins had taken the courier position a while back but had been robbed, then drowned under the bridge to Dakow. Rumor had it that the Vietnamese Sûreté was investigating and would certainly arrest someone. Not waiting to hear the gory details, Papa showed up at the delivery entrance of Saigon's premier opium factory.

During his lucrative years as a courier, Papa spoke little and kept a low profile. Purposely he made no friends or enemies. The contacts he had of necessity knew him as a shadowy figure who wore a hood sewn from cheap brown cotton. The roomy hood fell over his forehead, covered his cheeks, and threw shadows across his eyes, mouth, and nose. In full sunlight his nose looked long; in darkness his face was a brown hole. This unfashionable item began as a way to keep the sun off his head, but ultimately was more important. It obscured his features so much that if acquaintances were asked to describe him in detail, they would draw a blank. Even his name was unknown and he was referred to only as The Hood. After less than ten years, with a tiny bit of the dreamy, sticky stuff cadged here and there innumerable times, Papa made his fortune.

When he had enough to net him a million-piastre note, he didn't show up at the deeply perfumed opium factory but took the first merchant ship down the Saigon River, out to the South China Sea, and into the Gulf of Thailand. Docking at the Chao

Phraya River in Krung Thep, later known as Bangkok, without incident, he sold the opium on the open market, then successfully changed his appearance. He had worldly clothes tailor-measured at a shop run by an East Indian. He grew his hair long, worked out, and even put himself on a calorie-consumption program to bulk up. Eventually he grew a drooping Manchurian mustache that covered his sensually bowed upper lip, the only notable part of an otherwise totally forgettable face. Returning to Saigon in his new persona, he purchased a villa in distant central Vietnam and soon had an eminently suitable mate, Jade's mother, arranged by a marriage broker.

Papa's love for Jade was tainted. She was Maman's veritable reincarnation, and all Papa had left of his beautiful wife. Sometimes, half awake, Papa would dream of his wedding night and how he had carried Jade's mother up the sweep of the house stairs, her long hair trailing like strands of seaweed from a fisherman's net. Jade knew of this because Papa would tell her proudly about his dream, but what he kept secret was that at the grand moment, when it was time for his own hardness to enter his bride's malleable body, she turned into Jade and he'd awaken, feeling annoyed.

Jade's every whim was pandered to by her father. He showed her off as his trophy, but she knew he had no interest in her childish aspirations and problems. To Papa it was all inane chatter, woman's talk. What Papa did understand, like any other man who set eyes on her, was the attraction of her beauty. He compared his daughter, as he had his dead wife, to the most dazzling specimen of butterfly, something to be stroked at will but only when on display.

Jade thought of Papa as The Spider. Too soon she gleaned,

from the whisperings she heard both at the back door of the kitchen and outside her now-neglected home, that her father's position as *colon* had been bought by her mother's family in place of a dowry. Papa had already amassed his fortune, making the monetary aspect of his bride's offering wholly unimportant. With his marriage he had purchased a different commodity: respect.

Learning to scorn Papa came naturally to Jade. He said little to her except for clumsy endearments. Although he spoke French, he delighted in speaking Kinh, the language of his childhood. Jade thought him crude and refused to speak the lowly Vietnamese dialect with him. Taking for granted that her own linguistic talents came from elsewhere, Jade soon learned that Papa wasn't interested in her school subjects. Perhaps she had inherited her cleverness from Maman's family, but she didn't really know that for sure, either. What remained undisputed was that Maman had come from a royal Chinese family that had migrated to Vietnam during the fourteenth century. But after Maman's death, Papa refused contact with her side of the family. As for Papa's own relations, he maintained that his parents had died and left him with his great fortune when he was a mere boy.

Books became Jade's constant companions. All subjects interested her, but French romance novels were the books that she lay awake far into the night with. Dô would enter the bookstore with Jade on the first Monday of each month and wait patiently until Jade signed the receipt. Excited after her purchases, she dragged Dô home by the hand. The packages of books bound in leather and embossed with gold were delivered later in *cyclos*, the bicycle carriage's narrow leather seat top-heavy with volumes wrapped in paper and secured with twine. Only once did Papa challenge the constant bills he received. "They are for books the nuns say we must have for school," Jade answered, turning her back to make sure he knew the subject was closed.

Jade's secondary school at Sacré Coeur Convent was attended by the lucky four percent of Saigonese girls whose families were wealthy *colons* and government officials. The brick-and-plaster school library brimmed with religious books and French histories. Strict discipline meted out by the Catholic nuns ensured the girls behaved. Silence in class, at meals, and on the grassy grounds was rigidly enforced. All classes were taught in French, and Vietnamese was frowned upon, although the students' uniform was the white silk *aio dai* with fluted pants and an ankle-length dress slit on both sides to the waist. After school the young girls chattered faster than chipmunks, words cartwheeling from French to Vietnamese.

An unpleasant reputation dogged Jade. Not her own, but Papa's. Her fellow students weren't allowed to visit Jade's home after an unfortunate incident at a birthday party early in her school career. A classmate had mistakenly wandered off and through the doorway of Papa's cavernous bedroom. What the fourteen-year-old girl saw quickly became local gossip: Jade's father sitting on a carved blackwood chair, mouth open, eyes glazed, a naked whore humping him on his lap.

Jade hated the longing in Papa's eyes when they moved admiringly over her. At the same time he would cry out in a raspy whiskey voice, "Your mother was a mandarin's daughter and so beautiful, just like you!"

On Sundays Papa and Jade strolled together down Saigon's tamarind-studded boulevards. Her father took her elbow in his pampered hand, his long nails digging into her soft upper arm as Jade shook his hand away.

"Why can't I touch you?" Papa asked.

"Your hands feel so ugly," she replied. "I just don't like it."

Papa fell silent, his mouth turning down at the corners, making the spindles of his mustache droop lower. Quickly Jade grew bored with having no one to talk to, then she grabbed her father's hand and put it on her arm, saying, "Papa, feel how silky my skin is today. Would you compare it to the softness of a lotus petal?"

And Papa then did as she bid.

8

JOURNEY WITH NO END

Follow after—we are waiting by the trails that we lost.
—Rudyard Kipling, "A Song of the English"

Montpellier: April 1955

Holding the train ticket to Mont Ste-Odile tightly in her hand, Jade took her seat in an empty *supérieure* compartment of the train. She glanced at the Rolex she had received from Van for their sixteenth wedding anniversary. The train's departure was late. Studying the slender second hand of the watch, Jade was annoyed by the imprecision of the train and the precision of the timepiece. It didn't suit her, she thought. Why hadn't Van bought her the one she preferred—a Piaget, simple, elegant, and eighteen-karat Swiss gold?

Jade knew the answer. Van was precise and practical. Remembering that Jade had ruined her good watch by continually forgetting to take it off before she bathed, Van had thought it brilliant to get her the most durable timepiece available.

What would Van do if he were in her position? Jade wondered once more. Then she realized Van would never be in her position. He was too good, too moral, to allow himself an illicit love affair. He was an important man with huge responsibilities, yet he usually allowed her to do as she pleased. Van adored her and she liked that, too. Most important, her husband was kind and, Jade noted, easily manipulated by her. Yet even Van would have a hard time understanding her affair with Jacques, let alone the revelation that she'd had a baby.

Jade knew she had to act quickly and that was why she was going to the orphanage in Mont Ste-Odile. If she could find Phuong, or Phoenix, she could provide a lifetime stipend in exchange for the orphan's silence. The benefit of such an arrangement would be threefold: it would eliminate the possibility of being found out, ensure Jade wouldn't suffer public dishonor and humiliation, and relieve her of guilt.

Outside the train window an old porter wearing a blue cap struggled with an irate woman's trunk, finally turning it on its side and hoisting it up the metal stairs and into an empty compartment. Then the conductor called out "All aboard!" and the train's whistle blew shrilly in the mist. Jade could smell steam as the train lurched, then stopped. Rising, she reached forward and pulled at the heavy glass of the door. After a few seconds of struggle, the compartment door slid shut. Jade then bent to pick up her overnight case, which had tumbled over due to the train's motion. Once her business in Mont Ste-Odile was completed, she would return immediately to Paris. She had no desire to see Montpellier again ever. At that moment the train started again with a larger jerk and began its journey.

Jade observed the scenery as the train hurtled northeast toward the West German border. Through the outstretched limbs of trees and behind villages she glimpsed the Spanish hues she associated with Montpellier. For a few minutes the tracks overhung the Mediterranean, and the sea seemed to Jade to be an inky tongue licking a dark line of blue at its edge.

The train labored up a steep incline and the landscape changed to a study in vertical, with tall, triangular pines covering the slopes of the Vosges. The scene reminded her briefly of Dalat, and then she recalled how different Saigon appeared. South Vietnam had an exciting beauty, she thought. This part of France, the Alsace, was like a tall, cool European woman, while Vietnam was an energetic lady full of life. She wondered which race Phuong resembled, then pictured Jacques with his hair as dark as hers. Phuong, she imagined, would be dark-haired, too.

Mont Ste-Odile was submerged in shadow and neglect when Jade arrived. The orphanage Les Enfants de Ste-Marie hung off a craggy hilltop at the end of a twisted road. From a distance it looked like an overgrown monastery or antiquated château that had come unstuck from its perch. It might have seemed romantic in the distance to someone on a more carefree mission, but to Jade it was somehow sinister.

The orphanage was run like a military camp. Different age groups were confined to different blocks. Segregation went no further. There was no racial discrimination: black, poor white, or yellow, they were each and every one only orphans. The orphanage, like most such institutions in France, was funded by the benevolent whims of the Roman Catholic church and run by a sisterhood of nuns. The nuns were perpetually understaffed and the children were many. The doors were locked, but sometimes a brave or silly child would slip through a window in the dead of night in search of the elusive comfort of a remembered parent.

The sisters had the long-term character development of their young charges in mind. Discipline and physical labor were meted out to the orphans on a daily basis. This was meant to serve them well as adults but didn't fit the softer needs of the children.

Blocks of colorless plasterboard lined the walls of the orphanage, topped by high yellowed ceilings. Restless sleeping heads, the sighs of youth, and sometimes a cry from a bad dream gave surreal movement and sound to the iron cots that lay like caskets on the old stone floors. Peering through the windows of the dormitory-style buildings made Jade feel insecure and claustrophobic. As she passed Cell Four, she imagined that its dusty confines still retained the faint imprint of her mistake, an illegitimate child…

wrap your thin arms round your knees
and dream
of a father dead and gone who loves the child you still are,
of a mother you have never seen

wrap your thin arms round your knees
and know
of the barbs and cruel remarks that bombard you every night and day
till you know you're not accepted
no, not here in a world that counts your color like a rude remark
that shows on your face no matter what you say

until you dream that you can only escape
when you run away

When Jade was ushered into a small office, she said, "Excuse me, Sister. I'm Doctoress Jade Minh. I've come from Paris."

A nun, her habit obscuring her hair, ears, and sex put her pen down on a blotter. "It's a pleasure, Doctoress. I am the mother superior of this orphanage. On behalf of all of us who work for the good of our Lord, welcome." The woman bowed her head. "Pray with me for all the lost children. May they find a little peace in this world and more in the next."

Jade obeyed, bending her head and putting her hands together as she had when attending Catholic school. She felt embarrassingly near tears at the memory of those years.

The mother superior's well-scrubbed face was hopeful. "Have you come to offer your services to our needy lambs of the Lord?"

"I'm so sorry," Jade said. "I'm not a medical doctor. My title comes from a doctorate in languages. I'd be happy to leave a donation for this worthy institution." Opening her handbag, she extracted a crisp hundred-franc note and pushed it across the desk.

The nun folded the bill and pushed it up the loose sleeve of her robe. "Thank you, child."

"I'm trying to find a friend's child. She's the daughter of a cousin who died recently. I've been named the girl's guardian and was told she was left at this orphanage some time in the past year."

"A cousin or a friend—or were they both?" the mother superior asked but left Jade no time to answer. "What would you do for the child if she were to be found here?"

"The family has left me money to enroll her in a well-known girls' boarding school in Switzerland."

"What a lucky child! So many of our children live with the unhealthy delusion that they have family who will one day rescue them from this place. Quickly tell me the child's name."

"I'm not sure what name she goes by," Jade said, suddenly confused about what family name Jacques would have given the child. Not her own, she hoped, deciding to be vague so the nun couldn't penetrate her lies. "But her mother was of a good Catholic Vietnamese family and her father was a wealthy Parisian."

"How can you not know your cousin's name? That is most unusual!"

"Sadly my cousin's husband, Jacques, ran away with the child when my dead cousin's elderly parents wanted the girl to return to Saigon to live with them. Poor Jacques didn't want to lose the child to her wealthy grandparents. My cousin's parents never approved of the mixed marriage."

The nun shook her head. "Unfortunately that is the outcome of many mixed marriages. The children are not accepted by either race. It is a sign of evil that parents procreate without thinking of the child."

"Her mother is Vietnamese, her father is French, and the girl is fourteen."

"An impossible request," the nun said. "There are about a

hundred orphans here at this moment. In its short twenty-five-year history this orphanage has had thousands of children pass through the doors. Some live with us until they grow up, others only spend a short period with us. Forty percent of these unfortunates are half-castes who habitually spring from Asian mothers and European fathers. Many are half Vietnamese. The couples have been living together against God's wishes. The women are prostitutes with no care for the fruits of their sins. Some are depraved and have succumbed to the Devil's lure. But God forgives." The nun crossed herself. "Few of their unfortunate offspring have identification. Doctoress, you must provide more information than this. Could you at least give me her parents' full names?"

"Her father's name is Jacques Duras." I think her mother wanted her called Phuong." Jade hesitated. "It translates to Phoenix, but I can't really say what name the girl uses."

"I'll allow you to look in the unfortunates' registration book." The nun bent her head and pushed a book across the desk.

The heavy volume made Jade's hands shake. The mother superior sat silently, her face unmarked by human love. Her hands were folded against the cold in the room as she waited for her guest to search the pages of the old book. A square of paper had been glued to the leather cover. On it were the words THE BOOK OF ORPHANS.

The orphans were categorized by gender. Running her eyes over the scrawled entries, Jade moved her lips without sound as she searched. She traced the names with an elegant fingernail. "Duras Phuong—that's the one!"

"I am sorry, my dear, foreign names are so difficult. Let me see." Jade passed the book across the large desk to the nun. "Oh, my spectacles! I can't read without them."

"Phuong," Jade said slowly. "It means Phoenix."

Jacques had known it was the tradition in Jade's family to name girls after myths and precious stones. Her own translation was obvious. She was as costly and beautiful as a piece of jade. Jacques had told her the myth about the rare bird that sprang surprisingly from ashes. And in Vietnam *phuong* was the celestial bird—the head was the sky, the back the moon, the wings the wind, the eyes the sun, the feet the earth, the tail the planets, the whole of the phoenix symbolizing peace and prosperity.

And her daughter had Jacques's family name. Jade breathed a sigh of relief. The plan that she might view the girl safely in her guise as an old friend of Jacques raced through her head. She was elated. She had found her Phoenix. Her plan would work and she would have peace from self-hatred and protection from public humiliation.

Before Jade could speak again, though, the mother superior said, "I know the girl you speak of. The unfortunate child was not with us long. She ran away. I don't know why, other than that she was a particularly sad child. There was nothing we could do but pray. We knew little about her. She hardly spoke, not even to the other children. I do remember she had the most remarkable hair. Strange, that I haven't crossed her name out yet."

Jade didn't pay much attention to what the nun had said except the part about Phuong being gone. Crushed with disappointment, she excused herself and left the bleak, shadowy place.

On the night train to Paris, Jade could barely keep her eyes open. She stowed her purse and gloves on the metal rungs above and slumped onto the red velvet seat in her compartment. Her eyelids fell, then rose as she took in her slightly shabby surroundings. Jade stretched over the seat to open the compartment window. Cold air rushed in, slapping her fully awake. Immediately her mind set to work on her problem.

This was only a setback, she decided, a mere detour. If Phuong were still alive, Jade would rescue her from poverty, set her up in a comfortable life. She would be generous, and that kindness would eradicate the cringing humiliation of her mistake, as well as the fear of being found out. The child must never know Jade, but it wasn't thanks she wanted from the orphan, only escape from the past. What if Van found out and left her because of the scandal? She couldn't blame him if he did. But she knew what she must do. The child was near fifteen, the legal age, and Jade could arrange for a lawyer to draw up a legally binding contract of silence in exchange for a monetary settlement. Until then Jade would be an anonymous benefactor and the child would be safely tucked away in a Swiss boarding school.

After some brainstorming as to how she would search for the girl, Jade concluded she desperately needed help. Whom could she trust with such a delicate matter? Chou leaped to mind, but she immediately dismissed him on the grounds that he was too curious. More important, Jade didn't want to owe Chou any favors. He was liable to ask for repayment in any manner of indelicate ways. She would put nothing past the man. On the other hand, due to these traits, Chou could be invaluable tracking down the child. As legal adviser to the embassy, the man had made contacts with all sorts of shadowy characters.

Reflecting further, Jade decided it was fitting to get Chou to assist her. After all, he was the bearer of the telegram that had set her on this course. And Chou would be secretive about everything. He loved anything clandestine, and it was of the utmost importance to Jade that this matter remained hidden. How could she explain to Chou, let alone to her husband or to the world, the existence of a half-caste unfortunate who had sprung from her illicit love affair?

But with his penchant for intrigue, Jade reasoned, Chou

would make the perfect detective. His connections might know the whereabouts of her runaway daughter who, Jade believed, must be roaming somewhere in France. Still, she wouldn't tell Chou the whole truth. In fact, she'd extract a promise from him not to tell Van, Papa, or a single soul. Dealing with Chou like this was dangerous as it left her open to blackmail, but Jade was certain she could charm the lawyer.

As the train rumbled toward Paris, Jade determined that relating the same history she had concocted for the mother superior at the orphanage, with a few minor changes, would be her best bet when enlisting Chou's help. His running interference with her telegram had handed her the opportunity to involve him.

Jade would go to Chou's office at the end of the day when his receptionist left and his telephone was quiet. She'd tell him how she'd gone to the strange assignation in Montpellier and how worried she was about the outcome. Two dear friends from her university days, a Vietnamese and her French husband, died in a skiing accident in the French Alps, she'd say, holding back tears of grief. Chou would make a move to comfort her physically and she would step back. Then she would say the couple had no other family and had lost their fortune in an unsuccessful business venture immediately prior to the tragic accident. This unfortunate swing of fate had landed their half-caste daughter in an orphanage. The telegram Chou had given her was from a mutual friend who thought Jade would want to help the poor child for her dear friend's sake.

Recalling that she had told Chou it was a university professor who had died, Jade started again. She'd tell the lawyer that the message had come through her old professor and that her first impression had been mistaken. Then she'd let Chou know how she had gone to the orphanage where the child had been placed and found her missing. Listening to the steady roll of the train, Jade grew increasingly excited. Her plan would work.

On the way to Chou's office in the La Tour Building for the second time in only a few days, Jade took a secondary road, expertly working the Renault's clutch. The engine hummed in perfect tune, and she was glad she had shunned the main autoroute and its busy commuter traffic. It was five o'clock. Paris's populace would be leaving their office buildings to meet for Cinzano, Pernod, or a glass of wine in the cafés on the Left Bank, or they would amble through the theatrical enchantment of the royal forest of Versailles before taking in a musical comedy.

When she arrived at Chou's building, she maneuvered her car onto the sidewalk, the wheels rolling across the grass and over a patch of budding lilies. She slid to a stop under the stand of silver poplars, but this time she removed her gloves, tucking them into her purse before entering Chou's office. She didn't notice the tender stalks of the lilies crushed under her Pirelli tires.

Chou was alone when Jade entered his office. He stood by the window, hand on one hip, smoking and thinking. The interview began according to the plan she'd concocted on the night train, including her intuitive knowledge that Chou would try to give her a sympathetic embrace after she related her news. Predictably he moved toward her and, still holding his cigarette, put his arm around her shoulder. Jade stepped back too soon, then realized she had miscalculated. Chou's eyes became hooded, and when he looked up, Jade knew there was no desire in his face whatsoever to please her.

"Well, then, Doctoress, since you insist on confiding in me, continue."

Jade came straight to the point. "I want you to help me find the girl."

Chou didn't answer. His eyes were filmy and cold.

Distressed, she tried a new tack. "Chou, in the past my father has done you many favors in Saigon. I'm now collecting on those debts." The flicker of boredom in Chou's eyes made Jade falter. "I didn't mean that. Please forgive me for being so rude as to demand a favor. It's just that I'm at my wit's end. Chou, the girl's mother is Vietnamese, and the girl, she's only fourteen. She's completely alone in a dangerous and cruel world. If we don't find her, anything could happen. She could starve or fall in with the wrong types. She could even become a prostitute or be murdered. Although you probably feel I make light of it, your protection means everything to me. Think what your protection would mean to a defenseless orphan..."

Jade's eyes shone with tears as she moved closer to Chou. This time she allowed him to take her into his arms. A whiff of smoke trailed from his cigarette, and at that moment a fleeting vision of herself and Jacques came to her. Seconds later she disengaged herself, but it had been enough. "Chou, the Vietnamese community in Paris owes you a lot, and I know your loyalty to your motherland wouldn't allow you to let a Vietnamese compatriot down."

"All right, my dear Jade, you've convinced me to help you. And you're right. If we Vietnamese don't help our own, who will?" The question dangled unanswered.

Once again Jade moved closer to Chou. She took his hand and lifted it to her lips. The sight of his yellow nails didn't disturb her this time. In fact, his index nail, longer than her own and the sign of a wealthy and powerful man in Vietnam, gave her a feeling of security. "Please don't mention this to anyone, especially to Van and Papa. I hope you don't mind if I confide in you again?"

Chou backed up, his hand still in hers, and sat on the edge of his desk. Jade smiled, and she knew the beauty of that expression, with its curved corners and Cupid's-bow upper lip, enchanted Chou. "You see," she said, sure of herself now, "both Van and

Papa have always been disappointed that I put my career before having children. If Van knew I was going to take charge of someone else's child, he'd be jealous. And Papa's old-fashioned. He'd be prejudiced against the girl because she's of mixed blood. Besides, we may never find her. Promise me, on your honor, that you'll keep this a secret."

For once Chou didn't tap his nose, a habit Jade had found increasingly annoying over the years. He merely nodded, then slowly moved the hand she'd allowed him and lifted it to his lips. She felt the brush of his goatee on her hand. Chou's mouth didn't linger this time. Instead he raised his elegant head and said, "It will be our secret, my dear. You have my word as a gentleman."

Jade was elated. The heavy weight of responsibility she had suffered so intensely the previous night slipped away and she wordlessly gave thanks for having someone to lean on. It crossed her mind that maybe, just maybe, she'd misread Chou all these years.

When she related the few details she had about Phuong, Chou suggested his street contacts might know something concerning the runaway. Jade was assured. Since the bulk of Chou's work consisted of checking Jade's translated press releases for the possibility of libel, he had time for a lucrative side practice. Arguing Vietnamese criminal and illegal immigration cases was his forte. He dealt equally well with the Vietnamese ambassador, the French Sûreté, Communist cadres, and smugglers of heroin. He'd told Jade that he had amassed a great fortune from his legal work in France. He'd also told her he had no qualms about getting his hands dirty. As she thought about this, Jade smiled to herself. Chou would find her Phuong.

BOOK II
VAN AND JADE

The last time the Chinese came they stayed a thousand years! The French are foreigners. Colonialism is dying out. The white man is finished in Asia. But if the Chinese stay now, they will never leave. As for me, I prefer to sniff French shit for five years, rather than Chinese shit for the rest of my life.

—Ho Chi Minh, as quoted in *The Pentagon Papers*

1
HOMEWARD

Even in Saigon it is a war of random assassination, of grenades thrown into cafés, nightclubs, and cinemas. Life goes on, however, despite the grenades, although some people prefer to drink in an upstairs bar or grill, but these things are not major preoccupations. Unless one is unlucky, all one hears of the war is the occasional small explosion in the distance which might just as well be an automobile backfiring.

—Graham Greene, *Reflections*

Paris: November 1957

Jade sat in the back of the cab in silence. Her driver, an elderly Frenchman, his beret jaunty, chattered at her. He took the back route to Orly International Airport through streets that twisted like intestines. The taxi swayed as he muscled through the sporadic traffic, taking corners too fast and running stop signs.

"Slow down!" Jade told the driver. "I'd like to live long enough to fly back to Saigon."

She was taking service leave from her work at the South Vietnamese embassy and was completely thrilled to be returning to her native land. It had been three years since her last trip. This time she had chosen the tail end of the much cooler monsoon season for her visit.

The cab arrived at the airport a few minutes shy of the mandatory hour before her Air France flight. After the driver bowed with a charming flourish of his hand, she tipped him well and joined the short queue at the first-class desk in the terminal.

She would collect her boarding pass, have her luggage weighed, and be checked through immigration. Jade was laden down with an assortment of packages, as well as her leather-bound trunks. Behind her a harried Vietnamese matron inched a crate of strawberries toward the check-in with her foot. A pink puddle trickled. She noticed a contingent of French journalists in the economy line. They wore khakis and looked disreputable to her.

Jade was next in the queue. "The flight to Saigon," she said, flashing a practiced smile that put her lips at the center of attention. Charm and her embassy passport made quick work of the check-in/customs agent. With hardly a glance at her papers, but with an appreciative look at Jade, he stamped her passport with the place and the date and handed her a boarding pass. Now Jade had a full half hour on her hands before boarding would begin.

Passing through the security check, she waited while the female attendant searched her bag and checked her parcels. In the routine body search, a woman armed with a Colt .22 patted Jade up and down from her shoulders to the bottom of her straight skirt, then waved her through. Next Jade purchased a duty-free bottle of Révillon's Carnet de Bal for herself and a second-rate Houbigant *eau de cologne* as a token gift for Van's "niece," although she could have shopped just as easily at one of the many *perfumeries* on rue Catinat.

She took a seat at the gate and waited patiently in the claustrophobic holding room with her carry-on bags beside her. She could see the empty runway being cleaned by a worker in a jumpsuit. He pushed dejectedly at his shovel, the snow turning to water as it touched the ground.

Her thoughts turned to Chou, who had been playing detective for her for more than two years. Whenever she thought about the possibility of Chou finding Phuong, she had an attack of nerves. Jade didn't want to dwell on the matter, but she picked at it as if it were a sore tooth. Of course, she had planned for Chou's potential success: a boarding school and a settlement. The girl would still be an orphan, but at least a wealthy one. Still, what if Phuong were so far gone she had become a prostitute, or was addicted to drugs or liquor? She was that age, just turned seventeen, and from what Monique had said, Jacques had been an alcoholic. Jade had read that alcoholism was a hereditary condition.

Just the previous week Chou had informed Jade he was driving to the French Riviera in response to a lead he had received from one of his cronies. Jade had made a face, then had become calm, instinctively knowing this would end like Chou's other leads—nowhere.

As expected, Chou had enlisted his underground contacts to help him with his search, but the child seemed to have vanished. It was almost as if she didn't exist. And maybe that was the truth. Perhaps Monique was a blackmailer, had played Jade for a fool, but had been frightened away by the telephone call Jade had arranged through the pension's reception.

Jade thought more about Chou, and although she couldn't deny an unhealthy attraction, she felt she saw him too often these days. He seemed to show up everywhere she went. Her mind moved on to the hot topic of her country's leadership. The Vietnamese in Paris talked of nothing else. President Ngo Dinh Diem had suspended the elections mandated by the Geneva Agreements, and it looked as if there would be no repercussions. But who could foresee the future? In fact, the changes of government in the past decade and the fighting forces behind them had been dizzying.

Although Van talked politics, Jade knew he was too focused on his research to become much involved in its dangerous rigmarole. She was aware that the Communist Vietminh had assassinated more than four hundred South Vietnamese officials in the past year. She also knew Diem had cracked down on dissidents and Vietminh suspects. Her embassy position gave her an ear that most Vietnamese didn't have. Much of the information she gleaned was confidential.

From a personal perspective she was relieved that Van's scientific endeavors were so demanding that he didn't insist she return permanently to Saigon. Even innocent Saigonese were at risk these days. Van had written to her describing the scene since the French were defeated at Dien Bien Phu by Ho Chi Minh's Vietminh in 1954: armed guards were posted throughout the city, and wire nets protected the cafés from grenades. Still, like most Vietnamese, Jade was inured to fear.

In Paris her talent for translation was recognized, and although she wasn't a socialite by anyone's standard, she found the well-bred insouciance that Paris exuded attractive. In truth Jade had become accustomed to Gallic sophistication and to her own company. She ate truffles from Périgord, and shopped for gloves and scarves at the tiny Denise Francelle store on rue de Rivoli and for leather goods at Hérmes on rue du Faubourg-St-Honoré. In season she holidayed at Hôtel du Cap, the baronial English-style mansion on the extreme tip of Juan-les-Pins, or booked in at one of France's hundred health spas. In Paris she dined in the gold, burgundy, and white Art Nouveau atmosphere of Maxim's, or at the Tour d'Argent. Always there were embassy dinners she was invited to. When she chose to dine out, the *Guide Michelin* was her Bible.

La Doctoress enjoyed the best her francs could purchase. She supposed she could have accepted a position in Saigon as a government translator, but the work would have been rife with politics, and she, even more than Van, had no real interest. Van was fixated on science; Jade was absorbed in her own work. After hours she was content to shop in the exquisite fashion houses of Dior and Fath, and sometimes she'd slum at Henri à la Penseé, one of the less-dear boutiques. She wore hats from Paulette, the most expensive creations in the fashion world. Her Parisian lifestyle was based on her own salary. In her apartment she whiled away the time to the sounds of Claude Debussy, Erik Satie, and Igor Stravinsky. She read the works of Paul Eluard and Jean Cocteau, the literary heirs of Charles Baudelaire and Arthur Rimbaud.

But Van had thrown a wrench into the works. She was well aware that he didn't give a fig for a well-kept house. Anyway, he had Dô and a day woman, who acted as a cleaner-cum-cook. But that wasn't all. Van had taken on the responsibility for a young girl. Her name was Mui. Knowing Van had always been disappointed that they had never had a child, Jade wasn't all that surprised. Mui was the sole offspring of South Vietnamese parents whose background Van kept a secret, and with good reason. The girl's parents had fallen into the red snare of communism while studying for legal degrees in Paris. France was a hotbed of Vietnamese nationalists, past and present. In fact, it was commonly known in Paris that Communist strongholds were to be found in Ivry, Boulogne, Gennevilliers, Aubervilliers, and the area around the Renault plant.

Mui's parents had joined the Vietnamese arm of the Communist bloc in France and had returned to Saigon as members of the League for the Independence of Vietnam, the Vietminh. They were educated people and received orders from Ho Chi Minh himself. Back in Vietnam they disappeared into the jungle to toil like obedient and brainwashed peasants in their struggle against French domination, setting up secret bases in the impenetrable jungle. In an ironic twist of fate, both parents had died, but not in battle, though one could say they died for the Communist cause. Their brains had swollen with encephalitis, an agonizing death. Their only child, Mui, whom they had left in the paid care of a distant relative in Kratié, a Cham village on the Mekong River, had returned unscathed by politics except, of course, for the loss of her family. Oddly enough, it was Chou who had brought Mui to Van's attention, just after Jade had enlisted him to find Phuong, her own flesh and blood.

Chou had been alerted to Mui's plight by Madame Hoa, one of a handful of female barristers in Saigon. She had befriended Mui's parents, had drawn up the couple's will, and while doing so they had appointed her both executor and guardian. Thankfully the couple had saved a nest egg for their child's education.

Van, always the philanthropist, had immediately and without even consulting Jade taken this girl, Mui, as his niece. She called him Uncle Van. It irritated Jade still that Chou hadn't the courtesy to consult her before involving Van in this matter. It annoyed her, too, that Van had gone behind her back. And now Van's correspondence was filled with the tedious details of what Mui did and what Mui enjoyed.

Mui lived in residence at a French secondary school about ninety miles south of Saigon in a town called Sadec. Evenings in tiny Sadec, and for that matter in the ubiquitous "French" towns that had sprung up in the provinces, were humid affairs marked by languid hours on wide verandahs awash in yellow light. A short but memorable ferry ride across a branch of the Mekong from Vinh Long, the town was surrounded by vast plains of mud and rice fields striated by thin irrigation streams that splashed with jumping frogs. Mui took pleasure in the bird life. Herons, impossibly white against their muddy habitat, or the larger slate-blue variety, dipped their slim beaks and picked their way with high-stepping grace along the banks of the wide river, which was choked with water lilies. At sunrise the herons fluttered on ruffled wings above the pepper plantations and rice fields to stare down at the colorless conic hats that shaded the peasants' dark faces while they picked and planted, according to the season.

Mui was in her last year of secondary school, and Jade knew from Van that the girl would go on to attend the Sorbonne. Her teachers in Sadec, both the French expatriates and South Vietnamese nuns, pronounced the teenager brilliant. She had won top marks in her classes each year.

At the age of fourteen Mui excelled at her studies, but she was still so insular, so shy, that the school had contacted Madame Hoa and suggested the girl should have a suitable adult companion to spend her holidays with. It should be in a studious environment, the educational pundits agreed, where Mui could pursue her chosen pastimes of reading and studying, yet still have subtle adult attention. Because of rumors that linked her dead parents with the Vietminh, there were no takers until Chou solicited Van. And so Van had Mui home to their house in Saigon during long school holidays twice a year. This year the holiday coincided with Jade's return.

Twice in the past few years Van had flown to Paris to visit Jade. Neither trip could be deemed a true success, though nothing was outwardly onerous. However, Jade was always relieved when Van left Paris and she could once again concentrate on her chichi life. While in Paris Van spent his time at the university library making notes on the scientific journals that were slower to reach the Pasteur Institute in faraway Saigon.

Jade stared again at the slush on the airport runway. The sight of early winter made her anticipate her return home. She could feel it already, and knew when she stepped off the airplane's outdoor staircase into Saigon's tropical air, she'd stretch her arms to the sky and let her moisture-starved skin drink in the monsoon air. Jade reassured herself that Mui's visit wouldn't interfere with her long-awaited pleasures. The girl was only with them for a week.

To wash off the grime of the journey, Van knew to draw Jade's rainwater bath. It would be ready when she arrived. Jade relived a vague memory of herself and Maman sluiced with earthen ladles of rainwater, Dô spinning village tales as she dipped and poured. The reminiscence of Maman's hair—loose, almost brushing the ground—made a hard fist in Jade's chest. She thought of Van again, and how he loved and missed her, even though he didn't *need* her. They'd been "together" a long time.

Maybe, she imagined, Van would embrace her at Tan Son Nhat Airport. That would be the day! She smiled wryly and returned an errant strand of hair to her chignon. In Saigon young men strolled arm in arm, and women clasped hands as they walked, but members of the opposite sex didn't touch each other in public. Not like the French, who greeted with a kiss on both cheeks, or maybe on the mouth. But, she had to admit, in private the Vietnamese didn't stand on ceremony.

On her first evening home she knew Van would bore her with stories of his scientific experiments at the Pasteur Institute. Her husband was a man of passion when it came to science. He'd get carried away and instruct her in the scientific how-to of a discovery, something so important it would change the destiny of man, like Jonas Salk's polio vaccine. But she could put up with that. She could see Van's eyes magnified behind the thick lenses of his glasses, screwed up in concentration over his complicated formulas, Bunsen burners, and chemicals. Jade resolved to pay attention to her husband's words. Van, with his generous nature, had been a patient and good husband. She realized she really did miss him.

Just then an announcement blared from the Air France desk: "We apologize for the delay." Jade made the tsking noise that had become a habit and settled back in her chair. Her thoughts were already in Saigon. The first thing Van and she would do was to stroll the rue Catinat, the most elegant street in all the colonies. Quickly Jade corrected herself—Vietnam was no longer a French colony. But the French had left them their heritage no matter what the South Vietnamese, as the Republic of Vietnam, called themselves.

She continued to muse, stuck in the past, whiling away the time. Van had told her in a letter that Saigon's French street names were to be changed to Vietnamese ones. Then her drifting mind followed a different course. Until recently Saigon had been the capital of Cochin China. France's 1861 annexation of Vietnam, at that time known as Annam, was followed by requests from Laos and Cambodia to be put under French "protection." The three countries together were then called Indochina.

During World War II, the Japanese were allowed to occupy Indochina, and the French collaborated with them until 1945 when the Japanese interned French authorities and set up a puppet Vietnamese state under Emperor Bao Dai. Of course, that government collapsed with the defeat of Japan and was replaced by the nationalistic Ho Chi Minh and his Vietminh fighters. In 1949 a so-called "independence within the French union" was granted to the three countries of Indochina. In Vietnam Ho and his Vietminh persisted, trouncing the French in 1954 at Dien Bien Phu. And then came the Geneva Agreements and Vietnam's north-and-south division.

Now South Vietnam was a proud young republic, finally in charge of itself. Still, the country's division didn't sit right with most Vietnamese. With one finger Jade traced a cross over her left breast, a habit she'd picked up at Catholic school. She thanked God *and* her lucky stars that South Vietnam still had an embassy in Paris. She knew the French could have had hard feelings after their humiliating withdrawal from her country. But why was her nation still divided after three years? In July 1954 the cessation of hostilities in Vietnam had been hammered out and signed by France and the Vietminh. Surely the provisional separation of Vietnam into the Communist North and her beloved free South would end soon, though President Diem had refused to participate in nationwide elections, a decision backed by the United States.

Jade automatically crossed herself again. The French had completed their withdrawal last year, but their training role within the South Vietnamese army had been replaced by the

U.S. Military Advisory Group. She wondered if the American presence would be visible in Saigon. Pondering that, Jade removed her collection of letters from an alligator briefcase that sat dimpled on the tile under her shoes. She untied the ribbon and searched for a particular letter. It was one of Van's, and though she'd already read it, she wanted to look at it again. Van explained Vietnam's situation so well and without bias. She recalled he had cautioned her to keep the letters from prying eyes, but she knew her embassy passport ensured the authorities wouldn't dare search her personal effects.

As she unfolded her link to the past and to her country, the loudspeaker crackled again: "Air France Flight 20 for Saigon is now boarding." She returned the letter to its packet and realized she was famished. The flight's previous delay meant it was hours past her breakfast. Jade pictured a baguette, Vietnamese-style, and her mouth watered in anticipation. She could hardly wait to eat a rice-flour baguette with fresh papaya *confiture*. The Vietnamese baguettes were even more delicate than their French cousins, probably because Saigon's humidity kept them fresher.

Once more Jade indulged in a reverie about Saigon. While Van and she lounged at their wrought-iron table on the edge of the open-air verandah at the Hotel Continental, watching the world of foreign travelers in style, she'd have a *café sua* with a double dollop of sweetened milk. Of course, Van would insist they go to the stalls of Hung Vuong Street and eat *heo rung*, the famous wild pig. She pictured them perched on the childish plastic chairs that crowded the alleyway and anticipated the press of the diners and the steam and clatter of tin dishes that overflowed with rice noodles from the wheeled *pho* stands. Jade would veto ordering the specialty items: dogs, cats, snakes, turtles, and monkeys purchased from the live-animal market and prepared in numerous ways.

After that they'd stroll to Saigon's popular Nam Duong coffee lounge, and Van would order her ice cream concocted from *mang cau*, the green custard apple. Jade almost licked her lips at the thought. She coveted the trifling details of life that made Saigon her true home and Vietnam only her homeland. Given her lengthy absences from Vietnam, it always amazed her how happy she could still be living in France. Perhaps, though, that was what made her visits to Vietnam so tantalizing.

Putting aside her hunger and her memories, Jade followed the stream of passengers through the covered gangway and took her first-class seat on the plane. She was in for a long journey. The plane would stop in Teheran, Karachi, Bombay, New Delhi, Calcutta, Rangoon, and Singapore before it reached Saigon. As she got comfortable, the silver Boeing 707's engines hummed and soon the travelers were airborne, the aircraft's landing gear retracting into the belly with a clunk. She glimpsed the coppery top of the Eiffel Tower and then nothing. Paris had disappeared and she was glad.

Jade accepted a fluted glass of Dom Perignon and orange juice from the Air France hostess and tucked into a breakfast of *omelet fin herbs* served in a plate ringed with platinum. Balancing her champagne glass on the arm of her roomy leather chair, she rubbed at the tiny plane window and observed the wisps of clouds that pirouetted like ghostly dancers on a flat blue stage of sky. Jade allowed her mind to wander with the pale clouds as she continued her amble through the past. She wondered if her father still had his membership at Cercle Sportif, Saigon's French colonial club. Although he hardly ever took advantage of it, he was lucky to have it. Very few Vietnamese were allowed memberships; Papa's had been a present from Emperor Bao Dai himself.

She recalled a dinner at the club she'd attended with Papa many years before. Her father had been horribly rude. "I'll never waste my piastres in this place again," he'd informed the waiter, who wouldn't serve his disgusting arrack and water, only Martel and Perrier. Papa had pouted at her, the ends of his scraggly mustache wet with liquor and festooned with crumbs. "All they have is expensive French champagne to drink," he complained bitterly. "And to eat? Who would want old fish eggs?"

"Papa, it's caviar all the way from Russia," she'd explained, losing her temper. "If you embarrass me again, I'll disown you." But she'd wasted her breath. Papa didn't even know what *disown* meant. When she married Van, Jade had been relieved to get away from her father's rough ways.

But that exquisite dinner lived on in her mind. She visualized the Baccarat chandelier that had glittered like rain and tinkled like chimes from neighboring Laos when the breeze blew. The Lalique stemware had been heavy in her hand and bubbled effervescent, a spring of fragrant champagne. So gracious, so elegant, and so French! French life was even more seductive in Indochina than in Paris. She also remembered a big black limousine, a Morris Léon-Bollée. Even the chauffeur in his white cotton livery, was strikingly handsome. Yes, those were the good days.

On the morning of the flight's fourth and last day the delicate light of dawn daubed at the windows. The passengers were sleeping, reading, playing cards. A few had taken opiates prescribed by their physicians to endure the long flight; some had resorted to alcohol to withstand the ordeal.

Jade adjusted her footrest. The flight had become interminable. She rubbed her ankles and shifted position. Her leg was asleep. She stretched, then stretched again. What could she do? She knew! She'd reread her letters, prepare herself historically for Saigon.

Van's correspondence had become very important to her since

that time when she'd burnt her husband's letters to keep Jacques from finding out she was married. Jade thought of the ashes of Van's correspondence as her scarlet letter. His letters since had become her badge of respectability. She carried them everywhere, as other women carried photographs. Van laughed at her for this and joked that his letters were world travelers, hitchhiking through the mail, sitting in heat and damp, or wind and snow, then flying first-class on Air France. When Van picked Jade up at the Saigon airport, he would say something like: "I hope my letters didn't have too much champagne on the flight." Or "I hope my letters had an interesting companion to pass the time with."

Jade opened the storage compartment above her where the hostess had secured her alligator briefcase. All around her passengers snored. Once she had her packet of letters, she withdrew one at random. Rereading it would beat the boredom and prepare her for a changed Saigon. The letter that won her impromptu lottery was dated October 26, 1955. It was from Papa. She hated her father's letters; they were trite and full of complaints. But Papa's letters were important, too. They reminded her that not all South Vietnamese had wanted Diem as their leader. Papa's letter also reminded her that Chou was constantly talking to people, meddling and misrepresenting. She realized again that the lawyer could one day be a threat if he learned the truth about her secret.

Turning her attention to her father's letter, Jade reflected that it was fitting that his correspondence belonged to the past as he did. His penmanship was poor and he wrote in an old man's shaky hand through an old man's eyes.

Dear Daughter,

As you take no interest in politics and may not have heard, our revered Emperor Bao Dai was defeated by Ngo Dinh Diem in the October 23 referendum. This event bodes ill for our country. And now Diem has proclaimed himself president of the Republic of Vietnam. I was shocked when your husband insinuated that my good friend Bao Dai was a playboy and had squandered our country's money on gambling and women. Bao Dai has disappeared for his own good reasons, probably to your little heaven in Paris, no doubt where I should be, too. One consolation for you is, as you may remember, that Diem is a devout Catholic. By the way, Van tells me neither of you attend church often, but being Catholic will serve you well in South Vietnam. Myself? You know I don't dabble in politics or religion.

I do, though, believe what our friend Chou has told me. The election was masterminded by the Americans. They have been studying our ways: the ballots for Diem were red, the color of luck, although your poor dead mother would disagree, as red was her downfall. Our emperor's ballots were green, the color of misfortune. Even worse, Diem's agents were said to be present at the poll booths in the countryside. They told the people to throw the green away. The supporters loyal to my beloved emperor and friend were beaten and harassed. Some had pepper forced up their noses and water down their throats to choke the love for Bao Dai out of them. I suppose I'm lucky nothing happened to me, but I'm a useless old man no one cares about.

Chou visited me when he was last in Saigon. I hear more about you from him than from my only son-in-law. Chou says he was going to ask your husband to be guardian to a girl who has fallen on reduced circumstances. Her deceased parents were Communist. I'd be careful she doesn't usurp your place in the household, although I doubt you care. You seem only concerned with your life in France. Chou also tells me he has been seeing more of you on a personal basis. I know, Daughter, that in the past you have said you dislike him. Now I see you have changed your mind and agree that he is a powerful and important man.

You are lucky he pays any attention to you. His friends in high places count themselves blessed to be in his favor.

You may remember many years back, on Chou's advice, that I invested in Saigon's opium refinery. I have tripled my already substantial worth because of this investment. I always knew opium would be my future. Chou invested even more than I and must be an extremely wealthy man. If you had been willing to marry an older man, it would have been an excellent arrangement. Too bad!

You should ask Chou to tell you about Ho Chi Minh. Fascinating! You will be most impressed with Chou's stories of this man's life. Chou said he met Ho in Bangkok in, I think, 1928. Daughter, you know I am getting old and my poor mind is not as sharp as it used to be. He explained that Bangkok was a haven for Vietnamese dissidents at that time. Ho had shaven his head and wore the saffron of Buddhist monks, though now he supports the wispy beard of a Chinese mandarin. After mastering the Siamese language, he opened a school and published a newspaper in an expatriate Vietnamese community in the northeast. Ho speaks French, Russian, English, three dialects of Chinese and, of course, Vietnamese. Although Ho hates the Chinese, he was wise enough to accept their arms and troops.

This Communist countryman of ours has more names and talents than they say a cat has lives. He has been, among other things, a pastry chef in London and a playwright in France. Ho was born Nguyen Sinh Cung, received the name Nguyen Tat Thanh when he was ten, called himself Nguyen Ai Quoc for a while, and took the name he has now after he formed the Vietminh in 1941. That was after he posed as a local shaman to elude French security forces. It was close to Lam Song, and the French were doing their usual damage—capturing Vietnamese nationalists and torching villages in the area. Ho was setting up training courses and expanding guerrilla activities. The authorities soon stepped up their efforts to suppress the guerrillas.

When Ho posed as a shaman, he wore a black robe and carried black magic texts, joss sticks, and a live chicken. You may remember, Jade, from when your poor mother died that chicken blood cures diseases, though it didn't help her. Maybe Ho really is a shaman. After all, he vanquished the Japanese and the French with his Vietminh. Perhaps, though, he is an evil shaman, since he has kept our country at war. I only repeat what I hear in the *fumerie*. I have no opinion. To many people, he is Uncle Ho and revered in the Confucian way. To others, he is a Communist revolutionary dedicated to bringing everyone to his cause. Chou says, too, that Ho's current name, the one we know him by, means Bringer of Light.

Daughter, my health suffers and no one cares for me, least of all you, my own flesh and blood. Van never even inquires about my health. The servants stole the last of your poor dead mother's silks that I kept as a remembrance to give you if you were ever to have your own daughter. I am slighted in this as in other matters of life. I long for the day I am taken away to where my loneliness will end. If I didn't have my pipe and the den, I would have nothing.

Glancing at her watch, Jade sighed and put away the letters. They would soon land in Saigon. The waiting was almost over.

2

JADE MEETS MUI

Saigon is a French town in a hot country. It is as sensible to call it—as is usually done—the Paris of the Far East as it would be to call Kingston, Jamaica, the Oxford of the West Indies.

—Norman Lewis, *A Dragon Apparent*

Saigon: November 1957

The Air France jet bumped and jerked to a stop on the hot tarmac of Saigon's Tan Son Nhat Airport. As Jade had hoped, her so-called niece, Mui, and Van had made their way to the front of the crowd that was anxiously awaiting the return of friends and relatives from abroad. Jade's fellow jet-lagged travelers, excited but slowed by the blast of humidity and tropical heat that hit them as they stepped down from the plane, gave Jade the opportunity for a quick perusal of Van and the girl. It had been two years since Van had assumed responsibility for Mui. Jade knew from Van's letters that Mui was fourteen. Her husband had said the girl was like a daughter. He'd also said Mui was anxious to meet Jade. In a long-distance telephone conversation with Van, Jade had put her foot in her mouth. Jealousy had prompted her to say, "Van, if I wanted a daughter, I would have had one."

Jade now sized up Mui and knew this girl would never fall into the kind of trouble she had. Mui's lack of physical attractiveness precluded that. Even the traditional *aio dai,* famed worldwide for displaying the beauty of Annamite women, was unflattering. Her bones were too big, not delicate like those of most Saigonese. And Mui's *aio dai*, though it was roomier than normal, revealed her inelegant frame. Jade remembered how she'd caused heads to turn at Mui's age.

The girl's eyes were set too far back in their sockets and her nostrils flared. Her face was sallow and flat-featured. Even her hair was homely, and though it was freshly washed, it hung shapeless. Jade even thought Mui looked a bit like Van. Her husband's round face and flat nose always reminded Jade of the face in the how-to-draw book she'd labored over as a teenager.

Jade's startlingly changeable eyes studied her husband. Van never changed. His rumpled suit still fit poorly, though Jade had taken him to a Parisian tailor of good repute. Even then, when the suit was new and before the tailor had suggested fitting it with thick shoulder pads, Van's knobby shoulders had ruined its expensive lines. And the dark vertical pinstripes still couldn't camouflage the fact that he was short by French, if not Vietnamese, standards. Still, the suit didn't appear to be a wreck, even though Jade suspected Van's day girl banged it on a rock to get it clean. Sadly Van finally had to send old Dô back to her village. At least there she would have company and be well looked after.

As Van gazed at the throng of travelers, Jade noticed his eyes light up when he spotted her. Mui seemed to know Jade, too, and Jade was pleased by the girl's barely contained excitement when their eyes met.

Van and Mui made their way through the crowd. "Auntie, I've been dreaming of meeting you and having you with us," the girl said, blushing.

With Mui walking beside them, Jade looped her free arm through Van's as they went outside to his beat-up Citroën. Before they got very far into the parking lot, Jade stopped short and kissed Van on the cheek, then erased the perfect rouge likeness of her lips with her finger. Van was mildly taken aback; he didn't like public displays of affection.

The trio resumed their stroll through the crowded lot. *Cyclo* drivers stood in a row, smoking and calling in whiskey voices to the travelers. Motorcades and army vehicles, their cargoes covered with tarps to protect them from spying eyes, moved in and out of the traffic, horns blaring. Poorer travelers lugged their trunks in the searing heat on foot, dragging them across the pitted asphalt.

Jade knew that President Diem's omnipotent secret intelligence agency roamed everywhere. Diem's brother, Nhu, had created a covert network—Can Lao Nhan Vi Cach Mang Dang or Revolutionary Personal Labor Party—from Catholic refugees. His spies were placed at strategic levels to report on government officials. Can Lao infiltrated every aspect of life in South Vietnam and was headed by the powerful Dr. Tran Kim Tuyen, whose high-pitched voice belied his power and authority. Unlike the fun-loving gangster Bay Vien, Tuyen was all work and no play.

Tuyen had been handpicked by Nhu himself. Under Nhu's auspices the Can Lao chief had built not one but ten separate secret intelligence agencies that competed to bring him dispatches of traitors, spies, and plots, often fabricated for gain or self-protection. Worse, the manipulative Nhu financed his family's subversive Can Lao Party and intelligence agencies by engaging in extortion, waterfront piracy, exchange manipulation, and illicit trade in opium. Nhu was becoming an underworld lord and black marketeer similar to Bay Vien, his old enemy. The Ngo family ruled with creative mayhem, forming bandit groups and secret societies and creating warlords even they couldn't keep track of.

Can Lao agents always mixed in the crowd, the only key to their presence the telltale bulges of revolvers in trouser pockets. Some posed as *cyclo* drivers, but these were arrogantly obvious. They didn't mingle with the drivers whose livelihoods depended on their demanding trade. The real drivers were evident by their darker complexions, rough hands, tattered shorts, and worn rubber thongs. You could also tell a *cyclo* driver by his legs—bare and hairless, rippling with muscles and pumped with veins.

Van, Jade, and Mui passed an armed sentry with nary a glance. They took little notice of the commonplace.

"Auntie," Mui said, "it would be so wonderful if you'd live here with Uncle."

"My dear Mui, I'd love to stay home with you and Van, but I must keep my embassy posting," Jade said. "There are few women in the world who have as important a position as I do."

"But, Auntie, Uncle Van has his important work when I come to visit. We eat together and then he returns to his research and I sit alone. I don't have a mother and I'm lonely."

"You have a wonderful school in Sadec, and I promise I'll come home more often. We'll have lots of time to get to know each other." Mui 's words triggered annoyance in Jade. She had thought this girl was lucky to have anything. Mui could easily have joined the ranks of the many Saigonese street children hawking gum, cigarettes, or their bodies. Or she could have been stuck in the jungle with the Communist guerrillas, wielding a gun, sleeping in ditches and caves, dying of plague or malaria. Instead, fortune had smiled on her and brought this well-off orphan everything: a doting "uncle" and one of the most exclusive schools in South Vietnam. Jade knew Van pressed money on the girl to purchase anything she liked. He treated her as if she were his daughter. But obviously it wasn't enough. This girl craved a mother figure, a woman in her life.

Jade thought of Phuong, who was as elusive as her namesake, the mythological phoenix. She reflected that her own flesh and blood had nothing and was likely alone somewhere without even a father. Phuong had never known a mother, while Mui lived in comfort. Still, the girl beside her now did lose her parents, and Jade thought of her own lost mother. Mui was an orphan, and Jade decided she would be good to the poor girl. Perhaps that would atone in small some way for her past mistakes.

"Auntie, what's wrong?" Mui asked. "Have I upset you?"

Van intervened. "Jade, you must be exhausted from the flight. We'll take you home."

As they continued their trek to the car, they were forced aside. A Mercedes limousine, freshly waxed and as luminous as black water in sunlight, held up all traffic. Members of the Women's Solidarity Movement led the way in blue jackets and silk pants. Their fingers clasped miniature flags as if they were outstretched flowers. "We want only peace," they chanted, "to live quietly in friendship, but if the Communists come, we'll fight them and kill them." Hand grenades and knives hung from their belts. The Solidarity Movement was just one of many specialized political units the Ngo family had set up to further their dynastical rule.

"The car's windows are darkened," Mui said with awe. "It must be the presidential family."

Van put a finger to his lips, then said, "They say President Diem goes nowhere but spends sixteen to eighteen hours locked away in his study at the Presidential Palace. He's even said to sign every single exit visa issued himself." Van made sure no one was eavesdropping, then continued. "Chou tells me he can't separate the trivial from the important and oversees even minor details of government. Our president even chooses where shrubs are to be planted. He is mired in the deceptions and truths fed him by his army generals and secret police. His factions work against one another like Chinese shopkeepers trying to damage each other's business." Then, as the limousine slid by, he added with sly humor, "So that can't be our busy president riding in style."

"Look at the patriotic women in uniform leading the way!" Mui enthused. "They're members of Madame Nhu's Solidarity Movement. It must be Madame Nhu!"

"Mui, you're very observant," Van said. "It's too bad we're not in the terminal still where we could catch a glimpse of her. That woman is the talk of the town. They say she's a self-advertised, sanctimonious Catholic who shocks the elderly Vietnamese with her décolleté gowns. Until she married the fierce and intellectual Nhu she had no knowledge of Catholicism. The beautiful first lady takes much pleasure in having shows put on for her benefit and has built a special raised dais where she sits and applauds her women performing judo on men."

"Madame Nhu *is* a mandarin's daughter," Jade insisted. "Where is your car, Van? Will we ever reach it?"

3

RIVER RATS AND FOXES

A sacred respect is due the person of the sovereign. He is the mediator between the people and heaven as he celebrates the national cult.

—Ngo Dinh Diem

Saigon: November 1957

The bedside clock read a quarter to eleven. Jade wasn't used to the time change, not accustomed to the humidity of Saigon. Van stood over her with a plate of fresh figs.

"I'll feel better when I have some tea," she said, motioning him back to the kitchen. Then she got up, filled the ceramic basin with fresh water from the jug that stood nearby, and splashed her face and underarms. The adjacent bathroom was complete with running water, a bathtub, and a bidet, but she preferred to be artless on her first morning back and shunned the paint and powder of her Paris life. Slipping on the pants of her favorite *aio dai*, Jade pulled the high-necked, ankle-length dress over her head. The embossed silk was translucent, cool against her skin. She was glad of it as the air was heavy with heat. Dressed, Jade wandered into the sitting room in search of Van and the figs. The ceiling fan was still, so she pulled once, twice, thrice on its beaded cord. The blades remained motionless. Obviously there was a power outage.

"Van, do you know where I left my fan?" Not waiting for his answer, she returned to the bedroom and retrieved it. The woven fronds swayed as her wrist flicked the handle, the noise of the fan sounding like cane moving in the wind. As she fanned, she sighed, perhaps hoping the exhalation would help drive the close air away from her. Impatiently she walked by the open casement windows of her house on Bui Thi Xuan Street, muttering. Why had she left Paris for this stifling weather? Even though it was the cooler season, the birds themselves in the banana trees outside appeared lethargic.

Beyond the protection of the fenced-in yard and the greenery of leafy palm and flamboyant trees that sheltered their house from the heat, Jade could hear the clatter of a sole vehicle on the street. If she had cared to look, she would have seen a sober black Renault 4CV. Both history and blueprints set the automobile apart from its predecessors—the Juvaquatre, Novaquatre, and Vivaquatre. The 4CV was fondly nicknamed Puce or Pet. Puce beat its manufacturer's target speed of fifty miles per hour. Its 760 cc engine and four-speed gearbox were firsts. Invented in total secrecy while the Germans were occupying the Renault factory, the vehicle had caused a postwar sensation in France with its sleek appearance, economical fuel consumption, and sporting achievements. It was the type of vehicle that inspired lusty admiration. The only one of its kind in Saigon, it belonged to Chou.

Jade looked at the thermometer and noted the temperature: ninety degrees Fahrenheit. It was too hot for this time of year, and it was unusually quiet outside. The Saigonese were a hardy lot and far hotter temperatures didn't keep them indoors. She wondered if something was going on.

"I'm so tired," Jade complained to Van. "My flight from Paris was grueling. Why is it so stifling here?" Her feet were bare except for the lacquer on her toenails. One hand rested at her throat, showing her painted nails bright against her skin.

Van, with the infinite patience of his countrymen, replied, "Don't worry, my love, it will rain again soon."

Jade ignored this. "You should have the cleaner in more often,

Van. The ironwood floors look dull and my beautiful brocade couch that I had shipped from Paris needs a shampoo. And please don't put the newspaper on the couch. No wonder it looks dirty."

Jade picked up the paper and threw it on the floor. In reality she knew the house was more charming than ever. On the dining table a giant orange hibiscus floated its open petals and ruffled stamen in a crystal bowl. The wooden floors shone and the wrought iron that divided the rooms was free of cobwebs and dust. In a dragon pot placed under the window an orchid thrived. That was Mui's influence, she'd bet. Van had told her with barely contained pride that Mui had given the day girl strict instructions on cleaning and flower arranging.

"I don't notice such things, Jade," Van said, referring to her lecture on housekeeping. His eyes moved from the elaborately carved hardwood beam that was the backbone of the crabshell roof and stopped to rest on the splash of color of Jade's silk *aio dai*.

"What are you thinking, Van?" Jade asked, knowing the answer already. "Are you wishing I'd let you get on with your work?"

"Of course not, my dear. I'm happy you're home."

"I'm sorry, Van. I'm just tired—and hot! Where is Mui, by the way?" Jade threw herself onto the feather-soft couch.

Van picked up the newspaper from the floor and folded it neatly. "Mui is safe visiting Madame Hoa, her lawyer. I have a question for you. When will you come home to stay permanently?"

"Please, Van, I've just come back. Let's not discuss that now. Did I tell you I have to go to the Presidential Palace to deliver a package from our embassy in Paris?"

A dispatch case lay on the simple coffee table separating two uncomfortable high-backed chairs. They were carved with dragons and inlaid with mother-of-pearl. Van looked dwarfed in the one closest to Jade, who lolled on the couch's overstuffed goose feathers covered by French brocade.

"Jade, please don't go to the Presidential Palace today. It's the most dangerous place in all Saigon. It's bad enough that I'm worried about Mui all the time." Van thought carefully before he spoke again. "I don't like to do this, but I won't allow you to go outside. Anything could happen in times like these."

"Van, that's ridiculous! I'm only delivering some papers. It will barely take an hour. The only reason I'm getting extra time away from my work in Paris is that I agreed to be a courier. And I'm not about to let the ambassador down!" Jade sat up and glared at her husband.

"Jade, you've been gone from Saigon too long. Things have changed since Diem became president, especially in the past couple of years. Saigon is a sinkhole of corruption. What with the Hoa Hao, the Cao Dai, and the Binh Xuyen—all of them with their own private armies maneuvering to take power. Diem has crushed the two religious sects, the Cao Dai and the Hoa Hao. He even bribed the Cao Dai to join the South Vietnamese army. They're now three hundred thousand strong. The U.S. government has given Diem millions of dollars for bribes. Those river rats, the Binh Xuyen, tried to hold out, but Diem cowed them, too. The place is a tinderbox. Our embassy in Paris is living in a dream world. There's shooting in the streets every day. Don't you read my letters?"

Jade looked uncomfortable. "Yes, but surely you were exaggerating."

"Jade, this is serious. The streets are dangerous. There are criminals and dissidents everywhere. You have to be careful."

"I'm not stupid, Van. I know there's trouble because of that opium factory, illegal smuggling, and the Communists. But Saigon has always been a hotbed of illicit activities. What's new?"

Van interrupted. "Jade! If things go on like this, even Diem could be toppled. You can't *not* run into trouble on the road to the palace."

"Well, then. I guess—" A sharp knock at the outside gate didn't let her finish. "Who could that be? You've made me so nervous with all your talk about shooting and gangsters."

"I wasn't expecting anyone," Van said. "I hope nothing's happened to Mui."

He went out to open the gate where he found Chou leaning. The lawyer's attention was on the street. His Sobrane cigarette pointed a black-and-gold finger at the hazy sky. The burning ember of the cigarette was held to the black paper by the inch of gray ash he'd neglected to tap away.

"Excuse the intrusion, Van," Chou finally said, turning to look at his host. "Our chess game the other night wasn't finished and I just thought of my next move. I was hoping I'd find you at home." Chou's cigarette ash finally floated gently to the ground.

"Come in, old friend," Van said with a smile. "I always thought you were a madman. It's dangerous out there."

"If you mean the gangsters roaming the streets the past few days, don't worry about me. I've got a large share in their opium refinery and they count on me to get more investors. I knew Bay Vien and I know his successor, Big Boss, personally." Chou tapped his nose and stretched one eyebrow.

"That scoundrel?" Van said, shocked.

Chou moved with his streamlined gait into the house. "It pays to know everyone."

After the stifling noonday heat, the house was comparatively cool. The painted wooden shutters were fastened, yet a few rays of sunlight broke through and drew *X*'s on the bamboo birdcage that hung empty in the corner.

"Ah, Van, you lucky devil, your wife's home." Chou looked pleased. "I have the pleasure of seeing La Doctoress often when I'm in Paris. But to see her here in her own home with the objects she loves and the man who loves her paints her in a different light. She's even more beautiful." Chou turned to Jade. "Doctoress, welcome home." He took her hand in his. "I trust you're not overtired from your flight? Myself, I've been home for a week and have been butchering boredom by challenging your husband at chess. But Van's too much of a thinker and beats me every time."

Jade smiled. It was purely a muscular contraction, the kind she adopted when she wasn't amused. "You didn't tell me you were going to be in Saigon."

Chou looked meaningfully at Jade, and his black brows danced. "You know me. I'm here, I'm there, I'm always doing favors for someone."

Ignoring Chou's look, Jade said, "Van has sent Dô away. She's ill and old, you know. I'll bring tea." With some relief she headed for the kitchen.

Although her feet were bare, Jade was out of place in front of the massive gas stove. Her *aio dai* wasn't meant for the oil and spices of a kitchen. An apron hung on a hook, but she was too distraught to bother. She struck a safety match, but it broke. Then she tried again, and this time the match fizzled before she could touch it to the gas ring. Concentrating, she finally lit the gas. Her unsteady fingers placed the tea leaves in the pot. It had belonged to her mother. The three matching cups were handleless and painted with gilt snakes. Jade felt vaguely uneasy as she waited for the kettle to whistle. She detested Chou's offhand manner with her, his seeming flirtation in front of her husband.

She stared at the blue flame and deliberated, trying to fathom him, predict his actions. Jade was annoyed that he was hanging around Van. Before, Chou wouldn't give her husband the time of day. Now they were playing chess. She was confident the lawyer wouldn't dare tell Van about their secret search. He'd lose his power over her.

Arranging the tea things on a lacquered tray, Jade returned to the sitting room. Van and Chou waited in silence for her to pour. The tea was black and her hands now bore no trace of her anxiety.

She noticed that Chou was tieless and that his collar was open underneath his white tussore, the suit of coarse silk that was favored by Saigon's well-heeled bankers.

Once the tea was poured, she wound her fingers around one cup, covering its gilt serpents as she spooned sugar into Van's cup. Quickly she transferred the tea to his outstretched hands. Then, taking up the tiny gold spoon again, she asked, "Chou, do you take sugar?"

"Yes, I'm still Vietnamese. I take my tea sweet."

She dumped the raw cane sugar into his teacup, then placed the cup in Chou's hands, brushing his long, sallow fingers as she did so.

Van broke their relative silence. "Jade foolishly wants to go to the palace despite the current troubles. Chou, you must help me talk her out of this madness."

Chou's black-eyed gaze was curious. "My dear Doctoress, what would make you risk your life?"

"I promised the embassy I'd do them a favor."

"To deliver some papers," Van interjected. "Whatever it is, it can wait for a safer time." He directed these last words at Jade.

"I can take them," Chou said decisively. "I have to go by the palace on other business."

"No, thank you, Chou. They were entrusted to me alone."

"Nonsense, dear girl, I insist. I haven't forgotten the favor I promised your revered father."

Before Jade had a chance to speak, Van said, "Wonderful Chou! I was just impressing on Jade the danger of her mission. I appreciate and am indebted to you for your generous offer." Van withdrew a sealed manila envelope from the dispatch case that lay on the coffee table and handed it to the lawyer.

Chou drove his black Renault through streets that were as empty as a dead man's eyes. Even the new traffic lights at rue Catinat had ceased to function. Windows were locked tight with iron grilles. Businesses had closed. The streets were desolate except for scraps of the previous night's garbage. The charred remains of incense, a remnant of religion and hope, lay like heaped black pepper here and there. Paper and garbage were strewn in a filthy tumble as business owners and housewives alike valued their safety rather than the cleanliness of Saigon's evening sweeping ritual. Not a child or a beggar braved the streets today.

Negotiating the corner of the wide Boulevard Norodom that led away from Diem's abode and the place of government, Chou saw nothing as he maneuvered his car through a narrow alley. The alley was used to dry freshly made vermicelli, and when it was, the noodles were strung like white laundry over bamboo mats high in the air. But not this day.

Chou pulled up to the gutter, his practiced eyes sweeping the street as he pushed the lock buttons on all four doors. A dog, all bones under a mangy coat, glanced the lawyer's way, then foraged again through an upended garbage can. Satisfied there was no one to see him, Chou unlocked his glove box and removed a pistol. The Ruger .22 was standard-issue for the American CIA and Special Forces. He had received it from his Hanoi sponsor. "For emergencies," the sponsor had said cunningly. The Ruger's handle was well-worn.

He placed the weapon on the passenger seat, reached again into the glove box, and took out his onyx dagger. Then he neatly slit the wax seal on the manila envelope he'd usurped from Jade and her precious embassy. The envelope was marked CONFIDENTIAL.

Removing the contents, Chou read, his thin lips curving into a derisive smile: "A Communist-backed movement of Vietminh militants called the National Liberation Front for South Vietnam is being organized by a male intellectual, Tran Van Bo, alias Hai Cao, who is the son of a wealthy landowner in Ba Xuyen Province. The aim of the group is to topple President Diem and undermine the Republic of Vietnam. They may set up clandestine headquarters in Tay Ninh Province near the Cambodian border."

Chou grinned. He had heard much of agent Hai Cao or Second Tall One, whose true identity was unknown to all but Ho Chi Minh himself. Hai Cao was in charge of propaganda. In the interests of security he operated through an intricate command system and had one contact only—an agent who communicated with another and so forth.

Chou knew of the agent's secret movements, too. Although Diem had smashed many of the pockets of Vietminh guerrillas that hid in the Mekong Delta, he had become indiscriminate with his revenge. Former Vietminh who preferred to live in peace after the French left were arrested and imprisoned. Innocent peasants and city dwellers were denounced by jealous neighbors or imprisoned by corrupt officials coveting their property. The prisoners were tried by "security committees" personally appointed by Diem. They were always denied counsel and often tortured. Some were caged in Poulo Condore, the island prison built by the French to hold Vietnamese nationalists—the *old* enemy. The National Liberation Front for South Vietnam was a backlash against Diem's cruelty toward Vietminh "suspects." Hai Cao was rallying all those who hated Diem to Uncle Ho's side.

Stroking his goatee, Chou tried to think of the best use for this windfall. He knew Ho would reward him well and that Tran would be extremely grateful to him for intercepting this dangerous message. Chou stroked his beard again. Perhaps one day he might need this favor returned.

The lawyer opened the Renault's door. The automatic revolver was barely visible on the seat, black steel against black leather. He burnt the document, watching as its ashes joined those of the incense on the ground. As Chou straightened, he pricked his ears and narrowed his eyes. The *rat-a-tat-tat* of machine-gun fire was getting closer. Hurriedly he got back into the Renault, started the engine, and sped off, the mangy hound his only witness.

4
INCIDENT IN SAIGON

Five boys use two poles.
They chase a herd of water buffalo into a dark cave.
What is this? A hand using chopsticks to eat rice.

—Vietnamese Riddle

Saigon: November 1960

The streets were overrun by the military. Even so, Chou made progress in his black Renault 4CV, or the Shadow, as he called it. He was on his way to Van's to play their prearranged game of chess. When he arrived, he found Mui and Van in the living room reading, as if nothing was wrong with the state of their world. Mui's school in Sadec had been temporarily closed due to guerrilla movement in the area. Van's outdated RCA radio, with the etching of the dog on the front, blared and crackled over and over that the Presidential Palace had been besieged once again. But Mui and Van seemed oblivious.

"Van, come outside onto the front verandah," Chou said. When Mui started to follow, he added, "Stay inside, my girl. You never know when danger can appear."

Striding to the front porch, Chou leaned on the banister, the gray trail of his cigarette smoke mimicking the columns rising from the Presidential Palace. Van sat on the stairs, his hands folded in his lap. "The right of the dissident is an integral part of political change," Chou said, watching Van for clues to his political loyalties. But he saw nothing in the man's eyes and changed his tone. "My dear Van, there's a coup going on and I knew about it weeks ago."

Van searched his pockets and withdrew a tin of Juan Bastos. "Are you a fortuneteller?"

Chou tapped the side of his nose, then leisurely lit Van's cigarette.

"All right, Chou, tell me."

"I'll do better than that, Van. Accompany me on a mission!"

"Chou, you're foolhardy," Van warned, the wail of sirens corroborating his statement. "The streets are very dangerous, especially now that the American military is here. If a coup is happening, then wisdom dictates we stay behind closed doors." Van stubbed out his cigarette without even drawing on it. He was careful not to mark the stair.

Chou snorted. "You're the only South Vietnamese in Saigon I know who doesn't have a cache of foreign currency, diamonds, or drugs ready to escape with. But let me confess. I'm just kidding you—about a mission, I mean. Actually, I really must be going, or I'll have to rely on your hospitality and stay the night."

"You're more than welcome to stay as long as you like. Mui and I are happy to have you. But tell me, Chou, what do you really know about this coup?"

"My sources say it's an officers' revolt. Even the top brass in our army are convinced Diem and Nhu are ruining our country. Like the boa constrictor in the countryside, the Ngo family is swallowing our land and people whole. The only ones who get fat in this country are Diem's precious Catholics who have been given land." Chou dropped the butt of his Sobrane and mashed it into the wood with his shoe, leaving a mark.

"I agree with you up to a point," Van said thoughtfully, one ear cocked to the sirens that grew ever louder. "Our government imprisons innocent people on false pretenses. I tell you this in confidence, Chou, but I've asked Jade yet again to quit her work at our embassy in Paris. You, too, would be wise to give up your embassy contract. Jade's translating and your legal work are associated with the South Vietnamese embassy in Paris, and that could prove embarrassing if Ho Chi Minh is behind any of the factions trying to usurp President Diem. Politics is a most treacherous game in Saigon. Take my advice and keep out of it." A tiny lizard scooted under Van's bent knees.

Moving his sleek head back and forth, Chou said, "I'm surprised at you, Van. Maybe Uncle Ho and his Communists can reunite the North and South."

Van scrutinized the lawyer. "Are you a secret Communist, Chou?"

"I'm just playing the devil's advocate. Of course not!"

"Well, if you are my friend, don't tell me anything more. I'm a scientist and my work attempts to further mankind, not set it back. My research is more important to the world, and to Vietnam, than politics and fighting. My colleagues and I are almost at a breakthrough for a vaccine to combat malaria."

"*That* is truly a miracle," Chou said with a smile. "We're friends, Van, you and I. Friends shouldn't allow political ideology or religion to come between them. Or women, for that matter. And for you, Van, my future Nobel Prize winner, it's dangerous to talk like this out on the porch or anywhere else. Saigon has ears in every wall. Come see me to the gate. I must be off before I become a nuisance in your house."

"What about our chess game?"

Chou tapped his nose slowly. "Another time, my dear Van. Something just occurred to me and I must attend to it."

The headquarters of Big Boss, Saigon's organized crime lord, sat decaying at the foot of an abandoned wharf. The musky Saigon River oozed in the sunlight, creating a hothouse stench. The sun's rays bounced off the tangle of pistols and rifles in the ammunition dump. The arsenal was comprised of Japanese automatics that fired 8 mm Nambu rounds; Russian Tokarev pistols; and some old Mauser rifles. Many of the weapons had been used in the Chinese army; others were standard Russian issue. A mound of grenades lay beside the guns.

The street that led to the wharf was deserted. Chou had maneuvered his Renault in low gear, avoiding puddles he knew would bottom out under the brackish water. Chou wished he had his Citroën halftrack. He'd gotten good use from its unusual four-wheel drive fitted with two rear wheels that rotated like a Caterpillar tractor. Chou had been forced to abandon the vehicle months before. It had been up to fender level in the jungle's squelching mud when he'd been unable to ferret out one of the few remaining Moïs, the bow-and-arrow tribe that refused to submit to any authority and were once believed by city folk to have tails.

Here, at Big Boss's riverine headquarters, it had rained long and hard. Stopping the Renault directly in front of the gate, Chou removed his revolver from the glove box, made sure it was loaded, and stuffed it down his silk sock. "Hello!" he called out. "I'm here to see Big Boss."

Two ugly youths appeared. Each carried a Mauser rifle. The boys had rolled up their sacking shirts to cool their stomachs. They were streaked with mud and reeked of sweat. Even their mothers referred to them as river rats. The taller youth was all skin and bones. He leaned against the paddled handle of his weapon, the odd-looking C-96 7.63 mm Parabellum Broomhandle rifle used by the Communists during the first year of the Korean War. The other boy had a stomach girdled by an adolescent ring of fat. One chubby finger curled around the ring attached to the more manageable and shorter handle of his Schnellfeuerpistole, which he twirled like a baton. His plaything had been made for the military in China. Both weapons boasted twenty-round magazines.

Beckoning to the guards, Chou handed each a Babe Ruth chocolate bar. There were genial smiles all around. After a perfunctory body search that stopped at his knees, Chou was led to the back of the derelict building.

Big Boss sat at a metal desk built large and heavy. A Tintin comic book lay on his desk; it was popular reading in South Vietnam as well as in France. Big Boss, whom even Chou didn't know the real name of, reclined in a scoop-necked undershirt and a *lunghi*, the roomy wraparound skirt worn by men in India. The chair on rollers was designed to take his substantial weight, and the *lunghi* was specially fitted with deep pockets on the inside panels. "So, Little Fox, how does the CIA and army-backed coup fare against our haughty presidential family?" he rumbled, feigning disinterest. Chou was known to his comrades and cronies as Con Cáo Con, or Little Fox. Like his namesake, he was secretive and sinewy.

"We may soon taste the sweetness of revenge," Chou said. "The brave South Vietnamese paratrooper units are bombing their own."

Before the lawyer could say anything else, the shrill ring of the phone cut him off. Big Boss scooped up the receiver in his fat hand. After a lengthy exchange studded with profanities, he hung up. "That was the brilliantly conniving Dr. Tuyen."

Chou had admired Tuyen once but had reversed his opinion since Tuyen's appointment as the Ngo family's secret-service head. So he made no comment but curled his lips in disdain. Under Nhu's orders Tuyen had run most of Big Boss's men out of town. The chief spy was no friend to the crime lord.

"Are you deaf, Chou? That was Dr. Tuyen. He's offered a reward if we can throw a wrench into the army's coup."

Chou raised a black eyebrow and held it there.

The lawyer's calm drove Big Boss's blood pressure up, and his words tumbled out as quickly as a *cyclo* driver on the way home to dinner. "Tuyen needs our help. Without it the Ngo family will fall. Tuyen tells me the Presidential Palace is surrounded and communications are cut off. Diem can't get word to General Khanh and his loyal Mekong Delta troop, which is on alert in case an officers' coup gets this far. But Khanh won't march to Diem's aid unless he receives direct written orders signed and sealed by the president himself. And Diem can't get anything past his own palace door." Big Boss took a deep breath. When he exhaled, his stomach rolled in waves over the folds of his *lunghi*. "Tuyen has asked us to intervene."

"And why would *we* do that?" Chou muttered.

"For financial gain and exchange of favors—what else?" Big Boss looked aghast at Chou's question. "We're assured by Tuyen that Diem, the self-righteous pig, and his bloodsucking brother, Nhu, will be history, anyway—and soon enough. It's for our benefit, and not only Uncle Ho's, that we're *not* rid of the Ngo family just yet."

Finally Chou was intrigued. "How great is the reward for us to change horses in midstream?"

"Pretty good. They'll make it well worth a quick change in our loyalties. Money can buy an entrance to any country in the world, and I'm on my way out soon, anyway. Really, my friend, what's loyalty cost for people like you and me? Our skins come first and then piastres as insurance for our skins."

"How much?"

"Fifty million piastres each, and straight into a Swiss bank account. That's enough for us to think of a plan to save them this time, eh, Chou?" Big Boss pushed his chair back from the desk and leaned, the momentum propelling him forward to a standing position. His face beaded with the effort, rivulets of perspiration running down his forehead and neck. He dabbed daintily with a handkerchief and returned it to a deep pocket. His undershirt puddled even below the cutaway armpits and at the chest. As he moved, his contagion of sweat spread.

Big Boss rolled like a rowboat in a storm as his dimpled bare feet padded across the floor. A rat, brown coat gleaming, scrutinized his landlord's rollicking progress from a filthy corner. Chou went ahead, and the two men emerged into the sunlit yard, the river air putrid and thick in the lawyer's nostrils. Big Boss called two of his gangsters who had been squatting on the rough ground watching a game of *boules*, the French version of bowls. They smoked hand-rolled Gitanes.

"You!" the gangster leader barked to one of the hoods. "Get together a company of our best men and make sure Dr. Tuyen's house is safe. Be sure to go one at a time, so you don't attract attention."

"Yes, sir," the man answered, a cigarette clenched between his teeth.

Big Boss glanced at a third sharp-looking thug who leaned against an open box of grenades as if it were the backrest of his personal chaise longue. He was waiting his turn at *boules*. The gang leader instructed him to go to Thanh's rubber stamp shop at boulevard Charner and ask the proprietor to bring himself and his seal-making tools immediately to headquarters. "Tell the seal maker he'll be generously rewarded." Behind Big Boss's flesh-choked eyes the beads to a mental abacus calculated the seal maker's cut—it would be a pittance.

He eyed Chou. "My latest acquisition." He withdrew a custom-made .357 Magnum Smith & Wesson from the double leather holster rig accessible beneath the folds of his Indian-style skirt, then waved it at the lawyer. "The Americans hunt grizzly bears and their lawmen hunt human flesh with this." Big Boss guffawed, then produced a second Magnum with a shorter barrel from the endless mass of material ringing his hips. The cloth Hula-Hoop below his waist was a veritable gun cache. "FBI," he proclaimed, releasing a belch. "J. Edgar Hoover's personal weapon. This one's yours, my friend." Big Boss handed the short-barreled handgun to Chou. "A gift, no strings. For your collection."

Chou smiled and closed his hand around the Magnum, pointing it toward the men playing *boules.* Arm outstretched and legs planted firmly, he aimed and pulled the trigger. *Bing*—a silver-tipped hollowpoint drilled a wormhole in the metal disk rolling across the uneven ground. The man who had held the disk a second earlier scowled at Chou.

Big Boss howled. "Good shot! Too bad you didn't hit Co. He's pretty useless as it is."

Chou tucked his gift into the empty holster rig that lay flat against his bare chest, and the two men embraced, clapping each other on the back and chortling with pleasure.

Nightfall came like a wraith seducing the city. Saigon was overrun by carpetbaggers and touts circling the streets, picking fights, bickering, waiting. Confusion was paramount. Saigon was no longer the sophisticated metropolis of boulevards dappled with tamarind petals and busy with honest street merchants shining shoes and practicing the ancient arts of fortune-telling and ear-cleaning. The city was the Pearl of the Orient no more. It had degenerated into ignoble anguish, reinventing itself as the Peril of Southeast Asia.

But before the bloody tones of sunset mirrored their beautiful blaze on the river, before the purple neon of the bars turned Saigon's streets and alleys into a carnival of corruption, Chou and Big Boss successfully counterfeited a suitable message from Diem to the leader of the Mekong Delta troops, ordering them to save the Presidential Palace.

By the dinner hour, Big Boss and Chou had sent the bogus message to Tuyen. Wasting no time, the spy chief went into action to save his bosses and benefactors: Diem, Nhu, and the deliciously malevolent Madame Nhu, who wouldn't have needed saving if she'd flown to Paris to purchase a strip club on the Champs-Elysées as she had planned.

Joined by a handful of Tuyen's best secret-service men, Big Boss's handpicked ruffians piled into a cavalcade of Mercedes sedans and headed out on their mission to save Diem's faltering dynasty. The rescue message would be safely delivered to the loyal Mekong Delta troops within hours.

The smoke had dissipated by the next day, yet a legacy of burnt-out cars lay everywhere like half-eaten carcasses. Chou drove to Van's home and parked by the gate. He knew Van would be there. Listening, his ear close to the door, he heard the blare of the radio and gave a sharp rap. Van answered immediately.

"Ah, my dear and brave Chou! Mui and I worried about your safety last night. Come in and let us begin a new chess game."

Chou removed his shoes.

"Mui, Uncle Chou is here. Do you recall, dear girl, where I put the chessboard?"

"I'll get it, Uncle," Mui said. "You left it out and I returned it to its case for you last evening." Mui put her reading material down. She was enjoying a book of riddles.

Van looked fondly at her. "What would I do without my Mui?"

"Oh, Uncle, you're an absentminded scientist and I'm happy to look after you. I'll make some chrysanthemum tea and then Chou will tell us about yesterday's events."

Chou lit a cigarette, his fingers as yellow as the flowers Mui had picked from the garden to brew in Jade's teapot. "It's all over now except for Diem's inevitable revenge to search out and silence political opportunists as well as anyone who gets in the way—innocent or not. But yesterday talk had it that Diem was desperate." Chou grinned, enjoying the telling, though he made sure to keep some distance from his words. "Supposedly Diem sent a message to the rebellion's leaders, asking for a ceasefire for negotiations. But then, of course, Diem reneged when his loyal Mekong Delta force marched to his rescue.

"Even more fascinating," Chou continued, "when the CIA was informed that Diem's Mekong force was only six miles west of Saigon and that its coup would be unsuccessful, the CIA issued a statement saying it would continue to support Diem's South Vietnamese government, abandoning the rebellion's leaders."

"Those Americans are so disloyal," Mui said. "I think that's immoral. Don't you agree, Uncle?"

Van indicated that he did.

She turned to the lawyer. "Don't you agree, Chou?"

"Yes, Mui, one must have loyalties to something in times like these." Then he smiled and repeated something he'd heard bandied about the rooftop bar at the Majestic Hotel. "Sooner or later one has to take sides—if one is to remain human."

5

JADE'S SECRET

There is nothing men like more than a red moist mouth.
—Somerset Maugham, *Wit and Wisdom of Somerset Maugham*

Paris: November 1960

A dichotomy in signature red, Jade stared out the Republic of Vietnam embassy's window and down at the Parisian landscape. Then she looked up at the sky, her eyes narrowing in frustration. Life in the so-called City of Light seemed endless—and dull. There was no break in the accumulation of clouds. The weather made Jade's head ache.

She glanced down at the street below and across to a park, usually cheerful with lovers strolling, tourists snapping memories, and just yesterday the sweet voices of a children's choir trilling from the nearby Catholic church. Although it was noon, the embassy, the street, and the park were deserted. The violet clouds would bring stingy flakes of snow, like dry tears.

Jade observed an old man on a wrought-iron bench, his somber coat turned up at the collar. The man's mottled hands were covered to the knuckles by woolen gloves, the frayed fingers cut away to allow him to feed bread to the pigeons that flocked around his feet. The color of the pigeons mimicked the sky.

Turning away from the dismal scene, Jade made an effort to concentrate on work. She picked up the *Paris Gazette* and scanned the headlines, but all she got for her trouble was more about French President de Gaulle and the Algerian question. The question was independence. Nothing unusual. Jade thought of the years 1954 to 1956 when French newspapers had been packed with headlines and stories about France's lost colonies: Equatorial Africa, West Africa, Morocco, Tunisia and, of course, her own Indochina. Maybe France was finished, she thought, trying to focus on her work.

A tablecloth of papers marred Jade's desk. The door to the outer room was ajar; she was alone in the embassy. The receptionist, Miss Hau, was taking lunch.

Jade grumbled to herself. Where was she to begin? The embassy had given her too much work to do. She had a lot of translation work to catch up on and was constantly being interrupted by Vietnamese students who had stupidly forgotten to renew their visas. Now the ambassador expected her to write press releases meant to reassure South Vietnamese expatriates in France that all was well in Saigon. That wasn't an easy task after the November 11 attempted coup by Diem's own army units. Jade thought hard and began:

> Paris: November 1960
>
> France's hopes in Indochina ended in blood at the climactic battle of Dien Bien Phu just six years ago on May 7, 1954, but French culture still pervades on the wide boulevards of our lovely city of Saigon.

No, she told herself, that wouldn't do. She crumpled the sheet and started again:

> Paris: November 1960
>
> On June 20, 1954, the Geneva Agreements split Vietnam in two, leaving the North under Ho Chi Minh and communism. Our beloved South remained free under President Ngo Dinh Diem,

> who was nominated by Emperor Bao Dai. Our president is well supported by the United States of America. The years that South Vietnam has enjoyed after the Geneva Agreements have been relatively free of incident until a short while ago when Hanoi began sporadic attacks on our fair city. In the previous days our fearless President Diem's army was infiltrated, but unsuccessfully. Now the West protects us further and America has seen fit to send more advisers to our country.

Studying the words whose letters trailed like a peacock's tail down the paper, she sniffed a familiar scent. It was Chou. She hadn't heard him enter. "You startled me, Chou. You're as quiet as the Vietminh."

"Dear Doctoress, I'm a jungle cat or a fox, not a peasant guerrilla—but just as cunning. You should know me by now!"

Choosing to ignore Chou's braggadocio, Jade said, "My new position as public-relations officer is proving difficult. I'm so tired of repeatedly warning naive Vietnamese students who come to the embassy to renew their papers. But then I lecture them, no, advise them, that they're toying with disaster for our country if they attend support rallies for Ho Chi Minh. They allow themselves to be seduced by Ho's brand of communism. They all seem to think that since the French government backs Ho that South Vietnam must fall. I have to explain that Ho made a deal with France at Fontainebleau, giving him the backing of France if he took power in South Vietnam, and that's why so many rallies are held. Then I have to reassure the students that the Americans, who are stronger than any European power, back our President Diem." She looked up at Chou. "My own loyalties to France are being tested."

Chou said nothing, and although he looked relaxed, his gaze darted around her office like the sphere in a pinball machine.

Jade took no notice of Chou's eyes. She was worried about

the state of her country. "Some call Diem America's puppet. They also rant that Diem couldn't care less about the South Vietnamese. And now we have this coup attempt by a disloyal faction in his own army. I don't know how they can expect me to keep up with my job as translator *and* be a public-relations officer under such ridiculous circumstances."

Jade's new brief as public-relations officer for the embassy was to uphold the democratic and stable image of South Vietnam and to field questions from concerned South Vietnamese who resided in France. Simply put, that meant translating from Vietnamese to French and writing press releases for the embassy's newsletter intended to counteract the endless detrimental propaganda against South Vietnam disseminated by Ho Chi Minh's regime.

The embassy knew the situation was made even more sensitive by the fact that France was pro-Hanoi. As well, North Vietnam had imposed military conscription. Where South Vietnam was concerned, it was common knowledge that Diem had been petitioned by eighteen prominent South Vietnamese to reform his government. They had been jailed. All of Saigon was sick of the Ngo family and its paranoid repression.

Jade's mind clicked and she looked at Chou. He cut a dashing figure in black. She was aware that his cashmere jacket made him appear as sleek as a panther. Hands on slim hips, she asked, "How *did* you get by the security downstairs? They should have informed me that you were on your way up."

"Never mind about that, my dear Doctoress. I've got important news for your pretty ears."

Jade remembered the last time Chou had news; it had precipitated her trip to Montpellier and the revelation about Phuong. But she said nothing and waited in silence while her mind roiled with a set of constant fears that centered on being found out. Perhaps Phuong resembled her and people would see instantly that the girl was unmistakably hers. Phuong would be a young woman of almost twenty now—too late for a finishing school. Should she call Chou off the hunt? *But what if it was too late?*

"What news do you bring, Chou?" she asked, reeling with the words *too late, too late*.

"My dear, I can't tell you here. The information is too sensitive for a public place. I'll come to your apartment tonight." Chou's black patent shoes turned smartly on the office floor, and he was gone, shutting the door behind him.

Jade couldn't move for a moment. She pushed papers angrily to the floor, then hid her face in the crook of her arm. She was certain disaster was imminent. Why had she gotten herself into a predicament that would never go away?

Her fear at being found out sent her spiraling. Still seated at her desk, Jade placed her palms together, her long fingers curving, vermilion nails pointed toward her matching lips, elbows a tight triangle against her chest. Silently she prayed to God for protection, knowing deep down that she probably didn't deserve such consideration. After a while, she collected her wits and picked up the papers she'd swept to the floor. Mechanically she put on her chinchilla coat and left her office, noting that the receptionist had returned. "Miss Hau, I have to go home. I'm not feeling well. Please field any calls. I'll be back tomorrow."

The receptionist hardly replied.

When Jade got outside, the wind chilled her even more. She hid her face in the pelt of her collar. Her pace was slow as she stared at the cobblestones. The parade of elms that fringed the street shook their crimson leaves in a riot of red.

Concealed by the trunk of the farthest tree, Chou leaned, his jacket smooth against the rough bark. He was smoking, enjoying the peace of early afternoon and rethinking his evening's plans. He would make an excuse to Mona, the Parisian chorus girl he'd been seeing. She bored him.

The previous evening Mona had whined to be escorted to the popular Au Mouton de Panurge restaurant on rue de Choisel. But Chou was sick of the scene; he'd patronized the place too much. To him it was now a tourist trap. But Mona's slippery tongue down his throat and her accomplished hand that dangled, then stopped in his lap, had caused him to give in. Still, he was tired of it. He'd had enough of the restaurant's gouging, the dirty live sheep guzzling red wine in the corner, the bread rolls shaped like penises, the snails served in chamber pots. Worse than the contemptible familiarity was the hard-to-ignore issue that once there, Mona had ignored him for her young male friends who hung about the place. Finally he had gotten her out of the filthy hole and back to the bachelor pad he leased as Monsieur Graham Greene, a cherished pseudonym.

The name Greene tickled his fancy. He'd met the tall, lanky English author at the bar of Saigon's elegant Majestic Hotel. They drank with great gusto, downing vermouth cassis from Baccarat crystal glasses on the hotel's wrought-iron balcony. Greene divulged that he was writing about the French wars with Vietnam for London's *Sunday Times* and *Le Figaro*. But that was no surprise to Chou; there were plenty of European and Asian journalists in Saigon. He'd seen Greene again in the flickering light of the opium *fumerie* up the stairs from Arc-en-Ciel, the renowned Chinese restaurant in seamy Cholon. Immersed in their individual drug-induced dreams, they hadn't spoken.

Chou smiled as he thought about that opium night with Greene, a man almost as secretive as he was. But Mona was the problem at hand. Yes, she was young, but coarse and tawdry, almost a whore, he reasoned. She probably slept with every man who bought her a meal or a cheap dress. Chou was grateful that he'd used a condom each time he'd taken her, though he disliked the way the rubber desensitized his member. He only wore them with the dirtiest of whores, like Mona. If the girl was well dressed or, even better, was young, he'd risk disease for his pleasure.

Chou thought back. Yes, he remembered now. That first time he'd plied Mona with Pernod until she was loose. She undressed while he watched from the chair, unhooking the pins of her garter belt and rolling her silk stockings down her thighs. They were taupe. He would have preferred black.

That done he asked her to come closer, then turned her so her derriere was at his nose. He began by licking at her nylon panties. Pulling them down, he stuck his tongue in her hole, flickering it back and forth, in and out. That caused his penis to lengthen and harden impressively. Next, they traded places, and he told her to sit in the wooden chair, panties off and knees flung wide. He smoothed powder over his erect penis and slipped on the condom while she watched. It went well, but once he entered her she started chattering about her expectations, ruining his climax. She'd actually demanded he take her to the Moulin Rouge! Chou vowed again he would stop seeing her.

Now he leaned against a tree, wind stealing his trail of smoke and swallowing his breath. His instinct was to study Jade. He let her pass; she was unaware of his presence. Her face was muffled by her collar, eyes locked on the leaf-strewn ground.

Chou admired her gait, the way the ankle-length chinchilla swung to the rhythm of her hips. She was so elegant, so unattainable. That goggle-eyed husband of hers didn't deserve her, he muttered under his breath, imagining the length of Jade's thighs naked under her coat, conjuring up her flat, childless breasts, their pink nipples hardening to buttons when he touched them with his tongue. Chou pictured her naked legs again, this time his imagination drawing her derriere. He gave her a dimple on each cheek, then thought briefly of returning to his office to masturbate.

Instead he wondered where Jade was off to, what her mind was obviously troubled with.

Jade's pace had changed. It was quick and purposeful. Following with easy stealth, Chou kept a quarter block behind. He thrust his hands into his pockets as he trailed her, fondling himself as well as he could.

She was headed toward the Vietnamese Catholic church, Chou realized, surprised. Although Jade crossed herself like other Catholics, he knew she was a religious pretender who hadn't entered a church in years. Chou had made it his business to know every nuance of her life, from where she shopped for lingerie to how often she mailed letters to Van. He had a copy of Jade's lease and knew what salary she received from the embassy. Still, she remained an enigma.

Chou had often wondered if he could seduce Jade to his side. The idea that she might be a spy like him entered his head. Maybe Jade was a new agent. It had been a record month for recruitment and the new names were known only to Ho Chi Minh. Perhaps the elegant La Doctoress was passing embassy information to Father Nguyen, the Catholic priest who, like many Vietnamese in France, was sympathetic to Ho.

Father Nguyen used the confessional of his church to pass information. Chou had borrowed the dark confines from Father Nguyen for that purpose many times. Was Jade on his side? What a thought that was. Chou tapped his nose, musing on how good a team Jade and he would make in support of Ho and the North against dimwitted Diem. He forfeited the pursuit of own desires and let go of his penis. Abandoning Jade's trail, he made a dash to the back entrance of the church.

6

CHOU'S REVELATION

It is one thing to sing the beloved. Another, alas,
To invoke that hidden, guilty river-god of the blood.
—Rainer Maria Rilke, *Duino Elegies*

Paris: November 1960

Jade's apartment was heated seductively against the chill that swept the leaves from the tree-lined Quai de Tuileries. Jade was waiting for Chou. Earlier she had visited the Vietnamese Catholic church, a brisk walk from the embassy. She'd gone to confession.

The confessional had smelled of cigarette smoke and a strangely familiar scent. There, for the first time in two decades, Jade admitted her sin. The revelation gave her immense relief. Before the invisible priest, who puffed like an old man when he breathed, she bowed her head and clasped her hands. "I have sinned, Father. When I was young, naive, and foolish, I had an affair with a Frenchman and became pregnant."

Jade continued quickly, trying to ease the shame she relived as she uttered the words. "My lover told me the baby was born dead, but a few years ago I heard differently. I've searched all of France for the child. I've done everything I could. Now I believe my daughter has possibly come to a bad end."

The voice of the priest was barely audible, and for a second Jade thought he was snickering. But that couldn't be. It must have been children giggling from beyond the walls of the confessional. Then Jade heard the words she had come for: "You are forgiven, my child."

When Jade left the confessional, she had steeled herself for her appointment with Chou. Now she was sure the lawyer would tell her what she knew in her heart: Phuong, her Phoenix, was dead and lay buried in a pauper's grave. And if he didn't bring her that news, she would call him off. Her hunt had gone on long enough.

Chou arrived at Jade's apartment at six. "I have something very interesting to tell you," he said, wasting no time. Chou wore black, his turtleneck sweater and chinos flashing under his coat.

"Sit down, Chou. I'm listening." Jade's heart banged as she gracefully motioned Chou to the love seat. She took a seat herself, covering her legs with an English mohair throw she'd purchased at Galeries Lafayette.

Chou remained standing.

"Tell me! What is it? Has the girl I asked you to locate come to a bad end?"

"Have a cigarette. It's cold tonight." Chou lit his own cigarette with a practiced flourish of his Dunhill, but didn't offer Jade one. "A bit of absinthe would probably hit the spot." His smile oozed with false charm.

Annoyed at his game, Jade threw off the cover, her legs a bare flicker under her red-and-gold-brocade dressing gown. She removed a carafe and a glass from the liquor cabinet. "I've only got cognac."

"Well, I guess that will have to do. But it's not just for me, my dear girl. I thought you might need something potent to shelter you from my news. Here, let me do the honors." Moving lithely to Jade's liquor cabinet, he poured cognac into two snifters and handed her one. As usual Chou had wrested control of the situation.

"Tell me about the girl!" Jade demanded again.

Chou tapped his nose, irritating Jade further. "This has nothing to do with *your* girl, my philanthropic woman." The lawyer's smile was imperious and condescending.

"Well, *what* then?" Jade had formed her backup plan but would hear Chou's news first.

"A while ago, when I was in Marseilles searching for news of *your* girl, Phuong, a strange Vietnamese man paid me a visit. He wouldn't divulge his name but insinuated he had a law degree from the University of Bordeaux. He bragged he'd been jailed by President Diem for his earlier work with the Vietminh resistance.

"This Vietnamese stranger asked me to join a new covert organization called the Democratic Coalition for the Republic that would masquerade as an opposition party. In reality it would be under Communist control from Hanoi. He informed me that this fledgling underground organization would try to topple Diem's regime. He argued that it would bring together those in the South who were against Diem. He said it would bring Vietnam freedom from the American interlopers who were using our country for their own gain." Chou's black eyes glittered. "The seditious fellow offered me a position. He was obviously well aware that I'm quite valuable for my contacts."

Jade remained still. Although she hadn't forgotten her fear that Chou knew something, she was beginning to suspect his news had nothing to do with her.

The lawyer talked on. "This subversive related an interesting story about those mercenary gangsters who were quashed the very day I saw you at your husband's house in Saigon—looking like an angel, I might add."

"Chou! Please!"

"Remember, dear girl, it was the same day I did you a favor by delivering your embassy's envelope to the Presidential Palace." Chou paused for effect, his eyes flashing with importance. "I do admit, my dear, that I could have been caught in the crossfire. By the way, Jade, that was three years ago and you look even more ravishing." The dissatisfaction on Jade's face inspired Chou to continue." You must know how you attract me."

"Don't flatter me with your ridiculous remarks. I'm married and Van is your friend. Remember that."

"I didn't realize until recently what a loving and loyal wife you are."

Jade flinched, wondering nervously what Chou was implying. "Finish what you were saying and go."

The lawyer sipped his drink. "So, when Diem's forces defeated the gangsters that day, the ones who escaped hid in the countryside and some joined the Vietminh, just as the Binh Xuyen cutthroats had a couple of years earlier, making Diem's adversaries even stronger. Now there's a new faction in the South working against Diem."

"Well, Chou, what did you say to that fellow's offer of a position in this Democratic Coalition?"

"Naturally I was surprised by the man's audacity. I asked him why I should join his cause. He informed me again, this time with vehemence, that Diem was America's puppet and the Yanks wanted to take the place of the old French colonists and exploit the Vietnamese. He said Diem was a dictator, that South Vietnam was under the yoke of American imperialism."

Chou helped himself to another cognac. "Drink up, Jade. You're lagging behind me."

Jade took a delicate sip, her first. Calm now, she would tell Chou her own terrible news—that her friend's child was deceased—another time. "What position did this dissident have in mind for you?" she finally asked.

"Deputy minister of justice. Not bad, eh?"

"Did you accept the position?"

Chou's ploy was anger. "You underestimate me, Doctoress! I've been a friend of your family for many years and you still don't know me. Of course I'd never be part of such treachery to the South. You don't really believe I'm that much of an opportunist, do you?"

"Naturally I don't think that about you, Chou!" Jade said without conviction, reverting automatically to the rhetoric she heard and spouted daily at the embassy. "You and I don't think Diem's policies are perfect, but at least our president is trying to stop the spread of communism in South Vietnam."

Jade was a paragon of her own propaganda as she continued. "Our families are in Saigon!" That wasn't entirely true; Chou had no one else. "If Ho and his Communists take over, our people will be branded dissidents. Any movement attempting to overthrow Diem will give the Communists the opportunity to conquer the South."

"Jade, you must inform your embassy of this new movement and where they hide out before it's too late. I've written down what you have to say. We must ensure the message is clear."

Like one of his obedient concubines, she snatched up the telephone and dialed the number for the embassy. It was after hours, but the phone would be staffed by the evening receptionist. Jade was at a loss for the night receptionist's name, but no matter.

The embassy answered on the second ring. "Good evening. Paris embassy of the Republic of Vietnam."

"This is Doctoress Jade Minh. Please take down this message and have it couriered to our Foreign Ministry office in Saigon immediately." Jade read from the paper Chou had given her. "'A dissident group, the Democratic Coalition for the Republic, is being organized by Hanoi's leaders. Headquarters are being set up in the territory south of Pleiku. Their aim is to endanger the security of the Republic of Vietnam and topple President Diem. The information was reported by an unnamed Vietnamese intellectual who is a law graduate from a French university.'"

Chou finally sat. He crossed his legs and straightened his back in the upholstered love seat, the brass buttons of the brown leather an opulent contrast to the simplicity of his black garb. After Jade replaced the receiver in its cradle, he said, "I'm putting myself at great risk, you know. If the Vietminh gets wind that I passed this information on to the Foreign Ministry, I'm dead."

Jade's feelings about Chou softened dramatically. She moved across the room toward him, a consummate actress on her own stage. "Chou, I didn't know you were so dedicated to our country, or so brave. I can tell you now there was word around the embassy that you were a candidate for Ho's Vietminh cadres. I think you were being watched. I was even asked to report on you. How paranoid they are."

Chou scowled. "I can't believe those ungrateful pigs! I risk my life to further our cause and protect our beloved country from Ho Chi Minh and his Vietminh and look how I'm treated."

Jade leaned over Chou and took his hand. "Don't worry, my brave friend. In the morning I'll clear your name by informing the ambassador that you're the source of this important information."

Chou smiled and rose from his seat. He had what he wanted—for the moment. "Ah, Doctoress, I'm very late for an important engagement and I must bid you adieu."

7

VAN SPEAKS OUT

Shit! Diem's the only boy we got out there.
—Vice President Lyndon Johnson in an
interview with Stanley Karnow

Saigon: February 1962

In the early morning Jade dreamed of a man, faceless and smelling of almond hair oil, his body perfumed and smooth on her pliant nakedness. She hadn't protested, but groaned low with ecstasy, her own sounds unlocking her from sleep. The mosquito netting that swathed the bed under the open shutters was a translucent eclipse. She wondered where she was. Her eyes focused on Van's metal alarm clock on the night table beside the bed. The hands read 6:45 a.m.

A distant boom made her start. Was it Tet, the New Year's celebration of fireworks? No, it could only be an explosion, she realized, thinking how bad the timing was for her holiday home in Saigon.

Jade put her hand on her husband's disheveled pajama top and shook. "Wake up, Van!"

"What is it?" he asked, still half asleep.

"The VC are bombing!"

"That means the Vietcong are far away," he mumbled, retreating back into sleep. "Don't worry."

Another noise disturbed Jade, a diffident knock on the bedroom door. She wondered what it could be, then remembered Mui. It must be the girl knocking, frightened by the bombing.

Jade shook Van again and he sat up. "Come in, Mui," he called.

"Uncle! Auntie! I hear bombing."

"Don't worry, Mui," Van said. "It's miles away. We're safe in our little house."

Mui looked skeptical. "Uncle, Auntie, let's see what it is."

"Go wait on the couch in the outer room," Van told her. "We'll be right out."

In the streaky gray-and-mauve sky they saw the glint of a mechanical bird—maimed and dropping. It spun, trailing corkscrews of flame, and crashed near the Thi Nghe Channel, the old port. Spirals of smoke billowed above the Presidential Palace, obscuring the gilt edge of the roof.

After a short while, the radio droned: "At approximately 6:30 a.m. two Army of the Republic of Vietnam renegade pilots bombed Independence Palace in a protest. President Diem and his brother, Nhu, were not injured, but Madame Nhu has sustained a broken arm. Two bodyguards and a housekeeper are dead and thirty palace employees hospitalized. The building is damaged and the president and his entourage have been moved to Gia Long Palace, once the home of the French governor of Cochin China." The radio crackled. "The pilots were in command of ARVN aircraft, the World War II model AD-6 planes supplied to the ARVN air force by the United States. The pilots had embarked on orders to an air force mission against the Vietcong in the Mekong Delta. Instead they turned back to drop bombs on the palace. Both pilots had reputations as being the best in the air force."

"Unbelievable!" Jade exclaimed."

"The Ngo family is no longer being tolerated, even by their own," Mui said with an authority older than her years.

"Mui, you're too young to talk politics," Jade said, aghast at the girl's aggressive comment. But she, too, knew that Diem couldn't even trust his own armed forces. "Go to the kitchen and prepare tea," she said to Mui, looking sternly at Van as if he were the culprit.

"Mui, I'd like to speak privately with Jade."

"Of course, Uncle. I'll prepare tea and then read the lovely comic Auntie brought me." Mui held a French translation of the popular science-fiction magazine *Astounding Days*.

When Mui retreated, Van said, "Jade, I have grave misgivings about your posting in Paris."

"Don't be silly. It's just another incident. More Americans are coming and they'll save us from the Communists."

"Jade, I know this is hard, but look around you. It's no secret. President Diem and his officials have been imprisoning, torturing, and murdering the innocent, some of them our friends."

Jade twisted the ring on her finger. "Maybe these *friends* are secret Vietcong."

"There's more to it than you think. Diem announced he had to have special powers to stop the Communists from overthrowing his government, but now he's gone too far. For example, my assistant Vinh, whom you may never meet now, didn't show up for work last month. Normally he sleeps at his flat at the far end of Tu Do in Saigon, but I knew he had gone to visit his elderly mother and brother's family who have a farm in a small hamlet in Tay Ninh Province."

Van drummed his fingers. "To make a long story short, I traveled to their hamlet to make inquiries because I was worried that my assistant had fallen ill in the countryside. He's only a few years younger than I am and his only political move ever was to help in the fight against the French before Diem took over. Anyway, I found his elderly mother and his brother's children in a state of panic. Officials from Diem's secret police had come in the night and arrested my assistant and his brother under the president's anti-treason law. When his family got up the courage to go to police headquarters to find out his fate, they were told he'd only be returned if they gave up their land and paid an exorbitant fine. The police actually gave Vinh's mother a bill to pay at Land Expropriations in Saigon." Van stopped, then decided he must tell Jade.

"My assistant had been arrested, tortured with electric shocks—his fingers hooked up to a field telephone—and then badly beaten, all for some imagined slight against Diem's regime. He's very ill now and consequently useless to his family. Jade, these people are innocent of any political crime. Stories like these circulate daily about relatives and friends."

Jade's lovely face looked stricken.

Van hesitated, worried that he had told her too much. Then he continued. "The Buddhist monks are also on Diem's hit list. They're not allowed to worship these days. Rumor has it that the monks plan to revolt. What Diem doesn't realize is that this treatment sends these people over to the other side. Many are joining the Vietcong out of anger. Diem's repression knows no bounds."

"This is terrible. I didn't realize it was so bad."

Van opened his hands in appeal. "I'm concerned about Mui. She's totally innocent of any crime, but her parents were Vietminh agents. I'd like to send her away to Paris to live with you until things improve. But she refuses to go until she graduates from school and can begin her first year of university at the Sorbonne."

Jade's eyes dilated. This was the last thing she needed—a young girl to look after.

Van rushed on. "Jade, there's a wave of discontent in Saigon. It's not a small faction and it grows each day."

"But Diem is well liked by the Americans. Just last February Lyndon Johnson compared him to Winston Churchill."

"Jade, Diem refuses to field questions from anyone, even his own staff. Much worse, he's given far too much power to his ruthless brother. Nhu even spies on his own family, and he sends his so-called enemies to death as easily as he picks his teeth. The man's a monster."

"And what about Madame Nhu these days?"

"She's even madder than her husband."

Jade nodded. "In Paris she's the talk of our embassy. Gossip has it that some years ago, when Nhu returned from his studies in France, long before he married his wife, he had an affair with her mother, Madame Chuong, an aristocratic hostess who enjoyed illicit affairs. Nhu was six years younger than the mother and switched his passion to her daughter, fourteen years younger than Nhu."

"The woman is ambitious," Van said. "Madame Nhu touts herself as the reincarnation of the Trung sisters, those two brave Vietnamese women who led our struggle against China in the first century. They ruled as queens for two years until our empire was crushed by China. Then the Trungs sealed their place in history by throwing themselves into the river when the Chinese were at our gates. Madame Nhu acts as if she's a queen, which makes her all the more dangerous. It's not for nothing that the Americans call her the Dragon Lady.

"Amazingly the woman who's changed the *aio dai* to suit herself by cutting a low neck in the front has outlawed dancing, beauty contests, boxing, contraception, abortion, divorce, and adultery. But she still allows prostitution in the bars, though the girls are now made to wear white uniforms, like cleaners or nurses. Far worse, the woman interferes in government affairs. She tries to run the country through her brother-in-law, Diem."

Jade was becoming annoyed. She didn't blame Madame Nhu for all of her actions. But rather than argue with Van, she quipped, "*This* dragon lady must get dressed."

Van put a hand over hers and spoke somberly. "I never interfere in your life, but in light of this mess with our government, I ask you once more to quit your post and live as a lady of leisure in Paris. Your job is a sham. You're protecting a dictator who's murdering his own people. You must leave the embassy."

Jade's mood darkened, but she didn't say anything.

When she remained silent, Van touched her cheek. "Things have to change even if we don't want them to. Mui must leave school before graduation and fly to Paris to live with you, and you must leave your post."

Jade saw that he held little hope of convincing her, as he knew her character well. He'd often accused her of being like a child in that she had no sense of reality. He admitted, too, that when she didn't respond to advice he knew to be right, he felt the weight of it like a father.

She voiced an idea she knew he would turn down. "Van, why don't you ask for a transfer to the Pasteur Institute in Paris? Then Mui would be persuaded and you could come together."

Jade's suggestion obviously pleased Van, but he couldn't comply. "My dear, you know my research must go on here in Saigon. Scientists who research tropical diseases have nothing to do with politics. I'm one of the few people lucky enough to have nothing to fear no matter who governs our poor beleaguered country."

8

CITY OF SECRETS

> Just next to me was a bomb that had fallen. It was fat like this, just like a little pig. It hadn't exploded. It was just there. And I was just there, too.
>
> —Interview with Madame Nhu

Paris: November 1962

Jade yawned as she walked to her writing desk by the window in her apartment. The painted blooms that enlivened the lacquer of her desk made her think of home. Jade had thought she preferred her Paris life to the dangers of Saigon, but now she missed every aspect of her house on Bui Thi Xuan Street. She pictured the urns of rainwater that stood in the garden awaiting the pleasure of refreshing her...if only she were in Saigon.

The Saigon yard bloomed year-round with such opulent greenery that any noise from the street was muffled. The scent of the jasmine that blossomed behind her window would have wafted to where she slept, surrounding her with a fragrance more exquisite than any French perfume. In Saigon every wish was her command. If she were there now, she'd ask the servant to go to the Central Market and pick the most expensive durian fruit available. Jade's mouth watered at the imagined taste, her nose wrinkling at the smell foreigners found disgusting, the putrid stench belying the tender, sugary flesh inside. If only she were home. If only...

But she wasn't and she turned to the daily Paris paper that lay neglected on her desk: PRESIDENT KENNEDY FORCES SOVIETS TO

WITHDRAW MISSILES FROM CUBA. She looked past the photograph of a bearded Fidel Castro and thought Chou's clean look was more attractive. He'd shaved his goatee. But what of Chou? She knew that when he was in Saigon he kept company with her husband. But here in Paris the few times she had seen him he'd seemed odd. He no longer reported on his search for the lost child of "her friend." It was as if he had something on her, over her. She had read it in his eyes.

Jade perused the day's mail. She fished through the raft of bills from her masseuse and from Cadolle for her made-to-measure patented four-way stretch brassieres and girdles for a letter and her monthly check from Van.

"Damn," she muttered. She saw herself seated at the desk in her office at the embassy. If she had to translate one more bureaucratic paper, write one more press release, or counsel one more churlish Vietnamese student, she would scream. She was sick to death of work and finally bored with her life in Paris. She should resign her post. Jade pined for Saigon. But then, she mused, there *was* the safety factor.

Too vividly, Jade remembered the morning the Presidential Palace was bombed by Diem's own pilots. She recalled Van's words. But Jade and Van were members of the upper stratum of Vietnamese society. That, in itself, guaranteed safety. She thought it through. Van was a scientist and invaluable to any regime. She had proved her worth at the embassy, but if the unthinkable were to happen and the Communists took the South, as long as she wasn't in Diem's employ, she, too, would be safe and under Van's protection. *If* she were to return permanently to Saigon, she needn't worry.

And what about the danger from the Vietcong? Jade was aware that those surreptitious shadows sometimes struck in Saigon and took the lives of anyone, even innocents, unlucky enough to cross their paths. She had heard rumors that the VC rode in stolen ARVN and even U.S. vehicles, that they killed with stolen guns. There were many reports of VC victims ending up as corpses in the Saigon River, or as human fodder for the vultures on the roads that led in and out of the city. But she lived a different life in Saigon and had no need to place herself in harm's way. Jade was also aware that the United States had sent South Vietnam sixteen thousand American soldiers as advisers in the past three years. And no one could beat the Americans, no matter what Van said. Especially not a bunch of country bumpkins led by Uncle Ho.

Jade wandered about her apartment, then settled with a flounce on the velvet chair that matched the dressing table. The table was crowded with skin creams and vials of perfume. She saw herself in the mirror and found her reflection offensive. Exploring her skin, she noticed a telltale line and imagined her face aging, her beauty fading until she looked like a map, lines obscuring every feature. The image horrified her and made her think of her mother, dead before the humiliation of old age set in.

She upbraided herself for being in a morbid frame of mind. Perhaps it was the wretched weather but, no, it was the incident with Chou a couple of years ago. Daily she worried he knew something. But what? She could stand it no longer. She had to act.

Jade strode to the telephone on the night table, her robe flashing under the crystal chandelier. She lifted the receiver, took a deep breath, and readied herself for a performance, squeezing a tear out and dialing. The phone rang, then was picked up. "Chou, this is Jade. I have distressing news—"

"Ah, dear Doctoress, I'll come to your apartment tonight."

"No, I'll tell you on the phone."

"You can't argue with me, my dear. I'll be there at six." He hung up abruptly.

Jade stamped one bare foot ineffectually on the carpeted floor. "Damn!" she said out loud. "Now what have I done?"

Jade's wardrobe was a treasure chest. Above her shoes of satin and suede and crushed between the designer suits and gowns she never wore was her latest order, an *aio dai* she had designed herself. She knew it was stunning and that it would make Chou amenable toward her. She would be sad and helpless. She would say she had received word that Phuong was dead, which would end Chou's search or bluff out of him whatever he knew—if anything.

Smoothing the *aio dai* over her frame, she thought about her mother, who had told her so often when she was small that a famous Saigonese fortuneteller had warned that red was an unlucky color for the women in Jade's family. But that was so silly. Madame Nhu's red was a fashion statement. Even Coco Chanel, who had been stodgy with her designs, was showing red. Jade hadn't been able to resist having an *aio dai* of the finest red silk made, and with a low neck, if just to wear around the apartment.

Again, she wondered uneasily why Chou hadn't pushed his company on her for nearly two years, since that afternoon at her apartment when they reported the information about the Democratic Coalition for the Republic, the fledgling covert organization. The message had been too late. The illicit group's headquarters in Pleiku had been abandoned at about the same time Diem's publicists had come up with the pejorative label Vietcong. It was just another change of name, Jade knew. They were still the Vietminh to her. Jade had avoided Chou this last long while for her own reasons.

A little later, when Chou arrived, his eyes danced and his lips curled into an oily smear. "I see you're dressing Madame Nhu–style. I find that arousing." He pushed rudely past, tossing his coat over a chair, a half-empty bottle of Remy Martin in his other hand.

"Chou, this isn't the time for remarks like that, or for drink. I've had bad news. I've had word that the girl we've been searching for is dead." Jade touched a hand to her throat.

"My dear Doctoress, it must be a terrible shock to you. I know you loved the girl as if you were her mother." He ran a gloved finger across Jade's décolletage, tracing the swell of her breasts and causing her to step back. "I know everything," he said, tapping his nose, fingers clad in black leather. "I'll make you a trade. My silence for one hour of sex with you." Chou's other hand stroked the front of his slacks.

Jade raised her hand to strike Chou, but it fell. *Chou knows*, she thought. *I'm undone—he's discovered the missing girl is my illegitimate half-caste child.* "Where did you find her?" she finally asked.

"Dead. Very sad, just like you said. Dead in a pauper's grave."

"Oh, Chou," Jade sobbed with real grief, "I was going to confess my secret to you tonight."

"A confession. How amusing you should say that." Chou's smile was devilish. "But I'm not a priest. So what do you say, Doctoress? Will you, like any other whore, give me your body for one hour in return for my eternal silence on this, shall we say, delicate matter?"

Jade's own silence was his answer.

9
JADE SCHEMES

But don't begin it unless you are sure of winning.
—Ho Chi Minh to General Giap

Paris: August 1963

Jade was dreaming of a man again, faceless and stinking of sweet almond hair oil, his body pummeling her nakedness like a fist. She was unable to protest, as if he had pasted down her tongue. Yet she held a blade in her hand, ready to put it in his back, but not until she chose. The hard-bodied man's groans came louder and faster until he screamed and spent himself inside her. Then she raised the knife. At that moment the telephone's insistent ringing burst into her sleeping mind. She sat up straight in bed and groped for the receiver.

"Jade, are you still sleeping?"

"No, Van, I was reading." Jade couldn't admit her dream to Van. And though she didn't care what Chou thought of her, she was aware her dream was about him. He was the faceless man. But she was almost positive that now that he'd enjoyed her flesh in exchange for silence, he would keep their bargain. And the child was dead in a pauper's grave. If Chou kept his promise, nothing could hurt her anymore.

"Jade are you there?" Van shouted. Then he spoke with unusual authority. "I'm sending Mui to you in Paris. It's become too dangerous for her here. Besides, you'll enjoy her company. When you leave your posting, as I insist again you do, you'll want her as a companion. Think of her as the child we never had. She'll be happy studying science at the Sorbonne. It's all arranged. I'll telegraph you the flight number and her date of arrival so you can meet her at Orly."

The line went dead just as thoughts of her dream receded. "Damn," she said aloud, "what am I going to do now?"

Below Jade's apartment the trees that lined the Quai de Tuileries were studded with late-summer buds poking out furled tongues. The bank that tumbled to the Seine River was packed with lovers. Their fumbling ministrations were hidden under throws tremulous with fringe. The paths were slow with couples' hands entwined or arms encircled. Jade looked away from the scene. Although nine months had passed since her disgusting evening with Chou, she could still conjure up the lawyer's breath on her breast, and worse… For her, the apartment and even the embassy would always reek of that event.

Now Mui was going to live with her in Paris. Jade deliberated, hoping to think of something that could turn this insupportable situation around, but there was nothing. She sat at her writing desk, cupped her chin with her hands, and narrowed her eyes in thought. If Van had seen her, he would have been worried, as he knew that look. Jade's eyes became as fluid as the night sky, then she had the answer. It was simple and inspired, and afforded a way to escape being a chaperone to Mui and the boredom she'd endured since the ambassador had saddled her with public-relations work at the embassy.

And then there was Chou. She half wished he'd contact her in person so she could read his eyes. The lawyer had given his word he would keep their bargain, and he'd kept it so far—sex in exchange for secrecy. Certainly she had paid a high price that evening when she telephoned him to get everything out in the open. She thought once more about Chou and it was clear. If it ever appeared he would expose her—and maybe even if he didn't—she'd inform her government that he was a spy for Ho Chi Minh.

Chou would never suspect her of such an action if she remained friendly, and especially if she weren't working at the embassy. She would return to Van's protection and Saigon for good. She'd be just an innocent housewife and the wife of Chou's good friend, Van. It was her husband who had inadvertently given Jade the idea when he expressed his anxiety about Mui. Van had then gone on to tell Jade that Nhu's secret police had infiltrated their own families and friends to hunt down and punish any North Vietnamese supporters. Van had said that sometimes it was done for spite and revenge.

Jade had kept the idea of returning to Saigon in reserve as protection from Phuong, her own flesh and blood. It had been an impossibility that her illegitimate offspring would travel all the way to Vietnam to find her. But now the danger of being exposed in France was over and her suspicion that the poor orphan had come to a bad end had been verified by Chou, yet returning to Vietnam was still her best option for self-preservation in light of Chou's secret hold over her.

But what about the ever-present danger of North Vietnam? She was a scientist's wife, valuable to either side and privy to the same protection as he was yet had made herself in her own right. She had a doctorate in languages, especially useful in a place like Vietnam. But even if she had been an uneducated nobody she would have still been called La Doctoress because of Van's position.

On the Paris front, and that was how she thought of it now, if she ran into trouble making Mui's arrangements, she'd use her embassy connections. Jade stared at the riverbank, but the scene didn't interest her. Taking out the telephone book, she dialed the Sorbonne. The registrar's office would arrange an apartment for Mui in the Latin Quarter.

There was so much to do: arrange, pack, and maybe she'd have a holiday. Jade had read about a new health spa near Naples that used volcanic mud in their treatments. She'd book in there for a few weeks. Then she'd travel to Tuscany to a cooking school she'd heard about. And maybe she'd take a Mediterranean cruise. With all she wanted to accomplish, she calculated it would be a couple of months before she returned to Saigon and Van for good.

Five little angels around my bed
One at the foot and one at the head
One to pray and one to sing
And one to watch me night and day.

—Anonymous Prayer

1

PHOTOGRAPH IN SEPIA

Now is the time or never. I am trembling like a leaf. It takes cunning to open the door...

—Jack Reynolds, *A Woman in Bangkok*

Mont Ste-Odile, France: April 1955

Under the candied hue of dawn, Suzette left Les Enfants de Ste-Marie orphanage, saying boldly to herself that her father would be with her and that she didn't care what happened to her, anyway. She had waited on the highway, an unkempt demoiselle in ragged shirt and pants. The beauty of her face was both sad and wild, with a bow-lipped mouth, high cheekbones, and pewter eyes that mirrored her despair.

Catching a ride with a kind truck driver was easy—she hardly even had to wave her hand. After telling the driver, whose name was Pierre, her destination and thanking him for his generosity, Suzette feigned slumber for part of the journey to Paris rather than answer too many of his fatherly questions. Facing the window, her eyes shut tight, she momentarily missed the feel of the orphanage's hard cot and the gentle roll of snores that had sounded to her like waves on the shore. Then she recalled what the nuns thought of her and knew she'd been wise to run away.

When her father left her at Les Enfants, she had missed him terribly but had hoped she'd make friends, just as children did in the storybooks Papa had read aloud to her when he was "with her" and not drowning in his sorrow. Even when she was small it was apparent that his pain was brought on by his drinking.

He'd swig straight from evil-smelling bottles cradled in a blanket of brown paper, and if she went near him, he'd flail at her with his hands until he fell deeper and deeper under the bottle's spell and began crying like a baby. She, too, would cry, but quietly and from a safe distance, because his eyes by then had become hollow and he had changed into someone she didn't know. He would shake his fist and yell crazily at the sun or at the moon, saying, "You Asian bitch. You broke me. You killed me."

On her first morning at Les Enfants a nun had told her to stop sniffling and go to the chapel. She'd been surprised when the mother superior had announced, "You are all equal—white, yellow, and black. You are all orphans." But it wasn't true. The white children—she came to think of them as the whole children, the lucky ones—had shunned her.

And before that, when she and her father had roamed the backroads like Gypsies, if she'd found children to play with and she told them about her Vietnamese mother who'd run away, they spurned her, calling her bad things like "yellow" and sometimes even "bastard" or the ugly-sounding "slut."

Suzette had known what the nuns at the orphanage thought about her. She'd overheard those black-cloaked creatures, those wraiths of fear. The terror of what they had said had prompted her to flee. They were supposed to be religious, charitable, but they were mean in spirit. She'd seen it in their eyes when they looked at her that she was yellow, part Asian to them, even though Papa was white and her own skin was paler than his. Suzette would never forget what they had said early one morning during her third week in the institution after the mother superior had told her Papa had died. She couldn't stop crying for her father, and a girl with skin like breakfast gruel had laughed at her, calling her "Cry-baby chink." She'd run and hidden in a closet to get away from the words, huddled on the floor amid the cobwebbed brooms and the greasy rags. Secreted there, she had heard two nuns stop by the door. "The Vietnamese girls are the worst," one voice had announced imperially.

And the other had agreed in an even more authoritarian tone. "Yes, the Vietnamese girls are liars. They *give* themselves to the boys."

When the first nun chimed in again, Suzette had realized they were speaking about her. "We must watch that new half-caste Vietnamese, especially now that her father is dead. We need to control her. If we don't, she'll get herself pregnant and we'll have another illegitimate unfortunate on our hands. The boys are already eyeing her." The nun's voice dripped with disgust. "These Asian girls' flesh is weak. It's engrained in them, like their mothers. They can't help their sins."

Later, when the dormitory was black as ink, Suzette had spoken with one of the few orphans who deigned to be friendly with her. The girl had told her: "The nun means we're sluts and we let the boys fuck us. The nuns don't want anyone to love us, because the nuns aren't human and they have no husbands, no men for themselves."

Suzette hadn't slept that night, and when the sun came up, she'd run away, hitching a ride with Pierre to Paris.

The truck now rode high and hard above a road that twisted like an oiled serpent and rumbled under the tires like an earthquake. They traveled west, past the mysterious pagan wall of giant stone blocks and through the high woods called Hohwald. Suzette saw the snowcapped Bernese Alps, and Pierre remarked that she was "surveying Switzerland."

Racing like a greyhound over hills whose tops were crowned with morning sunlight, the truck rolled through villages she'd glimpsed in old picture books Papa had read to her, past monasteries, châteaux, cows, shimmying geese, and the ruins of stone churches. When nightfall came, the truck's headlights lit the damp road like a flashlight in a tunnel and Pierre gave Suzette his jacket. Placing her duffel bag under her arm, she said a silent prayer to her special angels.

Since Papa had deposited her at the orphanage, Suzette had repeated the prayer her father had taught her as if it were a lifeline. Elbows resting on the metal frame of her cot, she had held her palms together and pointed them to heaven. She always imagined Papa was with her when she prayed to those heavenly guardians: exotic angels with wings that flowed like wind and waves. *Please,* she now implored, *if you can't bring Papa back to earth, let me find my mother since I have no one left in this entire world.*

She awoke to the cacophony of a city. As the truck entered Paris, traffic slowed, and Pierre shook his fist, crying, "Women drivers!" Smiling, Suzette didn't think they were all female.

"Where should I drop you, mademoiselle?" Pierre finally asked politely.

"I'd like to go to the Gare du Nord," she replied, having heard this place mentioned at the orphanage.

"Here we are. You're very young to be on your own, but I suppose that's the way these days. At least you'll be safe with your friends in the city."

"Yes, thank you, I'm visiting friends."

"Well, that's something. And you've saved the fare. You'll probably spend it in the cinema like other girls your age, won't you?"

As she stepped down from the truck cab, she nodded. Pierre pointed through the cab's door at a yellow square. At its center sat an unadorned fountain, the alabaster veined blue and etched with primitive fractures inflicted by the curious penknives of countless boys and their girlfriends. An au pair, dressed in a worsted uniform, pushed her baby carriage by with spinsterly delight. Her charge was swaddled in baby bunting, its bawling face red beneath its infant's cap.

Suzette was drawn to the fountain. A raven squawked and

dipped its beak, lifting it to the sky, then shaking it to swallow. Bright disks stared up like silver eyes—the fountain's bottom was littered with bottle caps. The raven flapped and hopped away, and Suzette took its place. She stared into the water and was captured in the twinkle of the discarded caps. They held the sun's rays within their metal circles, and she was momentarily mesmerized by them.

Seating herself on the rim of the fountain, Suzette waited for what seemed like days. An ancient man, rambling incoherently about the coming of Christ, tossed bread crumbs to squabbling pigeons. She knew he was demented and looked away when he stood and sermonized. The forlorn look on her face attracted comments from passersby, but she was too shy to respond. She was becoming tired and her loneliness returned.

There was no one to find her here, she thought, hanging her head. Behind her half-closed eyelids she imagined Papa was with her, smoking, his free arm around her. She imagined the wispy rings he created for her pleasure were portholes she could float through—if she could make herself small, like Alice in Wonderland. And where would those portholes lead? Her imagination transported her and she was in the arms of her Vietnamese mother. Around her the air was luxurious like a warm bath, and the shadow of a beautiful kite shaped like a bird obscured her mother's face.

Lost in thought, she wrinkled her nose at the sulfurous burn of a wooden match, which brought her back to the fountain. Her lashes flickered, making shadowy fringes on her cheeks. When she opened her eyes, she spied a man standing before her. He had pale gums and gold teeth that flashed when he spoke. "Good day, my beautiful child," he said, smiling.

For a moment she thought it was her father back from the dead. But it was a stranger. Somehow, though, the figure that stood over her, pensively puffing, filled her with a crazy hope that she'd find the exotic woman who had stood in sepia beside her young father. Suzette had stolen a look at that snapshot once when her father was sad and sick and his mind floating away. Papa's dog-eared relic of the past was hidden in a medical textbook he had never sold, though they hadn't much more than two bundles of clothes. The photograph was old, like heritage. Fragile, like memories. Revered, like ancestors. Although her father had never told her, she knew the woman in the snapshot was her mother.

The stranger who now stood over her reminded her of Papa when he wasn't sick, for no better reason than because the man smoked and was middle-aged. Suzette was unfinished, unschooled in the ways of men, like any child.

Although she didn't have the photo of the exotic woman, Suzette did possess a picture of herself and her father when she was much younger. On its back Papa had written: "My Phuong and me." Phuong was her Vietnamese name, which neither of them ever used. It was easier to call her by the middle name he'd given her—Suzette. Of course, she knew that her Vietnamese name translated into Phoenix.

The photo was her talisman of love. In it Papa was tall and lanky, a half smile like a whispered secret on his lips. Suzette, only five or six, was solemn-eyed with silken hair as pale as straw and a dress that lifted up at the tops of her little knees like an upside-down open umbrella. The two stood together, as if defying even the camera to separate them, Suzette's small hand naturally curving within her father's protective one.

Her father had never spoken to her about her mother. Whenever Suzette asked, he answered that she might as well be dead. If pressed, he'd sometimes say, "Your mama was as beautiful and hard as a piece of jade. Her family name was a common one. She left us for her homeland, Vietnam. Don't think of her. She's gone forever and we're happier and better off without her."

Now she was faced with a decision. Should she trust this stranger who said such nice things to her, this stranger who reminded her of her father?

"You're a rare beauty," he told her, "and I'm famous for finding unusual treasures like you."

She should have wondered at his words. She'd been taught not to speak to strangers. Papa had warned her of evil men who stole young girls.

Then she told the stranger that she was trying to find her mother.

"My dear," the man said, "I know where she is. Don't despair. I know where many Asian mothers are."

It was a short drive in the stranger's maroon car. The cracked leather seat was supple under her thin legs and childlike hips. They flew up cobblestone streets smelling of evening rain to a place near rue du Bac. Passing the door of a villa and parking in the narrow path behind, the stranger took Jade's hand and led her up the iron fire stairs. When she hung back, he held tighter and motioned her up with quick movements of his head. He seemed different to her now, not friendly, but furtively nervous like the rats the boys would corner in the shed behind the orphanage dormitory. Leaving her in the room that was tucked at the top of the fire stairs, he said, "Be quiet now. If you stay here, I'll soon return and help you find your mother."

Nodding, Suzette managed a faint, docile smile. But she mistrusted her dream. How could he find her mother for her when she couldn't even tell him the woman's name? Turning, he closed the door, which rang hollowly as his footfalls clanked down the fire stairs.

Suzette looked around the room. Another girl was slumped in a corner. The first thing she noticed was the girl's eyes. Dead things. Worse than her father's were when he drank, she thought, remembering the meaning of eyes that were empty holes.

A row of chairs, rickety as the sticks she used to play with at Les Enfants, seemed disgusted with the stained walls and stood away. Why had she left the orphanage? she berated herself. At least it had been safe there.

The lone girl, not much older than Suzette, slumped as if in a waking dream. A stuperous cadaver, she seemed not to notice Suzette's hesitant entrance, nor did the conga line of cockroaches. They weaved like jovial drunkards down the greasy wall behind her and then turned, waving their antennae before retreating behind a skirting board.

After a moment of silence, the girl finally spoke. "If you don't go now, you'll be lost forever like me. The man will come back with his medicine and put you into another world that makes you tired and slow. See my arm? It's his pincushion." She looked up, and her pupils were as big as saucers. "I'm the only one left. Men come and give him money."

Suzette was stunned and couldn't move.

"Go now!" the girl shouted, rousing her to action.

Suzette pulled at the fire door and it opened. The stairs and the path to the alley were empty. The car was gone. Hurrying, she checked the number of the villa and stored it in her mind. Papa had taught her to notice things. Remembering a telephone box she'd seen from the window of the stranger's car, she ran in that direction. Her feet flew over the slippery cobblestones, her thin, worn soles soundless even in the rain.

2

AMERICAN DREAM

Monday's child is fair of face,
Tuesday's child is full of grace,
Wednesday's child is full of woe,
Thursday's child has far to go.
—Anonymous

Seattle: April 1962

A young man in a field of waving poppies graced the calendar. His hair touched his shoulders and his robes were suggestive of biblical times. The man's serene face tilted heavenward, his hand—caught by the camera—halfway to his parted lips and holding a joint.

It was Moon's place, a rented house at the cheap end of Capitol Hill's university district, though he wasn't a student but a musician. He'd thumbtacked the calendar to the wall and marked his gigs on it in a wavering hand. Across from his house, across Broadway, if you could have heard over his music's volume, you would have picked out the neighbor's goat baaing as it cropped the lawn.

Moon's spent Ruffino wine bottles were stuck with candles lined up like soldiers. They hissed as they piddled black wax on his wine keg. He had cleverly reincarnated the keg, with its metal waistband, as a bedside table. Suzette sailed beside the keg, a sloop on the stormy sea of Moon's bed. It was mid-afternoon.

Groaning as he pumped, Moon was the captain as well as the artist and engineer. Suzette's firm breasts were pinned under his thick chest. The short muscles of his buttocks beat with his rhythm, and the heated waterbed sucked and slurped as they made love.

Suzette's eyelids fluttered as she moaned and almost lost consciousness within the crazy high of her orgasm. At the same time she felt the smooth cream of his semen trickling down her thigh. They panted and sighed, twinned in mutual gratification.

Moon rolled off and reached for the joint. He took a drag, holding the smoke deep in his lungs. Always the gentlemen, he attached the roach clip so Suzette wouldn't burn her lips, then passed it to her. She inhaled and a seed exploded. Moon and Suzette slapped at the embers, trying to stop the sheets from scorching. Then they relaxed again, the bed still heaving.

Suzette's skin was translucent and her lips were swollen with the aftermath of sex. She drifted far away on the music, thinking about Geoffrey, who had whispered that she was ravishing after they made love. He'd been thrilled at how sexy she looked when her hair lay like a fan across the pillow.

Alarm suddenly entered Suzette's mind. She was in bed with a total stranger. She had gone to a pizza-and-beer bar last night and met Moon, who had taken her back to his place. If Geoff knew where she was, he'd freak. But then she remembered. Why should Geoff care, since he would never marry her, anyway? She hated him for being so weak, and her lips trembled at the memory.

It had been a spectacular morning. She and Geoff had wandered around Pike Place Market, sharing a freshly baked Russian meat bun, a *piroshki*, while listening to a busker strumming a folk tune on an acoustic guitar. Geoff had suggested they play tourist, and they'd swooshed to the top of the newly opened Space Needle in the ultrafast elevator. The viewing deck was disk-shaped, like a flying saucer. All around them glass skyscrapers mirrored one another and mountains clasped the city. The Olympics and the Cascades were as clear as crystal, and Mount

Ranier was gowned in white.

While Suzette photographed the landscape from their perch in the Needle, Geoff broached the subject of marriage at long last. It was a mutual decision and what she desired above all else. Papa's love had been taken from her, but now Geoff would love her without reservation and she him. She remembered the O'Brians and the release from loneliness she'd felt when her new mom had embraced her. And now their dream for her was finally hers. They were going to bite the bullet and tell Geoff's parents first.

She'd held his hand as they'd driven in his Corvette, an automatic with a souped-up V8. Geoff's father was an executive at Boeing. Suzette was silent and happy but nervous about meeting his parents and breaking their news. Geoff's hand was clammy, but his grip was firm.

Then they were there and he pulled into the drive. The Eastons' house was at the other end of Capitol Hill. She saw the new coat of brown paint and the stingy European-size windows on the second story. Geoff had jokingly described it to her as Americana Tudor. As they entered his realm, he squeezed her hand.

Geoff did all the talking. He introduced Suzette as his girlfriend and jogged his mother's memory, describing her as "the girl I told you about." And then he got to the point, informing his mother that he and Suzette were going to "shack up." When he was finished his commerce degree at the University of Washington and had a good job, he and Suzette would get married.

Geoff's mother seemed quite friendly. "How nice to finally meet Geoff's girl, but what a surprise," she said, smiling at Suzette. She'd just returned from her appointment at Alfonso's where she'd had her hair coifed and lacquered to a bouffant plastic sheen. But the next day, when Geoff picked Suzette up in front of her residence, he dropped his bomb—his parents had totally freaked. They'd sat him down on the little-used couch in the formal living room and read him the riot act, threatening to cut off his allowance if he and Suzette moved in together. And, they'd warned him, if that happened, he'd have to quit school.

Geoff told Suzette he could never marry or live with her. But he'd like to continue making love to her. He suggested they see each other secretly.

Suzette's mouth quivered. "Why?" she asked. "I don't understand."

"It's stupid. It's your background."

Being an American citizen wasn't enough. It was because her mother was Vietnamese. She should have known. It was because she was Vietnamese. "But, Geoff, I've never stepped foot in Asia. I was born in France. You know that."

"Sure, Suz, but you know my parents..." he said, beginning his defense again.

"Actually, I don't," she replied, realizing her smile was forced. "When I was adopted by my new mom and dad in what's supposed to be the freest country in the world, I told myself I was the luckiest girl on the planet."

"Look, Suz, let's just pretend this never happened and go on as we were. I love you."

But she knew Geoff's words were a sham. "My adoptive mother is a psychiatrist and Dad's a doctor. What more do your parents want?"

"Shit, Suzie, I don't know." But she knew there was something else and finally he told her. "My mom said that if we married and had children there might be a throwback and the kid might look Asian." His face showed his disgust with his mother. "I told her that our kids would be beautiful if they looked anything like you." He hesitated, then spoke again. "My mom also said your real father was an alcoholic and that maybe it would be an inherited trait." Geoff rolled up the car window, as if no one should hear.

"How could you tell them that?" Suzette cried out angrily. It flashed through her mind that it was her fault Papa had been an alcoholic. She had never deserved his love. Maybe her mother wouldn't have left if she hadn't been born. Her father would then have had a happy life and wouldn't have been saddled with a Vietnamese half-caste.

Geoff tried to take her hand. "Look, Suzie, I don't care what the old lady and the old man say. But I need to stay in university and they're serious. My dad's pussy-whipped. He'd take away my allowance for my rent and stop paying my school fees if my mom told him to."

"Maybe my real father was an alcoholic, but he did his best for me. He drank because he needed to wipe out the pain of my mother leaving him. I've told you that before." Then she continued with barely concealed bitterness. "You've never had to be without a mother. I don't know where or what my real mother is, except that Papa told me she was beautiful and well educated. She loved my father before she had me. I don't even know what my mother's name is or what she looks like. I saw her photograph only once when I was small. Papa slapped my face for glancing at the picture and called me a sneak. But he was drunk. When he was cruel to me and ignored me, he was drunk. It meant nothing to me. I loved him then and I love him now. You love people even when they have faults. But because the mother I've never known is Vietnamese, you can't marry me. I didn't realize that would be a black mark against me in your mother's eyes."

"Aw, Suzie, they're old-fashioned. Look, I know it's stupid, but I'll keep seeing you secretly. I really do love you. My parents don't have to know we're still seeing each other."

"Geoff, that's just not good enough."

"But, Suz, I couldn't stand not making love to you anymore. Please let me keep seeing you."

Suzette had reached for the door handle and flung it open. "Get yourself a Vietnamese prostitute if all you care about is sleeping with me." Slamming the car door, she had walked away in the direction of the dorm and hadn't turned back. Her tears had streamed when she heard Geoff's Corvette roar off.

Now back with Moon, Suzette felt her sad thoughts disperse when he held the joint to her lips. She pulled hard, but when Moon lay back on the waterbed, the pain of the past flooded her. After that she cried for days.

Suzette skipped all her classes. She locked her door and sat in silence, waiting for Geoff to call and tell her he really didn't care what his parents felt, that he couldn't exist without her. But her telephone was as silent as she was. Sitting dejectedly and cross-legged on the floor in a T-shirt and panties, she began sorting her jeans and looking at her sweaters. Then she tired of that mundane task and deposited the clothes back where they had come from. A semicircle peeked from beneath the pile. It was an old hat, a memento from her lost past. She dug for it. It was a dented but wearable black felt affair with a satin ribbon around the crown. She'd worn it when she came to America. The recollection made her lips curl into a wry smile, her first in a week. She'd been so proud and so hopeful when she disembarked the flight from Paris. Too grown up to let her escort take her hand, Suzette had locked her fingers onto the brim of her hat as if to prevent it from floating away. A woman in a Red Cross uniform and a couple, looking as nervous as she felt, waited in the customs hall.

"We're your new family," a serious but appealing woman with a confident smile said. "I'm Jenny O'Brian, and this is Russell O'Brian. Please call us Mom and Dad!" The Red Cross agent translated all this into French.

Suzette's eyes traveled between the strangers. She was disoriented by the long flight, the language barrier, and the third face that translated. But then the words penetrated and she saw what the woman's wide-open arms meant to her and what they offered. Suzette unclenched her fingers from the hat's brim and rushed into her adoptive mother's embrace.

"I'll call you Mom," Suzette murmured in French, her voice as thick as cream in her mouth.

"Honey, you'll have your own room," her adoptive father said, placing his freckled hand gently on her shoulder. "When you're bored with us at home and feel acclimatized, we'll get you an English tutor to get you ready for school in the fall."

Mr. O'Brian was as good as his word. Suzette's first summer in Seattle made her forget her sorrowful loss. Jenny and Russell O'Brian, a professional couple who couldn't have children, had taken a two-month sabbatical from their busy practices to devote to their adopted child. Preparing for Suzette's arrival, they had taken a Berlitz course in French.

The O'Brians were thoughtful, patient, and kind parents to the shy fourteen-year-old. When Suzette and Papa had roamed like Gypsies, Papa had isolated her, afraid of losing her to the childcare services or maybe to her real mother. Winters they'd lived in small villages; summers they'd camped in the countryside, Papa making short excursions to farmhouses and villages for supplies. He schooled her himself, and often they'd go months on end with only each other to look at. She had no idea how, but Papa had always made ends meet.

Twenty applicants had been interviewed by the O'Brians before they chose an English tutor for Suzette. And now that she was adjusted to their home, the tutor, a tall man with a dedicated face, rang the bell at precisely five o'clock each evening. Mr. Taylor was a retired professor who wore a tweed jacket with leather elbow patches. He and Suzette sat in the two armchairs in the formal living room near a wide window that looked out on the yard of firs and ferns. Suzette repeated his words, memorizing them, getting the accent right. She was a quick study, and Mr. Taylor gave good progress reports to her parents. Practicing in her room, Suzette read children's rhymes and storybooks aloud:

Mother Goose and Hans Christian Andersen at first and, when she was more familiar with the language, Enid Blyton's Adventure series. She loved the parrot Kiki and was transported especially by *Circus of Adventure.*

As a reward for her patience in being tutored, her new father purchased a three-speed Raleigh bicycle for her. Mr. O'Brian was an avid cyclist himself and attempted to teach Suzette to ride one afternoon. Embarrassingly she got on, only to fall off. So, under the cover of nightfall, he put on training wheels and led her up and down their long drive, holding the leather seat and the bicycle handles to steady her. And so Suzette learned balance. Each successive evening she and her "father" would set out side by side. After the last light, the moon would race with them over the tongue of road that glittered with luminous mist. The moon's pearly face would tease the shadows before taking refuge behind a film of cloud. Fir trees, their trunks wrinkled, lined the path, making it a private park for discussions and dreams of her future.

Then came late August and high school. Her exuberant adoptive parents spoke of little else. Mr. Taylor bragged about her, saying her English was already excellent. She had a facility for that language, and when she concentrated and wasn't nervous, she could even manage an American accent.

The O'Brians wove stories for Suzette of pajama parties and Saturday afternoons at bowling alleys, of innocently gossiping girls. And later they told her there would be the magic of prom night and first love. Still later, Suzette would, of course, marry and give them a grandchild, painting for her their rosy expectations and dreams.

Summer ended with a flurry of advertisements on television and in newspapers for school supplies. The stores stayed open until 9:00 p.m. every day that week, and Jenny and Suzette visited Dayton's young ingenue department to purchase her fall wardrobe. Suzette savored the mother/daughter experience—the slow ride up the escalator past the neat housewares and the disorder and shrieking in the toy department. She enjoyed immensely modeling numerous pastel sweaters, short skirts, and culottes, the fashion of that year. Jenny and the saleswoman agreed on her beauty each time Suzette emerged to get her new mother's opinion.

"Suzie, that suits you to a T!" Jenny would always say.

One last sale was made while the clerk calculated the bill, then folded, wrapped the items in tissue paper, and placed them in a shopping bag with Dayton's emblazoned on the front. It was Suzette's most precious purchase—a white leather jacket and matching white-backed mittens. Walking with Jenny to the underground car park, Suzette felt happiness was finally hers.

"We'll get to bed early so you'll be fresh on your first day," Jenny said. "The principal knows you're coming, but we'll stop in at the office first to get your schedule."

Suzette barely slept, and when she did she was visited by quixotic dreams.

Her debut at an American high school went well at first. Before long it was 11:00 a.m. Metal desks stood in a row on green linoleum in her homeroom. Behind Suzette a chair scraped on the floor. The noise made her remember for the first time in months her short yet unhappy time at the French orphanage. And that led to an image of her father's handsome, ravaged face.

Her teacher glanced around, irritated that a squirming student had dared interrupt his voice. His baggy green trousers and gray shirt looked institutional. Then his eyes settled on Suzette. "You! Are you daydreaming or asleep? Can you tell the rest of us what page I've just asked the entire class to turn to, or would you like to come up here and tell the class what's on your mind?"

Suzette shifted in her seat and felt the whole class staring, laughing. She knew if she spoke she would cry. Instead she ruffled through the pages of the text.

"Turn to page 12 before I lose my temper and boot you into the hall where you can dream all you like," the teacher threatened. "I don't put up with inattentive students in my class."

As Suzette turned the pages, the last class bell of the morning sounded, breaking the silence and propelling the students out of their desks as quickly as if there were a fire. Suzette rose with everybody else. Clutching her books nervously, she headed to her locker. A girl in a deep blue sweater stopped her and said, "Join our group in the cafeteria. We sit in the corner to the left. Maybe we can get you on the cheerleading team."

Later, when Suzette entered the noisy cafeteria, she had no trouble recognizing her new friend from the hall. The table where the girl sat was decorated with the most attractive females in her grade. All sported the same style of hair, shiny from a morning wash and poker-straight thanks to an iron. Their bangs tangled in their eyelashes, their lips were crayoned a silvery pink.

"Hi, I'm Patty and this is Georgie, Patsy, and Stephie. We formed a club called the Bachelorettes. To join you have to be a cheerleader. We do everything together, including date."

Stephie brushed her blond bangs back so she could see. "Were you a cheerleader at your last school? Your white jacket's the same one the cheerleaders at Altman High wear."

"Ah, no, I just came from France."

"Neato," the one named Patty said. "Are your parents with the French consulate?"

"Ah, no, but I am proud to be adopted recently by the O'Brians, who are Americans."

Suddenly it seemed as if the entire lunchroom was listening. Suzette dredged for the right words. "My mother is Vietnamese and I don't know where she is. My father is dead from alcohol and sadness."

"You're kidding," one of the Bachelorettes said, her face incredulous. Suzette hadn't caught all their names.

"No, I am not kidding."

"Well, that's weird. You don't look Chinese."

"I am *not* Chinese. My heritage is French and then Vietnamese. But that is the past. Now I am an American, just like you."

Stephie, the girl with the palest lips, said, "I guess it doesn't matter. Do you want to try out for the cheerleaders and join the Bachelorettes?"

"Wait a minute," Patty said. "Let the rest of us decide, too."

Suzette looked at the four teens and knew she wanted to be just like them.

Russell O'Brian's new Oldsmobile Skylark was parked on the boulevard by the basketball court. The court was concrete and reverberated with the fast bounce of the ball. Male legs scrambled, sneakers slapped, long arms waved.

Suzette fought to maintain her balance within the riot of faces that tumbled down the stairs. She was carried along in their midst.

"Hi, sweetheart, hop in," her adoptive father called through his rolled-down window. "I thought I'd save you the walk." He saw her books. "Have they stuck you with that much homework already?"

"Dad, I want to look at all the books. I want to get a head start on the work." Suzette's mouth was a splash of color in a pale face.

"Yeah, I remember the feel of nice, clean books at the beginning of the year. It's exciting, isn't it?"

"I want to be like them," Suzette blurted.

"Who, hon?"

"The other girls in my grade. The popular ones."

"Don't worry. Of course you will, honey. By the way, I brought you a present today. I know you're always taking out that little picture you have of you and your real father when you were little." Her new father hesitated. "Your mom and I thought you should have more memories to collect. We bought you a camera so you can take pictures of your new friends, record your new life."

He gave it to Suzette. "It's a Nikon SLR, the best camera in the world. You'll never grow out of this one."

Suzette stroked the camera bag and smiled.

"Did you meet anyone nice at school?"

Suzette deliberated. "I met some friends today. They might let me join their girls' club."

"Fabulous, honey. I knew you'd be a hit right off the bat."

Suzette felt the emptiness contained in the memory. She'd heard her adoptive parents refer to senior high as being the best years in their lives, and her mom still remembered the joys of being "sweet sixteen." Well, that certainly hadn't been the case with her years. She'd never joined the Bachelorettes. In fact, she'd never joined any club, not even a university sorority later.

Now it was too late, since she'd graduate at the end of the semester. Suzette didn't know what she would do then. She couldn't imagine getting a job, and though she loved the O'Brians, she certainly didn't want to live at home. She couldn't get into a master's program; the only thing she was good at and got good marks in was photography. At least no one could dispute that. Her professor had taken one of her photographs, a landscape of sky and mountain in striations of gray, and entered it in a Kodak contest. She'd won first prize and $500. But in the scheme of things that meant nothing. It was unfair. If she didn't get an overall grade-point average of 3.5, she wouldn't qualify for graduate school. And she was somewhat short of that, so there went any professional career.

After a while Suzette saw Moon again. He had wondered what had happened to her after their first date, which had led to sex right away. Now she watched Moon arrange himself in the lotus position on the cheap carpet that spread like fungus across his apartment floor. He was tripping with his guitar. Moon knew what he wanted, who he was. He'd come to Seattle for the spring and summer music scene, taking a train from New Orleans. Moon was a talented songwriter and singer, though success had eluded him so far. Suzette smiled as she watched him stroke the strings, tapping and caressing the Gibson as if it were a woman.

"Do you remember when we used to sing?" he serenaded in a gravelly voice, his boxer shorts brilliant white against the greasy red shag. "Sha la la la dee dah. Just like that." His head nodded in perfect time. "Dee dah la dee dah la dee."

Moon's voice drew out the last *dee*, and when he finished, he put his guitar down, stretched his muscled legs, and switched on the reel-to-reel tape deck. It was his latest song and he'd recorded the demo himself, hoping it would one day win him a record contract. His voice, sensual and melodious, emanated from four speakers.

The sound system was hot. Moon had traded amphetamines and Quaaludes for it. He loved cool music and romance, loved drugs and expensive things. Moon pulled a cigarette paper from a package and expertly rolled them another joint. "I'll need to score some more grass soon. The bags are empty."

"I feel so dreamy, Moon. I'll never get any studying done."

"Come here, Suzie. I'll give you a power hit."

"But, Moon, I can hardly move."

"So I'll come to you," he said, his muscular body nakedly animalistic. Rocking the waterbed, he crawled on all fours, the lit joint stuck between his teeth. When he maneuvered to Suzette, he pulled her to a sitting position.

Suzette giggled. "Moon, I don't know what to do."

"Suck it in through your mouth when I blow."

Still on his knees, he leaned over her. Suzette put her face close to his. Reversing the joint, he put the lit end in his mouth and blew. Pursing, Suzette inhaled.

"I'm going to ball you and you're going to love it, babe," he promised her, carefully taking the burning end from his mouth, reversing it, and taking short, deep drags. He peeled off Suzette's jeans and her panties. She put down her wineglass and obediently raised her hips and legs, then stretched her arms above her head for him to remove her sweater.

Her eyes followed his hand when he touched himself briefly. He tossed his boxers to the floor. When he turned back to Suzette, he was hard.

Feeling higher than ever before, Suzette allowed Moon to put her hand on his penis. The end glistened with a drop of semen. She rubbed it over his circumcised head. It was slippery, like lanolin.

Moon put his index finger in his mouth, then slid it inside her. Raising her legs so the bottoms of her feet touched his shoulders, he entered her from a kneeling position. Eyes blank with passion, she watched the muscles in his upper legs, arms, and chest dance, then ripple. She panted and let her eyes wander down again. The root of his penis, like a circular fist, pumped in and out of her. She could see her vaginal lips, pendulous and rosy. Suzette climaxed instantly and with an intensity that surprised her. Her longing for Geoff dissipated like the sweat that flew from Moon's hairy chest.

It was dark now, and Moon's bedroom was soft with candles and burping lava lamps. Moon and Suzette were in his kitchen, their faces illuminated by the red glow of the electric hot plate. Moon passed the knife, heated on the burner with its clump of smoking hash, back and forth between them. They sucked at the thin trail.

Still holding the hash in, Moon said, "Suzie, let's sell your car, buy a Volkswagen camper, and travel across the country. Maybe we should go to Mexico. What do you think?"

Suzette looked at her watch. "Moon, I've got to go! They lock the dorm at midnight."

"Fuck them! You're too stoned to drive, babe. Stay here." Moon was naked, his thick penis dangling between his legs. "Tell me who you are, Suzie Q. Stay and rap with me!" Moon began dancing around, strumming an imaginary guitar and singing, "I like the way you talk, I like the way you walk, my Suzie Q..." His tumescent penis bounced, then flagged in the air.

"I've really got to get back, Moon."

He held the knife under her nose and stroked her bare breast, then warbled, "Baby, please don't go," to an instant tune of his own making.

The weekend had been a sex marathon and time had melted away. Now, concentrating, she managed to recollect where she'd placed her purse and the keys to the Fiat Spider her adoptive parents had given her. Once outside, Suzette giggled, waved goodbye to Moon, and backed her little car out of his drive. Moon, still crooning "Suzie Q," had conducted her out in boxer shorts.

She had to be careful, she told herself as she tried to focus on the road. She was really stoned. The overhanging trees confused her as they threw shadows at her car. A distant stop sign looked like a lone man on the road. "Don't be paranoid," she muttered uneasily. "It's just the hash."

Through her jeans Suzette could smell sex. Feeling like the kid she was when her new dad had put training wheels on her bicycle, she drove tentatively down the black street. Moon had crooned jokingly, "Tell me who you are, Suzie Q." She pondered

Moon's request. She remembered the police at the station in Paris wanting to know who she was, too. But she had lied to them, had told them nothing about the orphanage because she had been afraid they'd send her back. And she had been right to do that!

Suzette had been lucky. A Red Cross worker happened to be at the police station when she arrived, and before she knew it the organization had found new parents for her in America. The O'Brians loved her and gave her everything. The Fiat convertible was proof of that, as was her place at university. But it wasn't enough.

She focused more fully on a sharp bend. The trees waved, their branches swinging in the wind like scythes. Suzette felt disconnected. She still didn't know who she was. She didn't even know who her mother was. Maybe, she thought sadly, she was as bad as her mother. The nuns in the orphanage had said the Vietnamese were sluts. And she wondered if that terrible word was a prophecy.

Hating the thoughts that crowded her, Suzette turned on the radio, cranking up the volume. It was set on 570, the first station on the AM dial. She heard the DJ say, "Here's a new talent named Mick Jagger doing his rendition of Willie Dixon's classic "I Wanna Be Loved."

Parking in the residence lot, Suzette passed through the dorm entrance and on to her room. She tossed her fringed purse on the bed, thinking her room could be anyone's under the fluorescent tube that flickered its bad light. Suzette felt lonely, and her desire to be with Geoff returned.

She stared at the telephone, picked up the receiver, then put it down. She knew she shouldn't, but she would, then got up her nerve. After more hesitation, she dialed the familiar numbers. It rang only twice and a female voice answered. Suzette didn't speak, nor did she hang up, only listened. She heard Geoff's voice call from the background, "Who is it, babe?"

The strange, harsh female voice answered, "Probably your chink girlfriend checking up on you."

Suzette gasped, then hung up.

3

FRIENDS AND LOVERS

I feel a sadness I expected and which comes only from myself. I say I've always been sad.

—Marguerite Duras, *The Lover*

Seattle: December 1962

Punctually at ten her alarm rang. Beyond Suzette's window the University of Washington campus was in motion. Pods of female students studied in cutoff jeans and tank tops near flowerbeds and fountains, enjoying the unseasonably warm and rainless weather, or wandered toward the classrooms. Suzette fumbled for the off button on the alarm. She hadn't really been asleep. Her thirst had woken her earlier, and she'd drained the glass of water beside the bed. "Shit," she mouthed. She couldn't believe she had a hangover. It was that cheap wine of Moon's. She had a morning math class today, her least favorite among classes devoted to photojournalism and the arts. In order to get her undergraduate degree she needed math, but she'd missed it before. Besides, it didn't matter. Suzette felt she'd never get her grade-point average up high enough to continue school, anyway.

Grimacing and at the same time stretching as though she had all the time in the world, Suzette became acutely aware of voices in the hallway. She clapped her hands against her ears. The laughing would wake a dead person. She could taste the carbonated sweetness of the bottle of pink Ripple she and Moon had consumed. She had to brush her teeth and pee. And in that order. Suzette searched for her robe.

While digging through her clothes, she turned on the portable television that balanced precariously on the empty built-in dresser. Lately Suzette had gotten into the habit of not hanging up her clothes or putting them in drawers but heaping them on the floor, as if she were in transit. The robe was on the top. Turning her head to see the small TV screen, Suzette became fascinated by the news. A distant sign announced the location—Tan Son Nhat Airport in Vietnam. She watched U.S. military men bending low under the spinning blades of a helicopter. Some had cheeky smiles and waves for the television cameras. The anchorman, his voice clear and self-important, read: "Earlier this year President John F. Kennedy increased American assistance in South Vietnam to 12,000 military personnel. Their assignment is to train the democratic South's army to combat the encroaching Communist North."

A light tap on Suzette's door swung it open. Val, a pretty green-eyed blond, leaned languidly against the doorframe. Suzette counted Val as her only girlfriend on the campus, or anywhere. She was a full-time assistant at the university library. Her husband, Jimmy, was a student in Suzette's Myths and Dreams course. Val was putting Jimmy through school. The two young women's friendship had jelled when they enrolled together in an on-campus dance class.

Smiling, Suzette turned off the TV and tied the belt of her robe. "Hi, Val, how come you're not at work?"

"I'm on my way. I just stopped in to remind you to bring a towel to our dance class tonight." Val absentmindedly scratched her arm. "Let's stay for a sauna. There's never anyone in there but us two heat-lovin' creatures, anyway."

Suzette looked closely at Val and thought her friend was even paler than normal. The woman's eyes were prominent in her vague white face. "Maybe you should go to the school clinic, Val. I think you must be catching something."

Val's green eyes were glassy and listless. "You don't know the half of it. But later. I'll meet you in the gym at seven."

"One, two, three, four," the lithe dance instructor shouted. "Curve those arms. Stand up straight. Val, your tummy looks like an olive on a toothpick."

Suzette smiled at the strange image, stood up straighter herself, and subsequently felt guilty that she'd smiled at the expense of her only girlfriend. Her smile faded as the class stepped gaily across the floor to the beat of a pop song, hands extended. Finally they halted and stood in place, imitating the instructor's rhythmic moves—shoulders and hips curved, isolated, rotated, and isolated.

After the warm-down and the usual resounding applause for the instructor, Val lay exhausted across the sauna bench, her bleached towel underneath. Suzette was stretched out on the bench below where it was a little cooler.

"How's Jimmy?" Suzette asked. "I didn't see him in class."

Val looked down at Suzette. "I know. Listen, I have to talk to somebody, Suzie. I don't know what to do."

Suzette waited expectantly for Val to confide in her.

"I'm having an affair and Jimmy's found out."

"But, Val, I thought you and Jimmy were so happy." Suzette didn't know what else to say.

Val wiped the beads of sweat from her face with the corner of the towel. "Are you trying to make me feel guilty, too?"

"Of course not, Val. I'm sorry."

"Okay. About a couple of months ago a cool-looking black dude came into the library. We flirted a bit and he asked me to lunch. I don't know why I did, but I went. I was pissed off at Jimmy that day for something or other." She shrugged. "Anyway, Suz, we went for lunch and smoked a joint. His name's Tyrone and he's a part-time commerce student. I met him once before when he sold Jimmy a couple of hits of speed to get him through exams. Tyrone also sells other things."

"You mean he's a dealer?"

Val sighed, ignored the question, then continued. "Anyway, Tyrone's gorgeous, and after a few more lunches, I couldn't resist him. Maybe Jimmy and I got married too young." Val giggled. "My black dude and I balled in the back of his car in the library parking lot. It was broad daylight!"

Suzette remained silent.

"Well," Val continued lazily, "the trouble is that Jimmy's found out. One day he came home earlier than I expected. He was supposed to be in class. You know he'd rather die than miss a class. It was bad luck, Jimmy catching us. He and I talked later, but I couldn't promise him I'd stop seeing Tyrone. I'm in love with my black stud. Tyrone's so different from Jimmy. But now Jimmy's gone and told his parents and mine, too. I think it's really only because Tyrone's black that they're all so upset. Jimmy's and my parents are ridiculously straight."

Suzette sat up. "But you're married to Jimmy!"

"Maybe I made a mistake. Tyrone's a great lay."

Suzette wanted to be close to Val. She loved both her friend and Jimmy. They were her only real friends, and she needed them. She would be lonely if she didn't have them. Lonely the way she'd been in the orphanage. "Val, do you want to stay with me at the dorm? Or we can even go to my parents if you want to get away from the university. Maybe you need time away from both guys to think things through."

"Thanks, Suz, but I can't picture myself anywhere but with Tyrone. He's on my mind all the time. I live to see him!"

"Then go to him!" Suzette knew there was no turning back for Val, and suddenly she envied her friend's passion.

"It's so complicated. Jimmy says if I leave he'll turn Tyrone in for dealing. Jimmy's threatening suicide, too, but I think it's only hurt pride. His mother phoned me and said he was serious. He can be such a jerk." Val turned onto her stomach and lay with the backs of her hands supporting her forehead.

Suzette frowned. "Poor Jimmy! What will you do, Val?"

"Nothing, I guess. I can't risk Jimmy turning Tyrone in to the cops. I'll have to bide my time and see what happens."

"Are you sure you don't want to come home with me at the end of the semester?"

"Thanks, kid, but no thanks. Besides, I have to work."

Suzette then voiced a hope she'd been harboring for a while. "I don't know what I'll do after this year when I graduate. The O'Brians are great and I love them, but I can't see myself back at home. It would feel too much like I was in high school again. I remember you and Jimmy were talking about taking someone into your spare room for some extra cash."

"Honey, when I move in with Tyrone, you can live with us."

"I love you, Val. I don't know what I'd do without you."

Her friend smiled. "Anyway, how's your guy Moon? He's got a far-out name."

It was Suzette's turn to confide. "God, I don't know. Moon's not my type. We have nothing in common. Sometimes I don't even like him, but he's great in bed. I probably shouldn't bother with him, but I can't say no." Rising from the bench, Suzette threw a container of water over the sauna's rocks. They sizzled.

"Honey, nobody's perfect."

"I'm seeing Moon this weekend. He called and said he had something important to tell me. He probably just got some wild new grass. He's into sex, drugs, and music in a big way. I guess I like all that, too. It makes me forget."

"About what, hon? That creep Geoffrey?"

"I guess… Val, it's getting late and I've got some photos to develop for an assignment. I have to get it done before they close the photo lab." Wrapping herself in her towel and bending to give Val a kiss on the cheek, Suzette left the sauna.

"See you later, kid," her friend said apathetically.

On a whim Suzette turned back to peer through the sauna's tiny square window. She wanted to make Val feel better and began to mouth the words, "Don't worry. It'll work out. I know it will." But she stopped. Val was far away. As she watched, Val gently scratched at her arms. Suzette turned away and headed for the photo lab, haunted by the memory of the fire stairs in Paris she'd climbed and the girl in the room at the top with eyes like the dead.

4

SUZETTE'S DREAM

Man, it was the Fourth of July—tracers coming up everywhere.
—American Chopper Pilot to Stanley Karnow

Seattle: January 1963

The Myths and Dreams course was described in the university calendar as esoteric. "Way out" was how the students and professor expressed it. Each week the students were to record their dreams, then analyze and discuss them in workshops in the manner of Jung and Freud. The class was full of poets and latter-day beatniks, and there was a waiting list. Jimmy, who marched to his own drummer, had red hair cut close to the scalp. Although he wore the standard blue jeans and lumberjack shirt, he did sport one thing that set him apart: the plainness of his gold ring gave him the distinction of being the only married person in Myths and Dreams. That included the professor, known to his students by his first name, Jack.

Of the young men, and Suzette thought of them as such, Jimmy seemed the most mature, as well as being the nicest. The others lolled in a cloud of their own making. They drank endless mugs of coffee and chain-smoked Winstons and Marlboroughs and littered their conversations with "Hey, man" and "Yeah, dude" and threw in "cool" or the brand-new "far out." They were too wise to try to pick up the prettier girls in the class. Their professor, Jack, was seriously on the make and the girls in class were bees to his honey. But when Jack invited Suzette to a special weekend group retreat—he and his bevy—at a hot springs on

Orcas Island, she declined. With Jimmy there was the safety of his wedding band. And so they had become easy friends.

Jimmy had invited Suzette home for dinner to meet Val, his wife. He was a hunter who had shot and prepared the pheasant dinner himself, arranging the iridescent male tail feathers into a centerpiece by wrapping the quills with a leather cord. Jimmy was an avid sportsman and hunted and fished every chance he got. On a subsequent occasion he prepared *lapin à la française* in honor of Suzette's heritage. Another time he grilled a deer filet and served it with a boiled-down sauce made from Chinese rice wine, soy sauce, and ginger.

Jokingly Jimmy threatened to serve them stewed squirrel, but that first night Suzette and Val had gotten to know each other over a bottle of Chianti that Jimmy had placed in a straw basket shaped like a duck. The girls had chatted intimately over their wine and fresh *pâté faisan au Jimmy*. Suzette and Val had struck up a close and sisterly friendship.

At the beginning of their friendship, on her days off from the library, Val accompanied Suzette on her photography junkets. And those were Suzette's happiest times. They would motor, windows down in Suzette's pumpkin-hued Fiat, to the Pioneer Square area, with its cobblestoned streets, frontier-style buildings, and underground system of roads. Here, Suzette would compose a picture in a split second, then click her camera to capture it. With her ethereal looks Val made an excellent model. Suzette would pose her friend under a lamppost, raindrops glistening on the cobblestones, or make her stand in profile, eyes as far away as the horizon.

Jimmy told Suzette constantly how talented she was and that he loved the photos she took of his wife. And she knew he did. He had them blown up to poster size at a photographic studio. Their living-room wall was adorned with a collection of what Jimmy and Val proudly referred to as "Suzette's Seattle."

Suzette always meant to keep a photograph of Val for herself, but Jimmy coveted every single one. He'd say, "Please, Suzie, I love that one. You're so talented." And then, when she showed the next one, he'd say, "That one's incredible, too."

She'd usually say something like "That's true." Then she'd smile and add, "Val belongs to you! And I love both of you. You make me feel like the most important person on the planet."

While the girls were off together, Jimmy fished the streams for salmon. Or he traipsed the countryside in a red hat hunting pheasant, quail, and even moose and deer in season. His hunting and cooking prowess reached legendary proportions, and the planning of everything required phone calls and get-togethers.

The night before Suzette and Jimmy's last Myths and Dreams class together Suzette had a dream so poignant that when she awoke her pillow was soaked with tears.

An earthen path bisects rippling shoots of green, and Suzette continues on, devoid of thought or reason. Her attention is taken by a bright figure whose waist-length hair tumbles like weeds on the sea. The female figure is resplendent in silk that flutes at the ankles like an upside-down red flower, and she keeps a distance from Suzette. The figure tantalizes with her aura. An uncontrollable urge to be close fills Suzette. She doesn't just want to talk to the apparition who appears to be flesh and blood, or to photograph her exotic beauty. She wants to be with her. Suzette calls after the apparition, but the figure doesn't hear, or maybe can't understand. Quickly the apparition glides on, with Suzette trailing.

The open sky has switched to a canopy of jungle. Silent parrots flash unreal color. A daylight moon throws spears on the earth that are silver slivers on volcanic sand. The apparition leaves no footprints but disappears around a curve shaped like an S. *Elephant leaves and lipstick palms frame Suzette's path, and then the rush of water is audible. She thirsts for it.*

Sheets of mist fall from the mouth of a cloud, and the figure stands brilliantly clothed behind a transparent curtain. The turquoise pool that catches the mist glitters like precious stones. The lovely phantom beckons, hands undulating in the dimming light. Suzette follows with a child's light step. She dips a foot, makes ready to wade across, then the pool sucks at her like quicksand.

Again the apparition entreats Suzette, this time removing her eyes from their sockets and offering them to Suzette. They are two kaleidoscopes of exquisite form with which Suzette is meant to play, maybe even see through. As Suzette ponders the risk of the crossing, the curtain of water furls back into the clouds. A marigold sun turns the treacherous pool cherry.

Suzette shakes her head, and the kaleidoscopes break up and dissolve in the apparition's hand. The woman's eyes are magnified. They are the agates Suzette played with and lost at the French orphanage. They are memories, and she is overpowered by emotion. Her chest knots, and the bliss she knew from being close to the apparition becomes complete desolation. The pain she feels ends the dream and causes her to wake up.

"It's hard for me to talk about this dream," Suzette said softly, studying a cigarette that lay like a charred elbow on the classroom floor.

Jack, her professor, drummed a finger on his bottom lip. "Don't worry. We'll all go through this before the workshop's over." He seemed strangely happy as he lit another cigarette. "Do you have any idea who the woman in your dream might represent?"

"I don't know. I just know I had this incredible yearning that I still get when I think about the dream."

"Okay, let's talk setting. Do you recognize the place from TV, or a movie, or a picture you could have seen?"

"Well, it could be someplace in Vietnam. I've never been there, but I know it's tropical and I imagine it would look like that."

"Good. Now we're getting somewhere. Someone take over for me." Jack crossed his legs and looked around the seminar room at his favorite students, all of them female.

Jimmy spoke up instead. "Suzette, I was thinking about some of the stuff you've told me about yourself." He stopped, and his eyes queried hers, not wanting to betray a confidence.

Suzette understood his meaning. "It's okay, Jimmy. Go ahead." She wondered how he and Val were getting along. As far as she knew, Jimmy was unaware that Val had told her about Tyrone.

"I could be way out of line, but don't you have a Vietnamese family member?"

Jack's eyes shifted back to Suzette. "Were you dreaming about a relative?"

"Maybe. I've never met my mother, but she's Vietnamese and the woman in my dream was Asian."

Jack swung his feet to the floor and jumped off the top of the desk where he'd been reclining. "So, were you dreaming of your Vietnamese mother in the place of her birth?"

"I don't know...I guess I could have been. I've never dreamt about my mother before, only my father."

"Suzette," Jimmy said, "I hope I'm not breaking another confidence, but Val told me that as a child you hoped one day to find your mother in Vietnam. Maybe the dream's as simple as that."

"Well, yes..." Suzette raked a hand through her blond hair. "But it was only a childish hope, a fantasy because I was lonely. I didn't really think of going to Vietnam to find her. I don't have any information. I don't even know her name. I mean, how could I go to Vietnam? There's a war going on there."

"Suzette, maybe one day you'll need to travel there to find your roots," Jack said. "It's important to every human being's sense of identity to see the cultures they spring from. An individual is richer for his cultural background. With a photojournalism major you'll have lots of opportunities to travel to Asia. It's a goldmine of salable images."

Suzette pondered the idea, her face alight with movement and thought. "That seems true."

Jack noticed the youthful trust in Suzette's eyes and he cautioned her. "But now's not the time. In fact, I don't know how many of you follow politics, but I came across an article in *Time* that said the Communist Vietcong defeated a South Vietnamese troop. It was somewhere in the countryside at a place called Ap Bac."

"It's all happening in the Vietnamese countryside," a political-science major interjected. "The South Vietnamese army, with U.S. air support, attempted to take a Communist radio center near the Cambodian border. There were fifty-one U.S. advisers along, and in spite of superior firepower and numbers they were defeated. They expected a victory, but everything went wrong. Instead of fighting a few jungle guerrillas, they were up against a Vietcong battalion of four hundred. The five American support helicopters sent were destroyed within minutes. Two of the five flew into direct fire to rescue downed buddies who were actually safe behind friendly lines. Later the South Vietnamese army accidentally shelled its own troops. The South was trounced. Three advisers were killed and sixty-five South Vietnamese."

Jack nodded, then smirked with false confidence. "Yup, we'll help them and that will be the end of the Red Menace!"

Another student, a plump young woman with turquoise bangles, said, "Well, look what happened in Cuba."

And the entire class began talking and arguing at once.

5
CONTINUAL DISILLUSIONMENT

I went to the sea—no ship to get across;
I paid ten shillings for a blind white horse;
I up on his back and was off in a crack,
Sadly tell my mother I shall never come back.
—Anonymous

Seattle: February 1963

Outside, rain had given way to sunlight. The morning was already half gone, but Suzette's class didn't start until half past ten, so she lay in bed regretting the date she'd made with Moon. She had been waffling about breaking off with him for a while now.

Why had she said she'd see him? Suzette chastised herself. Moon really wasn't her type. He was exciting and a nice guy, talented musically, too, but they had nothing in common except sex.

The last time she'd slept with Moon her brain had said no, but she'd ended up in his wildly rocking waterbed, anyway. Annoyed with herself for being so weak, Suzette still had to admit that making it with Moon was fun. The weed and liquor helped her shed her inhibitions like stripping off clothes in a sweltering room. It left her raw but open to sensation. Touch was accentuated, she thought—sex and grass really were far out. Still, it wasn't fair to Moon. She knew she was leading him on.

Suzette vowed this time she would tell Moon it was over and not see him again. Happy with her decision, she decided to ask Val to go swimming with her in the university pool. Picking up the receiver, Suzette called the library. The dial clicked through the numbers, and she waited for the ring. "Could I speak to Val?" she asked when the phone was answered.

"Val Owens isn't here," a professional female voice replied. "She called in sick a few days ago. Can someone else help you?"

Suzette declined the woman's offer and hung up. So Val hadn't been at work and was home in bed. Suzette thought about Jimmy, who hadn't been at class in a few weeks. Maybe he was sick, too. Suzette's thoughts were positive: maybe some time at home would get her friends back together. Still, she knew that was wishful thinking. Just last week Val had introduced Tyrone to her. He and Val made a striking pair, and they were obviously in love. Val had begged Suzette to take their picture.

She'd photographed them at Tyrone's pad. Val's normally straight hair had been curled and curved like the tresses of an old-fashioned cinema siren. She waited as Val used a comb to spruce up Tyrone's hairdo. Tyrone's skin was very black, and Suzette had to use her flash to catch his features. She'd used black-and-white film and the photograph glowed with intimacy. Val lay engulfed in his arms as if she belonged, had always been there. Tyrone had been strong and loving and had said Suzette was welcome to live with them.

Then she remembered poor Jimmy. Obviously he wasn't handling the situation well. But who could? She thought about the last time she'd seen him in her Myths and Dreams course. He was quieter than ever about his personal life. Suzette hadn't wanted to broach the subject of Val's love affair with a black guy, or her moving in with him. If Jimmy needed her to confide in, she knew he would. Suzette didn't want to get in the middle, didn't want to take sides. She wondered if it would hurt Jimmy if she did move into Val and Tyrone's. All she knew was that she didn't want to cause him further pain. She loved them both.

Dialing Jimmy and Val's apartment, Suzette counted thirteen

rings. She wondered why there was no answer and she'd almost given up when she heard Val's voice.

"Val, I almost hung up you took so long. Did I wake you?"

"Oh, Suzy, Jimmy did it. That idiot did it." Suzette heard Val swallow awkwardly, as though she had difficulty with thought. "I can't stay here anymore. You don't know what it's like. The cops have been all over the place. Jimmy's parents blame me. Mine do, too." She sobbed into the phone.

"Val, what are you saying?"

"Jimmy shot himself with his hunting rifle in the head last night. He's dead. Oh, my God! It's horrible. I had to come back here. There's blood everywhere. I guess I'm supposed to clean it up. I can't believe this happened."

"No, that can't be!" Suzette cried.

"Suzie, Jimmy blamed me and my having an affair with Tyrone. He left a note and said Tyrone was selling him heroin. We'd had a fight and I'd left him, gone to Tyrone. A neighbor heard the shot and called the police. They searched Tyrone's house when I was there. Thank God he'd hidden the stash the day before."

Suzette felt sick. She knew Val must feel even sicker. "What can I do? Should I come get you?"

"There's nothing you can do. You should probably stay clear of me until this blows over. The cops will be following us, and Tyrone said they'd be bothering all our friends to get something on him. He says we have to move, hide out somewhere where we can't be rousted. I gotta get out of here. The blood makes me sick. You can smell it. I'm going away with Tyrone now no matter what anyone says or does. I'm gone, Suzy. I know you care about both Jimmy and me. I love you for it. Don't call me. I'll find you later when I can." She hung up.

Suzette sat cross-legged on the floor, her back bent, one hand brushing away her tears. Then it sunk in. She'd never see Jimmy again. She should have been sensitive to him. Jimmy had been her friend. Maybe if she had been there for him… Now it was too late.

Suzette's mind raced to the old photograph she'd once glimpsed and the Vietnamese mother she'd never seen. Her mother would die, too, and she would never know her. Suzette panicked. Everyone she loved left her.

I can't go on
my life has dropped from me
and broken

I can't understand
why there is no one to warm me
I am freezing, improperly clothed

am I meant to follow
climb down
from this dreary world
and slip away unnoticed
like raindrops in the sea

Rising from her knees, Suzette went to the dresser. She opened her jewel case and removed the velvet-lined box. From underneath she took the only remnant she had of her childhood and her other life. It was her most beloved possession—the picture of herself with Papa. Tracing first her own image, then his face with a delicate finger, she saw both figures captured in a moment of sincerity, the simplicity and truth of their love befitting the old-fashioned black-and-white snapshot. She remembered Papa the way he had been to her when he had been really with her and not taken away by his unhappiness. And finally he came to her as he had when she was a child. She could feel Papa's nearness now and kissed the tattered picture, careful not to ruin it with her tears.

Suzette thought of going home to the O'Brians. She could be there in a half hour. But how could she tell them about Jimmy's death, especially the drug part? Her parents would be saddened, concerned about her lifestyle. They would want her to come home for good. Instead she dialed Moon's number. "Can I come over?" she asked, knowing the answer would be yes.

It was clear to Suzette that she shouldn't go to Moon. For one thing she had an important photo assignment to finish for her final portfolio. And then she'd made her decision to stop seeing him. But Moon would kiss her when she came through the door, and that was what she wanted. Suzette craved comfort. Maybe she even needed liquor and drugs. But she didn't care. She picked up her car keys and drove to Moon's.

When she got there, he was really stoned, even more than usual. He'd been drinking, smoking, and dropping LSD, a new drug to her. His mood was wild.

"Hey, babe, you gotta try this. They call it acid. Let's do it together." Moon was elated that Suzette was there. His voice made a song of his words, and he was good at that, too.

"No, I can't, Moon," she said faintly, knowing she sounded like a prude.

"Come on, Suzie. I want you to experience this with me," he coaxed, waving a tiny square of paper at her.

"Is that it?"

"Yeah, kid. Haven't you done blotter acid before?"

"I guess I haven't."

Moon held the tiny bit of paper up to Suzette. "That's what I love about you. You're so upper class."

"Listen, I shouldn't have come. It's just that—" Suzette stopped. She couldn't tell Moon about Jimmy blowing his head apart. She couldn't explain to him what Val must have felt finding Jimmy lying in their bed. She couldn't tell Moon they were the only friends she had and now they were both gone. She remembered Val's comment about the smell of blood. She wasn't sure if it was too important for Moon, or if she didn't want to say anything because it was so horrific. Or maybe she still didn't believe it was real. Instead she said, "I shouldn't have come. I've got an important photo assignment to do."

Moon pouted. "Come on, doll. I want to peak with you tonight. I'll ball you just when we're peaking. You'll love it." He danced around Suzie, his idea of a wanton ballerina. Suzette smiled. "You'll have to take this now, so we can get off at the same time."

"No, Moon, I can't. But give me a glass of wine."

"I'll give you the world, Suzie Q, 'cause I love you." Dancing to the fridge, Moon grabbed a second glass and another bottle of Ripple. He unscrewed the cap and poured. The wine fizzled with pink bubbles. "Suzie, you've got to be quick. We gotta experience this together. Don't worry. I'll take care of you."

"But, Moon, I'm scared." Despite her protests, she knew she'd do it. She'd do anything to forget. And she wouldn't talk about Jimmy to Moon.

"Suz, this will give you some real-life art to think about. When you start hallucinating on this stuff, the air will dance and your idea of color will never be the same. It'll help your art. All the arts profs do it, and painters, too. Acid primes your mind for creation."

"Well, it might be good for me artistically."

Moon laughed. "Only *you* would put it like that. Here, put this little dot of paper under your tongue."

Twenty minutes later she was in a fairy tale and nothing mattered anymore. Pleasurable fingers tickled and chased through her body. When she told Moon that, he said, "It just means you're getting off."

Moon lit an incense stick in the bedroom. Then she noticed that the scent of the joss stick was patchouli, and she was transported to a tropical garden of perfumed flowers that sweetened the room's air. Moon blew on the incense, and the little embers streamed like blowing rain. He blew again, entertaining her, and the flames that spewed from his lips had the intensity of a torch.

As Moon sang something to her huskily, she became lost in the caverns of his voice. He danced, jumping high, then fell to the ground. He was her acrobat, her carnival performer. His bare breast was tanned below the rainbow stream that whooshed out of his mouth when he sang his tune again.

When he grabbed his guitar, the red shag it lay on followed like a limpid train. He played and his guitar controlled the vibrations in the wall and sang inside her body. It was as if she'd been deaf and blind. Then the calendar with the smoking dude in biblical robes twisted like a secret door in an Enid Blyton story. The opening flowered. It was massive, not rectangular anymore; it was a hole and behind was a field of red poppies. No, it had become the powder-blue door of a mosque shot with stars. It was every shape, every hue, every movement, and it pulsated to the guitar riff Moon played for her. The colors in the calendar were so bold that she wanted to re-create them, be a painter. The smashing intensity gyrated, and the robed figure became a comic-book ghost with buttons for eyes.

Suzette braced herself. "I'm scared, Moon."

"Come on, I'm going to fuck the pants off you." He stripped off his shirt to the music. The bed lay like a lake before them.

"Moon, give me something to stop it. I'm not ready for this."

"Ride it out, Suzie Q. It's time for me to tell you my surprise. Let's sell your car and buy a VW pop-top. We'll camp through Mexico and into Central America. Great idea, kid. I really dig you. Better than anyone for a long time. We've gotta do it."

"I can't sell my car. How will I get back and forth from school?"

"Fuck your stupid school! University's bull. You don't need it. I've seen your photos. You're talented, and not just your gorgeous ass. We'll be in Mexico soaking up the sun, blowing our faces off, and fucking like rabbits." He put a hand on the crude night table to steady himself. "You can work selling your pics to my Uncle Jake. He's a far-out dude who owns this magazine in L.A. The magazine is cool, too. They're always looking for something on different countries and they're into anything exotic. They'll even pay your traveling money, expenses. They always pay airfare for good photo people like you. We'll live like kings, Suzie." He grinned. "My uncle's first-class. He takes risks on people he thinks are talented. He's helped loads of new photographers get famous. We'll probably get paid for pictures of marijuana fields, or pictures of the *federales* riding in jeeps over long sand beaches as blond as you. I've told him about you. He's willing to take a chance on you, baby."

Suzette tried to concentrate. "Moon, I can't handle this. I can hardly think or see."

"I know what you mean. I'm hallucinating like it's Halloween around here. You'll sell your car and give me the money. I'll buy a used van and we'll fly this coop."

"But I don't want to sell my car or go to Mexico."

"Sure you do. We'll have a ball."

"I'm telling you, Moon. I can't do it. I've got enough problems right now dealing with myself."

He touched her lips. "I think I love you, Suzie Q. I want you to come with me. You told me you don't feel comfortable here in the States. Mexico's a gas. Drugs are cheap and I can deal. Food's cheap, too. It actually grows on trees. With warm weather it's easy to live. I'll look after you, I'll carry your camera, I'll fuck you night and day." Moon kissed her. "We can pick fruit straight off the trees. You've gotta come with me, doll! We can pitch a tent, we can swing in hammocks tied to shady palm trees. We'll fuck five times a day. Come on, try to imagine it. Think of your camera itching to click."

Suzette tried to feel the warm sunlight on her skin.

"See the turquoise water against the white sand?" Moon asked.

"Yes, I do. The sand's so soft and white that it looks like baby powder."

"Now imagine my cock inside you, your body lying in that soft powder."

"Oh, yeah, I can feel the sweet breeze soft and gentle on my skin."

"Fuck the sweet breeze, Suz! Feel me!" He unbuttoned the fly of his jeans and put Suzette's hand on his penis. "Put your mouth on it, doll."

And she did.

BOOK IV

KIET AND SUZETTE

We bathed together in the cool water from the jars, we kissed, we wept, and again it was unto death, but this time, already, the pleasure it gave was inconsolable.

—Marguerite Duras, *The Lover*

1

KIET'S WORLD

Experience had taught him that reason could not be counted on in such situations. There was always an extra element, mysterious and not quite within reach, that one had not reckoned with. One had to know, not deduce. And he did not have the knowledge.

—Paul Bowles, *The Sheltering Sky*

Saigon: December 1962

Nguyen Son Kiet loved his life. He was charmed. Life had never been so exciting, so good. He was strolling down the newly named Tu Do, or Freedom, Street. It was a muggy late afternoon, but Kiet kept up a snappy pace, looking neat and handsome. He was one of many young men wearing "the blues," mandatory wear for all South Vietnamese government employees under thirty-five who had to be members of President Diem's Republican Youth movement.

Letting his eyes roam Tu Do, Kiet felt dwarfed by the huge American bodies, mostly black but some white. They strutted and slumped. Sweat stained their uniforms and trickled down their cheeks. They were members of the entourage known as the Military Assistance Command Vietnam, or MACV. Kiet was aware it was just a new name for Military Assistance Advisory Group, or MAAG, the same command structure that had been advising the French and training South Vietnam's Special Forces since the end of World War II. Now there were just more of them.

Rock and roll blared from the shacks that had been turned into shanty bars. Neon signs screamed the virtues of steam baths. Vietnamese beauties postured by the painted doors, their slender legs balancing on impossibly high stiletto heels. They called to one another in singsong voices. One by one the Asian beauties were claimed, the Americans touching them awkwardly with their hairy paws and leading them behind closed doors.

"Saigon's new boss, the American," Kiet grumbled, jealous of the men. He wondered if the women's actions were fueled by poverty or simply by ambitious desire.

Asian dolls with open palms
GI bodies black and strong
groan and push with dulled delight
easier for GIs to fight
Asian dolls with dreamy thoughts
of U.S. places where there's lots
of money
clothes
much food
and riches

turn child girls
to sleazy bitches

Asian men not good enough
too small
too poor
no U.S. tough

for Asian dolls
with dollared palms
who'd sell their souls
to boys who bombed

Kiet arrived at the popular Café Brodard at exactly the same time as his best friend, Kim. Seating themselves in a corner booth, they began their aimless talk. Kim ordered a bottle of 333, a popular Vietnamese beer, and offered Kiet one.

"Let's eat first. I'm hungry," Kiet said.

Kim had a wealthy father who fed him an endless supply of piastres but always berated him for not getting an education. "Okay, you eat, I'll drink and contemplate the girls out there."

Two Americans who sat in the booth behind attracted Kiet and Kim's attention. The boys listened eagerly and between them understood much of the conversation, which was conducted in English.

"As a military man, I see Vietnam's future improving," a lanky fellow in a lieutenant general's olive-green field dress drawled Texas-style. "Diem's been very successful in his bid to destroy the Vietcong."

The other American was a chubby civilian, possibly a diplomat, who wore heavily starched Bermuda shorts and a short-sleeved golf shirt. Physically he was a direct contrast to the sinewy military man. "You're dead wrong, Sam. Don't forget that before he left for his new position at the Pentagon, Colonel Ed Lansdale urged President Kennedy to send more aid to South Vietnam. Diem obviously needs it." The civilian sipped his coffee and continued. "I know Diem claims his brother, Nhu, has helped him eradicate the Communists in South Vietnam, but as far as I'm concerned, that's just typical government propaganda."

"Shit, Eldridge, you sure got a bee up your ass about Diem."

"General, you haven't got a clue. Diem's a paranoid weakling who doesn't trust anyone except Nhu and that gorgeous bitch he's married to. And Madame Nhu and her husband seem to be doing their damnedest to turn public opinion against Diem. If you ask me, Nhu's strengthening his *own* political future through his secret police. And look at the way Nhu lets his wife call the shots on social policy. I'm sure you know Madame Nhu's outlawed divorce just to stop Le Chi, her younger sister, from divorcing her husband and losing the family fortune. And as for Nhu himself, he works every angle and has his dirty hands in every pie."

"That's a load of horseshit!" the general spluttered over the clatter of plates being cleared at another table.

"Now come on, Sam, think! Nhu's secret police is above the law. His agents can imprison South Vietnamese citizens without a court order. And, worse, Nhu's usurping Diem's powers. I've heard Nhu described as a bloodsucking snake who hasn't got an ounce of humanity in him."

"What's the use of arguing with you, Eldridge? Still, you can't deny that Nhu's protected the countryside from the Commies."

Eldridge curled his lip in an undiplomatic sneer. "You call that protection, General? Let's face it, Sam, you don't understand this country. Those so-called *aggrovilles* meant to protect the farmers from the Vietcong have become fucking concentration camps surrounded by barbed wire. If you ask me, the ARVN's Colonel Pham Ngoc Thao, who heads the program for Nhu, is pushing the peasants into Ho Chi Minh's open arms."

"Goddamn it, you cock-sucking know-it-all! You're not the only one in this ass wipe of a country who knows the score."

Kiet understood the insult implied by the general's first words, and their violence caused him to drop the bottle of 333 he had seconds before received from the waiter. It crashed to the floor, spreading shards of glass and splashes of beer on the well-shod feet of the gentlemen the two Vietnamese friends had been listening to. Mortified, Kiet and Kim apologized and left the café.

When they were definitely clear of the Americans, Kiet grabbed Kim's elbow and steered him into a quiet alley. "Kim, do you believe what the civilian was saying?"

"Of course. But what do we care about politics and policy? It only concerns us because we'll be drafted and sent into the killing fields."

"You're right," Kiet said thoughtfully. "But how can we escape such a fate?"

"I know what you can do, Kiet. Go back to university, or buy yourself an officer's position. Let's be realistic. There are high-ranking, uneducated generals in our army. They were either born to the position or bought their stars! Besides, women won't give you the time of day unless you're an officer."

"Is that all you ever have on your mind—women?"

"Sure, what else is there?"

Kiet shook his head. "Anyway, you don't need to be educated to be a good officer. General Giap was expelled from school and he vanquished the French."

"That's different. Giap protested a French ban on national newspapers. Our army commanders above the rank of captain consider themselves above field service and have never seen battle. They refuse to lead on the front lines."

"It's not that bad, Kim."

"It's not entirely their fault. You can blame Diem. Officers also refuse to fight because they know Diem's attitude."

"What do you mean?" Kiet asked, confused.

"Come on. Are you telling me you don't know that our *beloved* president is so fearful that his own high-ranking officers might become heroes that he threatened to stop a colonel's promotion if he incurred any casualties?"

"But winning takes lives!"

"What's worse, I know for a fact that the brass registers more soldiers than they have to steal extra salaries from the government. And it doesn't stop there. The generals requisition supplies for their soldiers, then use the materials to construct villas for their mistresses."

Kiet put a hand on his friend's shoulder. "Kim, be careful! You're being brainwashed by Communist propaganda."

"No, Kiet, you're the one who's brainwashed! I'm not a Communist, nor do I support our current regime. I'm for myself! No one except an idiot would willingly sacrifice his life for an uncertain future. You and I, if we had a choice, would rather drink beer and enjoy our youth than fight in a stinking jungle."

"Kim, we'll have no beer if the Communists take over the South. No religion, either. We'll be doing hard labor in a reeducation camp in the stinking jungle."

"You know Ho Chi Minh that well?" Kim challenged.

"No, of course not. Neither one of us knows anything about Communists. But we're citizens of the South and we should do our duty."

"Go ahead, my friend, but I have different plans. It seems to me that you're already hoisting a bayonet and sleeping in a private's tent."

"Face it, Kim," Kiet said with conviction, "you can't live here and not be involved."

"That's absolutely right. So just watch me! Both sides are devils and I won't be trapped by either! The Communists will take away our money, jobs, and land when they come. And if things go on the way they're going, Diem and his armchair cutthroats will take our lives. That means there's no alternative except to leave."

"Where will you go?"

"To Cambodia. Come with me, Kiet."

Kiet gazed thoughtfully at his friend. "Remember Hung?"

"You mean Laughing Hung who's now with the Vietcong in the swamp on the other side of the Saigon River?"

"Laughing Hung was one of my best friends at school. We were like brothers. The day the Communists in the South were allowed to regroup and return safely to the North under the rules of the Geneva Agreements, Hung asked me to come with him and join the Vietminh. He wasn't a Communist. He just wanted adventure. But he's my enemy now. He sent me a letter saying that if he were to see me and I was still employed by the South Vietnamese government, he'd kill me with no qualms. You make fun of Hung because he joined the Communists. You think I'm stupid because I work for Diem. The three of us—you, me, and Laughing Hung—are from the South, but each of us feels differently. Regardless of all that, though, we're still Vietnamese!"

Kim looked at Kiet fondly. "You're my best friend. When I leave Vietnam, I want you to have my apartment. The rent's paid for six months. And I've got a year's lease. I'll make sure I leave the key and lease for you before I go!"

Kiet took off his sunglasses to look deeper into his friend's eyes. "I can't believe you're serious, Kim."

Kim slapped Kiet's shoulder playfully. "Don't *you* be so serious. Let's go have another beer, and this time we won't waste it."

2

KIET AT WORK AND PLAY

We learn resignation not by our own suffering but by the suffering of others.

—Somerset Maugham, *The Summing Up*

Saigon: December 1962

Kiet awakened on his familiar mat on the floor of his room. His mouth felt as if it had been stuffed with cotton wool soaked in liquor that tasted like sewer water. The beer had gone to his head and, of course, he and Kim had gone hunting for women. As usual they never found any. The good Saigonese girls were at home under lock and key, and the hookers had eyes only for white and black pockets bulging with dollars and the chance of a new life away from Vietnam. And if what his friend had said came true, who could blame them?

In Saigon greenbacks flowed as thick as the refuse in the citrine river's maw. Prowling navy boats and freighters streamed in and out of its filthy mouth. While children played on the open junks that were their homes, the ragtag fisher folk sluiced the river for cheap surprises: spent grenades and small armaments dumped before a customs search.

Focusing, Kiet lay on his naked back and stretched the length of the mat. Then he stretched again, his big toe knocking the smoldering mosquito coil. "Shit!" he said in English, mimicking the general he'd overheard the previous night. Jumping up, he hopped like an injured rabbit.

As usual Kiet blamed Kim for his troubles. His friend would

be the death of him, he reflected good-naturedly. Kim kept him out to all hours every chance he got. His friend had no job and no responsibilities and could sleep in his fancy apartment until the war ended. He, on the other hand, had a government job to get to. Scooping up his watch from the floor, he saw that it was 8:00 a.m. and realized he was late.

Kiet headed for the water closet in his boxer shorts. Both the bathroom and the adjacent toilet, a floor with two metal footholds, were unoccupied. Thank God, he thought as he brushed his teeth, swilling the brown water that dripped from the tap around his mouth. He spat. A myriad of diseases were carried in Saigon's water supply. He splashed his face, then dabbed some water under his arms. It was the best he could do. Sprinting back to his room, he delivered a well-aimed kick at a scuttling cockroach on the way, grabbed his blue uniform off a nail, and dressed as quickly as he could.

Kiet buttoned up and strutted in front of the mirror. Wetting a finger, he smoothed his eyebrows, then shook lime cologne from a bottle, picked up a jar that contained jasmine oil, mixed the two, and combed his hair away from his forehead. Next he put on his aviator-style sunglasses, which he kept safe in a pouch. Finally, before he made his way outside, he saluted himself smartly.

The sun stared down on Kiet as he dodged the bleating Suzuki and Honda motorbikes that careened between trucks and cars, *cyclos* and pedestrians. He gave in and hailed a *cyclo* immediately, pulling up the leather roof of the three-wheeled pedicab to protect himself from the glare. "To the office of the General Treasury Department on Ly Tu Trang Street and make it quick," he said to the driver.

As he rode, Kiet girl-watched through the lenses of his dark glasses. Pretty women passed on bicycles and on the backs of motorcycles with two-stroke engines. Those that wore the *aio dai* sped by like swallow-tailed butterflies clinging to metallic insects.

The rest of the scene didn't interest Kiet. He'd seen it often: peddlers selling Kleenex, Russian army knives, Chinese chopsticks, shoe polish, French newspapers, and automotive oil. One kid hawked distilled water on the curb, and Kiet threw some piastres into the urchin's hand. Then his eye caught a glossy flash of nudity—a pretty girl, no older than five, selling pornographic French postcards.

Kiet cursed. Trucks crowded with army troops impeded the progress of his *cyclo*. Military police, the Quan Canhs, led the way. They wore the same olive-drab uniforms the soldiers did but sported steel helmets emblazoned with a white QC on a red stripe. He knew the QCs were being equipped and trained by the U.S. Army Military Police Corps. Kiet guessed that Saigon's military police performed the same duties American military cops did in New York and Chicago, places he couldn't fully imagine.

His *cyclo* driver crossed, making a diagonal beeline across four lanes. Kiet congratulated the man. Then he whistled long and low: another army vehicle had turned in, blocking them again. It was a truck, a U.S. M-35 towing a 75 mm infantry howitzer. At this rate, Kiet thought, he'd never get to work. Just as he was set to abandon the *cyclo* and take to his feet, the pedicab's driver hopped off his bicycle and dragged the vehicle, with Kiet in the passenger seat, over the curb. Kiet applauded as the driver nipped back on, then expertly maneuvered through the pedestrians on Tu Do and around the army truck. When they finally arrived at the General Treasury, Kiet knew it was a miracle of navigation.

Kiet had been promoted to manager of lotteries and expropriated land compensation for the General Treasury. His duties were to pay the winners in the government-run lottery and issue funds to individuals for proven expropriated land claims. When he was given the new position, the general treasurer himself, a secretive man with a reputation for high political morals, had warned Kiet that his predecessor had been swayed by bribes. Given the fate of his predecessor—swift termination—the message was perfectly clear.

Hurrying into the building, Kiet called up his luck and didn't remove his dark glasses. He knew the general treasurer was a watcher, and out of the corner of his eye spotted Mr. Thé concealed behind a pillar in furtive surveillance, but looking the other way. Kiet gently swung the door of his tiny office shut and at the same moment breathed a sigh of relief. Safely ensconced at his desk, he opened a drawer to take out his pens and treasury stamp. A strange paper bag, bloated like a puffer fish, lay on top of the pens. He pulled it out, and a carton of Imperial cigarettes tumbled free. Underneath was cash fastened with a large paper clip.

Kiet counted the bills with damp palms. When he reached two hundred thousand piastres, his mind reeled. After all, Kiet was aware that the amount under his nose equaled twice the yearly French budget for hospitals and libraries throughout Indochina twenty years earlier. He knitted his eyebrows. Was someone testing him? There was no note. Was his assistant bribing him to turn his head while he brought in false land claims or lottery winners? He had heard rumors about his assistant's shady sidelines. Whatever the answer, Kiet knew the money signified danger. Nervously he stuffed the cash back into the bag and returned everything to the drawer.

At lunch he presented the money to Mr. Thé, then asked his boss to transfer his assistant and appoint a new one. Impressed by his employee's honesty, Mr. Thé agreed to the request and Mai Ling came into Kiet's life. She was a graduate of the Saigon Institute of Management, something she never failed to remind Kiet of. From the first day Mai Ling put her dainty foot down in Kiet's office, he became obsessed with her. Every morning when he arrived at work he looked forward to hearing the click of her heels as she walked by his door.

Although Mai Ling was habitually late, Kiet could never reprimand her. He felt her presence like a hot wind and perpetually dreamed of her, both in the office and at night. She permeated his every thought just as her expensive perfume pervaded the air around her and then lingered. Kiet imagined her mounted on him across his desk, her supple legs gripping his thighs, riding him like a stallion full tilt until they were both satiated. Thinking of her in such a manner, Kiet was tongue-tied in her presence. To his dismay she was married to a wealthy older man and related to Kiet's superior, Mr. Thé, something that made her even more unattainable.

Mai Ling was well aware of Kiet's admiration and of her husband's importance. Despite the fact that she was Kiet's assistant, she teased him about his lesser social status. Safe as a married woman and bored with her duties, which consisted mainly of typing Kiet's reports, she took to crossing her legs and letting her American-style short skirt inch up a little more than it should. To torture Kiet further, Mai Ling often dropped a pencil and bent low to titillate, allowing him a flash of breasts. Occasionally she turned her back to him and stooped. At that ecstatic moment she'd switch her shapely hips and derriere before straightening her skirt. Mai Ling's ploys were tremendously successful, causing Kiet to stammer when he spoke to her.

She teased him verbally, too, addressing him as *sir*. Kiet responded formally, calling her *madame*. Always when she spoke to her "boss," she pressed her face close to his, her minted breath almost causing him to swoon. Once she said, "Sir, you're my boss and I must obey you on all matters. So I have a question for you. If you were a girl married to a husband who was old and rich, would you take a young lover to keep yourself alive?" Before Kiet could reply, Mai Ling declared, "But, of course, the husband loves his beautiful young wife to distraction and would kill any man who glanced at her." Then she laughed and added, "Sir, would you risk death for me? A real man would, you know. But a boy doesn't know what he wants."

Mai Ling's comings and goings provided Kiet with moments of bliss. He would arrive at work early and leave late, always with the purpose of watching her mount or dismount her Velo Soles moped in tight skirt and high heels. Kiet went out of his way to torment himself, knowing full well Mai Ling was beyond his reach, consciously resigning himself to lusting for her from afar. Still, no matter how impossible he knew the situation to be, a part of him held out hope that his deepest desires would someday be realized.

Duc Tu's Tea House was an inexpensive meeting place for young Vietnamese on Saturday nights. Musical shows were one of the few entertainments not classified as immoral by President Diem's regime. Diem's sister-in-law, Madame Nhu, thought nothing of holding dance parties at the Presidential Palace but declared that pastime illegal for the rest of her countrymen. Overnight, dance clubs became newly dubbed tea houses so they could retain their liquor licenses. Madame Nhu's ever changing rules and regulations stated that tea houses were allowed to play only South Vietnamese songs and that dancing was strictly forbidden. Still, singers and musicians were in great demand and were paid good wages, among the highest in Saigon.

Kiet and Kim were Duc Tu regulars. They visited the tea house every Saturday night without fail and sometimes during the week. The friends enjoyed the privilege of being regular patrons and were addressed by name by the staff, including "Duc" himself. Tonight Kiet and Kim moved toward the stage, drinks in hand. There they could feel the music. The songs were infused with anti-Communist spirit and the heroism of the armed forces. Love songs and foreign tunes had been expressly banned by Madame Nhu!

The two friends stood at the front of the crowd. Kim tapped a boot-clad foot in time to the music. Kiet was rapt in the lyrics, attentive to the nuances of the singers. The night was in full swing. A particularly patriotic song was coming to a rousing end when Duc, the master of ceremonies, rushed onstage. Halting the musicians with a wave of his arms, he said, "Ladies and gentlemen, I hope you enjoyed our show. A private party has arrived and I know you'll leave quietly in honor of our important guests. I hope you'll patronize my tea house again tomorrow evening when our singers and musicians look forward to entertaining you. Thank you and good night!"

"I can't believe this!" Kim said to Kiet. "No one has the right to spoil our Saturday night."

Kiet patted his friend on the arm to calm him. "We'd better go, Kim. These VIPs obviously want the place to themselves."

The other merrymakers were leaving quietly with only a few murmurs of discontent, but Kim refused to budge. "Our money's as good as theirs and this is supposed to be a free country."

A half-dozen thugs loomed in a dark corner by the bar.

"Kim," Kiet whispered, "when we're millionaires we'll buy this place. Let's go!"

Kim ignored his friend and called out brazenly, "Mr. Duc Tu, four bottles of 333. I have enough piastres on me to finish your stock of beer. So give us our drinks and don't worry about money."

"Duc Tu won't serve you or anyone else!" a smooth voice emanated from the knot of brutes.

Kiet frowned nervously, but Kim only laughed and repeated his order.

Duc Tu intervened, attempting to usher the boys out. "Boys, you don't want to make trouble. Believe me. Come back tomorrow and I'll give you drinks on the house."

Kim stood his ground. "Our money's as good as theirs. We're entitled to your services as much as—"

Before Kim could finish, three men wielding Tokarev semi-automatic sniper rifles surrounded them. One thug poked Kim with his barrel. "You heard the man. Leave or we'll blow your empty heads to pieces and feed your brains to the chickens."

Blood drained from Kiet's face but somehow he said, "Gentlemen, let's all remain calm. My friend is a little drunk. Put your guns away. We're not your enemies."

Kim sneered at the thugs and spat, his saliva wetting the hard face of the ruffian closest to Kiet. The hoodlum responded, and as fast as a silverfish his gun barrel connected with Kim's gut, making him retch and bringing him to his knees. Then the blunt end of the rifle found Kim's ribs while another man's barrel tap-danced on Kiet's chin as a warning. Without thinking Kiet yelled, "Put down your weapons, cowards, and fight like men!"

"Leave them alone!" the arrogant voice they'd heard earlier shot from the bar. "I'll handle this! I won't introduce myself," the voice in the shadows addressed Kiet and Kim. "My name is my own business. But let me ask you something. Do you know whose party you're crashing?"

As he said this, all eyes in the bar settled on a fat man crammed into a nearby chair. The obese man's shirt, big as a balloon, was tucked into gargantuan pants. The chair he sat in looked as if it would collapse under his weight. Every Saigonese, including Kiet and Kim, knew who the corpulent man was—Big Boss, the Vietnamese godfather, the most notorious gangster in South Vietnam! His name was synonymous with greed, corruption, brutality, and terrorism.

Kiet groaned but nevertheless said to the fat man, "I'm not surprised your bodyguards beat unarmed men. We know your name and reputation all too well."

"Apologize to Big Boss and go!" the smooth voice from the bar ordered.

Big Boss rocked in his unstable chair and laughed. "Young man, it's easy for you to criticize, but never mind. Don't worry. I think my men will apologize instead. I believe they were a little hasty." The gang lord chuckled, waved his handkerchief for a truce, then swung his swollen body out of the chair and lumbered toward the kitchen, calling out, "Duc Tu, bring me a field telephone!"

Duc hurried out of the kitchen, a telephone clutched in his trembling hands.

Across the room Kim was doubled over in a chair, while Kiet massaged his aching jaw. Both were silent and wary.

"Hello, Dr. Tuyen? Big Boss speaking. Come to Duc Tu's Tea House right away. We have some new friends here, but they're a little damaged. You need more men. I'm sure these young men would be useful. They've proved their bravery, if not their brawn."

Kiet knew that Tuyen was head of the regime's covert intelligence apparatus.

As he conversed, Big Boss lumbered to the bar, his sagging flesh following like an overflowing soufflé. He faced the dark figure. "What do you think, Little Fox? Will these two make good recruits for Tuyen's secret police?"

In answer the dark figure took the receiver from Big Boss's hand and replaced it. Leaning over the fat man, he tapped his nose. "Be careful what you say," he warned.

"Don't worry," Big Boss said, unperturbed. "You're among friends here. No one lives long in Saigon if they tell tales." He flapped his handkerchief and called out, "Duc, a round of the best cognac in the house for everybody!"

Fish-bowl glasses were delivered into the hands of Kiet and Kim.

"Let's drink to reconciliation!" Big Boss boomed magnanimously. "Accept my apologies, *please*."

Kim sat up, groaned, and drank, but Kiet said, "I don't understand. Why are you apologizing? You have the upper hand."

"Believe me, my naive young friend, I'm not apologizing because I'm afraid of you. I'm not afraid of anyone or anything. Killing is my business and as pleasurable to me as eating and drinking." Big Boss downed the cognac with a slurp, his mouth puckered like the orifice of a jellyfish. "I like your spunk. If I decide to squash you like a bug, I'd find you no matter where you tried to hide." He pummeled his chest with a beefy paw. "But I'm looking for men with guts, not dead enemies." His eyes seemed as innocent as those of a well-fed baby.

"Let's go, Kim," Kiet said. "This man's not fit for our company."

"You wound me, my young friend," Big Boss said mockingly, and his hand fumbled for the revolver in the wasteland of his shirt. "I could do a lot for you, but if you insist…"

The shadow at the bar intervened again, catching Big Boss's wrist in midair. "Let them go," he said. "There's no harm done. We'll have our sport later with women, not boys."

Big Boss glanced at the man in the shadows and smiled, nodding slightly.

Kiet and Kim kept their eyes glued to the floor as they were escorted out of the tea house.

3

HOME AT LAST

These people may be the world's greatest lovers, but they're not the world's greatest fighters! But they're good people and they can win a war if someone shows them how.

—U.S. Adviser Lieutenant Colonel John Paul Vann
to David Halberstam

Saigon: April 1963

It was so beautiful, Suzette reflected. She was almost there, finally flying over South Vietnam. Suzette pressed her camera lens against the plastic window and clicked the landscape below. She saw a child-size checkerboard awash with the ruled green of canals and irrigation ditches. She imagined she was in her own hopscotch game, one foot tucked up, jumping from square to square, with a scribbled Mekong River the largest leap. Suzette remembered the silly rhyme: "Step on a crack, break your mother's back."

She noticed an irregularity in her private board game and looked more closely. There were craters of water. At first she thought they were lakes or swimming pools, then she heard the passenger behind say, "Look at those holes. The Vietcong's been busy dropping bombs on all those American advisers down there."

Suzette wondered if Moon would end up in Vietnam against his will. She doubted it. She recalled his promise that if the draft were ever brought in and he was chosen, he'd shoot himself in the foot. Suzette doubted Moon would have to worry about that.

She didn't think the situation, whatever it really was, meant much to America. It was just more strife in some faraway, unwanted backwater, similar to how she felt about herself.

Suzette was miles high over her birth mother's country, and it was comforting to be on the way somewhere. Her life had gotten lost. Or maybe it had never been hers. She was like an empty concrete chamber that resonated with her own loneliness, echoed with her own footsteps that went nowhere. Merely being alive wasn't enough. Her fling with Moon had been an escape, an American-style freefall into sex, marijuana, even LSD. It had thrown a thin facade over her loneliness, and Moon had dulled the pain.

"I've put my old beater up for sale, Suz!" Moon had said the last time she'd seen him. He'd been drinking Pink Ripple straight from the bottle. Sucking on a joint, he'd burbled, "That acid we did the other day was far out. Did you get off like me?"

She had. And then she had a flashback and was tripping all over again. They had dropped at noon. Moon had checked the time, noting how long it took before they began to buzz. It wasn't long. He ran the water in the bathtub. It hit the porcelain, improvising a guitar riff with a super-loud splash. She was definitely getting off. The bath wasn't just a bath; it was a pool of warm rain. As if she were out of her body, she watched herself undressing, her jeans and blouse landing in a rainbow heap on the floor. She was wide-eyed in a dream that played itself out in 33 1/3 rpm.

Moon drew her to the bath. She was afraid she would fall or disappear. Her legs wobbled, and he steadied her and helped her into the crystal pool. The water on her skin was her only reality. Distances were altered, colors primary. Suzette watched Moon from the bath.

He strummed an invisible guitar and sang, "Half a mile to the countryside and the rain came pouring down..."

She hadn't even realized he was naked until her eyes discovered his cock, which seemed to grow from an innocent sapling to a prehistoric tree crowned with an enormous mushroom cap, everything blooming out of a burnt landscape.

Moon climbed into the tub and lifted Suzette onto his lap. Putting his tongue in her mouth, he entered her, a half inch at a time. He stop kissing her and sang again, softly into her ear, the same jazzy tune, making up the words to mimic her desire: "Oh, the water, ooh, the water, let it run all over me…"

Through a haze she heard herself moan, the music a rush. The water ran unseen hands over her breasts, and her nipples hardened. The liquid lapped and licked as Moon crooned in her ear: "And it stoned me to my soul, stoned me just like a jelly roll…"

Their bodies made love to the lazy words, the bathwater flowing with desire. Moon sang on: "And it stoned me to my soul, and it stoned me just like goin' home…" They had moved in and out of each other until Suzette had climaxed with one orgasm after another, the song's refrain echoing in her mind: *stoned me just like goin' home…*

She knew even then that she needed to feel *home*. But not in the United States. That wasn't her true home, nor was France. She wanted Saigon. She corrected herself—she needed Saigon. Suzette wondered if she would look into the faces of all the women in Vietnam, wondering which one was her mother. She would swim in the South China Sea. It would be the same temperature as her body, and to feel the water around her would be like being born again. Suzette smiled inwardly and shook her head in disbelief. She was almost there. Silently her lips formed a single word: *home*.

The airport touts sized up the crowd while they waited and smoked. Oblivious to the sun's rage, insensible to the oppression of the heat, the touts were middlemen who hawked all manner of services. They got first kick at the can in their bid to bilk travelers and appeared well heeled in comparison to their downtown counterparts. They wore trousers, long-sleeved shirts, and real shoes.

Touts received a "service tax" for luring customers to a hotel, to a girl, to a stolen U.S. Huey or H-21C Shawnee helicopter bristling with rockets, to a weapons dealer, to an afternoon at an opium *fumerie*. If desired, they could supply customers with a lid of Mary Jane, a pound of Saigonese blond, a spoon of coke, or a dime bag of heroin. A good tout bragged he could get you anything. He was clever and spoke a smattering of at least three languages, like most Vietnamese. The "tax" he received for his long, drawn-out sales pitch was miniscule.

The touts were cacophonous in French, Vietnamese, Russian, Chinese, and English. "You need hotel room, lady, lady?"

Suzette stared straight ahead as she propelled herself out of airport customs past the touts and toward the steam of Saigon. She made a beeline to the beat-up cabs that queued by the curb.

"Où, mademoiselle?" an elderly driver asked as she got into his antiquated Citroën.

"Hôtel Majestic, s'il vous plait."

The Majestic rose from the elbow of Tu Do Street. As Suzette got out of the cab and paid the driver, she marveled at the grand hotel's marble splendor. Inside, the desk clerk was busy on the telephone. "If you no like me no more, I know important American who be happy buy me present, take me dinner. I know lots."

Suzette waited patiently, wondering who the young woman was talking to. After a short silence, the clerk slammed the receiver down with a bang that belied her delicate appearance. She wore a translucent silk *aio dai*. Turning back to her job, she beamed and said, "American men no good. Vietnamese men make love better. I give you right advice—find rich Vietnamese."

Not quite sure what to say, Suzette replied, "I haven't met any Vietnamese men yet, but I'm sure you're right."

When the clerk handed her a registration card, Suzette noticed the lobby was quiet. She seemed to be the only guest. The American military advisers rented villas and apartments, while reporters patronized the Rex and Continental hotels a few blocks away.

After Suzette completed the form, the clerk studied it for a moment. "Su-zette O-Bri-an." Then the woman stroked the cover of Suzette's passport. "You lucky. You American girl."

Suzette followed the bellboy to the lift. She'd seen elevators like this one in old movies. Glancing back at the desk clerk, who was dialing a number on the telephone, Suzette recognized the woman's traditional dress from a lost dream. Déjà vu, she thought as the bellboy shut the wrought-iron grille and worked a brass lever.

The elevator rose slowly, then stopped with a shudder on the third floor. When they reached room 304, the bellboy unlocked the door and deposited her suitcase and a small knapsack with an American flag on a foldout table. Then he waited with expectant eyes. Suzette pushed a two-dollar U.S. bill into the boy's white-gloved hand. It was overgenerous and he was overjoyed.

When the bellboy was gone, Suzette closed the door. She'd been given the hotel's Majestic Suite. The mahogany posts of a concubine's bed spiraled. The head and footboard were lyrical with carved wooden hummingbirds, their beaks half obscured in ruffled flowers. Mosquito netting, fine and white, billowed. A ceiling fan spun lazily. The room was exquisite.

Suzette went to the windows, an entire wall of frame after frame of glass. Outside the old-fashioned casements a balcony beckoned. Her eyes lit on a strip of park fronting the wide river. To her right was the wharf. There, watercraft roved, the oddest being the *thung chai*, a gigantic round wicker basket sealed with pitch and used as a rowboat.

Traffic paraded on Tu Do Street and on the adjacent river road: mini-Peugeot and Renault taxis painted white and blue; *cyclos* like baby carriages piloted by sinewy men on bicycles, their arms outstretched to signal turns. Suzette leaned out of the window, her hair a yellow curtain in the sunlight. She could just see to her left the Rang Hung Dao Circle with its newly erected statue that was infamous because the faces were said to look like President Diem's sister-in-law, Madame Nhu. Suzette wondered briefly what historic figures the beautiful statue actually represented.

She thought she could take enough photographs from her hotel balcony to fill Moon's uncle's magazine. That was how she had come to be here: on assignment for Jake Frazer's *View*, a glossy pictorial. Below her the scene on Tu Do laid itself out before her like a living gallery. Children hawked small items; women squatted and cooked *pho*, noodle soup, on sidewalk braziers; men worked diligently on shoe and bicycle repairs; beggars, thin and ragged, sought charitable handouts; and *cyclo* drivers napped, feet up as they waited for passing trade. It was a house with no walls, and she let Saigon into the room and subsequently into her heart.

Suzette laughed out loud. She was exhausted. The flight had taken three whole days, but she was finally in Saigon. She'd nap and then get a recommendation for the best restaurant in the neighborhood. She would celebrate. Get to know her countrymen.

4

FIRST FRIEND

> Is there any solution here the West can offer? But the bar tonight was loud with innocent American voices and that was the worst disquiet. There weren't so many Americans in 1951 and 1952.
>
> —Graham Greene, *Reflections*

Saigon: May 1963

Suzette descended the curve of the Majestic Hotel's stairs directly onto Tu Do Street. She held a copy of *Fielding's Guide to Vietnam*. The cover and paper weren't quite up to Fielding's normal standards, but then the thick book had been illegally copied and bound at a nearby printing press. For the equivalent of twenty-five cents, however, it was a bargain.

Kitty-corner from the Majestic's columned entrance and bright white promenade, the usual flock of *cyclo* drivers lounged in their vehicles, arguing and smoking. "Mademoiselle Suzette, take me, take me!" they called in unison when they saw her bright figure across the confusion of the road. Pushing and shoving, they pulled their carriages toward her.

She smiled and said in French, "Next time. I'm only off to the Continental."

"Tomorrow! Tomorrow!" they chorused.

Suzette laughed. "Tomorrow I'm going to Hué."

As she strolled by Maxim's, she slowed to inspect the photographs of scantily clad Vietnamese beauties on the club bill. Suzette was leisurely making her way to the travel agent desk in the lobby of the Hotel Continental to pick up a train ticket. She planned to journey the next morning to the ancient city of Hué.

In the few weeks Suzette had spent in Saigon she'd explored its slightly run-down colonial core. Buildings and balconies wriggled with intricate motifs, and jalousied windows opened and closed their shutters like painted wings. In the daytime the colonial part of town seemed relatively sedate, but after dark the city rocked, especially Tu Do Street. Neon signs flashed in red and blue, the shades of a psychedelic American flag. The homeless retreated into doorways and alleys, leaving the street to after-hour barkers, pimps, and hookers. When night covered Tu Do, the scene leaped and quivered under a licentious purple flush.

Suzette inhaled. A bouquet of joss sticks, French perfume, and the previous night's liquor, made the edges of her lips lift charmingly. She wandered along the street, her camera bag against her hip. It was still morning. As she walked, she felt she was finally, truly, *in* life. Suzette stopped to pat a small dog, someone's pet, and noticed the leather strings on her sandal had unraveled. She stooped and wound the laces of her huarache twice around her slim ankle, then tied a perfect bow.

"Mademoiselle Suzette, Mademoiselle Suzette!" the street urchins cried, tugging at her pockets. "You buy postcard?"

Taking out her camera, Suzette snapped them, tousled their dusty hair, and walked on. The morning was now in progress. She clicked an American who stood in the embrace of a Vietnamese girl. The soldier's hair was cropped so close that his skull glowed like a cola nut. Suzette watched as the prostitute counted the American dollars the soldier had given her for services rendered.

"I see you tonight?" the girl asked. Then, when the soldier looked for an escape route, she flashed her eyes provocatively. "You go me. I take you round world again." Giggling, she added, "You come me. Other Vietnamese girls, they low. They want only money, they no good. Me, I love you. I make you happy. I your girl."

Suzette turned into Le Loi Street, dodging the *cyclos*, bicycles, and cars as if she'd been born in Saigon. She saw the city through her camera, her real eye. Nothing shocked or surprised her. She made no judgments; she saw only the bustle, the sensual hustle. A beggar in a shred of ARVN camouflage garb stared up at her, eyes glazed. His trousers were cut off and tied where his legs should have been. One arm was missing and the elbow was round at the end like a scarred and scabby knee. He was propped on a low wooden platform with wheels. A battered tin cup hung around his neck.

She watched the beggar with the eye of her camera. Through the lens she focused on his background: a glass window and behind the window a bustling café. Suzette viewed the maimed veteran in relation to his surroundings. She saw the picture within its frame. Through the café's window well-dressed men and women, mostly Saigonese and a few Americans and French, chatted. They sipped coffee, black and steaming, from the pure white circles of their cups. A few, mostly American men, drank imported Hamm's and Budweiser from pilsner glasses with thin gold rims. White-suited waiters served croissants and rosettes of iced butter.

Putting her subject, the amputee beggar, in the foreground, Suzette focused. She pressed her finger, clicking the shutter, then repeated the action. Approaching him, she stuffed a crumpled wad of piastres into the man's hand. He looked up at her with incandescent eyes, laughed softly, and scooted away.

Suzette was thirsty. She would have freshly pressed lime juice with soda and people-watch while she sat in Girval's. Her loneliness was at bay. Saigon's exotic ways and the locals' endearing, though poverty-induced friendliness, along with her purpose, her photography, pricked her to life again. To be truthful, she felt higher than a kite every hour in Saigon, minus Moon, minus Geoff, and minus LSD.

She opened Girval's glass door and waited to be seated. There were no single empty tables and she was led to a gentleman's booth. Looking aloof and reading a paper with what seemed like voracious speed, he waved her away, hand up, palm out.

"Oh, I'm sorry," she whispered in French, turning to go.

The gentleman stood in a hurry, dropping his papers on the floor. He gestured again and she stopped. This time he motioned for her to come back, his palm facing in. She saw that he was small in stature and wore eyeglasses with thick lenses.

"You speak French?" he queried uncertainly. When she replied affirmatively, he said, "I was concentrating so hard on this scientific treatise that I didn't look up at first. I thought you were Vietnamese. To a Vietnamese the gesture I made means, 'Come sit with me.' But then when you spoke and began to walk away I looked closer and realized my mistake. You're American, aren't you? I know that in the Western world my gesture means, 'Go away.' I should have been paying attention. Please accept my humble apologies and join me."

Suzette felt his acute embarrassment and sat opposite him in the booth. He introduced himself as Van Minh and told her that his wife lived and worked in Paris, where he had recently sent his niece so she could attend the Sorbonne. Van said he missed them both. He was obviously pleased to have her company and she appreciated that.

They talked for some time and Suzette learned that he was a scientist at the Pasteur Institute. She told him about her photography and her planned trip to Hué. The afternoon flew by, and eventually she said she had to leave. Before she got up Van invited her to dinner on Saturday at the Soi Kinh Lan Restaurant, saying he'd treat her to the best Chinese dim sum in town. Suzette happily accepted, agreeing to meet him at the restaurant at 7:00 p.m.

Back on the street she continued on to the Continental, picking up the thread of the day's errand to purchase a ticket for the morning train to Hué. As she passed the Opera House and peered up at the beautiful alabaster angels, she realized something—she had made her first Vietnamese friend.

5

DEADLY INCIDENT

There is no explanation for evil. It must be looked upon as a necessary part of the order of the universe. To ignore it is childish, to bewail it senseless.

—Somerset Maugham, *The Summing Up*

Hué, South Vietnam: May 1963

Kiet hadn't received a draft order from the army, but he expected one. It was merely a matter of time. It would come by way of the post and then his landlord. Kiet checked the return address on each letter he received with trepidation. Kim had received his order and fled to Cambodia rather than be a private in the front lines. Kiet wondered why Kim's wealthy father hadn't bought him an officer's commission, though he doubted Kim would have accepted, anyway. Kiet viewed Kim's action as cowardice, but when he discovered the key and paid-up lease to his friend's apartment he was elated. Kim had slipped them under Kiet's door as promised with a note vowing eternal friendship. Although he disagreed with Kim's flight, he knew his friend had a good heart.

The weekend loomed long and dull. Without Kim who would join him for beers? So Kiet was ecstatic when Mr. Thé, the general treasurer, asked him to travel to Hué. He'd never been far from Saigon, and besides, he figured fresh scenery might distract him from his lustful thoughts about Mai Ling. Kiet had heard much praise for the famous Huong, or Perfume, River, that ran through the Central Region of South Vietnam and through Hué. The river was reputed to be the cleanest in the country.

Kiet decided that after his trip to Hué he would move his few belongings from his rented room to his new digs on Le Duan Boulevard. His rooming house was a derelict building and he was thrilled to be moving up in the world.

Shopping was in order. For the cooler temperatures of the Central Region he purchased a wool sweater of French origin in the Ben Than Market. When he returned home, he modeled the sweater for his own satisfaction. "I could be mistaken for that dashing American movie star, Cary Grant," he said to himself. "For sure some clever girl will notice me in Hué." He rifled through a box on the floor. Underneath his prize possession, a much-thumbed copy of *Playboy*, he found what he wanted—a map of Hué. One more thing and he'd be set. He placed the land-compensation check that he was to deliver in the inside pocket of his case. Smiling at the prospect of his impending adventure, he chuckled. "It's going to be my lucky day. I know it!"

Lavender mist was strung like hammocks between Hué's mountains. Nearer to Kiet a male peacock, feathers spread, shrieked. A Vietnamese family, obviously on a pilgrimage to culture, fussed in front of a peach tree, making ready for a portrait against the blossoms.

Shaking off a headache that had begun on the bone-crunching bus trip, Kiet wandered about, soaking up the atmosphere. Basket boats with hooped roofs of woven rushes were anchored by the riverbanks, and orchids, the color of the mist and the water, hung with parasitic grace from banyan trees that lined the shore. But he wasn't impressed. Kiet preferred the nonstop action of Saigon's river where long-necked boats slid between navy ships and flat freighters anchored splendidly in their sienna cloaks of rust. However, he did admit that Hué was romantic.

Kiet picked a frangipani and sniffed with appreciation. A cluster of Hué's traditionally garbed women passed by, and his eyes settled on their conical poem hats. The braided rattan was translucent, and delicate tracings of birds and pagodas were revealed in the sunlight, making Kiet privy to their palm-leaf secrets. The women's hair fell down their backs like satin ribbons.

When Kiet reached the Citadel, Vietnam's legendary Imperial City, he knew from his history lessons that the splendid royal tomb and palace had been built in the early nineteenth century by the Nguyen emperors. Kiet dug in his pocket for a match and lit a cigarette beside the canal that surrounded the Citadel. Its glazed tiles gleamed yellow, the imperial color that only royalty was customarily allowed. With a man's eye he admired the impenetrable walls and their ten gates with watchtowers.

Kiet consulted his map again. Enough history, he decided. Like the past, history was a colossal bore. A drink was called for, and he'd go girl-watching in the town. He walked and smoked, not thinking about anything in particular, but appreciating the change of scene. Nearing a plaza, he saw what he at first thought was a hallucination: saffron robes hovered like a stain, their hems making a bold stroke on the gray square. Blue and white flags twitched in the breeze. Kiet picked up his pace to see what the commotion was.

A crowd blocked his view. He stood on his toes, attempting to see over the shorn heads of the Buddhists, but couldn't. "Excuse me," he said to a fellow standing beside him, "what kind of demonstration is this?"

"The Buddhist monks are asking for broadcasting time from the local radio station," the man explained. "They were denied and they're angry because President Diem has forbidden them to mark Buddha's birthday by displaying flags. The Catholics are flying their papal banners, as you can see, to celebrate Archbishop Thuc's ordination twenty-five years ago."

Kiet was perplexed. "Who is this Archbishop Thuc and what right has he to interfere with a celebration of Buddha's birthday?"

"Who is Thuc? He's only Diem's older brother, which means he has the right to do anything he likes."

The rumble of an army motorcade interrupted their conversation. Five armored military vehicles pulled up near the radio station. An officer got out of one of them and spoke through a loudspeaker. His assembled troops stood behind him. Some of the onlookers dispersed, allowing Kiet to see. He moved farther from the motorcade and to the right of the saffron bonzes where his attention was drawn to a young woman. She dropped a matchbook as she tried to position her camera to take a picture. Kiet couldn't see her face properly, but her hair was yellow, the royal hue, and her mouth curved deliciously.

The Buddhist chanting and the officer's angry voice from the loudspeaker faded as he admired the girl. He watched her as her camera clicked. He wanted to *be* the camera caressed by her hands; he wanted to *be* the camera bag slung over her shoulder and touching her hip. Kiet stood so still that he could feel the cotton of her jeans against her legs, as if *he* were that cotton.

A glint of metal touched the periphery of his consciousness and broke his rapture. A small metal object left a soldier's hand and flew through the air toward the plaza and radio station. Kiet knew what it was instantly and pounced on the camera-wielding girl, pushing her down onto the ground. She fought for a moment, then became rigid when she heard an explosion, screams, and rifle fire. The wounded fell as quickly as autumn leaves, the monks' saffron robes blossoming red as if dipped in dye.

soft flesh
and sharp-edged metal
like open virgin thighs
drips red-hot blood
that blinds the senses
and gouges out the eyes

Ambulance sirens shrieked, almost blotting out the terrible moans and cries of the injured. Kiet felt a warm trickle in his mouth. When he touched his face, his hand came away bloody. He reached into his pocket for his handkerchief but couldn't find it. On the pavement in front of him, though, he spotted the photographer's matchbook. But the girl had vanished.

6

COUP AFTER COUP

I don't think the war can be won unless the people support the effort, and in my opinion, in the last two months the [South Vietnamese] government has gotten out of touch with the people.

—John F. Kennedy interview with Walter Cronkite

Saigon: May 1963

Every Saigonese under twenty-five years of age knew about Club La Danse, and every visiting foreigner under fifty frequented the nightspot. There was foreign music and dancing. Saigon's Big Boss received plenty of protection money to keep Madame Nhu's vice squad away. The illicit club boasted brazenly, advertising its name and address on matchbooks distributed in hotels and shops throughout the city. The *cyclo* drivers recommended it and received an incentive of piastres from the management for each customer they dropped at the door.

Finding himself in front of La Danse, Kiet fingered the matchbook he'd retrieved in Hué. He'd been to the club before, but not often. The drinks were too expensive for his meager government-clerk salary, and he hoped he wasn't wasting his hard-earned piastres.

The door shot open and a couple tumbled into the street. Kiet propelled himself in and through the blue haze. Liquor teased, shoulders shimmied, and feet and hips imitated the bongo beat. Kiet loved music, especially French love songs. Kim had teased him unmercifully, calling him a foolish romantic. As if by magic, he heard the words of his favorite song: *I'll be waiting, I'll be waiting for you.* The lyric transformed his mood. It was his lucky day for sure, he thought, his eyes searchlights in the crowd.

Kiet threaded his way through the throng to the bar and leaned against its polished wooden length. There, just a few bar stools down, was the young woman who had mesmerized him that terrible day in Hué when he saved her life.

In Saigon, after he got back from that trip, he'd scanned the newspaper headlines and been dismayed. The media falsely reported that the Vietcong had thrown a grenade into the crowd during a simple Buddhist gathering. But everyone there knew that one of President Diem's own soldiers had set off the massacre.

Kiet could have kicked himself for wandering away that day in Hué rather than staying to find the girl and make sure she was all right. He'd been in shock and wasn't thinking straight. He remembered feeling stupid about not having a handkerchief to clean the blood that had flowed down his face. But that didn't matter now. His dream had come true—he'd found her again and she was more than all right. She looked wonderful. He kissed the matchbook and placed it carefully in his pocket.

There was no mistaking this young woman. He couldn't miss those long legs in their tight American jeans, not after he'd covered them with his own in the square of the city he now knew was the most romantic on earth. How could he forget those lips that curved like spiraling notes played by the *dan*, Vietnam's lute? How could he forget her royal hair? He moved closer and noted that her chin rested in one hand. She was deep in thought.

The throb of the music became mere background to Kiet as he stepped nearer. Finally he stood behind her and waited. Then she twisted her body and it happened again: nothing else existed. As her head turned, he memorized every inch of her face. Just to be certain, Kiet snapped his fingers to get her full attention, and she smiled.

"Hi," she said casually in English with an American accent.

"Do you want me to call the bartender?" She stared at Kiet. "I've seen you before, haven't I!"

"Do you speak French?" Kiet replied in his halting English.

She switched to French immediately. "My name's Suzette O'Brian. I'm a photographer for *View* magazine."

Kiet called on the image he saluted every morning in his mirror. "I am Nguyen Son Kiet, but you can call me Kiet. You're the most beautiful woman I've ever seen."

Suzette's lips curved upward in the sweet way she had. "Where do I know you from?"

"I am the man who saved you in Hué!" Kiet said, knowing it was the best opening line there could ever be.

"My God! I'm so glad you're here. I wanted so much to thank you. In all the confusion and smoke, somehow I couldn't find you. Please sit down." Suzette gestured at the empty stool beside her. When he sat, she saw the bandage on his forehead and reached out to touch it.

"It's nothing. All that mattered was you," Kiet said, then went on to speak of his love of dancing, music, and poetry, charming Suzette.

They talked against a background of swirling couples. The women wore elegant dresses and the men sported crumpled white silk suits. When Suzette admired the men's attire, Kiet told her the slubbed fabric was called tussore.

The dancers were mostly Vietnamese. They tangoed cheek to cheek and then angled their necks as if listening to a mutual inner voice. They danced as if there might be no tomorrow. But the feeling, the tango, and the war were nothing new to Saigon, and dance clubs were just another illegal element in an already louche and edgy city.

"It must be fate that you saved my life in Hué," Suzette said softly around a sip of her vermouth cassis on ice. "I'm half Vietnamese, you know. I feel that Vietnam is closer to me than my American or French heritage."

"But you're lucky to be an American!"

"I'm not so lucky. And besides, I'm more Vietnamese and French. I carry a U.S. passport, but I hate America and what it stands for."

"Why do you say that?" Kiet asked, leaning closer to hear her above the club's din.

"I'm not accepted in the States because I'm part Vietnamese."

"I don't believe that. You outshine any woman in the entire world."

Suzette was silent, but he knew by her face that his outspoken admiration had cheered her.

He laughed. "It's hot and smoky here. I'll take you to Saigon's best nightspots."

"Sounds good. It's about time I saw Saigon through the eyes of my hero *and* my countryman."

Kiet and Suzette roved from nightclub to nightclub. At each underground spot they had a drink and an illicit dance. Kiet's footwork was smooth and lithe. He drew Suzette closer with each step. Their mouths were at exactly the same height, and when she turned her head, their lips brushed.

"It feels like an eternity since I've had so much fun," Suzette said, her mouth by his ear.

While they sat at quiet tables their talk became serious. Kiet was amazed about her adopted American family, but he was saddened by her past. She explained her burning need to look for the Vietnamese roots she'd never known, telling him about her French father and how she loved him totally, even when he wasn't himself and behaved like a devil, or a dead man. She said she didn't know why, but that her love for her father hadn't been enough for him, how it wasn't his fault that he drank, that it was the unhappiness of losing the Vietnamese woman he loved, her mother, that filled him with so much pain. Most of all Suzette told Kiet about the mother whose name she'd never even heard, the mother who had supposedly returned to Vietnam when Suzette was just a baby.

Kiet listened attentively, his eyes never leaving hers while she exhausted the telling of her life. She included her sadness about Jimmy's suicide and her powerlessness to help her friend Val. He knew she was voicing every thought she'd ever tried to bury.

At their last club they eventually looked around and realized the music had stopped and they were alone. When they left the bar, Saigon's streets were dark and silent. "I'll take you to your hotel if we can find a *cyclo* driver," Kiet offered. He still had a few piastres in his pocket.

Hand in hand, they strolled the slumbering street, Suzette unaware of Vietnamese custom and Kiet not giving a damn if all Vietnam saw them. Beneath a street sign a lone *cyclo* driver slept, the cracked soles of his feet a reminder of his station in life. Kiet woke the driver and chatted amicably with him in Vietnamese, arranging a few hours of his time.

"I'll get in first. You sit on my knee," Kiet said to Suzette.

The *cyclo* driver dipped the worn leather carriage, and Kiet hopped in. Suzette followed, allowing him to encircle her with his arms as the driver pushed them through the city.

"Shall we watch the sunrise?" Kiet asked.

Suzette nodded, and when she glanced up, she saw the moon trailing tattered clouds like a kite. They pedaled by buildings and balconies tumbled with shadows. They rolled past winged porticos and lofty columns of pale marble and ocher plaster. Then, suddenly, the countryside beckoned with green fingers. Bats flitted by, their cloaked bodies on a mission to a midnight snack. The air was rich with the perfume of night-blooming flowers, and the landscape appeared to be carved out of jade. Tiny spears of rice rippled in the mirrored stripes of irrigation. The rows repeated until the scene broke at a horizon that was as dull blue as an evening sea.

"We shouldn't go any farther," Kiet said. "The Vietcong are out there."

Suzette frowned. "I don't believe it. We're only a mile from Saigon."

Kiet made a scary face. "The VC are everywhere and they're out to get you!"

Suzette looked surprised, so Kiet spoke seriously. "Actually it's true. The Vietcong are everywhere."

As she snuggled into Kiet, he placed a hand on her bare midriff. They passed a dike with newly laid giant concrete pipes, ready for the government's distilled-water project. Then there were more rice fields displayed like green carpets.

"A place to make love while the sun's still sleeping," Kiet murmured, chancing a kiss on the nape of her neck.

"Shall we stop and walk and give the driver a rest?" Suzette suggested, smiling.

Kiet asked the driver to stop, instructing him to return when the sun rose. He handed the driver his remaining piastres, not bothering to count them, then took Suzette's hand and pulled her across the road and beneath a stand of trees.

"I'm lucky to have met you, Kiet," Suzette whispered, putting her arms around his neck and pulling him close, tracing his lips with the point of her tongue.

Untying Suzette's blouse, Kiet said, "If you mind, I'll stop."

She slipped off her blouse in answer and took Kiet's hands, placing them on her braless breasts.

He shuddered. "You have the breasts of a goddess, but your nipples are so pale. Vietnamese women have flat chests and dark nipples."

Suzette smiled. "Do you prefer Vietnamese girls?"

"No," Kiet breathed. "I could never look at a Vietnamese woman again after being with you." Removing his jacket, he placed it on the ground. The gold buttons dug into the black earth.

Suzette unzipped her jeans. "Help me take these off. They're too tight."

Kiet knelt before her and tugged. She lifted her feet for him like a helpful child, and he saw that her leather sandals were tied at the ankles with bows. When Suzette abandoned the ruffled panties she wore, Kiet's eyes widened. He smiled at her suggestively.

"Yes," she said in a soft voice, no longer hearing the tiny lizards that sang *chick-chack* in the fields.

With his tongue he explored the rosy lips and pink bud that poked from her thatch of pubic hair. "Vietnamese women are like hairless Chihuahuas compared to you," he muttered.

Suzette wriggled on Kiet's jacket as he thrust his tongue deeper and deeper. Her eyelids fluttered and he kissed his way up to them, feeding her senses.

"God, you're good," she murmured. "I've never been so excited."

"I'll show you how much *you* excite me. My pants are tight, too." He winked as he unbuttoned his fly and let loose his penis.

"Oh, Kiet," she said breathlessly, "I've never seen anything like it. It's so smooth, no hair at all, and such a color!"

Kiet chuckled. "I may not be six feet tall, but my cock thinks it is." He took it in his hand and rolled it against Suzette's thigh, then brushed it lightly over her pussy. Gently he teased her clit, coaxing, tantalizing, causing her to moan. "Are you ready?"

"Oh, yes," she said, sighing.

Kiet entered her, pulled away, entered again until his cock filled her. He could feel her change inside, as if her senses connected, streamed, and connected again. Then she stiffened and cried out, tumbling back to earth in a gradual spiral.

When she opened her eyes, she marveled at the early-morning

workers gliding across a distant paddy. They appeared to walk on water, and she imagined she was one of them. She wore a peasant's pajamas and conical hat and swept across the horizon like a triangular boat on the sea.

he touched my soul
I was mad with desire
he made me whole
lifted me from the mire

Together they heard the primeval husking of a Saurus crane's wide wings, and at that moment Kiet orgasmed.

Afterward, he lit a cigarette and leaned on his elbow, exhausted. Above them the night had left behind wisps of vapor that had begun to catch the rays of the sun while it was still below the horizon.

"Let's celebrate," Kiet said. He had purchased a can of beer at the last club. Now he flipped it open and offered her some. "American women are so different. You, Suzette, are a tigress."

"No thanks to the beer, but I'll try a cigarette," she said, grinning at him. As he bent over to light it, she asked, "Do you have a girlfriend?"

Kiet smiled. "I've known a few women, but none make me feel like you."

She glowered in mock jealousy. "Well, then, I hope I'm the last woman you know."

"Aren't you a beautiful boss!" Kiet ran a hand over her upturned hip. "If you keep that up, you'll remind me too much of the Vietnamese woman who cut off her husband's cock while he slept. She was punishing him for making love to another woman."

Suzette laughed. "I admit that's a little extreme. But I've found my Vietnamese lover and I'm going to keep him. How many girls get to go steady with a man who saved their life?"

Kiet kissed her. When the slow tonguing ended, he stroked her cheek. "If I don't watch it, I might fall in love with you."

"Would that be so bad?" he asked.

She gazed into his eyes. "No, it wouldn't."

Kiet ran a hand through his hair. It was slick with dew. "I must tell you more about myself, Suzette. My father's dead. He was educated in France, and most of his life he slaved as a public servant. He's the reason I'm lucky enough to have my government job. My father loved gambling. His terrible habit eventually ruined all of us. If he wasn't betting the money from my mother's dowry at the Casino du Grand Monde, or the Parc des Attractions in Cholon, he was at neighborhood cockfights. If he couldn't bet on a cockfight, he'd play mahjong or cards, usually *vingt-et-un*, for our grocery money. My father's addiction eventually killed him. When he came down with a deadly type of malaria, there was no money left for medicine."

It was her turn to stroke his cheek. "You can't believe how much I understand what you feel. We're alike. Our history's the same. As I told you, my own father ruined his life because of sadness and alcoholism. He's dead, too."

"I wish I could take all your unhappiness away, Suzette. I can't stand to see you sad. But I must tell you more. I had an older sister. She'd have been thirty if she'd lived, probably married with kids. But our politics robbed us of her, something all too typical in this unfortunate country. My sister joined the Vietminh in 1954. She died fighting the French that same year. My mother's never been the same. When my mother finds out I have to go into the army, I don't know what she'll do. I don't go home often. It's too difficult. My mother hates my dead father for not leaving her any money. She's forced to live in a slum. I send all the piastres I can to her."

Suzette lay on her stomach, one hand supporting her chin. For the first time she could remember she was conscious of seeing life clearly. She was there with it, not looking in through someone else's window. It was as if the icy glass pane had been removed from her vision.

"I finished my secondary schooling with honors," Kiet continued. "I studied and had hopes of continuing my education, but my plans were shattered when my father died. I was so disillusioned that I joined a friend who was sailing to the North after the division of Vietnam. Even though I'm not a Communist, I was going to throw in with Ho Chi Minh and the Vietminh, thinking that was what my sister would have wanted. But I changed my mind fast, mainly because of guilt at leaving my poor mother destitute. So I jumped off my friend's small boat right in Saigon's muddy harbor and almost drowned. Soon after I accepted a clerical job at the General Treasury. It's my father's old position."

"Don't be sad. You're a hero, remember? You saved my life in Hué. You must have been fated to protect me. Now I'll make it my fate to ensure you're happy," Suzette said, lifting her head.

"Suzette, I must warn you that I have no future. My mother brought a fortune to my father as a dowry, but I'll inherit nothing thanks to my father's gambling debts."

"But, Kiet, you've got a government job. Don't worry about it. In the U.S. kids make it on their own. So, you see, you're just like any American. You're just like me."

Kiet's manner was jaunty again, but then he remembered something. "I have another confession. My parents arranged a marriage for me, but my change of fortune made me an unsuitable mate. Her family reneged on the agreement. In their eyes I'm not worthy. So there, now you have it all. I've never told anyone these things before."

Suzette recalled how Geoff had dumped her because his parents wouldn't accept her Vietnamese heritage, but she didn't care about that anymore. In fact, she was glad of it. The experience had pushed her out of someone else's nest and over to

Vietnam in search of her roots.

"I really could fall in love with you," she said again, believing in her own words and consequently in the future.

He smiled, almost wistfully. "It's too late for me. I've already fallen in love with you." And in a sunlit curve of road their *cyclo* appeared, looking like an antiquated chariot.

7

BEDROOMS AND BAPTISMS

Let them burn and we shall clap our hands.
—Madame Nhu

Saigon: June 1963

Kiet and Suzette's apartment—actually Kim's—was compressed within identical two-story villas, leftovers from the French regime. The buildings' exteriors had deteriorated and their builder wouldn't have recognized them. The finish was gangrenous from monsoon weather and a century of peeling plaster and paint, but the complex's location on the tiny extension of Nguyen Du Street across from a hospital and touching on Le Duan, the boulevard that led to the bombed Presidential Palace, was perfect. It was close to public transport that enabled Kiet to get to where he worked, and the Central Market with its foodstuffs was a few minutes by *cyclo*, as was Tu Do Street with its shopping and nonstop action.

The second-story apartment in Kiet's villa was marked number 10, and the ground level of the building had been converted into a convenience store that sold sodas, bottled water, plastic toys, and rain ponchos to the nuns and physicians who worked at the hospital. The upstairs of the villa was divided in half, but the apartment next to Kiet's, number 11, remained empty. It wasn't comfortable enough to attract the American advisers who rented or purchased the better villas across town, nor were the physicians interested. The apartments had never been renovated, and the wail of hospital sirens limited their rental value.

As soon as she moved in, Suzette set about making the apartment into a love nest for herself and Kiet. She sanded and buffed the wide plank floors and unpainted wooden shutters, finishing them with a coat of palm oil, then primped and prepared the pocked walls and transformed them with red lacquer. In no time at all she replaced the ceiling fans with enormous models made in nearby Singapore. Once switched on, they spun like tops. When she was pleased with her decorating, she scoured the markets for equipment and supplies to develop her film, hoping to transform the bathroom into a darkroom. But for the first while she had her negatives developed in town at a small lab near the General Post Office. That delightful ocher building was close by, too, and located at the head of Tu Do.

The arrangement was very convenient for her work. The editor of *View* was publishing a pictorial series on Asia for his quarterly glossy. Few magazine photographers traveled to Vietnam at that time, and Suzette received a stream of checks, almost as if she were employed in-house. She cashed them at Saigon's Banque Indochine, located beside the Office of Information and Propaganda. Her dollars went a long way, and she and Kiet ate in local restaurants and frequented every single nightclub that was popular in Saigon. However, it was through the eye of her camera and in Saigon's streets where she observed the culture that she now desired to be part of but that had never been hers. And it was in the apartment with Kiet that she so fervently attempted to change her past by embracing her Vietnamese heritage.

One morning, as always, the humid air lay on Saigon like a woolen blanket. The honeycombed mosquito netting flickered above Suzette and Kiet's bed to the ceiling fan's rhythm and click, not unlike the snap of fingers. Suzette sat on Kiet's knee in a sea-grass chair, and they could both still smell the paint and palm oil of Suzette's renovations. The scent lingered longer than she thought possible. Everything loitered like a slowly unraveling dream in the torrid heat.

Kiet was talking to her about Kim, saying that he would trust his best friend with his life. She adored the safe feeling of sitting in Kiet's lap and stroked his hair as he reminisced about the good times he'd had with his friend. He told her that Kim was like the brother he'd never had. But as he spoke, Suzette was reminded of Seattle and her girlfriend Val, which caused tears to well in her eyes. To avoid Kiet's gaze she cradled her head in the crook of his neck; she didn't want him to see her sudden sadness.

She now understood how Val felt about Tyrone and how nothing else mattered when you loved a man deeply. But then she thought of poor Jimmy and of her father, too. She'd never cheat on Kiet, hurt him as Val had done Jimmy, hurt him the way her Vietnamese mother had her father. Lives had been ruined by their actions.

Suzette also blamed America where Val was concerned. She believed couples thought too little of loyalty in America. They were selfish and spoilt. But then she didn't like to blame anything on Val. Her friend had been good to her. Val had been her only girlfriend. She was like a sister. Why hadn't Val met Tyrone first? Everything was fate, Suzette realized. She always laughed at Kiet and his talk about luck, but she now believed in it. Luck and fate. And death.

Kiet talked on, and Suzette pushed memories of Jimmy and his suicide away, replacing them with reflections on her lucky new life in Saigon. She remembered that day in Hué in May. She'd been really lucky then. Kiet had saved her life. She could have been blown to smithereens. In some ways, back then, she wouldn't have cared. But now Kiet and Saigon had shaken away her horrible sadness.

Suzette thought about Kiet. He was the missing piece in her jigsaw puzzle of a life. He made her feel loved, even more than Geoff had. Kiet made her feel like only her father could when he'd *really* been with her. She wanted to be Kiet's life, and she loved every bit of him: his eyes that she wished she could both drown and swim in; his mouth that made her yearn to lick it like a piece of sweet Vietnamese candy; his hard body whose color she couldn't yet find the proper word for—not gold, not bronze, not black like Tyrone's, but beautiful, anyway, with pale blue veins running down the inside of his arms and through his chest.

She loved his silly humor, the way he cut up for her each morning in front of the mirror like an actor in a movie. He'd jump out of bed, a naked jack-in-the-box, and clown for her under the rollicking fan. She'd watch him, a smile lingering on her face as he'd salute in the mirror, wink, kiss her lips, put on his aviator glasses with a flourish, and proudly head for work. Kiet bragged to her that because he loved her he could tackle the world.

And she loved and admired the Vietnameseness of him. To her it had come to mean being hopeful, being happy, even when life treated him shabbily or didn't measure up to his expectations.

Suzette would emulate Kiet and his culture and one day have his children. Vietnamese children. And here in Saigon they would never be called half-caste. They would never be taunted as she had been all her life until now. The Vietnamese weren't racist, she believed. Kiet loved her and didn't care that she was half-caste. He accepted that about her, and so did someone else: Van, the friend she had made before she met Kiet. From that first Chinese dinner she'd had with Van and on all the occasions she'd enjoyed with him since, Suzette had felt as if she'd always known the gentle scientist.

As Kiet spun more tales about his adventures with Kim, Suzette thought about family. Kiet and Van were her family now. Vietnam was her birthright. It was fate, and luck, that had brought her home.

To Suzette Saigon was an earthy hothouse. It had been clear to her from the moment she had gazed down on Tu Do from her fantasy suite at the Majestic that the streets were an extension of the buildings the people inhabited. The locals performed their toilet in public, and even in the bigger houses the doors were thrown welcomingly wide. She wandered the city, snapping frame after frame of the precocious street urchins selling leather-bound books of postage stamps from when the Republic of Vietnam was still Indochina. They hawked Chiclets, postcards, and hairy coconuts with cheap plastic straws. Suzette wheedled smiles from beggar children with round eyes, their tiny palms invariably thrust at passersby. She coaxed grins from and put glints in the eyes of men who worked like pack animals, bamboo rods as strong as steel shouldering their burdens. She shot roll after roll of film of wizened old men with French berets twinkling with war medals, of crones with faces like Kiet's crumpled map of Hué, of girls enveloped in the poetic *aio dais*. And she captured Buddhist monks in robes so vivid that even against Saigon's ocher buildings they leaped off the photographic paper.

Foreigners contributed to the city's character, too. She snapped handsome Americans in uniform hanging out in front of the Continental's glittering globe and looking as if just standing there would make them famous. Vietnamese girls, some as young as fourteen, solicited the soldiers incessantly. The girls forsook the *aio dai* and strutted in skirts that ended a few inches below their thighs. They wore cheap nylon blouses, binding pantyhose, and whatever else they thought fashionable American women wore.

In the middle of the afternoon Suzette returned home to their apartment, her mind still reveling in the sights. She retreated into the tiny bathroom where her developing fluids brought her visions to life. She usually finished before five o'clock so Kiet wouldn't see or interfere. She hid her equipment in the cupboard beneath the sink. Whenever he caught her at it, he argued with her, or if she attempted to show him her photographs, he sulked and walked away. Maybe Kiet disliked her photography because he wanted to protect her from Saigon's streets where she roamed too freely, or perhaps, like her father, he had a need to keep her to himself. She understood that.

But sometimes when she stared at her creations, a fear that her photography was meaningless, that it meant nothing, would creep over her. What if her art meant she would always be alone, always be an outsider, a spectator merely watching from a safe distance? Suzette loved to take photographs, especially in Saigon, so she hoped that wasn't true. She blamed herself when Kiet argued with her about her art and the evening was ruined. So it was easier to hide her work and say nothing, even though she longed to talk with him about her photography.

He disagreed with her about Saigon, too. When she'd say she was going to stay with him in Saigon forever, he'd answer that she must be crazy and that only a fool like him would stay in Vietnam by choice. And he'd roll his eyes at her, meaning he didn't understand her.

Sometimes Suzette penned letters to the O'Brians in answer to their worried correspondence that attempted to persuade her to come home. Suzette ignored their pleas and stuck to the innocuous and happy parts of her life in Saigon. She told them how her photographic skills had blossomed and that it helped her to feel connected to her Vietnamese heritage. To her, she wrote, photography was a joy. She said little about Kiet and less about what he told her went on in Saigon. Suzette knew better than to worry her adoptive parents with stories of politics and danger. She thought often of asking the O'Brians to call the university library to hunt down Val's address. She hated to lose touch with her friend for good. But she knew she couldn't face Val's pain yet, so she never actually put her request into words.

Suzette delighted in Vietnamese cuisine and experimented with it using a French-language cookbook. She had mastered *cha gio*, Vietnamese spring rolls, and *pho*, Kiet's favorite rice-noodle-and-beef soup. The secret was freshness. She took a *cyclo* to the nearby Central Market most days and chose pungent coriander and white stalks of lemongrass, haggling over cash amounts that were equivalent to less than an American penny, something Kiet had told her always to do. With trepidation she braved the market's bloody butchers' avenue. Holding a handkerchief discreetly to her nose, she selected the slab of meat that crawled with the fewest flies.

Kiet tried to teach her to speak Vietnamese, but the lessons began with Suzette in his lap and ended with a duet of wild laughter at her strange pronunciation. He would hoot and say, "You can't pronounce it that way. You sound like a North Vietnamese. Like a Vietcong." Then he'd beg her to say it again, holding her slim waist so she couldn't get away.

When Suzette met her friend Van, they got together in a restaurant or café, but one day he began inviting both her and Kiet to his house, with its wooden door carved with a dragon for luck and ceilings that soared to cathedral heights. Kiet had taken to Van and called him "Uncle" in the Vietnamese way. Van's exotic garden was even more beautiful than the rainforest Suzette had known in Washington State. Kiet informed Suzette that the district beyond central Saigon where Van lived was the most elegant residential section in the entire city. Tropical birds were attracted to the garden as if it were a natural aviary. They swooped and fluttered, flashing emerald and ruby tails. It seemed to Suzette that these little birds that sang so sweetly represented the happiness derived from nature and friendship in Vietnam.

Suzette taught Van to play backgammon, as she had done with Kiet. They would challenge one another after sets of three. One Saturday afternoon Suzette practiced Vietnamese cooking with Van. Kiet was hilarious with his bumbling attempts at being their sous-chef.

After living in Seattle, it was astonishing to Suzette that she embraced Saigon's Third World lifestyle so passionately, with its never-ending poverty, open sewers, sporadic electricity, and water that was unfit for human consumption. But she didn't mind all that; in fact, quite the reverse. She wasn't spoilt in the least and her early nomadic life with her father on the backroads of France had encompassed poverty.

Suzette loved their simple apartment. The windows had no glass and the louvered shutters ran the length of the place. She found it ingenious the way a simple twist of a pole changed the slats' angle to let in the street scene below, or screen them from sight. When Saigon's rain was light, the noise and clatter of pedestrians, bicycles, and *cyclos* was a muffled whisper through their windows. When the rain became a torrent and the ditches in the street were flooded, they'd watch the locals take shelter in doorways or continue pedaling their bicycles and *cyclos* under the cover of scratched, barely translucent plastic. Suzette loved everything, minded nothing except what Kiet called *gián*, the saucer-size cockroaches that marched across their apartment floor.

Once Kiet laughed uproariously when Suzette asked, "What's that, Kiet?" But when he felt her shudder under the thin cloth of her Chinese-style robe, he took action and smashed the giant insects with his shoe, chasing them as they scattered under the shadow of his raised hand. He deposited their corpses outside at the same time telling Suzette to sleep and that he would return in the blink of an eye. It was already near midnight, but he scoured downtown by foot, looking for a late-night convenience store. The shop below their apartment had been shuttered since the dinner hour. Kiet returned a few hours before sunup with a box of boric acid. He sprinkled the white powder along the cockroaches' routes while Suzette watched warily from the couch, having left the protective enclosure of the mosquito netting to wait up for Kiet.

When he was finished his task and scrupulously washed his hands, he swept Suzette into his arms and carried her back to their bed stuffed with raw cotton and shrouded with diaphanous netting. He disrobed her as if she were a child. And while the rain drummed a song they played a game. Suzette was the Saigon River at the beginning of time. Kiet's light kisses were the caresses of a thousand purple water hyacinths floating on her smooth skin to the South China Sea. When Kiet put his thick cock inside her, she imagined he was the water hyacinth trying to take root. She was the shore, feeding and pulling him into her depths. She was the rain-soaked earth. When the rain finished, the air was layered with the early-morning rites of animism and the scent of spicy joss sticks lit to appease the gods. The next day Suzette went shopping and purchased a new pair of sunglasses for Kiet. They were genuine Ray-Bans, aviator-style, of course, and they cost her a horrendous sum at the Central Market. But the look on Kiet's face and his actor's flourish when he donned them was worth every dollar.

Suzette never tired of the market's long concrete aisles and throngs of vendors selling silk faintly embossed with medallions and flowers like watermarks on stationery; dried fish wrapped in palm leaves; bottles of liquor with snakes embalmed in the sweet overproof liquid; and aphrodisiac powders made of tiger bone and rhinoceros horn. In out-of-the-way corners pockmarked crones read palms, tea leaves, and skulls, while scribes wrote letters and love poems in longhand for those unsure of the value of their own words. The huge market milled with bargainers from dawn to dusk. It had been built of reinforced concrete by the French in 1914 and was still referred to by the older Saigonese as the Halles Centrales, or Central Market. The belfry and clock that stood at the main entrance across from a roundabout was an incongruous sight as was the equestrian statue that raised its hooves above the busy traffic circle. It was a representation of the first person in Vietnam to use courier pigeons.

Each time Suzette visited the market the items for sale were different. Sometimes she saw green pith helmets with little red stars that Kiet informed her were Communist issue. Along with these there might be grenades like black pinecones; AK-47s; boxes of slugs marked for use in M-16s; metal Zippo lighters engraved with wild epigrams about death, sex, and Vietnam; and even jeep tires. The only part of the market Suzette refused to frequent was the live-animal section that sold monkeys, cobras, bats, turtles, dogs, and peacocks for dinner. They were shut up in cramped, dirty wire cages and were Vietnamese delicacies.

Suzette and Kiet's neighbors were clerks and a few Chinese shopkeepers. The Chinese had a reputation as nose-to-the-grindstone entrepreneurs unaffected by causes, good or evil. And because of the volatile political situation, their Saigonese neighbors didn't embrace strangers. They were afraid they might be spies trying to ferret out traitors to a failing and paranoid dictatorship. For their part, Kiet and Suzette were content with each other and with their occasional forays to Van's house on Bui Thi Xuan Street.

It was that hour of the morning when lovers cuddled like spoons. Kiet liked to contemplate the past with Suzette in his arms and reflect on the future before he really woke. Sunlight streamed through the window slats above the bed, and a fly buzzed near the mosquito netting. Suzette waved the insect away and looked at the clock. "Mmm, I love your body next to mine," she crooned, "but I'm late and I think, Kiet, you are, too."

"Xau!" Now Kiet was really awake.

Suzette blinked. "What does *xau* mean again? You're always saying that."

He grinned. "*Xau* means, 'Shit, I'm going to get fired and end up in a mosquito-ridden foxhole waiting for the Vietcong because I'm late.'"

"Do you know that we've been together now for a whole month?"

"Yes, and every day I love you more. I never tire of you. I could make love to you now...and then at noon again...and then before dinner, and—"

Suzette looked at him sternly. "We can't now! Let's get dressed. Can you put me in a *cyclo* and tell the driver to take me to the Cambodian consulate, just in case he's from some faraway village and doesn't speak my languages?"

Kiet frowned, his sexual gleam fading. "Why are you going there?"

"Don't you remember, Kiet? You told me yourself there was going to be a Buddhist demonstration this morning."

"Don't go! There's talk that our Catholic president and his brother are harassing the Buddhists again."

Suzette picked up her jeans from the floor and shook them for centipedes. "Don't worry. Nothing will happen. The Buddhist demonstration is in front of a consulate and reporters will be there. Nhu's secret police and the army aren't going to shoot innocent people with the world looking on. I'm dying to get some good shots of the monks. I can't miss this."

Kiet finished buttoning up his uniform. "I wish you'd stay home."

Suzette looked at him imploringly. "I can't."

With surprising suddenness Kiet threw her back on the bed. "Stay home and wait for me!" he insisted, his eyes unusually serious.

"Why?" she asked, alarmed at his fervor.

"It's not right that you run around photographing the way you do, and besides, Saigon gets more dangerous every day. Thanks to the Americans we have even more pimps and drug dealers. Suzette, you can buy bombs, grenades, even automatic weapons in the alleys these days. Do I need to go on?" Kiet struck his forehead in frustration. "You're no innocent anymore. You know what's going on. Remember Hué? Do I need to say more? I want you to give up the photography."

"I love you, Kiet," she answered slowly, thinking. "But for the first time in my life I've found something I'm really good at. And this is where I'm meant to take pictures. I enjoyed photography back in the States and hoped to make it a career, but the subject matter here makes my life more important. Taking photographs in Saigon makes me feel real to myself and, even better, helps me be Vietnamese. When I look through my camera lens at the street children and they smile for me, I feel connected to them. And the Vietnamese women, when they allow me to photograph them, they're accepting me. It sounds weird, but it's true."

Suzette kissed Kiet, attempted to extract herself from his grip, then changed the subject. "If you don't leave now, darling, you'll be late for work and I'll be late for my cultural experience." Try as she might, though, she couldn't get Kiet to let her go. The look in his eyes was beginning to scare her.

"Didn't you listen to anything I said? A Vietnamese wife would stay home and wait for her husband."

"Good for them!" she retorted. "Look, I don't want you to be late for work and I don't want to miss the Buddhist demonstration, so let's go."

Kiet spoke again. "You're only concerned with your pictures, aren't you? I don't agree with your photography whatsoever. Not only is it dangerous for you to roam the streets the way you do, but you're taking advantage of my people. Your pictures don't show the truth of their lives. It shows their beautiful big eyes and their smiles that are meant to please, but not their poverty and fear of our own leaders as well as the fear of the Vietcong. But what would you know about fear? You're an American. You don't really understand what it means to live in Saigon. You don't have any real ties to this country. You could buy a ticket any day to leave, so the danger here isn't real to you."

"Kiet, that's cruel!" she said, staring back at him. "You know I belong here, that this is my true home. You know that before I met you I didn't care much about my life. I never felt that I really belonged in America or France. And so many of the people I cared about left me. I never knew my mother. Papa abandoned me in the orphanage and then died. Jimmy died, and Val is gone from me, too."

Kiet scowled but finally released his grip. "I can see that you couldn't care less about anything I say. Fine, have it your way. Go."

The Cambodian consulate was packed with onlookers. Buddhist monks sat on the curb. Their eyes were directed downward in prayer and their ears were oblivious to the honks of cars, the rattle of *cyclos*, and the *ding-ding-ding* of bicycles. A black Peugeot sedan parked amid the crowd of Buddhists, and Suzette aimed her camera at the expensive car. As she did, a door in the sedan opened. Three young Buddhists helped an elderly monk out, carrying him to an empty spot in the middle of the intersection. His helpers sat him gently on the asphalt, crossing his legs in the lotus position and arranging his saffron robe over his knees and calves for modesty. A younger monk returned to the automobile and unlatched the trunk. When Suzette's camera eye caught the young Buddhist again, he was pouring gasoline from a plastic container over the elderly monk, who remained immobile on the pavement. The younger Buddhist then lit the gasoline with a plastic lighter. The flame ignited and rose, devouring the elderly monk's robes, turning his skin to char, baptizing him with heat, burn, and stink. He moved not an inch, emitted no sound. The greedy yellow tongue consumed the old man and his mouth became an inky hole.

flames consume human flesh
stinking woven piece of death
eats and gobbles Buddhist skin
immolation's not a sin
for martyrs, monks of Buddhist fame
to beat the infamous Ngo Dinh Diem

The elderly monk's body crumpled and fell. A young bonze spoke loudly into a microphone, saying "A Buddhist priest burns himself to death. A Buddhist becomes a martyr..." over and over in Vietnamese and English.

Like an automaton, Suzette continued to take pictures of the self-sacrifice. A Buddhist woman walked through the crowd, handing out biographies of the old monk whose name, she said, was Thich Quang Duc. Suddenly Suzette realized what she was doing and stopped clicking. Without thinking she ripped out the film and hurled it into the gutter. Then she held her long blond hair away from her face and threw up.

Suzette waited for Kiet in their apartment. She listened for his step from her seat in the sea-grass chair. As soon as he came through the door, she ran to him and cried, "Someone should have stopped it. I should have stopped it."

Kiet took her in his arms. "I heard. All Saigon knows."

"I saw a monk let himself be burned to death today," she said, pulling away and covering her face. "I still can't believe it. No one did anything. No one stopped him. I even overheard another photographer say that the monk's suicide was planned and it had to be. But why didn't someone stop it?" Her sentences bumped together.

"Suzette, don't think about it."

"The Americans there just watched." She began to cry. "And why didn't I do something? How could I photograph it? How can I touch my camera again? I took pictures of a man killing himself. It makes me sick. I must be sick to have done that. Sick, like the other American photographers. It was immoral not to prevent him from taking his own life."

"Don't forget, Suzette, what you told me yourself. A reporter's job is to record events, not interfere with them. And you're just a young woman. No one would have listened to you, nor could you have done anything. The Buddhists knew what they were doing. You shouldn't have gone in the first place."

Suzette stared through Kiet. "You didn't see it or smell his flesh," she said bitterly. "I hate all Americans. What kind of people can take pictures of monks burning themselves up?"

Kiet held her hands tightly in his. "It's no one's fault."

"But I'm responsible, too. I was there…" Her eyes grew wide.

"I know. It's terrible, but it was the monk's choice. This kind of thing is part of their culture. It's their way of protesting politically. The monks often burn fingers and toes as a small protest. Suicide makes the Buddhist monk a martyr for his faith."

"If that's their culture, then they're sick, too."

"Suzette, you don't understand the Vietnamese."

"So what does that mean? That I'm just another Yankee interfering in something I don't understand?" She pushed him away. "But maybe you're right. I'm as bad as they are. I'm an

American, too. And I hate them. I hate myself!"

Kiet was shocked by her vehemence and didn't know what to say, or how to comfort her. He could only watch as she sobbed inconsolably.

Suzette remained awake the rest of the night. She stood by the open shutters, watching the rain and the street. When she finally went to bed, she'd stopped crying, and when Kiet moved close, she hid in his arms.

She grieved for two days, refusing to eat. Not even Kiet's usual teasing could make her smile, make her forget death, what she'd seen. And then he told her he had a surprise for her. They would go and visit his mother in the country. They would take a trip to see the real Vietnam.

8

INTO THE COUNTRY

The mysterious East faced me, perfumed like a flower, silent like death, dark like a grave.

Joseph Conrad, *Youth*

Thu Bang, South Vietnam: June 1963

There was no bridge to access Thu Bang. Kiet paid a few piastres to a boatman, who ferried them down and across the river and up the canal in a long-tailed canoe from the waterfront café at Point des Blageurs.

His mother's village begged in the shadow of its colonial cousin, Saigon. The huts were constructed of tin or old-fashioned mud and thatch. Kiet disliked going there and had done his best to move his mother to Saigon, but to no avail. His mother was typical of his country, and he had told Suzette that maybe she would understand him and his culture more if she would get to know his mother.

The swamp that had been controlled by Communist guerrillas since 1941 was now in view. In Ty Le the Vietcong waited, guns trained. Dressed in their trademark peasant garb of black pajamas, they hoisted Russian AK-47s and stolen American M-16s, unwieldy weapons for their smaller frames. An explosion boomed from that direction, and Suzette and Kiet shot looks at the boatman, who steered his craft onward, unfazed.

"Just the VC getting ready to fire their usual evening shells at Saigon," he explained in Vietnamese. "Nothing to worry about."

Kiet translated for Suzette, trying to apprise her of the danger that lurked everywhere in Vietnam. The boatman, Kiet told her, risked his life each time he made the crossing. But as the poorer Vietnamese said, a slow death from starvation was worse than a quick death at the hands of the Vietcong.

The river was becoming a no-man's-land, as was the countryside and even the roads to Saigon. The VC were moving in with surreptitious speed, cutting through Laos and Cambodia and into the South, encroaching on Saigon. Weapons, ammunition, military supplies, and thousands of guerrilla soldiers crowded the Ho Chi Minh Trail. The North Vietnamese government was becoming increasingly arrogant and audacious with each passing month. But as the boat made progress, Suzette and Kiet soon put thoughts of the Vietcong aside. They puttered by a village of sampans moored along the shore. These were true houseboats with flowers blooming in wooden crates on the decks. Hens pecked at kernels of grain, and cages of canaries hung from eaves. Women in conical hats tended their miniature floating gardens, while under the shade of canopies men quietly played cards and threw dice. Other women cooked and chatted, and babies in small hammocks swung in the slight breeze. Suzette was enchanted by the sight of a naked child jumping from the deck of one houseboat. She laughed as he endeavored to land on top of his older sibling, who splashed gaily in the soupy water.

"Kiet, would you live with me on a sampan?" Suzette asked teasingly. "If you want, I'll go to Hué on that boneshaker of a bus and buy myself a poem hat and you a fishing rod."

Kiet chuckled but told her that sampans were a way of not paying rent and taxes. It was cheap, he said, to build a little house over a boat.

On the bank people fished with bamboo poles and walked pigs on leashes. They were taking their exercise. When Kiet and Suzette's craft was out of the harbor, the water became a looking glass in bronze. Hawkers in small boats called out in melodious voices and beat gongs to attract attention to their live wares of mud crabs, river prawns, and frogs. Around a bend they entered a canal and the scene changed: prawn fishermen with wicker baskets toiled, black slime ringing their waists.

They landed on a shore where the gaiety was gone. Suzette wore her sandals and had to pick her way along a track strewn with coconut husks and refuse. Kiet was quiet, embarrassed at the poverty of his mother's village. Suzette felt badly for him and told him she didn't care. She knew his mother had been forced here after his father lost the family fortune and died of a horrible strain of malaria that she couldn't pronounce but sounded something like *falciparum*.

Kiet gently clasped her wrist and led her past a group of women in cheap black calico squatting silently. A skinny cur with open sores lay at the side of the path. Kiet knew Suzette was afraid of rabies, and he picked up a dried chunk of mud in case the dog came near.

They squelched down a path past a line of deserted shacks, all with similar pitched walls, until they came to a platform on a pole next to a small front door. A burning joss stick and a package of unfiltered Vietnamese cigarettes had been placed on the platform. The brand was Les As, with a depiction of a diamond, a spade, a heart, and a club on a gold package.

"For my dead father's spirit," Kiet said in response to Suzette's inquiring gaze. Then they entered the hut, which was small but clean. Its dirt floor was covered with rattan mats, and on a low table there was a tin print, a photogravure, of a handsome couple barely past puberty. Both were dressed in silk tunics with mandarin collars. Trousers peeked out beneath the tunics, and the boy wore Western shoes. The child bride's fingernails were very long, the length indicating she'd come from an extremely wealthy family and had never known housework.

Kiet greeted his mother with a kiss on each cheek. They took off their shoes, as was the custom, and he and his mother spoke in Vietnamese. Kiet had sent word earlier with a boatman that he was coming to visit and was bringing his American girlfriend.

Suzette noticed Kiet's mother's graying hair was twisted in a complicated chignon and that she was perfumed with jasmine. Her *aio dai* was worn, the embossed silk like parchment. Taking small, barefoot steps toward Suzette, she kissed her once on each cheek. She had to stand on tiptoe to do so. Then she began to weep and wail.

Suzette was startled. "I hope I haven't made you unhappy," she said in French.

Kiet's mother answered in Vietnamese, requesting Kiet to translate. "I am thrilled that my son has an American friend from such a good family. My tears are tears of joy."

"But I'm not really an American," Suzette protested in French.

"Suzette, let her think you're American," Kiet said. "After all, you *do* carry a U.S. passport. It'll make my poor mother proud. It doesn't matter."

"But it does," Suzette insisted, only acquiescing when Kiet motioned her to be quiet.

The old woman served tea, and they sat side by side on plastic chairs small enough for children. Her stove was a coal brazier, and the smell made Suzette queasy. Kiet's mother faced her, and when Suzette took the cup of tea, it spun before her eyes. She remembered Kiet had instructed her that it was an insult not to take tea with a Vietnamese, so she sipped.

Kiet's mother noticed Suzette's sensitivity and fetched a tiny box similar to a makeup compact. She opened it and selected a ball of areca nut parings and betel leaves mixed with lime, offering it around with long, gracious fingers. Kiet declined for both of them, and Suzette attempted to smile, then tried to finish her tea.

Suzette didn't mind that Kiet and his mother spoke so rapidly in Vietnamese that Kiet had no time to translate. She was sleepy, anyway. The hut was dark and her hips and legs were stiff from the child-size plastic chair. She wondered why Kiet and his mother didn't feel the plastic bars in their flesh as she did. Finally Kiet asked Suzette if she was ready to go home. She was.

Later, when she and Kiet discussed their day, she wondered aloud how she would ever get to know his mother. She vowed to learn Vietnamese, but it was such a difficult language for her. Kiet told her not to worry so much. His mother was perpetually sad from the disappointments she'd had in life and she'd forgotten her French. Kiet told her, too, that his mother complained that since the French were gone the language would soon be lost to Vietnam. But, of course, he said, she and his mother had much in common: they both loved him.

The spell was first cast, I think, by the tall elegant girls in silk trousers; by the pewter evening light on flat paddy fields, where the water buffaloes trudged fetlock-deep with a slow primeval gait; by the French perfumeries in the rue Catinat, the Chinese gambling houses in Cholon; above all by that feeling of exhilaration which a measure of danger brings to the visitor with a return ticket.

—Graham Greene, *Ways of Escape*

1

MAN OF DECEIT

A man's most open actions have a secret side to them.
—Joseph Conrad, *Under Western Eyes*

Saigon: October 1963

Chou arrived at Van's door on the pretext of playing yet another game of chess. He held a cigarette between his lips. He'd chain-smoked since his espionage training in Hanoi. It was there that he'd received his code name, Little Fox, and where, among other things, he'd learned how to write communiqués in invisible ink made from starch and put down on folded foolscap. It aided his cover that he wasn't a great admirer of Ho Chi Minh and, in general, looked down on the North Vietnamese. He found them ridiculous with their pith helmets studded with palm fronds. He thought the Americans an offensive race, too, meddling and naive, but larger than life and a force to be reckoned with. As Chou railed inwardly against their intrusion in Vietnam's history, Van opened the door.

"I felt the need to play chess with you again, my friend," he told Van. He removed his shoes, then padded in. His black silk socks matched his pants and shirt.

"Good man! I was going to telephone you, anyway. My wife telegrammed that she's arriving in Saigon tomorrow and I'm arranging a small homecoming dinner for her the following night. We'd be honored if you'd attend." Van was visibly delighted to share his news.

"I'm afraid I have another engagement, but as we play, I'll

think about it. I certainly wouldn't want to miss a chance to greet your beautiful wife."

"But surely the two of you saw a great deal of each other in Paris?"

Chou tapped his nose. "Ah...yes, but remember she's been traveling for quite some time."

"Of course!"

The two sat down to their game over a couple of brandies. Chou moved a piece and said, eyes gleaming, "By the way, I ran into Big Boss yesterday and he told me the most fascinating story about Nhu's secret police chief, Dr. Tuyen."

"And what would that be?"

"He's plotting a coup." When Van seemed unconcerned, Chou asked, "Have you met the good doctor?"

"I hope never to meet that sinister devil. If I did, I'd be afraid of torture or a bullet in my heart."

"Well, then, my friend, I'll enjoy describing the scene in detail, though you should know that, like you, Tuyen's a Catholic who abhors communism. I've confided in you before that Tuyen and I are friends and that he and Big Boss are like brothers. Tuyen has repeatedly reported General Khanh and Air Vice Marshal Cao Ky to Diem as traitors who are plotting a coup, but Diem and Nhu refuse to believe they're disloyal."

"That's strange. Wasn't it General Khanh and his Mekong Delta Force who saved Diem from that attempted coup three years ago?"

"Van, you're not just a talented scientist. You're a pretty good political analyst, too."

"So why has Tuyen turned against his benefactors?" Van asked, seemingly interested now.

Chou took another gold-tipped Sobrane from his cigarette case and lit it with a match. His brand had been created by a Russian grand duke. "After the 1960 incident, when some of

Diem's own army units tried unsuccessfully to overthrow him, Tuyen's position as the head of the secret police was usurped by a newcomer. Diem and Nhu were so obsessed with gathering more and more information about their enemies that they decided they needed two secret police forces and two chiefs."

Van laughed. "Two? What folly!"

"Of course, the second secret police force was meant to spy on the first. For the sake of secrecy I'll call the head of Diem's second secret police, Tuyen's rival."

"Believe me, Chou, I don't want to know his name."

"Anyway, since then Tuyen has made it no secret that he's disenchanted with Diem's regime and with its CIA backers. Consequently the good doctor has offered himself to British intelligence as a double agent."

Van took off his glasses and polished them. "Really?" He poured them both some more brandy.

"It becomes even darker. Tuyen and Britain's MI6 are plotting a coup with a dissident colonel, but what they don't know is that the colonel's a secret Communist. This colonel's even more conniving than the whole pack of plotters and has completely fooled Tuyen. The doctor's aim is to keep Diem as chief of state and send Nhu, elder brother, Bishop Thuc, and Madame Nhu, into exile."

"How do you know all this, Chou?"

The lawyer let a smile dart across his lips. "Let's just say that I have my ways."

"So, does Tuyen really think his coup will succeed?"

"Tuyen's no fool. If his coup fails, he has alternative plans and piastres to escape." Chou leaned closer to the chessboard to examine a move Van had made, causing his chair to scrape along the floor.

"Chou, please be careful. When Jade returns tomorrow, you know she'll notice if the floor is scratched."

"You shouldn't let your wife rule you. In Vietnam a man tells a woman what to do."

"You don't know Jade… But enough of politics. Will you come to Jade's homecoming dinner? It's at the Soi Kinh Lan Restaurant in Cholon the day after tomorrow at 7:00 p.m. I've invited some young friends, as well. You'll enjoy their company."

Chou knew he'd relish seeing the look on Jade's face if he turned up at her homecoming dinner. He hadn't seen her since that evening at her apartment in Paris. "As I said before, I'm afraid I have previous engagements. I have a meeting with some important people, and afterward Big Boss has invited me for drinks and a game of cards. You know how I love gambling. But if I'm able to, I'll come to your dinner between engagements. As you know, I'm always delighted by the sight of your lovely wife."

2

CELEBRATION

It's a terrible thing to be alone—yes, it is…it is. But don't lower your mask until you have another mask prepared beneath—as terrible as you like—but a mask.

—Katherine Mansfield, Letter to John Middleton Murry

Saigon: October 1963

Jade Minh gathered flowers in her yard on Bui Thi Xuan Street. As she bent to pluck a lily, the gruff call of a heron reverberated from the canal behind their house. Jade saw the beautiful creature fly off, its legs a streamlined arrow behind a dusky silhouette. She was thrilled to be home for good. Jade looked as lovely as her garden in her summer frock, though the dress she really wanted to wear lay crinkled across her trunk. The offending sight of the travel-stressed dress had prompted Jade to apply a cream made from turtles taken in the South China Sea to her face and décolletage. But she had no need to worry; her skin was as youthful as the advertisements for beauty creams.

When the afternoon rains began, Jade went back inside and fussed with her hair, sweeping it into a complicated French twist and securing it with jeweled pins shaped like daisies. Outside her window, the rain bounced off the foliage, causing tiny frogs to sing. Finally Jade finished her hairstyling to her satisfaction and flounced into the living room where Van was reading. She pirouetted, mimicking a fashion model.

Van beamed. "You look exquisite, Jade, and I'm glad you've finally come home for good. Still, I was hoping you'd stay in

Paris with Mui."

Jade opened her eyes wide in mock surprise. "But, Van, you've been trying to get me to quit my job for a long time."

"Yes, my dear, but I meant for you to stay in Paris. I'm worried that it's too dangerous for you here in Saigon."

"I'm sorry, Van. I must have misunderstood you." She pouted. "I've been without you long enough. I want us to be together. I've been lonely for you! Haven't you missed me at all?"

"Of course I have, my dear!" Van smiled now, all trace of annoyance banished by Jade's words.

"Don't worry about Mui. I arranged an apartment close to the Sorbonne for her. There are two other Vietnamese girls living in the building. I was sure that was better for her—to be living with Vietnamese girls her own age. I met Mui at the airport and we opened a bank account for her the day she arrived. And I saw her once again when I returned from my Mediterranean cruise. Mui was very happy and has made a lot of friends."

"You're right," Van said, a hint of worry still in his voice. "I'm sure she'll be fine. She's a smart girl."

Jade looked into Van's eyes as she stood above him. "You still sound anxious about Mui. Believe me, the girl is old enough to be on her own. We were married at her age and I'd gone off to France to get my degree. I was fine on my own in Montpellier, wasn't I?"

Van removed his glasses and rubbed the dent in the bridge of his nose. "Yes, yes, I guess so. However, one thing you should be aware of is that the political situation in Saigon is even more dangerous than the last time you were here."

Jade ignored what her husband had said. "You'll see, Van. I'll be a good wife to you here. I have a contact at the Presidential Palace who might throw some freelance translation work my way."

Van hesitated, then spoke. "Jade, I don't think that's a good idea. I want you to stay away from anything political. You must consider the situation. There are spies from both camps everywhere. Sometimes I even suspect our old friend Chou."

Dropping the issue, Jade leaned over and kissed her husband.

"That's my girl," Van said, smiling. "I think you'll be pleased with the arrangements I've made this evening. As I said earlier, it'll be a small dinner, a party for you, and I've invited some guests."

"So you've told me. But who did you invite?"

"You remember the young American woman, Suzette, I told you about? The one I met at Girval's earlier this year? She's coming with her friend Kiet."

"Oh, yes, I remember now. The half-caste photographer who lives in an old French apartment with a Vietnamese boyfriend who works as a clerk for the government."

"You sound so judgmental, Jade. What do you disapprove of? That she lives with a man? Or is it that she has mixed blood?"

"Van, you know as well as I do that no one accepts a half-caste. Look at the children in the street. Many are from Vietnamese mothers and French fathers. No one wants them, not even their own mothers. They're shunned by Vietnamese society. People should stick with their own races and cultures."

Van was quiet, but Jade was aware by his face that he was upset. Her husband had often told her how he wished he could do more for Saigon's street children. He frequently gave them money and had once or twice tried to find homes for them, but never with any luck. Van was constantly picking up strays. She couldn't stop him and didn't care as long as it didn't affect her life. She reflected that Van's new friend, Suzette, was less odious to her than Mui. She knew Suzette couldn't possibly encroach on their lives. The American girl already had a home and a boyfriend. Besides, she remembered Van had told her that Suzette had an American family to fall back on, while Mui was an orphan and Van was her guardian. No, she reasoned, Suzette wasn't a threat. When her photo assignment was over, the American girl would go back to the States.

"You're right, Van. Perhaps I'm being a little hard on the girl. I don't mind your innocent friendships with the strays of the world. Not at all. I'm sure she's a delightful child." Jade's smile covered her lie.

"Oh, I almost forgot. I also invited Chou to our dinner, though he wasn't sure he could make it. He said he'd try."

"Oh, no, not Chou!" Jade cried before she could think.

"But why are you so alarmed? Chou always speaks of you with such affection." Van studied his wife for a moment. "If Chou does join us, we must make him feel welcome. Come now, let's both get ready for this evening."

As they drove toward Cholon and the restaurant, Jade reflected that the drizzle that continued to fall complemented her dismal mood. Van was too busy paying attention to the traffic to notice her dejection. "I wish you hadn't taken so long to dress, Jade. We're late for our reservation. What time is it?" A bicycle with a cargo of trussed chickens squawking in baskets careened into their lane on Le Loi, and Van dodged right.

"Not quite 7:30," Jade said, consulting her Rolex's oyster face. A honking glassless bus crammed with a big-eyed sea of small children crossed diagonally through the lane, and Jade waved them away.

"We'll celebrate your return with French champagne," Van said as an old Chinese woman ambled across the road, clutching an offering of goldfish in a plastic bag. She was likely on her way to the pagoda that honored the goddess of the sea. They drove in silence, and when they passed the boarded-up Parc des Attractions, one of the city's two infamous gambling casinos, the electric signs switched on and the Chinese characters gleamed like trickles of blood.

Damn, Jade thought. *I might as well be going to hell if Chou shows up at this dinner.*

Immaculately clad waiters in tuxedos zigzagged through the tables. Chopsticks tipped with sterling silver flashed like the scales of flying fish. The only music was the clatter of china, the click of chopsticks speeding from bowl to mouth, and the hubbub of diners chatting.

Suzette and Kiet had arrived at seven. They sat at a large table obscured by the swing of the kitchen doors, sipping tea and waiting for Van and Jade. A waiter flew through the doors with a flaming dish in a cast-iron wok. Another waiter followed. With French flare they served a heaping portion of sizzling beef to the table directly in Suzette's line of vision. Sadly the scene reminded her of the old Buddhist monk's flame-engulfed body. She'd been plagued with nightmares since she'd witnessed that horrible event months earlier.

"Maybe Uncle Van isn't coming," Kiet said. "It's unusual for him to be late, and if I was in his shoes, I'd want to spend the evening alone with my wife. Why don't we skip dinner and go back to the apartment? I'll make love to you as if it were the first time."

Suzette smiled and looked around the restaurant again. And then she saw Van moving toward them with an elegant Vietnamese woman. "There he is!" Suzette waved. "And that must be his wife."

Van, too, was searching the room with his eyes. "Oh, my goodness, Jade, Suzette and Kiet are already here. I hope we haven't kept them waiting too long."

Jade scrutinized the table Van was directing her to, and relief flooded her. Chou wasn't there!

When they reached the table, Van made the introductions in French. "Suzette, Kiet, this is my wife, Jade. Jade, this is Suzette O'Brian and Nguyen Son Kiet."

Jade took stock of the couple. She saw a young woman dressed casually like most of the young people she came across. Wrinkling her pretty nose, she thought how unsuitable the girl's jeans and madras blouse were in such a posh restaurant, even if it was located in disreputable Cholon. The young man with her, on the other hand, wore his government uniform well. She also noted that Suzette's boyfriend had gotten to his feet immediately. He appeared to have had some breeding.

"Pleased to meet you," Jade finally greeted Suzette, her eyes objectionable with a supreme and impersonal disdain.

After Jade had shaken Kiet's hand, they all sat down. "What an honor it is to finally meet your wife," Suzette whispered in Van's ear. "I'm so happy for you that she's finally home."

In short order Van had an ice bucket containing a magnum of Dom Perignon delivered to the table, along with a spray of orchids the same shade as his wife's mauve frock. When champagne was poured all round, Van lifted his glass and said, "To my lovely wife, Jade."

Jade sipped and studied the young man across the table. He was certainly handsome, she admitted. It was beyond Jade's comprehension why such a good-looking and upright young Vietnamese man would keep company with a half-caste American girl who could barely dress herself.

3

JUST ANOTHER WHORE

The truth has never been of any real value to any human being—it is a symbol for mathematicians and philosophers to pursue. In human relations kindness and lies are worth a thousand words.

—Graham Greene, *The Heart of the Matter*

Saigon: October 1963

In a smoky backroom Chou sat among men of distinction. Dr. Tran Kim Tuyen, North Vietnamese Politburo member Phung Ham, Colonel Pham Ngoc Thao, and National Liberation Front leader Tran Van Bo parlayed across a felt-covered table often used for cards. Chou had organized the secret meeting. He'd arranged it with the owner who was also a covert Communist. On another night the room would have been hired out for illegal gambling, or the table removed and sawdust spread over the floor for a cockfight.

Chou was tired of the men's rhetoric and tuned out their repetitious complaints about Diem and Nhu so he could analyze his own motives. He didn't have to think too hard on the matter; he knew well it was the element of danger that made all his clandestine games worthwhile for him.

He'd changed the location for the secret meeting at the last minute. His reasons were obvious. He'd switched to the backroom of this place for convenience. Chou had been invited to join Van for a celebratory homecoming dinner for Jade and to meet some new friends of Van's. And this establishment was close to the Soi Kinh Lan Restaurant, where the dinner was being held.

Chou's lips twitched when he recalled his last encounter with Jade. What an hour that had been! A vision of himself, naked and hard, straddling Jade on her precious chaise longue, entered his mind unbidden, and the memory stimulated his sleeping penis. He had experienced difficulty entering her and had been forced to rifle through Jade's medicine cabinet, hunting for something slippery while she waited like an obedient concubine, or like any other paid whore. At last he'd found a jar of Vaseline that he'd greased his penis with. He'd used that opportunity to stroke it, first pulling back the uncircumcised foreskin, then grasping it tightly in his fist and kneading until it stood like an arrow in its bow, waiting and ready to shoot.

Chou's penis stood at attention again just thinking of Jade naked, but he forced his mind back to assessing the danger of being at this meeting of Communists. It was risky gathering so many secret supporters of Uncle Ho in one spot. But just about anything went on these days in Saigon. Well, *almost* anything, he thought ruefully, recalling the 1960 incident at the Caravelle Hotel when eighteen prominent and stupid politicians had drafted a letter to Diem asking for civil-rights reforms. Of course, they were arrested, tortured and imprisoned. What had they expected? Chou's mouth turned down in disdain.

He acknowledged that taking political risks thrilled him almost as much as fucking Jade had. At this meeting, however, the risk was low. There were more secret Communists in Saigon these days than Diem supporters. Besides, Dr. Tuyen, the head of one of Diem's secret police forces, was present. Chou had initially disliked the boyish Tuyen, and it didn't help that the man's voice was as annoyingly high-pitched as a boy's before puberty. But Tuyen owed them. A few years earlier Chou and Big Boss had saved the idiotic Diem from extinction in an odd twist of fate at

Tuyen's request. Now the good doctor was on their side. And anyone with brains could figure out that no one would dare accuse Tuyen or his compatriots of a crime against Diem.

Chou laughed silently, bony chest heaving, mouth widening. The Ngo family's latest palace, Gia Long, was surrounded by an ever-growing pack of "wild dogs." Soon they would tear Diem and Nhu to bits. None of the men at the table seemed to notice Chou's reverie. They were making big plans.

Seeing that the bottle of Mekong whiskey was empty, Chou rose from his chair with his usual streamlined grace. He went to a sideboard in a corner of the windowless room and grabbed another bottle. As he unscrewed the top, he assessed his compatriots.

Comrade Phung Ham, the leading member of the North Vietnamese Communist Politburo, could easily be mistaken for a typical farmer. His bumpkin looks held no clue to his power, except that he went nowhere without armed bodyguards. Lucky devil, Chou thought. Colonel Pham Ngoc Thao, of the South Vietnamese army, was a handsome man and dressed the part. The colonel had once been a Vietminh officer in the war against the French and was now a great favorite of the Americans. Chou knew Thao was a covert Communist and was proud that he and the colonel had much in common: neither man ever stopped plotting.

Chou filled the famous Tran Van Bo's glass. Bo sat directly across from Chou and had a capacity for treachery the lawyer admired. He was both a high-ranking official of Diem's administration *and* the undercover leader of the Liberation Front named in the top-secret document Jade was to have delivered to the Presidential Palace years earlier. Only a privileged few knew Bo's true identity.

The lawyer congratulated himself on that long-ago affair. His action had been worthy of a spy novel. He had been brilliant when he took the secret document from Jade. Ever since, no one had been able to link Bo with the Front. Chou had saved the man's skin. Then, when the Liberation Front was much stronger, Chou had made an even more dazzling move. He'd saved himself by taking credit for reporting similar information using a false name—the Democratic Coalition for the Republic. Chou had even fabricated a headquarters for them, saying it was in the unexplored territory near Pleiku. Of course, there was nothing to find and the South Vietnamese army had wasted a great deal of time searching.

Chou had taken a chance when he had Jade notify the Foreign Ministry in Saigon about the bogus guerrilla group. The secret document's initiator could have followed up, but Chou had known that wouldn't happen. There was a reason it had been unsigned. The informant had wanted to remain anonymous. So no one had been the wiser, either at the South Vietnamese embassy in Paris, or even those under Diem's nose at the Foreign Ministry. What a pack of idiots! And it was a good thing, too. Jade had let Chou know he was suspected of being a traitor. But after that brilliant ruse he'd become one of the South's golden boys. He'd left his position as legal adviser to the South Vietnamese embassy in Paris in a blaze of glory and had actually received more immigration cases through embassy recommendations.

Bo suddenly interrupted Chou's self-congratulatory thoughts. "As an official in Diem's government, I'll allow the opposition party to send a written demand that Diem expel his relatives from government positions and appoint new cabinet ministers. And, if the public seems favorable to all this, then we'll strike!"

Looking across the table, Bo fixed his attention on Colonel Thao. "I know you're anxious, Colonel, but the time isn't quite right to demand Diem's resignation and conclude our planned coup. We must employ patience. Let's stir up trouble among those few who are still loyal to Diem and his brother. It's easy enough to turn people against Diem because of his continuing habit of doling out postings to his relatives, not to mention his arrogant handling of his cabinet. Some of his cabinet ministers are Buddhists, and we all know what Diem thinks about them." Bo directed a level gaze at the North Vietnamese Communist Party member. "Comrade Phung Ham, what's your opinion?" His voice showed deference for his political superior.

"The instructions from the Politburo are that our armed forces in the South are to remain hidden. At this point we agree with your mandate of posing as an opposition party and merely requesting a cabinet shuffle. Our grass-roots military installations aren't strong enough yet to resist the South Vietnamese army and their backers, the Americans, especially now that the ARVN and the Yankees have become even more formidable with the addition of Australian jungle warfare specialists. But our own military force from the North is on its way down the Ho Chi Minh Trail and they'll ensure our position in the battlefields when the time comes."

Ham looked at each man at the table. "Comrade Bo, as leader of the Liberation Front and with a key position in Diem's government, take extra precautions to maintain your status as a double agent but continue your good work in turning your peers against Diem. Colonel Thao, more than ever, you mustn't let anyone know you're on our side. You'll be invaluable when the fighting starts because you'll supply us with a great deal of precious military information. As for you, Dr. Tuyen, you're one of our most important assets. Your position as head of Diem's secret police means you can save our supporters from prison and death. We'll contact you weekly. And, Chou, continue to bring us any information that comes your way. You're the sly fox in this game of ours or, as the Americans would say, our ace in the hole."

After Ham's instructions, the men left one by one via the back stairs. Chou exited last and then sauntered down an alley toward the Soi Kinh Lan Restaurant, hands deep in his pockets.

As he entered the busy eatery, he spied Jade immediately. Who could miss such a beauty?

Chou couldn't help being smug as Van introduced him around the table. He greeted Jade first and admired her self-control when she flicked him her embassy smile. How brazenly cool she was, he thought. Next he acknowledged Van's new female friend, Suzette. As he bent to kiss her hand, he got a better look at her face and was shocked. It was unmistakable. This young woman had exactly the same Cupid's-bow mouth Jade had. Certainly the girl was taller and her hair was blond, but Chou saw Jade in those features. With the swift intuition that had made him such a successful operative for the Communists, he knew Suzette must be Jade's illegitimate half-caste daughter.

The lawyer was momentarily confused. Surely Van could see the resemblance, especially with the two women practically side by side. But then Van, with his Coke-bottle lenses and scientific air, had never struck Chou as being visually perceptive. The man always had his head in the clouds and worshiped his precious wife. But what about the girl? Did she know? And if she did, how would Jade keep her from revealing the secret?

The others had already begun eating, so Chou ordered a vegetarian noodle dish and a beer and settled down to consider the incredible situation he found himself in. The other four people at the table were engrossed in conversation and didn't think anything of his silence. Chou thought back to that time in Paris three years ago when he pretended to be a priest in the confessional and Jade revealed she had an illegitimate child. Inadvertently she had told him then that she believed the girl had likely had a "bad end." Then, just last year, the bitch had phoned him in Paris and lured him to her apartment to tell him that her friend's "orphan" was dead. If she hadn't pushed her luck, hadn't thought she could beat him at his own game, he might have left her alone and not told her he'd known all along about her illegitimate child with a French lover. Nor would he have gone to her place drunk and struck the bargain of one hour of sex in exchange for his silence.

Had Jade really believed the child was dead only to have the girl turn up in Saigon and find her? Chou watched the two women with a practiced eye as he made light banter with Van and the young man named Kiet, obviously Suzette's lover. He heard Jade ask Suzette how she was finding Saigon.

"I'm a photographer on assignment for an American magazine called *View*," she told Jade. "But my real reason for coming to Vietnam is to discover my roots."

From the way Jade was acting, Chou was now certain the Doctoress had no idea who Suzette was. Then he heard the girl drop the key in Jade's lap.

"I'm half Vietnamese and I've always felt my life to be a riddle that I could only decipher if I came to Vietnam," she said in impeccable French.

Chou thought the girl's candor was typically American, but her command of French was obviously that of someone who had been born in France. Impatiently he waited for Jade to grasp the key Suzette had given her.

"My dear Miss O'Brian," Jade finally said haughtily, "I suggest you study Vietnamese culture. When you return to America, make sure you take a course on Asia." Jade then turned away from Suzette and joined Kiet and Van's conversation.

It took all of Chou's willpower to stop himself from laughing uproariously. Jade was so stuck on herself, so prideful and arrogant, that she couldn't see her own daughter right in front of her. She didn't just have a frigid body; her heart, too, was frozen.

The American girl had obviously been stunned by Jade's rudeness. Her mouth hung open at La Doctoress's pretentious words. Chou almost felt sorry for her, but with the sight of her pink tongue he sensed a stirring in his penis. Maybe he would fuck the daughter, as well. She was only in her early twenties...but too malleable, too soft for him. She was slave material. And he craved conquest.

Chou surveyed the table. What a group! He was now certain that neither mother, nor daughter, nor cuckolded husband knew just how connected they all were. Chou then remembered that when Jade had enlisted him in her search for the child, she had said the girl was named Phuong, or Phoenix. The girl had risen from nowhere, from ashes, despite La Doctoress's efforts to bury her alive.

What should he do with this knowledge? Chou wondered. Then he had it! He would write Van and reveal that his beautiful wife, who wouldn't have a baby with him, had had an illegitimate daughter with a Frenchman. And that the illegitimate child was the American girl he'd befriended in Saigon. But what would Van do with this information? He might forgive her adulterous relationship. He might even forgive his wife for having an illegitimate child. But what Van would never forgive was Jade's seeming abandonment of her half-caste child. And what would the gentle scientist think if Chou told him about his one hour of unrestrained sex with Jade in exchange for his silence about her secret? But, no, he'd never tell Van that. He had enough on Jade, and there was no need to demonstrate his true colors to Van.

But why tell Van anything at all? Cause and effect, Chou thought. If he blackened Jade's name first, no one would really believe her if she tried to denounce him as a spy or a traitor. Chou would write the letter tonight and then post it. Let the deluded husband know the frigid Doctoress was just another whore. Let the Doctoress learn that actions had consequences. Let her discover that her illegitimate daughter was living in Saigon right under her nose for all to see.

Chou was satisfied with his plans, so he excused himself from the table, announcing that he had a previous commitment to honor. After he said goodbye to Suzette, Kiet, and Van, he looked Jade in the face, examining her with cold, ruthless eyes. "Welcome back, Honorable Doctoress. Saigon has missed you. We've all missed you, I'm sure." As he spoke, his mouth twitched with mirthless disdain.

At his villa in the embassy district Big Boss was thoroughly enjoying a game of cards with Chou. The two men drank whiskey, smoked cigars, and told stories. Chou had a large pile of chips and was obviously winning, but that didn't seem to bother Big Boss.

Suddenly there was a knock on the door. Both men eyed each other, then the gang leader called for his manservant, Hông, to check the windows.

"It's the secret police! They've got the house surrounded."

Big Boss snorted. "Calm down, Hông. It's Dr. Tuyen coming to join our game. Open the door!"

Hông returned quickly, this time even more alarmed than before. "I'm sorry, boss, but it's the *other* secret police head. He told me to inform you that he's sent some of his men to arrest Dr. Tuyen. He insists that he speak with you in person. His bodyguards have their weapons drawn. He knows Mr. Chou is here and says that if either of you try to escape his men have orders to shoot you on sight."

Chou spoke first. "He's gotten wind of Tuyen's coup and is taking the opportunity to rid himself of the doctor, you, and me."

A telephone was on the table, and Big Boss's tiny eyes flickered over it, though he seemed relatively unperturbed. "Don't worry, my friend. The last laugh's ours again. Everything has been taken care of ahead of time." Big Boss pointed a fat finger imperiously at Hông. "Bring him here and draw your weapon."

A man in a white suit, accompanied by a bodyguard, followed Hông into the room. All three men had weapons drawn.

"Come in, come in, I finally meet you," Big Boss said cheerily, motioning the newcomer toward a chair. "Join us for the next hand. Have a whiskey and a cigar." He dealt the oily cards with quick grace. He'd left a joker face-up at his guest's waiting chair.

Tuyen's owlish rival looked down at them, the barrel of his automatic pistol pointed at Big Boss's amused face. "You're both under arrest. The house is surrounded, as is the home of your accomplice, Dr. Tuyen."

"Yes, Tuyen and I are like brothers," Big Boss said, "but I prefer to say we're as thick as thieves." He chortled, and Chou joined in, their mouths twisting in laughter. Then Big Boss got dead serious. "You're not a stupid man. You know Diem and Nhu will soon be gone one way or another. My friend Chou here has a great sense of humor and refers to those two as the Siamese twins. He says they need a doctor to cut them apart. You'd be wise to make sure you're on the right side in what's to come."

Tuyen's rival wasn't intimidated. "Get up. You're both under arrest for treason."

Big Boss and Chou remained seated. Sneering at the rival police chief, Chou said, "You're a stupid man. Dr. Tuyen will at least guarantee Diem and Nhu safe passage out of Vietnam. Some of the other plotters in this country wouldn't be so agreeable."

The rival police chief was silent for a moment, then he said to Big Boss, "It's too late for Tuyen. He's finished."

The fat gangster picked up the telephone receiver and dialed a number.

Chou smelled a whiff of fear emanate from Tuyen's rival, watched as a bead of sweat formed on the man's receding forehead, chuckled when he noticed the secret cop's toothbrush mustache wilt. The visitor's eyes widened perceptibly with each number Big Boss dialed.

After a moment of silence, Big Boss said, "Good evening, Ban, are the lady of the house and the children still well and happy?" His tone was buoyant and charming. "Wonderful!" he said after listening. "Carry out our prearranged plan if I don't call you back in the next two minutes."

Tuyen's rival looked as if he were going to faint.

"I think you know what number I just dialed," Big Boss said to the defeated secret police chief. "Now call off your men and let Dr. Tuyen go. Propose to Diem and Nhu that Tuyen be sent overseas. Tell them he's loyal to the Ngo family, as are Chou and myself. Then tell them you're tired of having two secret police forces. Say you'll be more efficient when there's only one. If you value your wife and children, you'll get a move on and do everything I just said."

Although it was well before breakfast, Tan Son Nhat Airport bustled with the custom-tailored white suits of the Can Lao secret police who watched with sharp eyes as Dr. Tuyen waited for his flight to Cairo. Tuyen had been assigned the post of South Vietnam's consul general to Egypt, with the blessing of Lucien Conein, the French-born CIA representative. Chou had accompanied his friend Big Boss to say goodbye to Tuyen.

As Tuyen and Big Boss had a last conversation, Chou removed a letter addressed to Dr. Van Minh, Pasteur Institute from his inside breast pocket and dropped it in a mailbox. The lawyer had spared no detail in his condemnation of Jade and the lengths she'd gone to keep her illegitimate daughter a secret. The letter would be in Van's hands shortly. And himself? After one last mission, he'd be sailing on a junk, hidden by the riddle of the green water and the thousand karst islets of the Baie d'Along. There he'd be safely out of reach of his enemies until Ho Chi

Minh was triumphant in the South and appointed him minister of justice. Thinking about his perceived rosy future, Chou turned back to his comrades, his lips curled in a secret smile.

"Disappear before you reach Egypt or you'll be carrion for the vultures!" Big Boss advised Tuyen in a whisper as he kissed him on each cheek.

But when Big Boss turned back to Chou, the lawyer had vanished as though he'd never existed.

4

JADE GOES SHOPPING

Of course the evening would be a disaster. Even supposing he found the girl in the next hour or so, the contents would certainly not stand up to the wrapping.

—Ian Fleming, *For Your Eyes Only*

Saigon: October 1963

A lipstick flower and one perfectly balanced palm frond stood in the four-foot-high vase in Van and Jade's house on Bui Thi Xuan Street. The traditional *canh dan*, or cockroach-wing, vase was inlayed with eighteen-karat gold in a dragon motif. The ceiling fan spun, cooling the morning air, and the window's wooden louvers threw stripes of early light across the floor.

Van prepared an early breakfast of star fruit and coffee for Jade. They sat in silence, sharing the paper. At 8:00 a.m. she would have Van call a *cyclo* for her planned day of shopping for antiques in Cholon. She wished she were already on her way, but the shops weren't open yet.

Jade was on edge: her mind kept dredging up the events of the previous night's homecoming dinner. She'd ignored the American girl after her silly comment about coming to Vietnam to find her roots, but it was Chou who had really disturbed Jade. She knew from the lawyer's manner that he'd make trouble for her. Jade could still see the cold-eyed look he'd purposely given her at the homecoming dinner. He was up to something.

At least Van hadn't noticed anything. Her husband had always been blind that way. Van had said on the way home that he'd thought the dinner had been a lovely, happy occasion. What a joke that was, but she was relieved. Still, she knew now she'd have to take action to preempt Chou. She'd write a letter to her old embassy in Paris, denouncing the lawyer as a traitor. Jade would blacken Chou's name, and then if he did expose her past to Van, she'd say he was a liar. Van would believe her.

Jade chewed slowly on the yellow flesh of her fruit, then she had an idea. She remembered the evening at her Paris apartment when Chou had told her about the man who had approached him to join a new Communist resistance organization in the South. The movement was called the Democratic Coalition for the Republic and was to masquerade as an opposition party. She recalled reporting this information under Chou's direction to her embassy. Her action had saved the lawyer's skin. There had been rumors then that he was a spy for Ho Chi Minh, but that report had cleared his name. In fact, it had made him something of a hero.

In the end the Democratic Coalition proved to be a chimera, and it was eventually thought by many in the South Vietnamese government that Chou had been fed false information. Now she remembered that there had been an embassy rumor about another Communist resistance movement—the National Liberation Front of South Vietnam. Jade would say that Chou had bragged to her that he had been offered the post of deputy minister in this outfit and had accepted it.

Of course, she'd have to make Van understand she had no choice but to turn Chou in. After all, he was a traitor. And then it would be too late for Chou. She knew that innocent people were jailed daily for invented political crimes. Doing this to the lawyer would be easy.

Van looked up from his newspaper. "Jade, here's something odd. It's an announcement that Dr. Tuyen, Chou's friend and the secret police chief whom Chou told me was planning a coup against our president, has been made consul general to Egypt. That's very strange indeed. But it gets stranger. The paper says Tuyen disappeared en route to Cairo. I must telephone Chou." He picked up the telephone receiver and dialed the lawyer's number.

Jade felt suddenly ill and could hardly breathe. "Why are you telephoning Chou? What does it matter?"

"Jade, you know I have a responsibility to him as a friend. I'll inform him of Dr. Tuyen's odd appointment just in case he hasn't heard. It might mean trouble for him."

"Van, I must speak to you now!" Jade cried. She would tell Van her story before Chou could say anything. But her husband was already speaking into the receiver. It was too late. She watched his eyes for clues. He spoke a few words and looked worried when he hung up. "Well, then," she asked, ashen-faced, "what did Chou say?"

Van shook his head. "I don't know what to make of it. Chou's landlady answered the phone. He's disappeared."

Jade's fear lifted and she almost cried out with joy. There was no need to write a letter now. Still, she thought, why not put a knife in the lawyer, anyway? "I've always suspected Chou of being a secret Communist."

"My dear, judging men by their politics isn't our business. Of course, I suppose it was only a matter of time. Chou kept company with the most dangerous characters in Saigon. Nevertheless, I hope he's safe."

"I wouldn't worry about Chou. You told me yourself he was planning an escape if he needed one." Life could go on, Jade thought, sighing quietly to herself. "Van, do you mind calling a *cyclo* and organizing it for the day? I'm off to purchase a few antiques." She kissed Van goodbye.

Just last evening Jade had decided on a new pastime to suit her lady-of-leisure lifestyle. It would be gratifying and it would keep her away from the house on Saturday, the day Van had entertained friends when she lived in Paris. Saturday was the day Van said he socialized with Suzette and her boyfriend. It had been the day he played chess with Chou. But Saturday was also the only reasonable time for purchasing collectibles and antiques. All Saigon knew that deliveries to the stores came on Saturday and that by Monday the best pieces were in the hands of collectors.

Although Van had said nothing yet, Jade suspected her husband would one day resent her coldness toward Suzette. But Jade couldn't help it. The girl was too brash, too typically American, and had no idea how to dress among sophisticated people. Hopefully Suzette's assignment would be finished soon and she'd return to America where she belonged.

So Jade set off on her search for antiques. In the first store she visited she discovered a concubine's bed from the Ming dynasty, a Steinway piano, and a set of Chinese opera masks. As she shopped, Jade planned her evening with Van.

She would silently celebrate being rid of Chou and ask her husband to escort her to the rooftop bar at the Caravelle Hotel for a glass of cassis. Sunset from the Caravelle's rooftop was always superb with its outlook across the river and nightly light show of tracers riding ruby across the tinted sky. The danger from the Vietcong's rocket fire was picturesque and peripheral and largely ignored by the Saigonese. Then, she decided, they'd dine at the Continental's terraced café. There, too, danger seemed a lark, and Jade found the presence of the heavy-drinking journalists who made these establishments their hangouts added to the thrill.

As they drove by the Ong Pagoda and Saint Francis Xavier Church, Jade told the *cyclo* driver to stop and raise the shade. The sunlight was a hot club on her head. The afternoon heat was exhausting. Worse, she realized she was still jet-lagged and shouldn't have taxed herself so soon. With that realization Jade changed her mind: she and Van would spend a pleasant night at home. And besides, that way she could admire her purchases.

When Jade finally ceased her shopping, she had bought only a single item: a one-hundred-year-old French clock, which followed her home by cart. It struck four as the delivery boys placed it in an appropriate corner of her house.

Van was sitting at his desk when Jade went into his study. "Ah, you're back, my dear! I was writing a letter to Mui to tell her about our homecoming dinner for you and to let her know about Chou's strange disappearance when I had a delightful idea. With Tuyen out of the picture, and now I hear that Big Boss has fled the country, I think the political climate will improve here. Surely Diem can't last much longer and his government will be replaced by a more stable regime. And if that happens, our Mui can come home. I've suggested that she could transfer to the University of Saigon. Wouldn't that be wonderful?"

Jade had a sudden need to sit down. Why did Van have such a need to surround himself with insufferable young women? When she figured out a way to rid herself of Mui, he had replaced her with the annoying American Suzette. And now he was scheming to get Mui back to Vietnam. Jade felt all the joy her shopping had given her vanish in an instant.

"Are you all right, Jade?" Van asked, looking at her quizzically. "You look so pale. I knew you shouldn't be out under that hot sun so soon after your return. I know what! I'll go out and get some durians, that fruit you like so much. That will refresh you. And while I'm out I can post this letter to Mui."

Jade only nodded as she watched him go. She would have to think of some other way to keep Mui in Paris. Then she heard her new clock chime and smiled. Now where should she put her latest acquisition...?

5

COUNTDOWN

I thought with more sympathy now of the southern President Diem. One pictured him there in the Norodom Palace, sitting with his blank, brown gaze, incorruptible, obstinate, ill-advised, going to his weekly confession, bolstered by his belief that God is always on the Catholic side, waiting for a miracle.

—Graham Greene, "The Marxist Heretic," *Collected Essays*

Saigon: October 1963

It wasn't Kiet's lucky day. He had received his draft notice. Kiet said nothing that morning, but left the General Treasury early, taking a *cyclo* home to his apartment. He surprised Suzette at her developing work, but instead of his usual moody anger when she tried to explain about her love for photography, he told her he was happy she had something that was so important to her. In fact, for the first time, he assisted her in the makeshift darkroom.

The air in the tiny space was humid, moribund, and Kiet's mind was far away as he stood behind her. Then he noticed she wore her ARVN-issue jumpsuit that she'd paid too many piastres for to a black-market vendor. The knee of the outfit was torn, accentuating her wanton look. Her appearance made his throat catch, and he kissed her neck so she wouldn't see his emotion.

When they were done, Kiet said, "Come into the living room. I have something to tell you."

Suzette sat in his lap, draped her arms around his neck, and looked at him expectantly.

Kiet cleared his throat. "This morning the notice came."

"What notice?" Suzette asked, but he could see by the change in her eyes that she knew.

"I've finally been drafted. In seventy-two hours I have to report to the Reserve Armored Infantry Officers' School at Thu Duc, eight miles northeast of Saigon."

"Oh, no, Kiet!" Suzette cried, her eyes filling with tears. "You can't leave me. We'll run away like your best friend Kim did."

Kiet frowned. "Suzette, there's nowhere safe to run, and though I don't want to go, it *is* my duty. I have no choice."

"Then we'll get married and I'll take you to America."

Kiet's face was set with his decision. "You hate the United States. Besides, you yourself say you're not accepted there because you're part Vietnamese. Think what it would be like with a Vietnamese husband."

"All I care about is you. I love you and I want to marry you."

"To marry you would be my greatest happiness, but I can't do it if it means I have to forsake my country. Suzette, I must obey the orders. It's my duty as a Saigonese. I don't want to go, but I know I could never live with myself if I ran away." A nerve beat in Kiet's cheek. "You'll have to go back to the States. After the war is over, you can come back. You'll be my wife. Or, if you want, maybe I can try to come there to you."

"I'll never leave you. You *are* my home. And Saigon is, too."

"It'll be too dangerous for you here alone and, anyway, you'll probably end up a beautiful widow." Outside, Kiet heard a siren, and it was as if the long wail echoed his fears. "Besides, you'll tire of me. I have no future, Suzette. No job now, only the possibility of rotting in the army."

Suzette shook her head reproachfully. "That's not true! You told me yourself you'll be an officer. Marry me, Kiet. Then I know you'll never leave me."

Kiet thought for a moment, then said, "The Vietcong would

assassinate me for sure if they knew I had an American wife."

"I'll rip up my passport! I'll tell the VC I'm Vietnamese!"

She pulled away from him angrily to search for her passport and destroy it, but Kiet held her. "Don't be ridiculous, Suzette. You don't even speak Vietnamese. You won't fool anybody, and besides, look at you, you're blond." A dark look suddenly clouded Kiet's face. "I just thought of something even worse. The VC might even try to get you to spy for them, and if you said no, they'd kill you."

Suzette was silent. She didn't know what to say.

"I can't stand it when you look so sad," Kiet said, seeking a way to satisfy her. "Maybe you're right. When I become an officer, marrying you will give you some security and protection."

Suzette looked up, a flicker of hope in her eyes.

He knew how to cheer her now. "I'll be dashing in an officer's uniform and you'll be an angel in a red wedding gown. Suzette, I must take you to see my mother again."

"Oh, Kiet," she said dreamily, "we'll buy your mother a new *aio dai* for the wedding and Van could give me away."

"Uncle Van would be perfect. And my mother will have something to live for again when I tell her the news. What's more, when I'm away at military school, Van can keep you company and make sure you're safe. My officer training will last two months, then I'll be in the reserves. And, if we're very lucky, after my training, I'll be posted to Saigon and we won't be separated. At least not often."

Suzette was lost in her dream. "Kiet, I've seen the Vietnamese brides in front of Notre Dame in their red gowns. I'll look good in red, won't I? And red is a lucky color in Vietnam, isn't it?"

"Yes, it is! And you'll be the most beautiful bride in all Vietnam."

At lunchtime on his last day of work, November 1, Kiet finished the spring rolls and rice Suzette had prepared for him the night before. He had penned a letter of resignation to his boss, saying he had been drafted, but Mr. Thé was nowhere to be found. As Kiet wondered where the man could be, the front door of the General Treasury opened, revealing a smaller number of people than usual queuing for afternoon services. Like Kiet, many were unaware of the sudden curfew that had been ordered, though there was a definite tension in the air.

The previous night had been traumatic, and today heinous plans were still afoot. Nhu, who had fallen further under the influence of heroin and opium, was embroiled in all manner of schemes. Always an extremist, those who saw him believed him demented, his woodenly handsome features a mask and behind the facade, a devil. His brother, Diem, plotted, too, in the name of Catholicism. Various ARVN generals schemed for love of power and war. Everyone was jockeying for position, and all the while Ho Chi Minh's Vietcong were strengthening their cause and firing rockets with even greater abandon. Something was about to happen. Kiet could smell it.

Like most South Vietnamese, Kiet had no real idea about what was going on. As they had been before the French were vanquished, Saigon's cafés were once again wrapped in wire mesh to prevent damage from grenades. But the Saigonese and visitors alike still gathered on the rooftop of the Caravelle and the Majestic Hotels, seemingly oblivious to the escalating danger. Diem had declared martial law at the behest of his generals. Unknown to Diem, the generals hoped to strengthen their control as they prepared another coup against him.

Diem had agreed to the generals' request to declare martial law, but only to further Nhu's strange plot. At the stroke of midnight Nhu's secret forces would swarm in armored vehicles across Saigon armed with tear-gas grenades, submachine guns, and rifles. Disguised as ARVN soldiers, they would raid Xa Loi Temple, the city's Buddhist sanctuary, burning and looting and arresting four hundred monks and nuns. The Buddhists were turning public opinion against the Ngos. There had been six immolations since the one Suzette had witnessed, each covered by television, and a burned bonze's heart was displayed under glass for the public. Nhu's plot was a bid to turn the people against the ever-rebelling ARVN and quiet the dissident monks in one fell swoop. Madame Nhu, too, was doing her part. She was on a speaking tour in America where she referred to the immolations as "barbecues" and the monks as "hooligans in robes."

Meanwhile, Nhu was engaged in a second bizarre plot. Diem's brother was planning a "coup," a pseudo-Communist takeover of Saigon in which a few prominent Vietnamese and American officials would be assassinated. Then forces loyal to the Ngo family would march into the capital and "crush" the bogus Communists, restore order, and appear to save the day, thus reaping more support from the Americans and proving once and for all that Diem and Nhu were the only leaders capable of thwarting Ho Chi Minh's designs on the South.

But Kiet was completely unaware of the nature of the sinister events unfolding throughout the city. Instead, he rocked back in his office chair, lost in thought, daydreaming about his beautiful blond fiancée.

"Mr. Manager Sir," Mai Ling, his assistant, said as she entered his office.

Kiet raised his head and put the front legs of his chair back on the floor with a thump. "Um, what did you say?"

Mai Ling giggled. "There's a famous movie star awaiting Your Highness."

Kiet glanced behind his assistant and saw Suzette, his American beauty in blue jeans.

Pinching Kiet's arm with unnecessary vigor, Mai Ling whispered,

"What does *she* want with *you*, Mr. Manager?"

"She's my fiancée!" Kiet announced with pride, then went to greet his bride-to-be.

Suzette buried her face in Kiet's neck.

"Please, Suzette!" Kiet cautioned, noting Mai Ling's greedy eyes. "It's inappropriate to show affection in a government office."

She looked up at him, her eyes wild with fear. "But I was so afraid for you!" The shriek of ambulances from the nearby hospital had started soon after Kiet left for work. Not long after noon she'd heard the curfew announcement on Radio Saigon and rushed to Kiet, even though the announcer had warned that Americans should stay off the streets.

Kiet dismissed Mai Ling, who withdrew in a huff, then closed the door to his office. "What is it, darling?"

"Don't you know? I heard it on the radio. Tanks and soldiers have surrounded Diem's palace."

"What?"

"There's been a coup by some army generals. Their soldiers have captured Saigon's radio station, and Diem and Nhu are trapped in the Presidential Palace."

"Well, that's it for us!" Kiet ran a hand through his gleaming black hair, trying to think. "Are these generals Communist?"

"I don't know."

"Suzette, go to the American embassy! You can't stay here. It's too dangerous!"

"The roads that way are blocked. I'll go back to our apartment and wait for you there."

"We'll go out and get my usual *cyclo* driver. He's always at the front of the building. Give him this if he's afraid to break the curfew." Kiet dug in his trouser pockets and pressed the piastres he found into Suzette's hand.

"Don't worry, Kiet. I'm safe. I have an American passport."

"That's the problem, Suzette. If the generals are secret supporters of Uncle Ho, you're in grave danger. If you're stopped, whatever you do, don't show your passport."

They walked to the General Treasury's main door. Impulsively Suzette kissed Kiet, then looked at him imploringly. "Why don't you come with me? It's dangerous for you, too, to be out in the streets while all this is going on." She tried to smile. "Besides, you could protect me."

"Believe me, I'd like to do nothing better, but I have to finish a few things here first. My *cyclo* driver will make sure you get home safely."

They went outside and found the driver and Kiet gave him instructions.

"Please be careful, darling," Suzette said, leaning out of the *cyclo* toward him.

He saluted her smartly, then blew her a kiss. "Be careful!"

She waved goodbye, her hand thrust high in the air.

On his way back to his office Kiet was cornered by Mai Ling. "You and your fiancée were so romantic, just like Richard Burton and Elizabeth Taylor."

Kiet frowned, his mind still on Suzette's departure. "I have to tell you something, Mai Ling."

"Then take me into your office like you did her. Or are you afraid to be alone with me, Mr. Casanova? Whatever it is, you can tell me in the privacy of your office."

"Okay, fine."

Shutting Kiet's office door behind them, Mai Ling moved close to him. "Do you want to kiss me, too, Mr. Casanova?"

"I haven't got time for this, Mai Ling. There's a coup going on. Suzette came to warn me that the Presidential Palace is surrounded by tanks and soldiers. They could be ARVN units sympathetic to Uncle Ho."

Mai Ling studied her long red nails. "Your fancy American girl is pretty stupid. It's just another curfew. Everyone but you and your Yankee baby doll have known about it for hours."

"Suzette is far from stupid, Mai Ling." Kiet scowled, then smiled. "If I'm not mistaken, you sound a little jealous."

"Me jealous of your American whore? Who do you think you're talking to, Mr. Manager? I spit on the ground she walks!" Mai Ling's pretty mouth twisted. "I'll have my husband's brother fire you."

"You're too late. I've been drafted. And if this is a Communist coup, there won't be any ARVN or government jobs for anyone. We'll all be doing hard labor at a reeducation camp."

"You're really certain about this coup, aren't you?" Mai Ling said, doubt invading her face. Then her glare turned to a seductive pout. "Why do you want that American girl when you can have me right now in your office?" She unbuttoned her blouse, revealing a white lace bra, the edge of which Kiet had once so ardently admired. "Take me here on the floor by your desk." She unzipped her skirt, letting it fall to her feet as she stepped gracefully out of it.

"Are you out of your mind? Put your clothes back on. I haven't got time for your foolishness."

Mai Ling flushed, then stooped to pick up her clothing. As soon as she finished dressing, she hissed, "You and that American bitch deserve each other. You're not good enough for me." With that she turned on her high heels and marched out of the office.

Jade and Van sat in their living room, listening to the radio for further news of the political situation. "You shouldn't have come back to Saigon, Jade," Van said fretfully. "If you'd listened to me, you'd now be safe in Paris."

"Quiet, Van!" Jade said. "I'm trying to hear the news."

"Poor Suzette. She's probably all alone in her apartment. I tried to phone her, but the lines are apparently down."

"Don't be silly, Van. I'm sure, like you, Miss O'Brian's boyfriend was informed about the coup and the curfew and has returned home by now. Now let's listen to the radio. They're about to make an announcement." Jade fanned herself nervously.

General Duong Van Minh's voice boomed from the radio as he launched into his victory speech: "In this change of government we have received total support from ex-President Diem's own army and from the people of South Vietnam..."

Van couldn't help himself and interjected, "The general's right. Our people are tired of Diem's harsh rule. It's time for a new government, and at least it's not a Communist one."

Yes, Jade thought, maybe it was the beginning of a new era. Perhaps now the chronic uncertainty would end and the country could get down to business as usual. Tomorrow would, indeed, be a better day.

Kiet listened intently to the news on the General Treasury's radio and was thrilled, no, relieved that the coup wasn't Communist-backed. His gaze roamed the empty offices of the General Treasury, and he wondered if he'd ever see them again. Satisfied that all was well outside, he placed his few personal possessions in a handkerchief, locked his office door, and headed out of the building.

The streets were wild with revelers celebrating Diem's downfall as Kiet hailed his usual *cyclo* driver. Earlier the man had told him he'd delivered Suzette safely home. Now, quickly, he pedaled toward Kiet's apartment villa, weaving in and out of the carnival of tooting trucks, automobiles, and motorcycles. The cavalcade careened around the traffic circle, cruising Nguyen Hue and Tu

Do, skirting the Majestic Hotel, and flowing past the bare-breasted alabaster angels that graced the Opera House.

Turning away from the river, Kiet's *cyclo* traveled down Thong Nhat Street, passing the foreign embassies. Kiet smiled to himself. He and Suzette would have a double celebration: their engagement and the new regime. They would party until dawn. When the *cyclo* reached his apartment villa, Kiet jumped out and told the driver to wait for him. Then he sprinted to Suzette, who was waiting on the steps of their building.

"We're safe, Suzette!" Kiet cried. "It's an ARVN coup and the new leaders are anti-Communist. Come, I'll take you out to celebrate our engagement and the new government. All Saigon's going to be celebrating tonight and I'm starving."

Delighted, Suzette extricated herself from Kiet's embrace and attempted to drag him inside and away from the noise. "I have to eat," she said. "I'm so hungry I could eat a dragon. But, Kiet, I didn't want to do anything without you."

"Well, I'm so randy for you I could eat you all up. But let's go out on the town first. I feel like being with my people on this incredible night."

"You're right, Kiet. We're Vietnamese and we should be at the party, too."

Together they hopped into the *cyclo*'s single seat, and their driver maneuvered his vehicle through the milling crowds. He squeezed the pedicab into a lane thick with bicycles, motorcycles, and *cylos*. Streaming with the joyous and interflirting traffic, they passed the Opera House and Lam Son Square. Then their driver turned out of the flow. A motorcycle swerved and Suzette closed her eyes. When she opened them, they were circling the pink-bricked Notre Dame Cathedral.

The *cyclo* driver pedaled on past swarms of citizens pulling Diem's portraits down. They rode by Bach Dang harbor and past the statue of the Trung sisters that resembled Diem's sister-in-law,

Madame Nhu. It was being smashed to pieces while onlookers cheered. Then they were back on Tu Do, where they marveled again at the quick-change artist that was Saigon. It was still light, yet the front doors of bars and clubs were wide open and their patrons flooded the streets.

"Suzette," Kiet said, "you *are* lucky for me. Look what's happened. Just yesterday I received my draft notice and we were so unhappy. But today there's a coup and everything changes. Don't you see? I would have lost my job, anyway. No doubt about it." Kiet snapped his fingers and explained. "When a regime falls, all new government staff is appointed. The old staff is never rehired. But at least now I still have a future. I'll have a reserve officer's salary to fall back on. If I hadn't been drafted, I'd have been made penniless by this coup."

"You'll be the handsomest officer around," Suzette said wistfully. "But I still don't want to be without you—even for a minute."

Kiet said nothing. In a mere twenty-four hours he was expected at the Reserve Armored Infantry Officers' School in Thu Duc. They both knew that after training, unless the war ended, Kiet would be called up. Just because there was a change in South Vietnam's government didn't mean the threat of Ho and the Vietcong would go away.

The driver passed by the river, and although the crowds still milled, and the carnival atmosphere remained, the sun was long gone and the river was like pitch.

Suzette voiced an idea. "Kiet, let's go to Club La Danse."

Finally the *cyclo* came to the club, the underground haven for Saigon's young people, music lovers, and high-stepping dancers. It was the place where Kiet and Suzette had first talked. For the first time the front entrance of the nightclub was open to the public. American and ARVN soldiers in fatigues and heavy boots mixed on the dance floor with civilians in jeans and suits. Suzette and Kiet couldn't get to the front, but they could see the

Saigonese wild to proclaim their new public freedom to tango, gyrate, gamble, drink, fight, even to be seen with prostitutes. The Americans hadn't been under the rule of Madame Nhu's puritanical laws, but their behavior was more audacious than ever. As Kiet and Suzette watched, a soldier stripped, mimicking a hooker who stood on a chair. He ogled her, pulling off his underthings in lewd imitation. But it was the sight of the uniforms and the sound of heavy boots striking the floor that upset Kiet and Suzette, reminding them of tomorrow.

"Let's go home," Kiet said, wanting to keep their thoughts away from his leaving. They'd buy beer and a bottle of Mekong brandy, then stop at an all-night food vendor for Suzette's favorite dish, *gio*, lean pork seasoned and pounded into a paste, then wrapped and boiled in banana leaf, and his own favorite, *banh cuon*, ground pork and *moc nhi*, edible fungus, rolled into a rice pancake.

By the time they returned to their apartment, they were exhausted. They opened the shutters and threw themselves onto the bed. There they lolled, Suzette resting her head on Kiet's thigh.

"Sit up and help me finish what's left of the brandy," Kiet said, finding a suitable subject. "Then tell me what happened this afternoon when you were here alone."

Suzette took the glass Kiet held out to her. "I listened to Radio America for a while and they translated Minh's victory speech. After that they made a few announcements. As you know, Minh and his junta have occupied the Presidential Palace, but Radio America said that Diem and Nhu have disappeared."

"But what about that sexpot Madame Nhu?" Kiet asked, wanting more news.

"She's in the United States dancing in a low-cut *aio dai*."

"Where could Diem and Nhu be hiding?"

"No one knows… Kiet, do you want to play a game of *vingt-et-un* or maybe backgammon? Whoever loses has to be the other's slave for a day!"

Kiet's eyes turned serious. "I wish you'd go home to your parents in the States—at least until after my training is finished."

"Don't, Kiet. You know I won't leave."

He kissed her mouth to stop her words, and to make the time last they played cards and talked, but only about their wedding, keeping their pact. They wouldn't waste precious hours being sad about Kiet's drafting into the ARVN.

At eight o'clock it began raining. Chou pulled up the hood of his cassock and raised his umbrella; he had an appointment to keep. He'd received last-minute orders to report on the coup. The Ngo brothers had scurried like rats through an underground escape tunnel after slipping out of the Presidential Palace and into the courtyard. They'd crisscrossed the deserted streets in an unmarked Land Rover, then crouched on the back-seat floor of a Citroën, avoiding the rebel troops' patrols. The brothers had arrived safely at a villa in Cholon outfitted by the secret police with a telephone connected to the palace's communications system. Chou admired the ingenuity involved, how the insurgent generals never knew the Ngos had flown the coop. And then, while the generals' forces assaulted the empty palace protected by the presidential guard, the brothers had taken refuge in Cholon's Catholic church.

Chou folded his umbrella and entered Saint Francis Xavier Church. He could hear the choir beginning the Latin litany. A priest in black soutane furtively directed him to a back room. Chou put his eye to a hole drilled in the stone. The brothers were already there, and he could hear their every word.

A dull thud sounded in Chou's ears as the porcine Diem fell to his knees, his trademark white sharkskin suit pocked with grime. Nhu huddled near, his face masked like one of the vultures that scrapped by the river. Their voices croaked as they begged God and the Americans who had so recently backed them for a last chance. Chou heard Diem say, "They're praying for us, brother. Today is the Day of the Dead, All Souls' Day."

"Brother, it's *our* day and *we* are dead," Nhu moaned, covering his empty eyes with his hands.

"We've protected the Catholic faith, Nhu, so let's take the prayers for our ourselves. With the whole congregation praying for us we'll soon be in heaven. We now have no recourse. We've tried everything. Last night I called on the military phone for help. You know I called on all who owe us favors and who I thought were loyal. I called army commanders, province chiefs, our own secret police, anyone and everyone. No one would answer. Now only God and maybe the Americans are with us."

Diem continued, though his voice seemed devoid of hope. "I spoke to the American ambassador. I asked what attitude the United States had toward the rebellion. Ambassador Lodge told me he believed those in charge planned to give us safe conduct out of the country—if we resigned. But I knew that was a lie and that we had no hope but to flee by the underground escape route."

Nhu fell to his knees beside his brother. They clasped their clammy palms in prayer. And then, as quickly as a pistol crack, it was over. A junior army officer, eyes as dead as the Ngos', fired at them, and fired again. The other drew a blade and stabbed Diem and Nhu repeatedly. As they died on the stone, Chou reflected that the ill-fated brothers' lifeblood ebbed slowly, as did their prayers. The lawyer began making personal notes in a cramped hand, detailing the Ngos' fervent pleas and wild eyes. Then he wrote a secret communication in invisible ink to Ho Chi Minh, and was satisfied when he was finished.

Chou's timing was perfect. The church service was over. He

reappeared and handed the priest a Bible. Stuck in the Old Testament, in the story of Cain and Abel, was a seemingly blank and folded sheet of foolscap destined for Hanoi.

Outside, the morning was overcast. There was little traffic, and Chou surmised that most of Saigon would sleep the day away after the previous night's good-riddance party in honor of the Ngos' overthrow. The lawyer accelerated on a sharp corner, taking the Shadow up to fifty. He still wore his borrowed cassock. Ahead was the oily brown river and Big Boss's recently abandoned headquarters. He parked the Shadow one last time and shut the door. *"Chào anh!"* he called loudly through the fence topped with barbed wire and shards of glass. When there was no answer, he unlocked the gate's deadbolt with a borrowed key, entered, then pushed the bolt back into place.

Chou sat in the abandoned ammunition yard. He admired the river through a telescope. Across the bank vultures sparred, claws first, their faces grotesque in black feathery masks. A bloated corpse stripped of earthly valuables drifted by, tangled in the river's wreath, a funereal festoon of hyacinths and lilies. Chou thought nothing of it, though he pondered the man's demise. Was it the handiwork of the Vietcong, or the last victim of the Ngo regime? Regardless of the perpetrator, the river worked on, gently floating its cargo to the South China Sea, where Chou would be. As the lawyer watched, he observed the clouds mirrored in the river and noted that they moved as slowly as ancient mandarins.

He heard the noise first, the roar of the speedboat slicing through the muddy water. As the boat came closer, he recognized Co at the wheel and swore under his breath. But maybe Big Boss's man had forgiven him. Chou replayed the incident in his mind. He'd tested the Magnum, pointing it toward the men playing *boules*. He'd aimed and pulled the trigger. *Bing*—a silver-tipped hollowpoint had drilled a wormhole in the metal disk. The man who'd held the disk had scowled at him. He remembered Big Boss howling, "Good shot! Too bad you didn't hit Co. He's pretty useless as it is." And Co had shot him the evil eye.

There was no other way. Co and the speedboat were his only means of escape. They would travel out the mouth of the river, Chou hidden in the hold, and then north along the coast to Haiphong. He'd ferry across the Red River and then row a boat to where the junk waited behind a karst's shadowy skirt.

With no time to lose, Chou leaped into action, kicking off his shoes and removing his socks. He discarded the cassock, donned flippers and a rubber mask, and squished through the river's slime. Stroking the hip pocket of his shorts, he felt the reassuring length of his switchblade before he submerged himself. Co would be fish food.

Then, while he bided his time on the Baie d'Along, he'd begin a book about his adventures. And with that thought his lips did their thin, dry dance.

6

RED DREAMS

So runs my dream: but what am I?
An infant crying in the night;
An infant crying for the light:
And with no language but a cry.
—Alfred Tennyson,
"In Memoriam A.H.H."

Saigon: November 1963

Their time was up, flown by in a flurry of embraces and sweet words. The day Suzette and Kiet dreaded had come. Kiet had packed his duffel bag and made ready to leave for officer training in Thu Duc. Both lovers attempted to reassure each other.

"At least you're not going to be a private and you'll be in the reserves. After your two months of training, you'll come home to me." Suzette saluted, her hand raised to her ear. "You'll be the best officer South Vietnam has ever seen."

Kiet teasingly saluted back and tumbled her gently back into bed. "I'll have a better-looking uniform than my old government-issue blues. Maybe one day I'll even be decorated with medals."

"When can I come and visit you?" Nothing else mattered to her.

"I don't know. Maybe if you were Vietnamese… But, no, it's too risky."

"But your school's so close. It's almost in Saigon and it's staffed by American military advisers. You told me that yourself. I know I'd be welcome."

"It's not that simple. I've heard the area's dangerous. And the

Vietcong seem to be getting bolder every day."

Suzette's mouth played on his lips like a butterfly and her kisses stopped the rest of his words and thoughts. "Kiet, I can't think of anything except how I'll miss you."

"I have to go now, darling," he said, getting to his feet and shouldering his bag.

They kissed long and hard, and for a while it seemed as if Suzette wouldn't let him go. Then, finally, she stepped back, tears in her eyes.

When he was gone, she began to cry in earnest. Her loneliness multiplied each hour Kiet was gone. Even her photography didn't interest her. She worried that Kiet had been right when he told her the work was meaningless and that it took advantage of the poverty plaguing the Vietnamese. She couldn't bear to leave their apartment, so she slept away the rest of the day and those that followed.

Kiet's officers' school was under the direction of the U.S. Department of Military Instruction. It softened the blow of being drafted when he discovered his new uniform was the same as an American would wear, as were his insignia and weapons. He came to appreciate, as well, the camaraderie of his fellow trainees and the paternalistic attitude of the commanders, though it was common practice for officers dismissed from combat operations for corruption or incompetence to be posted at Thu Duc and at the military college at Dalat.

Thu Duc was a military camp that had been set up in 1952 to train local Vietnamese reserve officers for the French armored forces during the war against the Vietminh. By 1956 the existing ARVN armored units had reorganized as armored cavalry regiments according to U.S. precepts. They had adopted further

American training programs and methods, though U.S. news sources had announced that a thousand American advisers to the ARVN would be withdrawn.

The armored units, each comprised of two reconnaissance squadrons, were intended to support anti-guerrilla operations and to ensure security along the main roads, while tank squadrons were trained to repulse an all-out conventional invasion from the North. The Vietcong had stepped up terrorist activity in the South, and their bases, intelligence network, and political infrastructure were widespread and sophisticated.

Although Kiet was designated a reserve soldier, there was no doubt he would be called up permanently. Since late 1961, the military situation in South Vietnam had deteriorated considerably. The Vietcong moved at will throughout the country and threatened the approaches to Saigon.

Kiet was at the beginning of two months of intensive basic training using pre-World War II French reconnaissance armored cars, halftracks, scout cars, howitzer transports, and light tanks. The equipment was dilapidated, but fortunately the U.S. military had shipped thirty-two M-113 armored personnel carriers before Kiet's arrival.

Because the Thu Duc school had supported the coup that overthrew the Ngo regime, its detractors referred to its students and staff as "coup troops." But even with the appointment of corrupt and inept officers, Thu Duc had forged an impressive reputation. Between June and October 1962 the Seventh and Twenty-first Infantry Divisions trained and based there had been sent to operate in the Plain of Reeds. They had killed 517 Vietcong and captured 203 at a cost to themselves of only four dead and thirteen wounded. The reason wasn't just luck. Thu Duc's mechanized troops fought from their carriers, only dismounting when an enemy position had been overrun and then only to ensure that a thorough and complete search of the area was made. The troops of Thu Duc were heroes, sung about in Vietnamese songs Kiet had tapped his foot to at the tea house that night with his friend Kim.

Even the American advisers were impressed, and contrary to the old method, where soldiers riding in the armored personnel carriers had to dismount to fight, the ARVN commanders fought with their men firing from the hatches of their vehicles. This tactic transformed the M-113 into a real battle tank against the lightly armed guerrillas. The Americans eventually adopted this technique, too.

Kiet was anxious to master the use of the American APCs. Dashing into a Huey with the blades beating over his head or gripping the wheel of an M-113 was every man's dream, wasn't it? And he even enjoyed bayonet practices and marching drills. In a month's time the newly commissioned ARVN reserve officers from his school would parade in Saigon. He'd only been gone forty-eight hours and he could hardly wait to see Suzette's face when she watched him march down Tu Do in his new uniform.

The armored vehicles and the idea of being on parade thrilled Kiet, but his picture of the situation wasn't completely rose-colored. The VC threat was real and he knew enough to fear the guerrillas' tactics. They were insidious and hid contraptions studded with nails in flooded rice fields and perpetually muddy paths. Kiet was relieved that trainees were issued thick-soled boots.

A legend of sizable proportion was bandied about by the American advisers who taught the Vietnamese trainees baseball as well as how to fight. It concerned a special group of American and Vietnamese soldiers trained at Clark Air Field in the Philippines and their undercover actions when the Vietcong were called the Vietminh. The covert group was spearheaded by Colonel (later General) Ed Lansdale and headed by Major (later Lieutenant Colonel) Lucien Conein, the same man who had given the go-ahead to the recent successful coup against Diem.

Conein's squad was reputedly as tricky as the jungle guerrillas. Back in the 1950s the covert group had laced the oil destined for Hanoi's trams and fuel systems with acid and had blown up the regime's coal, sabotaging the North's transportation systems.

Some Vietnamese members of the clandestine team who had infiltrated the North had been designated stay-behinds. They had buried arms in Hanoi's cemeteries, going to great lengths to stage funerals and sealing the equipment in coffins. Their mandate was to harass the Vietminh, but a number of these men had been caught and tried. The rest had just disappeared. All of their fates were unknown.

Another rumor that alarmed Kiet also circulated at the school. It concerned Cu Chi, which was being considered as the location for a new armored infantry headquarters. The former site of the Michelin rubber plantation, Cu Chi was northwest of Saigon and had been targeted in 1962 by the Fortified Hamlet Program or Operation Sunrise. The operation was based on British counterinsurgency programs against the Chinese Communists in Malaya. Like the British program, Sunrise trained and armed Cu Chi villagers against the Vietcong, then relocated them with promises of better land. But the Cu Chi area was fast becoming a free-fire zone. Worse, underneath the Cu Chi district were tunnels first used by the Vietminh and now infested with the Vietcong. The tunnel network ran all the way to the Saigon River. It was said the VC used the subterranean passages to hold meetings, train, sleep, cook, and even make love. Air holes and entrances were booby-trapped with mines.

Kiet thought too much. He lay down on his bunk and fell asleep, only to be enveloped in the same dream he'd been having for the past few nights. He saw the VC, mud-faced and stinking of slime. They wore black pajamas and crawled from a dark hole beneath his bunk and strangled him with boa-constrictor hands before he could make a sound.

It wasn't quite light outside Suzette's apartment where she slept alone. Behind the closed slats of the blinds Saigon's hot air percolated like spores of mold. It was still early, a Saturday, and Suzette's neighbors hadn't yet lit their joss sticks and put out their offerings to their dead and to their animist gods.

Suzette curled herself into a fetal ball. She'd lain in bed for forty-eight hours, depressed. Kiet was gone and nothing was right. When she opened her eyes, she needed to eat and had to seek out company. Suzette was afraid to sleep any longer. She'd dreamed of the burning Buddhist monk and the empty black hole of his mouth. Then she'd dreamed she was back with her father. Suzette was small again and they were on a dusty road that led nowhere. She knew that her places were all mixed up. In the dream she had pointed out to her father a girl pedaling a bicycle: the girl wore an *aio dai* and behind her thin figure was the wasteland of Vietnam's history, playing out like the reel of an old war movie. When Suzette and her father stopped to rest, he took his bottle of liquor and turned his back on her. His eyes were dead things and she knew he was drowning and that she was alone. Behind her the movie reel that was Vietnam had become the never-ending destruction of war. When she awoke from the nightmare, she knew she couldn't bear to be alone.

She would go to Van's and announce her engagement to Kiet. She'd also tell him about Kiet going away to officers' school and how they wanted Van to do them the honor of giving her away when they married. Suzette got out of bed and went to the kitchen where she found some crackers to eat. After that she got out her knapsack and began to pack. The only wrinkle in her plan to visit Van was the likelihood of running into his wife, Jade, again. Suzette had gotten the feeling the woman looked down on her, maybe even disliked her. Jade had virtually ignored her the night they'd met at the homecoming dinner Van had arranged. She had no idea what she'd said to the woman to deserve the cold shoulder. But it didn't matter. She'd bring presents for both Jade and Van and would win over Van's wife.

Suzette hoped Van would insist she stay for dinner and spend the night rather than go back to an apartment without Kiet. She planned Sunday. To take up the afternoon she'd stop at the Jardins Botaniques on the way home from Van's. Sunday was the day Saigon's secretaries had their bicycle outing. In their white silk *aio dais* they'd appear like human swans floating down a shady river of road. With that in mind she put extra film, a toothbrush, a change of clothing, a T-shirt for bed, and a bottle of water in her knapsack, then added her passport and the old photograph of herself as a little girl with her father. She never went far without the tattered snapshot. It was her talisman of love.

Zipping up her knapsack, Suzette noticed she still had the American flag she'd sewn on it before leaving Seattle. She'd meant to remove the flag but just hadn't found the time. Suzette turned the bamboo pole and shut the louvers on the window. When she returned, it would be cooler if she left them closed. She locked the door and was on her way.

A *cyclo* waited by the curb, and she pictured Kiet with her, saying, "It's our lucky day." It wasn't ten yet, so she decided to stop first for flowers at the Central Market. After telling the *cyclo* driver to wait for her, she walked under the old clock, camera in hand. She snapped a male fortuneteller with a full set of flashing gold teeth. He made educated noises while examining the eyes of a lady client with a magnifying glass.

The aisle of flowers beckoned with their thick perfume. Some blooms were button-shaped, while others spiraled like crinolines. She changed lenses and photographed the single blooms. Suzette spied stems of tuber roses, their pale green knots scented the way she imagined heaven must smell, and chose six heavy stems for Jade. Next she spotted calla lilies, their angular blooms edged like curls of white silk. She purchased a half dozen, then finished the bouquet with sprigs of white mimosa. Her bouquet was as pale as the inside of the seashell Kiet had purchased from an urchin who said it was taken from the green depths of the mystical Baie d'Along. Finally Suzette headed for the fruit stands to buy a smelly durian, Van's favorite fruit.

Her flowers trailed scent as she hailed a *cyclo*. Suzette relaxed with her purchases and watched the city scene roll past as the driver pedaled. A monk twirling a sun umbrella ambled by, and she thought she now understood the importance of their terrible deaths by fire. Their suicides were the ultimate sacrifices for freedom. As the *cyclo* driver zipped down the street, the tamarind trees above them rained petals of yellow.

When she neared Van's luxurious home, she conjured up the delightful time she would have with him. They would prepare some delicious dish, and in the evening they'd while away the hours with a game of backgammon, discussing Kiet's future as a reserve officer, Mui in Paris, and maybe even the shadowy Chou. The *cyclo* arrived at the gate to Van's villa and Suzette got out. She paid the driver, knocked at the gate with its prettily carved dragon, and smiled at the thought of seeing Van. After a minute or two, the door swung open to reveal Jade in a dress that reeled with color.

Suzette was at a loss for words at first, then stammered, "Oh…ah, is Van home?"

"Miss O'Brian?" She stared at the white flowers in Suzette's hands. "Are you on your way to a funeral?"

"Ah, no, these are for you. And the durian is for Van. I came to tell him something and hoped I could visit for a while."

"Well, whatever you tell Van you must tell me first. Come in."

Suzette removed her sandals and followed Jade into the

kitchen. Taking the durian and the flowers from Suzette, Jade placed them on the counter. Then the two moved into the living room where La Doctoress motioned Suzette to sit on the straight-backed chair. "So what do you want to tell my husband?"

"It's good news. Kiet and I are going to be married and I want Van to give me away."

"So you'll marry here and then fly home to the States?"

"No, we'll live in Saigon. Kiet's been drafted and is training for the next two months to be an officer. After his training's finished, we'll get married."

"That's ridiculous. You should go back to the States. Van thinks so, too."

"But why would I? I wouldn't leave Kiet. Saigon's my home now."

Jade clicked her tongue. "You're an American. Why would you want to ruin your life by trapping yourself in a mixed marriage?"

"I don't care about that."

Jade stared coldly at Suzette. "Then you're blind. Your children will suffer. No one wants or loves a child of mixed race."

Suzette's head spun: *No one wants or loves a child of mixed race.* How many times had she heard that? "La Doctoress, I'm illegitimate as well as being of mixed birth. My father loved me and he made me happy. I loved him for having me and for taking care of me the best he could. I don't care about being half-caste, or even that I was born out of wedlock. It was his love that mattered, that made me who I am."

Jade's eyes flared with disdain. "Ah, that explains a lot. I wondered how you could live so brazenly without the benefit of marriage."

"In the United States it's not that uncommon for a man and a woman to live together before marriage."

"Miss O'Brian, that may be so where you come from, but not here in Vietnam. You're marked as a loose woman and of the lowest class if you live with a man outside of marriage. You obviously know nothing of our culture. Even worse, the children of mixed marriages in Vietnam end up abandoned and unwanted. The sins of the parents are suffered by the children."

Suzette was both angry and close to tears. "My father didn't sin by having me. I'll prove it to you. I'll show you the most valuable thing I have—an old snapshot of my father and me. You'll see our faces and then you won't be able to say that just because a child is half-caste she can't be loved."

Suzette's chin trembled as she bent to open her knapsack and take out the photograph. She believed that when Jade saw the snapshot the woman would realize she was wrong. The photograph represented both who Suzette was and where she had come from. It was an integral piece of her life and demonstrated without a doubt that her father had loved her. She knew love radiated in her father's face and in hers.

Jade sat on the love seat, her legs crossed European-style, her eyes as hard as stone. "Dear child, I have no interest in your past. Please don't speak of this in my house again. I say this for your own happiness. I think you'll find the past is best left dead and buried."

Suzette returned the photograph to her knapsack. "Tell Van I was here. I only came because I was lonely and wanted to celebrate my engagement to Kiet. I thought seeing Van would cheer me up."

Suzette left the house in a daze, tears stinging her eyes. Jade was so wrong about her, she thought as she heard the mournful call of a cuckoo in Van's garden. She blinked and wiped her tears away with the back of one hand. Suzette had hoped a visit with Van would bolster her flagging spirits, but now she felt lonelier than ever. She needed to be with someone who loved her, and Kiet was only eight miles away. That wasn't far. She could be there in an hour, maybe less. Perhaps Kiet could ask permission for them to get married right away. Yes, that was the thing to do. She'd go to Kiet, her love, her life…

7
PHOENIX RISES

"Phuong," I said, which means Phoenix, but nothing nowadays is fabulous and nothing rises from the ashes.

—Graham Greene, *The Quiet American*

Thu Duc, South Vietnam: November 1963

Kiet closed his eyes in his bunk in the airless Quonset hut. Everyone else could sleep. The snores of the men around him seemed to eat up the stale air like a swarm of mechanical flies. Kiet couldn't stop envisioning everything as if he were Suzette.

He saw her two snapshots, the one she had of him and the one of herself and her father. He smiled at the thought that she'd loved him so much. She'd carried his picture everywhere and kept it beside her most beloved possession, the only remnant she had of her father and herself as a child. In that photograph Suzette was a beautiful waif, solemn-eyed with pale hair like straw. She wore a dress that turned up at the top of her tiny knees like an open upside-down umbrella. Suzette was holding the hand of a thin, handsome man whose eyes glowed and who bore a half smile like a whispered secret on his lips. The pair stood together straight on as if defying even the camera to separate them, Suzette's hand naturally curving within her father's. She called the snapshot her talisman of love.

Was it Suzette's fault that her mother had abandoned her at birth and that her father was dead?

Kiet recalled she had once said she knew she'd been born to a mismatched, miscultured pair. She had said that maybe her mother was some Vietnamese whore!

He saw his love again as he'd seen her first in the imperial city of Hué when she melted his mind and indelibly imprinted herself within him—her camera slung from her hip. Then he pictured her in the bar when luck had smiled on him and he'd found her again.

Kiet knew Suzette had taken a local bus to Thu Duc as far as she could. He knew she'd ridden patiently while she'd been jostled by the crowds of peasants, some carrying clucking chickens, their feet tied, their red and brown feathers flapping against wire baskets. He knew she'd probably taken out her damn camera and snapped a picture of a child, or a beggar, or a group of marching schoolchildren.

He followed her route in his mind, watching her step down from the bus, looking elegant and tall like the picture of a single red rose she'd once shown him. He knew she'd had to walk the last couple of miles to get to his school.

Kiet saw her in blue jeans and a simple white blouse. She would have worn her sandals with the leather straps and walked the dusty road with her long-legged gait, her camera bag against her hip. Then she would have heard the engine of a jeep behind her, revving in the still air, the only other sound the derisive shriek of cicadas.

Suzette would have turned around, a trace of a smile on her lush lips, her perfect teeth gleaming. She would have taken her American passport out of her knapsack and raised it with one hand, casting a shadow behind her. She would have waved the blue passport she half hated, half loved, because it would help get her a lift to his school. Then, in her best American accent, she would have said something like, "Hi yah, guys, how's about a lift?"

Kiet hoped she hadn't seen the glint of the M-2 rifle that emerged over the broken windshield. He hoped she hadn't heard the Vietcong guerrilla yelling in his poor excuse for English, "You America, lady?"

But Kiet knew she had probably heard and that too late she'd seen the man's black pajamas of death. She might even have realized he had probably stolen the M-2 from a dead American soldier. Kiet saw it all again in slow motion: a dirty yellow thumb pulling back the trigger, small, merciless eyes hard and unyielding.

He heard her anguish, her voice heavy with fear as she cried, "I'm Vietnamese!" And he couldn't stop the *rat-a-tat-tat* of the glinting M-2 that felled her and left her abandoned on the dusty road that led to him.

The light from the latrine shone on his bed. Kiet put his hand under the pillow and pulled out Suzette's leather wallet, which was stained with her blood. His fingers stroked her face in the passport photograph. Behind the passport he saw his own snapshot and her other prize—the picture of her as a child with her father. He turned it over and looked for the last time at the inscription: "My Phuong and me." Then he began a hastily scrawled note.

Dear Uncle Van:

Thank you for being Suzette's first Vietnamese friend. I know you'll be as shattered as I am about her death. I loved her so much, as I'm sure you did. A Vietnamese family was so important to her. I blame myself for her death. I should have made the danger clearer. Please find enclosed a photograph of Suzette and her real father. Something tells me she would have wanted you to have it—Kiet.

Kiet couldn't write or think about Suzette anymore. He put the note and the photograph in the envelope and addressed it and shut his eyes to forget. Then, rising from his bed, he shuffled like an old man to the officers' post box and slipped the envelope into it. It would be hand-delivered that afternoon.

Jade walked the leafy path to her mailbox, thinking about Suzette. Before Van had a chance to see the white flowers the American girl had given her, she'd thrown them away. They were just further proof that the half-caste had no idea about Vietnamese culture; after all, white was the color of death and funerals.

The cast-iron box was empty except for a single letter. Jade took it inside the house and went into the kitchen where she lit the gas ring and put a kettle of water on to boil. She waited for the steam to begin, knowing full well that Van wouldn't be home from the Pasteur Institute until dusk. When the kettle whistled, she held the letter in its moist breath to soften the glue.

Opening the envelope, Jade found a letter and an old photograph from Kiet. She stared at the snapshot and saw a beautiful little girl holding the hand of her half-forgotten French lover. On the back of the picture, scrawled in Jacques's still-familiar hand, were the words "My Phuong and me."

Then she heard the front door open, and before she could truly react to the photograph in her hands, Van stood before her, his face etched with anger and shock. With trembling fingers he held out a letter to her. Instantly Jade recognized Chou's cramped signature.

EPILOGUE

> We, too, have become strange, and the same sluggishness that has overtaken my mother has overtaken us, too. We've learned nothing, watching the forest, waiting, weeping.
>
> —Marguerite Duras, *The Lover*

Paris: April 1964

Jade Tu Minh stood at the window of her apartment overlooking the Seine River. Although it was Thursday and already mid-afternoon, she hadn't bothered to dress. There was no need—she was a lady of leisure. The thought that she could do what she pleased flickered through her mind as she watched a couple outside kissing. The path where they embraced was ablaze with blooms.

Uninterested, Jade moved to her desk where her mail waited. Her eyes glittered like black stones underwater as she recalled the long-ago days when she received Van's letters from Saigon. She turned from the raft of bills and faced the window again. The afternoon light hurt her eyes, and when she drew the heavy drapes to shut out the world, the room fell into darkness.

she turned
she stared
her life was bare
the woman was alone

Victoria Brooks is creator/editor/contributor to the *Literary Trips: Following in the Footsteps of Fame* series. Recently she received the Excellence in Caribbean Travel Writing 2001 Award. Victoria counts among her many honors her meetings with Sir Arthur C. Clarke in Sri Lanka and with deceased literary lion Paul Bowles in Tangier. These experiences are chronicled in *Literary Trips*. Victoria is the editor of *www.GreatestEscapes.com*, the Internet magazine for travelers. She lives in Vancouver, Canada, with her husband and son when she isn't traveling the globe.

PRAISE FOR VICTORIA BROOKS

"Victoria Brooks's storytelling is excellent."
—Sir Arthur C. Clarke

"The most poignant and effective contribution [in *Literary Trips 1*] is editor Victoria Brooks's piece on Paul Bowles in Tangier."
—*Quill & Quire*

"Her glowing homage to Bowles's life, his work, and the mysterious Moroccan ambiance provides a fitting epitaph for him and sets the bar very high for the literary quality of the 22 vignettes that follow."
—*The Mature Traveler*

"Victoria Brooks's [stories] take you on an adventure in magnificence and style…she provides explorations for the spellbound traveler and a philosophy of literature born out of the delight of discovering remote places."—Former *Millionaire* and *Elle* editor Vanessa Berkling

"Victoria Brooks and her crew have done it again. *Literary Trips 2* continues the high standards established by the first enticing collection."
—*Chicago Tribune*

Travel...and Reading About It
Life's Greatest Escapes!

Greatest Escapes Publishing is a multimedia company that produces online content as well as traditional books. We are passionately devoted to the very finest in travel writing, seeking to inspire the wanderlust of our readers rather than simply giving them a list of sights, restaurants, and hotels. Read the Greatest Escapes travel webzine (*www.greatestescapes.com*), a monthly compendium of award-winning travel stories from around the globe.

Literary Trips

Following in the Footsteps of Fame
edited by Victoria Brooks
ISBN: 0-9686137-0-5
$19.95 U.S.; $29.95 Canada

If you liked *Literary Trips 2: Following in the Footsteps of Fame*, be sure to check out the critically acclaimed first volume, *Literary Trips.* Following the same format, it's packed with 23 stories about famous writers and the locations around the world they're associated with, including Ernest Hemingway's Cuba, Bruce Chatwin's Australia, Tennessee Williams's New Orleans, D. H. Lawrence's New Mexico, Ian Fleming's Jamaica, Agatha Christie's England, and much more. The remarkable Paul Bowles, the subject of an essay in the book, also wrote the foreword—his last piece of writing prior to his death in November 1999.

"...irresistible..."—CHICAGO TRIBUNE

Literary Trips: Following in the Footsteps of Fame is available online at *www.literarytrips.com* (in whole or by the chapter), in bookstores across North America, and by calling 1-877-474-6743 (toll-free in North America). To order by phone outside of North America, call 604-683-1668.

Greatest Escapes
PUBLISHING